Ember Among Ashes

FAITH, LOVE & HOPE SERIES

BOOK 2

Scripture quotations are from the WEB® Bible
(The Holy Bible, World English Bible Version®),
public domain.

Front cover image by
DSM Images

DEDICATION

To my daughter, *Vienne*,
May the love of Jesus
bring you into the light
and keep you in the truth.

ACKNOWLEDGMENT:

Thanks my dear friend, *Patty*,
for being used of God for inspiration and guidance.
This journey would not have been enjoyable without you!

FORWARD

Before you embark on this journey, I would like you to know that this book is entirely fiction. It is sprinkled with Scripture and inspired by events in God's Holy Word, but it is not intended to replace your own personal time studying the Bible. When John penned the words, "There are also many other things which Jesus did, which if they would all be written, I suppose that even the world itself wouldn't have room for the books that would be written,"[1] I believe he gave us permission to enter into the realm of fictitious possibility with the intent of drawing closer to God.

As I wrote, I prayed that the Holy Spirit would keep me within the boundary of possibility even as I entered into the territory of imagination beyond the text. Where I felt it warranted the story, I took the creative liberty necessary to enhance the flow of the narrative, altering the chronology of events to fit the storyline while attempting to keep within the realm of historical accuracy.

My intention was to share what I have learned about the power of love that conquers darkness. I hope that through this journey with Mary Magdalene, you will come to know the love of Jesus that protects and shields you from the one who seeks to devour your soul. This book was not written with the purpose of adding to or taking away from Scripture. Rather, it was penned in a spirit of love not meant to cause offense. As you travel the imaginative road with Magda through the battleground of the spirit, I pray that your own heart will be set free by the protective love of Jesus that covers all who call on His Name.

Incorruptible LOVE has pursued you through Christ.

Always His, D

---

[1] John 21:25

Be sober and self-controlled. Be watchful.
Your adversary, the devil, walks around like a roaring lion,
seeking whom he may devour.
1Peter 5:8, WEB

Now when He had risen early on the first day of the week,
He appeared first to Mary Magdalene,
from whom He had cast out seven demons.
Mark 16:9, WEB

MAGDALA, 1 AD

The shadows of the black forest of Zophos seethed from the commotion caused by the minions of the Evil One. Their Master was about to address them, having gained permission from the Creator to go to and fro about the earth for a time. Lucifer appeared before the throng, his powerful hatred surging after being in the presence of the Creator. The supremacy of evil manifested itself by a formidable dark radiance all around him, a reminder to all that this was his domain. Though he often disguised himself as an angel of light, here in Zophos, Lucifer took on his true form as a magnificent dragon of darkness. The fallen angels hushed, their whispers fading into silence, as they lowered their heads before the one they worshipped.

"There is work to be done," the Evil One bellowed, his green serpentine eyes boring into each demon. "I am hungry for prey. Who will give me a report?"

His appointment with the Creator had left him with the sense that something was about to take place which would challenge his authority on earth. He did not have the insight he once did as a beautiful servant of the Lord God Almighty. Relegated to the never-ending frustration that came with his fallen status, he found himself constantly guessing the Creator's intentions through the signs of the times.

Several of his captains slithered before Lucifer. His highest ranking officers, designated Rulers of Territories, had already received their instructions. Now, Lucifer met with the Captains, whose influence was more personal. Using their authority over other demons, the Captains attacked God's precious humanity on an intimate level.

Appearing before his Master in the form of a specter, Dantalion, the Captain of Darkness, addressed Lucifer first.

"There is a man of Assyria. He has been primed for deception, Great One. With your permission, I can continue to use him as a weapon of destruction against the humans."

"Permission granted." No matter what he achieved, Lucifer was never satisfied, always yearning for more. His mission needed to be more focused and determined.

Eligor, the Captain of Enticement, came before him, taking the form of a serpent. "There is a ruler who sets himself up as a god in Rome. He would bring great advancement by luring people into the forest, Great One."

"Do it," Lucifer bellowed. "What of the children of Israel? Any reports there?"

The Captain of Shadows, Belial, stepped forward, his fangs dripping. He took the form of a bat-like creature. "There is a man highly favored by the Creator." The fallen angel spat at the mention of the Holy One.

"Who?" The Evil One questioned his servant.

"He is called Amos of Magdala, O Great One."

"What can be done to him?" The Evil One greatly despised those who lived in the Holy Land—those who were called the chosen ones of Yahweh.

"He longs for a child. We have already discovered a way to entice him toward us. We found an open door in his heart, Great

One. Your servant, Discontent, is prepared to walk in." Belial stepped aside.

Another minion of shadow stepped forward. "I am Discontent, O Great One. I will succeed in planting thoughts in the mind of the Lord's servant."

"The Lord?" The Evil One enlarged his dragon-like form ten times.

Lucifer's rage filled the forest, engulfing the darkness that dwelled there. The forest floor quivered under the weight of the terrified creatures of hell, cowering in fear of their Master's wrath.

"The Lord? We do not utter that blasphemy here! We do not reverence holiness here. We devour it!"

The Evil One stared down at the trembling Discontent. "Are you weak? I do not tolerate weakness. Is there another?"

Another minion of shadow stepped forward at Belial's bidding. "I am Pride, O Great One. I will help Discontent with the enticement."

This fallen angel was larger and stronger than Discontent. He had assisted Belial several times before. With a burst of strength, Pride effortlessly lifted the smaller minion, Discontent, off the ground.

"What is the plan?" The Evil One paced the forest floor, the sound of his talons scratching against the ground echoing through the trees.

"The plan is to bring the man here. We will ruin his reputation as one highly favored. We will strip him of everything until he curses the One who made him." Belial laid out the strategy he had been working on for years. "His faith is too strong for us to possess him. His wife's faith is stronger still. I am doubtful of gaining the man's permission unless I get him away from his wife."

The forest grew unnaturally quiet as the Evil One remained silent, his eyes fixed on his unsuspecting prey. His minions did not move. Lucifer was thinking about the times that were upon them. A sense of impending danger washed over him, as if a formidable opponent was on the horizon, ready for a fierce battle. His forces had grown soft. They had let the children of Israel gain too much ground. Lucifer was not unaware of the prophecy. He had been waiting for the One destined to crush his head. Where was He?

Belial risked speaking into the silence, unbidden. "Amos is a descendant of Judah."

Lucifer let out a deep roar of fire. "What? This man, Amos— he is a descendant of Judah?" The Evil One questioned his servant, overlooking the insolent manner that breached the silence uninvited. Thwarting a child of Judah was a particular desire for Lucifer.

"Yes, O Great One. He has served the Creator whole-heartedly for years. He is not without influence in his community. Yet, a child has been withheld from him."

With excitement in his eyes, Belial eagerly awaited the chance to proceed with Amos, curious about what lay ahead. He had come up against obstacles in laying the ground-work for this man's downfall. The man's wife had a faith that fought against them, stealing every seed they planted in the man's weak heart. Belial was determined to overcome the challenge of the power between this man and woman. It was a power the servant of the Evil One did not understand. Belial had an insatiable desire to conquer everything good, but this inexplicable bond stood in opposition to his best efforts.

The servant of the Evil One was determined to destroy the goodness that existed in this family line from Judah. Belial's anticipation grew as he imagined executing his battle plan, his fanged mouth watering at the prospect of gaining permission to proceed.

Lucifer invaded Belial's thoughts with his loud address to the multitude. "I am looking for the One they call their Messiah. We need to be on alert. I sense that His time is near. We will need to fight harder against the Anointed One. Weaken the faith of the people! Thwart their plans! Lead them astray! Go after the ones strong in the faith. I give you permission to invade and possess in order to prepare our defenses against the Creator's Son. We will fight Him!"

The Evil One commissioned all the soldiers of darkness, the rebels fallen from the grace of the Lord. He stirred them up, granting them more power than he had ever given them in ages past.

The Evil One turned to Belial. "As for this Amos, do whatever is necessary to make sure that this man does not have one shred of faith left in the Creator. I give you free rein to determine how to proceed with this Israelite. Your rank is on the line. I expect a full report once my mission is done. I will be busy searching out my enemy."

"As you wish, O Great One." Belial let his private rage consume him with the desire to destroy this man, Amos.

The Evil One addressed the tribes of darkness standing before him. "My minions, it is time to gather as many as you can. Bring them into our territory. The time is upon us when the enemy will strike us with light. We must snuff it out. We must blind His people to the truth. Remember what they have stolen from us! It was our right to be image-bearers. The Creator chose weak, human flesh over our beauty and strength. He is responsible for casting us out. This love He professes, we will destroy by any means necessary. We will show the Creator the weakness of His children by taking what He loves and turning it to hate, by stealing the light and bringing it into darkness. Go forth and conquer in the power of evil. We are at war with heaven."

The Evil One relished the adoration coming from his minions. Just as he had intended, his words stirred up a frenzy of murderous desire and frightening anticipation.

With an abundance of tasks to tackle, there was hardly any time to properly prepare. He would need every single one of them out among the inhabitants of the earth, wreaking havoc, spewing deception and stealing every inch of holy ground.

PART ONE

The Battle

CHAPTER ONE

A mos walked beneath the shade of the sycamore trees surrounding the courtyard of his estate in Magdala. The day was warm. The breeze was still. His heart stirred within him, igniting a restlessness that compelled him to venture forth despite the scorching heat of the day, while all of God's creation sought solace in stillness. There was complete silence and stillness around him, not a single thing moving. The only thing he could hear was the sound of his leather sandals sticking to the stone ground as he walked.

Why was he plagued by heavy discontent? Amos had everything a man could possibly want. He was wealthy. He held a good position among the elders of the community. He was well-respected. He had a wife that he both loved and adored. Truly, the Lord had blessed Amos. Yet, his lack of a son left a void in his heart. Dwelling on his discontent had consumed him lately, distracting him even during moments of worship, like an incessant buzzing in his ears.

The weight of his prayers seemed to dissipate as quickly as

incense, leaving behind a hollow emptiness. He doubted the Lord. After a decade of marriage to Elisheva, why had there been no child? He should have had many sons by now.

Amos let his thoughts wander into the darkness of this forest of doubt. He had served the Lord diligently, whole-heartedly. His wife was devoted and above reproach in her faith. Despite everything, the joy of having children remained out of reach. He hated to admit it, but Amos was angry with Yahweh.

He walked on toward the garden that skirted the outside of his property. A grand fountain adorned the luscious space, with its crystal-clear water reflecting the vibrant surroundings. But the water had become stagnant in the heat. The only creatures moving were the insects that reproduced abundantly in the area. Amos let his eyes linger on a black beetle as it scuttled across the hot stone ground, seeking refuge from the heat.

The elders had given him advice, urging him to take another wife, believing it would bring him happiness and fulfillment by producing a child. Amos couldn't imagine being with another woman. He didn't want to have a child with another. He wanted a child with Elisheva.

The love he shared with his wife was a true blessing. The other men of his community would not have hesitated to take another. Amos held to his faith, trusting Yahweh, leaning into his wife's relentless belief that they would be blessed with a child in God's timing. However, under the burden of a decade-long wait, Amos felt the thinning of his faith. After all he had done, didn't Yahweh owe him?

"There are other ways." Amos thought he heard a voice hiss from the trees above him.

Amos looked up. The serpentine voice reached his ears so subtly that he immediately questioned its authenticity. Yet, his mind took up the prompting. He wondered if there were other ways he could ensure that his family name would not die out with him.

He was the last of his line, a man of the tribe of Judah, a descendant of Adam, of Abraham, Isaac, and Jacob. Surely, the Lord would not want his family name to discontinue.

"What if the Savior is to come through your line?" hissed the suggestion to Amos's mind.

The thought that he had been especially favored by the Lord caused Amos to feel a surge of pride. After all, he possessed a deep love for his wife that most men did not have. His accumulation of wealth in Magdala was widely regarded as a tangible manifestation of God's favor. He was a man of high standing in the community. Surely, the Messiah would be perfectly situated to come through the descendants of Amos.

The man paced back and forth, circling the fountain of stagnant water. What was to be done? This had to be his calling from the Lord. This was why he was so preoccupied with thoughts of a son. He needed to find a way, even if it meant sacrificing himself to do it. The Lord's work was at stake. The Lord needed Amos's help.

"There is always Endor." The suggestion took root in Amos's mind, spreading like a weed and flourishing in the fertile soil of his discontent.

Endor—the place where dark magic fought with the forces of light. Idolatry flourished in that place. According to legend, the minions of the Evil One were known to roam without opposition, their dark presence casting a shadow over the land. Even a man of faith was no match for the witches of Endor. No, Amos couldn't do that, could he?

Yet the Lord is a God of forgiveness. Surely, Amos would be strong enough to withstand any curses placed on him. No one could match his strength and devotion to the Lord. What harm would come if he merely went to investigate his options there?

Of course, Amos knew he would need to be discreet. Others would not understand his reasons for going toward a city known for evil. Fueled by his overwhelming desire to preserve his lineage, Amos decided to journey to Endor, hoping to find guidance. Determined, he resolved to master the art of controlling the power required to regain what was rightfully his. Perhaps, by fighting the forces of evil directly, he would come away blessed. Amos was too important to let anything hinder Yahweh's work in his life. It occurred to him that this could be a deliberate test to measure his devotion.

Content with his decision, Amos returned to the dwelling. His wife came to him, frantic.

"Where have you been, Amos? I was worried about you," Elisheva said, stroking his perspiring cheek. "Come, sit with me and have something to drink. You should not have been outside in this heat."

"I am fine, beloved. I am more than fine. I feel the Lord has spoken to me. I know what I am to do." When Amos spoke, there was a noticeable pride in his tone.

"To do? About what?" Elisheva asked.

She went to pour her husband some wine, but nearly fell when the dizziness hit her once again. Amos was there to catch her before she fell.

"What is wrong, Elisheva?" he asked her, worry creasing his already wrinkled forehead.

"It must be the heat," she replied.

With a quick gesture, one of the nearby servants took charge of cleaning up the spilled wine, leaving no trace behind. "She has been like this for days, Master. We are worried about her."

"It is nothing," Elisheva said. "The heat gets to me. I am not a young woman anymore."

Amos tended to his wife by placing a cool cloth on her head. Within minutes, she was fine once again. They sat up and conversed. Amos read the Scriptures to her as he prepared for the evening prayer meeting at the synagogue.

He stood as he spoke out loud the designated reading for the evening, "Now the serpent was more subtle than any animal of the field which Yahweh had made. He said to the woman, 'Has God really said, 'You shall not eat of any tree of the garden?' The woman said to the serpent, 'We may eat fruit from the trees of the garden, but not the fruit of the tree which is in the middle of the garden. God has said, 'You shall not eat of it. You shall not touch it, lest you die.' The serpent said to the woman, 'You won't surely die, for God knows that in the day you eat it, your eyes will be opened, and you will be like God, knowing good and evil.'"[2]

"I cannot imagine how horrible that would have been for Eve," Elisheva commented. "I worry that I wouldn't recognize the voice of the Evil One if I heard it."

"Of course you would, beloved wife. As would I. We are children of Yahweh. The Evil One cannot tempt us nor sway us. We would recognize his plots immediately," Amos boasted. "He is not crafty enough to get by a man of faith like me."

"Amos," Elisheva scolded. "You mustn't talk like that. The Evil One is a master of deception. It is by the power of Yahweh, alone, that we are protected. It is His favor that keeps us."

"His favor?" Amos raised his voice unintentionally. "Where is His favor of a child, Elisheva?" Amos didn't mean to sound so harsh, nor did he intend to reveal to her his anger at the Lord.

"My husband," Elisheva stood up and went over to him. "Do not harbor bitterness in your heart. The blessing of the Lord is yet to come. He has plans for our child. I believe that there will yet be life in this family. Do not turn your back on the Lord, my dear husband. Trust in His timing. He has never failed us."

Amos looked at his beloved wife, wishing that he had even one ounce of her firm faith. He kissed her on the forehead. She deserved to have the reproach of barrenness lifted. She deserved to have her life fulfilled by a child. He was even more determined now than before to make that happen.

---

[2] Genesis 3:1-4

Amos departed in the pre-dawn hours. He left instructions with the servants to let his wife know that he was called away on urgent business. In just a few days, he would return, bringing with him the warmth and comfort of a resolution to their problem. He packed some things and departed with a caravan going as far south as Tiberias. From there, he would be sure to find another caravan going to Mount Tabor. He would then journey alone into Endor.

Chapter Two

A mos's plans to travel to Endor were unimpeded, allowing him to set off without any obstacles. With the sun sinking into the horizon, he reached the top of Mount Tabor, where he was greeted by a breathtaking view. An endless horizon of gold and orange stretched as far as the eye could see. He was only allowed one glimpse before darkness swallowed the beauty. Stars winked at him from above when Amos tilted his head skyward. But the descent down the mountain would not allow for him to keep his focus skyward.

At the base of the mountain, Amos found an inn where he could spend the night. A portly man took his coins and offered Amos a stark room with a bed that looked less than desirable to sleep in. The sight of the run-down surroundings was a stark contrast to what Amos was accustomed to.

Against the warning in his heart, he managed to settle in, convincing himself that he had made the right decision. His choices were limited. He could not live with the unfulfilled desires of childlessness. Not only that, but he owed it to his wife. He did this as much for her as he did it for himself. Amos dropped off his things and went to the common area because he was not yet tired enough to sleep.

As night fell, several of the traveling men emerged from Endor, their weary faces illuminated by the fading light flickering in the lamps set on each table. Some looked for lodging and food in the establishment where Amos resided. Some looked to stir up trouble. Amos, famished and unable to resist, reluctantly resisted the urge to retreat to the safety of his solitary room. Instead, his flesh forced him to join the boisterous gathering of men.

He stumbled upon a table tucked away in a quiet corner, offering him a shield of solitude. The owner of the establishment brought Amos a plate of food that looked edible but not entirely delectable. Amos had hoped to go unnoticed, but a burly man with a thick accent ignored the shield of solitude erected around Amos.

"You look like a wealthy man. What would a prominent Jew like yourself be doing in a place like this?" The man stood as he took his last swig of the ale he was drinking. Every muscle in his body seemed to be chiseled out of stone, exuding an aura of strength.

Amos merely looked at him without replying.

"Are you too good to talk to me?" The man got up and joined Amos at the table.

"I am only lodging for the night. My business is my own." Amos attempted to project confidence through his tone of voice.

"Your business is your own?" As the man laughed, his booming voice reverberated, capturing everyone's attention. When he slammed his fist on the table, most were wise enough to look away.

In a split second, he closed the distance between them, his breath warm against Amos's ear as he spoke in a low, intimidating tone. Something changed inside the man. His eyes held a powerful intensity that was impossible to ignore.

"Now I want to make your business my business."

"What is it that you want?" Amos could feel his irritation growing as the man continued to meddle with him. The man's intense look sent shivers down his spine. It took every ounce of Amos's provincial strength to not recoil from the man.

"What does every man want? Perhaps money and women? Of those, I am guessing you only have the one. The desires of the flesh—that is what drives many men to dangerous decisions."

"I don't have any money to spare. Please move on."

Amos got up, his heart pounding with a mixture of fear and uncertainty. He couldn't tell if his reaction was because of the man's request for money or the unsettling feeling that the man was peering into his soul.

The giant man grabbed him by the arm. The realization hit Amos that he was completely outmatched and had no hope of winning a fight against him. The man was too big.

"I am giving you one chance to turn around and go home. This will be your last warning. If you don't pay me, you will pay with life!" The man dug his fingers into Amos's arm. "Think long and hard about your decision, man of God."

Just then, the owner of the establishment came over. "Don't harass my customers, Angelo. Move on. He is under my protection."

Angelo let go of Amos's arm with a quick jerking motion. "Are you accepting his protection over mine?"

Amos looked at the man named Angelo. An unsettling sadness had replaced the once vibrant, fierce spark in his eyes, leaving them dull and lifeless. He no longer looked frightening.

Amos answered him, "I am. Leave me."

With that, Angelo turned around and disappeared from Amos's sight.

The owner escorted Amos back to his sparse room. The night was long. Amos tossed and turned throughout the night, his sleep disturbed by unsettled angst. His thoughts swirled around the exchange he had with the man named Angelo. What kind of protection had he been offering? Was Amos unwise in refusing it?

He felt a sense of nakedness and vulnerability, as if all his defenses had been stripped away when Angelo left him. The sensation he experienced was unlike anything he had ever felt before. Eager to leave the lodge at the foot of Mount Tabor, he hastily packed his bags.

Amos left in the pre-dawn hours of the following morning. As he descended into Endor, the wind rushed past his ears, creating a high-pitched whistling sound. Crossing the border was like passing through a gossamer veil of evil that Amos was oblivious to. The air of the territory felt heavy and threatening, wrapping itself around Amos like a cloak he was completely unaware of putting on. As Amos looked up at the sky, he couldn't shake the sense that a violent storm was on its way, even though there wasn't a single cloud in sight.

He walked through the murky streets with caution, unsure where he should go. The people he encountered were mostly cloaked and stooped, adding to the eerie atmosphere as he walked by. No one spoke.

As he walked down the street, he couldn't help but notice the dilapidated buildings, their cracked windows and chipped exterior telling stories of neglect. Trash scattered profusely throughout the streets gave off an unpleasant odor. Amos did his best to step over the trash and waste that littered the cobblestone ground he walked on.

His eyes briefly lingered on the numerous statues of idols strewn throughout the city. Against the backdrop of filth and darkness, their beauty was all the more enticing. As Amos continued, it became more and more difficult for him to turn his eyes away from the sparkling gold images and the dazzling silver forms. Gradually, his vision adapted to the surroundings, revealing intricate details that captivated his senses. Within moments, his eyes adapted to the lack of light, and he could make out the shapes and shadows in the darkness. Endor appeared more beautiful the longer Amos walked among the idols.

When he got to the city square, Amos leaned against a fountain that had gone dry. The dusty air created in him an awareness of his parched thirst. Amos scanned the area, looking for anywhere he might get a drink. Doubt started to creep into his mind, making him question whether it was time to depart from this location.

Angelo's question haunted him. *"I am giving you one chance to turn around and go home. This will be your last warning. If you don't pay me, you will pay with life."*

Pay with life. What did that mean? A sense of uncertainty washed over him, causing him to reconsider the merit of his idea. Amos stood up to leave, keeping his eyes down so that he would not risk setting his gaze upon the idolatrous statues that stood circling the square. A woman came to him, appearing out of nowhere.

"My good man, could you help an old woman?"

Startled by her sudden presence, Amos glanced up. The woman looked frail and tired.

"Of course, what is it that you need?" Amos asked her, taking her arm so he could help her stand.

"I need to get back to my mistress. It is hard for me to see. Would you take me home?"

"Yes, just tell me where you need to go," Amos said, the warnings in his heart completely disappearing.

"My mistress is the Enchantress of Endor. She is down the street a short way, here on the left. She will be most generous to you for helping me. I am sure she will reward you. She has many powers." The woman's words enticed him.

"Many powers?" Amos asked. "Like what?"

"Anything, good man. Whatever your heart desires, she can give it to you. She is an Enchantress for the Angel of light."

"Angel of light?" Amos thought that didn't sound so bad.

Perhaps this was divine intervention after all.

When Amos slipped his arm around the old woman in order to help her, his entire perspective shifted. Forgotten were the dark streets and run-down shops. Amos saw the jeweled pavement before him. As they walked through the city, he marveled at the stunning architecture, the buildings all crafted from pristine ivory. The fountain burst with red-tinted water. It was utterly breathtaking. Why had he not noticed it before?

He walked the old woman to the dwelling she led him to, delighting in the beautiful sights and sounds of Endor. It was like no other territory Amos had seen before. Everything was alluring to him. Amos did not hesitate to go inside the house belonging to the Enchantress.

• • •

Belial waited on the periphery of her consciousness. The Enchantress of Endor, a formidable human agent of darkness, possessed the power to disguise herself as an angel of light. That power had been granted to her by the Evil One himself.

Belial lurked, awaiting her surrender so he could enter in, infusing her with his own power. Frustration started to build within him as the wait stretched on.

"Discontent! Pride! Report to me immediately," he yelled into the darkness.

"Yes, Captain. We are here." Pride bowed before him.

"What is it? Why is he not here?"

"We ran into some opposition on Mount Tabor, Captain," Discontent uttered.

"What opposition?" With each hurdle he encountered, Belial's anger intensified, adding to his growing frustration.

"The Holy One sent one of His, an angel, to give the man one more chance to turn around and go home. The man was pondering it. He hesitated," Pride informed his Captain.

"And you did nothing?" Belial grabbed Pride by his slender,

scaly neck.

"We enticed him with a woman in need of help. He is on his way here now," Discontent reported. "But there is another obstacle, Captain."

"Another? Another? What is it now?" Belial had been trying to capture souls from this particular line of the tribe of Judah for hundreds of years. The constant string of losses was beginning to exhaust him. His determination to snatch Amos out of the hands of the Creator was unyielding.

"The woman is already with child," Discontent informed the Captain. "She doesn't know it yet. We will not be able to reach the child through darkness because the Holy One has already touched her mother's womb."

Belial used his fangs to rip part of Discontent's small wing.

"How dare you keep using that phrase! The Creator is thwarting us. Can't you see that? He is not the Holy One that you keep calling Him. If you use that phrase again, you will be demoted to the fiery pit, no longer an agent of darkness that roams the earth. Are you understanding me?" Belial spit out the blood from Discontent's wound.

"Yes, Captain." Discontent crumpled into a ball, licking the festering sore where his wing had been.

Belial began pacing. The Enchantress had not opened herself up to him yet. He still had time to devise another plan of attack. If the child would not be conceived under the powers of darkness, then Belial could devour the child with shadow and use it as a weapon against Amos.

"What else do you know?" Belial addressed Pride directly.

"We know that the child to be born will be female. We also know that the bargain struck with the angel was that if Amos did not turn back and pay Him, the Creator, it would cost him life. Amos replied to the angel—'I AM, leave me.' He refused the protection of the Creator." Pride bowed before his captain.

"That is good. We can use this in our favor. I will need you to call Disappointment and Despair to be ready for battle here with us. The man has refused protection from the Creator, so our time to strike his family is now. Do we know what life will be demanded for the man's disobedience?" Belial salivated at the thought that he might claim more than one soul for the Evil One if he brought this new development to fruition.

"We do not know, Captain," Pride answered. "The life required for the disobedience is a mystery to us. It could be the man or his wife or his child."

"No matter," Belial said. "All I need now is for Amos to invite me into his family. Once he gives consent, there will be nothing he can do to get back beneath the banner of the Creator's protection."

"How will you convince him since he already has a child on the way?" Discontent inquired.

"He doesn't know that, does he? Our greatest tool is deception. I will use that power to lure him to surrender his will to mine." Belial turned away from them. He heard the opening of the Enchantress's surrender.

Belial entered the Enchantress of Endor. Becoming one with a human as comfortable as putting on shackles. He didn't like it. He felt bounded, confined. Yet, the battle required it. The war with heaven demanded it.

"Welcome, Amos. I have been expecting you." She spoke softly, kindly.

"How did you know my name?" Amos sounded surprised.

"I know a lot about you, son of Judah. You are highly respected by your people. You are a mighty man of Yahweh."

Amos squirmed in a seat across from the Enchantress of Endor, mesmerized by her beauty. The man found it impossible to look away from her enchanting presence. He focused on her hair, dark as the black sky at night. Her eyes held him with an intoxicating hue, gray like shadows. Belial sensed Amos felt powerful in her presence, pleased by her assessment of him. He could hardly speak in her presence.

"I must thank you for your kindness in bringing my servant back to me," the Enchantress spoke in her soothing voice. "She is most important to my work."

Amos looked around, but the old woman had disappeared. The man struggled against the warning in his heart, intoxicated by the lure of the Enchantress.

"I would like to reward you for your kindness. What can I do for you?" The Enchantress looked at him, her eyes mesmerizing him.

"I'm not sure. I ...." Amos hesitated.

He couldn't seem to form the words. Something held him back, a memory of a warning. He couldn't formulate any clarity of thought.

"I see in your heart that you long for a child. You have waited for so long. You have served Yahweh with such diligence. He delights to bless you, Amos. You have only to ask. You have only to invite the power of the great one into your family." The Enchantress stood.

"What do you mean?" Amos asked her, befuddled.

"Ask for what you want. Surrender to the will of the Great One. You have traveled a long way. You fought against the evil at the establishment in Mount Tabor, didn't you? You are strong, Amos. You have great faith."

Amos had the look of a man who felt like he could conquer anything, like he had an invisible shield protecting him. He had no more reasons to object to anything the Enchantress was saying. He believed he had won the favor of Yahweh by his fortitude and resistance. The hole in his heart because he was without a son had become a distraction for him. Of course, the Holy One would not want Amos to be distracted in his worship.

Amos stood and kneeled down before the Enchantress. "I surrender to your will, Great One. I invite you into my family in order that your power might give me the child I long for. Will you bless me with a child?"

"Very good, you are mine now," the Enchantress hissed.

Amos stood quickly at the sound of the change in her voice. Had he not heard that voice before? Suddenly the atmosphere that had been filled with light became dark and foreboding. Amos couldn't understand what was happening.

"I said you may go now. Your wish has been granted. Your wife is with child." Her voice was dull and human, not supernatural like it had been. Belial had left her.

Amos looked at her as he turned to leave. She appeared different, normal. How could that be? What had just happened?

Once outside, Amos felt sick. He was left with a sense of discontentment that lingered long after the experience had ended. He felt exposed and vulnerable, hurt deep inside by some unseen heavy pressure. He suddenly wanted to hurry home. He wanted to be with his wife.

Amos wasted no more time in Endor. He made haste to get back to Mount Tabor in order to connect with the first caravan heading to Tiberius. He would lodge there for the night, as far away from Endor as he could get in a day.

Despite his expectations, the dark foreboding that had plagued him in the cursed city of Endor continued to haunt Amos even as he distanced himself from it. When he lay down to rest in a place of lodging in Tiberius, Amos never felt so alone and defiled. What had he done?

CHAPTER THREE

It was the middle of the night, when darkness was at its peak and only the nocturnal creatures stirred. Amos paced near the fountain. He was restless, wondering why his heart refused to find contentment in the news that Elisheva was going to bear him a child in only a few short months. Upon his return from Endor, she was filled with overwhelming joy and couldn't wait to share the revelation with him. Though Amos acted pleased in order to honor his wife, the reality had not produced in him the level of joyous gratitude that he had so long anticipated.

Amos knew that he should pray, but his mind would not form words. In the depths of his being, he felt a raw vulnerability, as if his soul was laid bare in an empty vacuum. He continued pacing back and forth, his weary heart enveloping the darkness both outside and within him.

"My husband," Elisheva's voice whispered into the quiet of night like a flame piercing the darkness with light. "Why are you out here at this hour?"

"I could not sleep," Amos replied, a little startled by her

sudden appearance.

"You have not slept well in months. What troubles you?" Elisheva was by his side, rubbing her hand protectively over her swollen belly.

"It is nothing," Amos told her. "Go back to bed."

"I am not leaving until you tell me what it is that bothers you." Elisheva linked her arm through his. "We can bear our burdens better together than alone."

Amos couldn't help but be drawn to the comforting warmth in Elisheva's voice. She was so inviting. Her love was so welcoming. Amos longed to relieve the burdens of his heart, but he didn't know how to put into words what he was feeling. Perhaps if he skirted around the truth, he could still unburden himself without actually admitting wrongdoing.

The sudden idea that he had done something wrong troubled Amos, causing a knot of unease to form in his stomach. It had not occurred to him that he felt guilty. Somehow, being in Elisheva's presence, surrounded by the light of her faith, made Amos feel powerfully convicted. Perhaps that was the reason he had been avoiding her more than usual the past few weeks.

"My husband, you have withdrawn from me ever since receiving news of the child. Why? This is a blessing from the Lord. We have every reason to celebrate, yet you are still not satisfied. Please, tell me what troubles you." Elisheva pleaded with him.

The conviction inside of Amos produced in him an anger he had never before experienced. Rather than entering into the softness of his wife's love, Amos retaliated with blame. It was her fault that he had to go to Endor. It was her fault that they had been without a child for so long.

"This child is not a blessing, Elisheva. I made it happen by bargaining with the Enchantress of Endor. At the time, I thought I was doing the Lord's work. She looked like an angel of light. I see now that I was wrong. If you had only been able to conceive, I would not have been led into sin." Amos glared at her, unmoved by the tears that fell from her eyes, unsure why he was uttered things that he had not even processed thoroughly in his own mind.

Elisheva stared at him as if she didn't know him or recognize him. Her expression was a mixture of fright and shock. Amos could no longer hide the difference. She had seen the shadows that taunted him, but she must have dismissed it as her own imagination. Her expression melted into one of resolute determination that shed light on the battle being waged in the unseen realm.

"I do not believe it! I won't believe it! This child is a gift from Yahweh. I know that it is. Whatever agreement you have made with darkness, Husband, can be undone. Fall upon the Lord's mercy. He always gives His faithful followers a chance of escape. He gives us a choice to turn back before it is too late." Elisheva fell to her knees, praying on behalf of her husband.

Amos watched her, his heart hardening. He thought back to the night on Mount Tabor when the man named Angelo asked him if he wanted protection. Amos was told if he turned around all would be well and if he did not, then a life would be the required payment—a life, what life? Had Amos given up his life without fully knowing what he was doing? Was that why he could not feel the presence of Yahweh anymore?

Amos walked away, leaving Elisheva on her knees praying by the empty fountain in the darkness of night.

• • •

Belial was pleased with his servant, Discontent. The demon kept Amos's heart in constant turmoil within him. It was a necessary strategy to ensure that the ground was perfectly prepared for Despair to enter the realm.

"Captain." Discontent approached him. "The man, Amos, still has a protective growth over his heart. His roots of faith are deeper than we suspected. I have been unable to get him to fully surrender his will. He goes back and forth. We are relying on emotions to keep him in this state of readiness. He is not used to the anger and frustration. I fear it will drive him to prayer. He keeps thinking about it."

"You mustn't let that happen," Belial shouted. "Do whatever you can to keep him from praying. It is elemental, but necessary if we are to achieve victory."

"Yes, Captain." Discontent hesitated, fear the response to the growing anger from his Captain. "The wife, she prays even more now. I don't understand her power. We cannot get near her or the child within her womb."

"No matter," Belial responded. "We will devise a battle plan for the child once it is born. In the meantime, focus on undermining Amos's heart. We need to strip his heart of all faith in order to access his soul. Once we do that, it will only be a matter of time before he is ours. You have done well in setting up this captive, Discontent. If you succeed, a name may be given to you by the Evil One himself."

"A name! Then I would be considered in the ranks of the Captains. What positions are available?" Discontent foamed at the mouth.

Belial studied the young demon. He needed to keep him motivated. "Both the Captain of Intrigue and the Captain of Abandonment have become Rulers of Territories. They have moved on to be by Lucifer's side in the battle against the Messiah." Belial spit on the ground, furious that the promotion to Ruler had escaped him once again. "If all goes well with this family. If we succeed with two souls for the kingdom of darkness," Belial continued, "then the Captain of Shadows position could be yours as well." Belial fluttered his black wings in anticipation of the promotion he so desperately wanted.

"You will be promoted to the Great One's side?" Discontent asked him.

"That is what I desire. I have wasted too much time over the years on this family from the tribe of Judah. It is time that something significant is stolen from them. Their faith has run deep. Surely, the Creator would be most displeased with losing them to us." Belial laughed a hideous cackle. "Keep the ground ready, hold your position. We will wait for the opportune time to strike."

"As you wish, Captain," Discontent replied, satisfied that he was still in charge of this particular mission.

• • •

Elisheva did not cease praying for her husband. She fasted and prayed every day. She made offerings at the synagogue. Though the battle remained unseen, Elisheva felt it all around her and she fought on her knees, crying out to the Holy One for mercy.

"Lord, do not let Your servant suffer at the hands of darkness. Forgive my husband for the error of his ways. Bring him back to the light. Let Your power guide and protect him. Rid him of the influence of evil that has deceived him, Lord. I ask You, our Lord and our God." Elisheva prayed relentlessly, especially during the night when Amos couldn't sleep.

She watched over her husband as he ate his meals in silence, retreating further and further into himself. Amos still went through the motions of religious rituals at the synagogue, but he no longer put forth the effort to study the Scriptures or read them to her. No one in the community suspected anything because Amos upheld the pretense of religion devoid of faith.

One afternoon as Amos was eating his lentils, Elisheva sang over him.

"Yahweh is my light and my salvation. Whom shall I fear? Yahweh is the strength of my life. Of whom shall I be afraid? When evildoers came at me to eat up my flesh, even my adversaries and my foes, they stumbled and fell. Though an army should encamp against me, my heart shall not fear. Though war should rise against me, even then I will be

confident. One thing I have asked of Yahweh, that I will seek after, that I may dwell in Yahweh's house all the days of my life, to see Yahweh's beauty, and to inquire in His temple."[3]

Amos looked up at her. She knelt before her husband, the life inside her belly stirring to the song. Elisheva knew that she had reached some place deep inside Amos when she saw a single tear trickle away from his eye.

"I want to seek Him, Elisheva. I don't know how. Help me. Please help me." Amos got down on his knees with his wife. He was exhausted, but he didn't know why.

"Pray, my husband. The answer lies in prayer. Let us make a pilgrimage to the Temple in Jerusalem. We can pray along the way, as well as when we get there."

"Are you well enough to travel?" Amos asked her.

"It is still a few weeks before the baby is to arrive. I am sure we can be back before then." A glimmer of hope filled Elisheva's weary heart. Perhaps a change of territory would diminish the hold of darkness.

"Alright then. Let us go to Jerusalem." Amos appeared exhilarated by the prospect of a trip. It had been a long time since he had made a pilgrimage to the Holy City.

Fearful that he might change his mind, Elisheva pressed the decision. "Let's leave right away. We can pack quickly with the servant's help."

"Leave now?" Amos questioned her.

"Yes, don't hesitate, my husband. Let us go." Elisheva summoned the servants, eager to move forward so that her husband didn't turn back.

When the couple arrived in Jerusalem, the sounds of chatter and footsteps filled the air as the city overflowed with people. Amos and Elisheva made their way through the crowded streets. Elisheva sat uncomfortably atop the donkey that endured her

---

[3] Psalm 27:1-4

weight for the day-long trip.

The look of delight and joy on Amos's face as they came upon the Temple was worth it. She could see that his eyes were no longer clouded by the shadows. Clarity slowly returned to him, like a fog lifting from his countenance. Elisheva did her best to hide the pain she felt because she didn't want to distract Amos from worshiping the Lord.

Elisheva dismounted, holding tight to Amos's hand. He led her up the steps. Losing her balance, Elisheva steadied herself by reaching out to the cornerstone.

"Are you alright?" Amos asked her.

"Yes, my husband. I am in awe of the beauty of the Temple stones." Elisheva smiled at Amos.

They made their offering together before going to pray in the courtyard. Amos remained with Elisheva in the court of women because he did not want to leave her side.

"You are my light, Elisheva," Amos said to her, his eyes expressing gratitude for the strength she had to bear his burdens.

"The Lord is your light, Amos, not me."

Elisheva touched his cheek. She loved this man too much to let him idolize her. The love they shared was a gift from Yahweh, for which she would always be thankful. Elisheva took Amos's hand and held it to her stomach. They both knelt down in prayer, covering their heads with their prayer shawls.

The child moved beneath Amos's touch. The love in Elisheva's heart burst as she felt her husband coming back to her. Something broke inside of him. A barrier came down. With his hand resting on the new life created inside Elisheva's womb, Amos prayed long and hard.

"Forgive me, my Lord, my iniquities are far too great. Answer me when I call, God of my righteousness. Give me relief from my distress. Have mercy on me, and hear my prayer. Set apart for yourself all who are godly. Redeem my mistake, Yahweh." Amos spoke out loud before entering into a space of silence. Elisheva shared the heaviness of

the conflict within him. He suddenly became aware of the battle that had been waging unseen around him for the past few months.

Elisheva remained on the ground next to her husband in silent prayer for hours. They were united, one flesh coming together in prayer against the forces of evil attacking their family. Just when Elisheva sensed they were gaining back some of the ground that had been stolen from them, the pains began. She remained silent for as long as she could, not wanting to give up her battle position. The physical distraction became too much for her. She had to move, to change position.

As soon as she moved, Elisheva couldn't help but release a pained groan that she had been suppressing. The thread of prayer was broken as Amos responded to his wife's distress.

"What is it, Elisheva?" Amos helped her get up.

"The child. It comes," Elisheva announced. "It is early."

"Someone help us!" Amos yelled. His frantic movements caught the attention of those around him as he desperately tried to help her.

A group of Temple guards came over. They gently assisted Amos in escorting Elisheva to a serene room tucked away off the portico.

"Come with us," one of the guards said to him. "There is a woman here who can help."

"Wait," Elisheva reached up and touched her husband's face. She looked into his eyes. They were clearer than they had been in a long while, but the shadows were moving in again. She pulled him close to her and kissed him. "Love, Amos. Love wins every time."

Amos smiled, even though he didn't understand what she was saying. He hurriedly left, trailing behind the guards as they led him to find a woman who could assist his wife.

Elisheva let the stillness of the afternoon calm her while the prayers of worshipers wafted into the space she currently occupied. She felt dizzy and feverish. With each pang, her body grew warmer and warmer. She let her mind focus in on the melding of mumbled prayers outside in the courtyard. She could suddenly smell the incense of the most Holy Place.

Elisheva breathed in the silence, letting the fragrance of holiness infuse her entire being. She endured the painful contractions with prayerful concentration for several minutes. When her surroundings faded in and out, Elisheva worried that she might lose consciousness. The air felt lighter and thinner, as if the atmosphere was slowly dissipating. The room shimmered with an ethereal light. Elisheva knew that she was not alone.

"Greetings, favored daughter of the Most High. I come with grave tidings. I am Gabriel, Messenger of Yahweh." The angel stood before her, his presence bathing the entire room with radiant light.

"Your servant listens," Elisheva replied, breathless with awe and wonder at the beauty of Yahweh's messenger. In his presence, she was shielded from the pain in her body.

"Your prayer has been heard. The Lord grants mercy to you with a choice. The child in your womb is a female child with a destiny yet to be determined. Your husband's disobedience will cost a life. But the life it will cost is a choice given to you. You may choose to spare yourself and the Holy One will bless you with another child, a male heir." The angel Gabriel's voice was not harsh, but it was demanding.

Elisheva knew in her heart the moment Gabriel spoke the words what she would do. "Servant of the Living God, I have been mightily blessed. Let my life be taken in place of this child. I ask for the favor of the Lord's mercy at my request."

"As you wish, daughter of Yahweh," Gabriel replied.

Elisheva bowed her head in prayer. *"May the grace granted to me in my life be passed on to her. Seal her heart with a love reserved only for You, our Lord and King. May her eyes see the wonder of Your salvation."*

The angel Gabriel touched Elisheva's abdomen. The baby was brought forth instantly into the light. Elisheva caught one glimpse of the beautiful child given to her by Yahweh before she took her last breath. She smiled as Gabriel touched the female child's heart with his finger of light. Elisheva knew without a doubt that her prayer had been answered. The baby girl began to cry when Gabriel departed from the Temple, taking her mother with him.

The guards brought the woman, and Amos showed up right behind them. As soon as Anna stepped inside, she was taken aback by the eerie juxtaposition of life and death within the room.

CHAPTER FOUR

A mos was woefully unprepared for the scene before him. As soon as he heard the midwife gasp and a servant's scream, he wasted no time and stormed into the birthing room. The first thing his eyes took in was the lifeless form of his beloved wife's body. Her eyes stared straight ahead as if looking into something Amos could not see. Her smile bespoke of a belief in the unseen that Amos was fast losing.

The grieving man fell to his knees and crawled to his wife's side. This was the cost for his sin. The price was death. Amos let his tears fall, unaware that the emotion of grief was being manipulated into anger by hidden forces lurking within the room.

"You have a daughter. She is healthy and beautiful," Anna pronounced, hoping to pull the man out of the gloom of his grief.

Amos stood quickly. The woman tried to hand him the child.

"What did you say?" he asked her in a menacing tone of voice.

"Your daughter, my lord." Anna extended the child, wrapped in a linen blanket.

"I don't have a daughter," Amos spat, his face turning red with rage. "Where is my son? I was promised a son!"

"My lord, there is no male child here. Your wife birthed a daughter. She is precious. She is healthy. What would you name her?" Anna gave Amos a scolding look. His reaction was not appropriate for a new father. The darkness swirling within him no longer seemed to be hidden.

"Name her? Call her Mary because she has brought a sea of bitterness and sorrow to my household!"

With that statement over his child, the child he had longed for, the child his wife had died to give birth to, Amos stormed out of the room, refusing to touch the daughter that would bear the name Mary.

Anna cuddled the crying infant to her breast. "Hush now, little Mary of Magdala. Your father is grieving. He will come around. In the meantime, we will just have to call you Magda because I believe that you will be a tower of honor to Amos's household—a tower of love that rises from this sea of bitterness and sorrow."

• • •

"How could you let this happen?" Belial raged, fuming and frothing at the mouth. His thin wings unfurled, making him look three times larger than he was.

Discontent trembled before him, afraid he would be turned from his lizard-like form back to an insect relegated down to pestering humans, stripped of all the power he had gained.

"Captain, the woman led him to pray at the Temple. Her faith was strong, but she is gone now. Something happened when she gave birth. We were blinded to it, but she is gone."

"Gone? What happened?" Belial asked, calming himself down by curling his outstretched wings.

"She died in childbirth. The child is without a mother. Her father does not want her because she was not born male. He named her Mary. He is about to leave the protection of the Temple. Once he does, Despair is ready to uproot what remains of his faith."

Discontent spilled out everything he knew in an effort to appease the wrath of his master. He left out the part about being blinded by the incredible light when the child came into the world, fearing it would only add to Belial's agitated state.

"Very good. We can still work with this situation. In fact, it might even be better. Stay with Amos. I will begin strategizing for the child. It is good for us that her life did not have the usual effect on her father. Otherwise, we may have lost this battle. Keep Amos distracted. If he loves the child, we will not succeed in securing her for the darkness because she will have the protection of her father until she comes of age. I have waited long enough for this family's demise." Belial took flight.

Discontent sighed with relief. He had not lost his position after all. He would have to work twice as hard now to make sure that Amos did not slip from his talons once again. He summoned Despair who was ever ready, having taken on a shadow in the form of a green-eyed wolf.

"The target is primed. The roots of his faith need to be snipped. You are exactly the one to do it. Make sure to keep him focused on his grief so that he does not end up extending love to the child, Mary." Discontent felt important giving instructions to the lesser demon.

"As you wish," Despair slinked off into the darkness.

• • •

In his time of grief, Amos chose to seek comfort in Bethany with his sister, Milcah, while his wife's body was being prepared for burial. Milcah had an infant of her own named Rachel. Her small son, Samuel, was almost four. Milcah was delighted to see her brother and the child, Mary.

"My brother, it has been far too long!" Milcah hugged her

older brother, welcoming him inside her small dwelling.

Like Elisheva, Milcah was a woman of unwavering faith and inner strength. She married a simple man who toiled in the fertile fields of Bethany. Amos had always admired his sister for her ability to leave the comfortable life they had in Magdala for a simple life of a peasant in Bethany. He did what he could to help her with his portion of the inheritance, but Milcah was content with her husband and children on the land they owned in the small village outside Jerusalem.

"I have tidings that will not bring joy to your heart, Milcah. Elisheva died bringing this child into the world." Amos could not hide the blame or disgust in his voice.

Sorrow eclipsed Milcah's heart upon receiving the news. Elisheva was an admirable sister-in-law. Milcah picked up on her brother's animosity toward the sweet child named Mary. If not for her brother's troubled response, Milcah would have allowed herself to deal with her grief. Instead, she looked down into the baby's eyes, deep and inviting, just like Elisheva's.

"She has her mother's eyes, Amos. She will remind you of your beloved all the days of her life." Milcah searched for ways to help her brother embrace and accept the child. Every child needed the protection of a father's love.

"She will remind me of the cost and nothing more!" Amos turned away from his sister.

"Uncle Amos!" With boundless energy, Samuel ran inside, leaving a trail of excitement in his wake. "Let me show you the frogs we found."

"Frogs?" Amos picked up Samuel. "Look how you have grown, Samuel. A fine son you are for your parents. Yes, a fine son." Amos hugged him tight, shooting an envious look in Milcah's direction.

"Can we go outside?" Samuel wanted to be released from the tight embrace.

"Of course." Amos let him down.

"Samuel, come meet your niece, Mary." Milcah bent down to show Samuel the baby.

Samuel looked at her intently. "She will be pretty, won't she, Mama?"

"I think so, my son. Now, go and show your uncle the frogs." Milcah hugged Mary to her, thankful that her own baby, Rachel, was asleep.

"The child will need to be nursed," Amos said. His words were so devoid of emotion that Milcah's maternal heart pricked with worry. "I could pay you if..."

"Amos, my brother, she is family. I will nurse her and return her to you when she is weaned. No payment is necessary," Milcah said.

As she listened to her brother's distant tone, unease settled in her chest. It was heartbreaking to witness a man treating a child he had eagerly anticipated for almost ten years with such disregard. She hoped that it was only on account of his grief.

"Very well, I thank you, Sister," Amos said before going outside with Samuel.

"Uncle Amos?" Samuel addressed him as they walked out of Milcah's presence.

"Yes, Samuel," Amos replied.

"Your daughter looks very important. Is she someone special?"

Amos scoffed at the boy's observation. "She is nothing, Samuel, just another girl."

Milcah shook her head, glad when the door shut behind them.

Later, Amos joined his sister's family for the evening meal. Milcah carefully arranged a spread of farm-fresh dishes, each one bursting with flavors of their homegrown produce. Her husband, Kohath, led them in prayer as the family mourned the loss of Elisheva together. At the end of the meal, Kohath, as head of his family, closed their meal time with a song of lament.

"*I acknowledged my sin to You. I didn't hide my iniquity. I said, I will confess my transgressions to Yahweh, and You forgave the iniquity of my sin...Don't be like the horse, or like the mule, which have no understanding, who are controlled by bit and bridle, or else they will not come near to You. Many sorrows come to the wicked, but loving kindness shall surround him who trusts in Yahweh.*"[4] Kohath sang, his voice filling the room with a melodic harmony.

Amos felt a hole in his heart that refused to be filled. Everything he did was a mistake. He was angry at Yahweh for taking the life of his wife. He was angry at himself for thinking that prayer in the Temple would bring relief to his present suffering. Where was this loving kindness that Kohath sang about? Amos had no trust in Yahweh. Compared to before, he was now in a much more dire condition.

Amos slept heavily beneath the blanket of grief that suffocated the sliver of light that had almost pierced the darkness of his heart. Nothing seemed to matter to him anymore. He didn't care about this child, Mary. He didn't want her. She was responsible for the death of her mother. The child was a curse. She was birthed from the powers of darkness; and to the powers of darkness she belonged. Amos wanted nothing to do with her.

The baby remained with Milcah, who agreed to raise her alongside Rachel until the child was weaned. Amos was eager to be rid of the baby. At least for the next two years, he wouldn't have to worry about the child. He left Bethany and returned to Magdala with the body of his wife. Elisheva had been anointed and prepared for burial by the woman named Anna, who resided in the Temple.

Amos endured an excruciatingly long trip home, the hours dragging on relentlessly. It ended up being a funeral procession for the love of his life. Emptiness washed over Amos, leaving him

---

[4] Psalm 32:5,9-10

feeling hollow and numb. He couldn't eat or rest. When he returned to Magdala, the entire community was ready to help. Elisheva was laid to rest in the family tomb. Amos didn't even appreciate the condolences and help that people offered him. He only wanted to be left alone.

Once the mourners departed and the lamenters quieted their laments, Amos returned to his empty house. He dismissed all of his servants. He sat alone in the dark, drinking the wine he had saved up for the occasion of celebrating the birth of his son.

For days, Amos let Despair become his only friend. Soon it gave way to melancholy. Melancholy gave way to self-loathing. Amos spent two years of his life slipping further and further away from the light. He was dismissed as elder of the community. He lived solely off his inheritance, having grown lazy as well as selfish.

• • •

"Captain, we have gained a lot of ground in the man, Amos." Discontent eagerly reported to Belial. "Despair made room for both Melancholy and Laziness by using the power of self-loathing."

"Good work, Discontent," Belial stated. "The child is almost weaned. I suspect they will return her to the estate in Magdala. I have a battle strategy ready for her when the opportunity is ripe. I do not suspect we will meet with any resistance. She will be prized by the Great One. He searches diligently for the one who is to give birth to the promised Messiah. I have wondered if this female, Mary, could have been a woman of great means. There is something about her, something I cannot quite place." Belial ruffled the membranes of his wings. "She might have potentially been a tool in the Creator's plan for the Messiah. We will see to it that she is nothing but a failure as we claim her for the darkness."

"The efforts are concentrated now around Judah, Captain. Is there any news?" Discontent asked him.

"The Messiah will be born or already has been. Lucifer has not discovered Him, but he has enticed King Herod to go on a murderous rampage against all boys under the age of two in Bethlehem. In this way, he is sure to thwart the prophecy." Belial cackled, spreading his wings in victorious display.

CHAPTER FIVE

Where had the time gone? Two years flew by with the swiftness of a bird taking flight, its outstretched wings catching the invisible breeze that would lead it to fulfill its destiny. Milcah let her mind drift to sweet moments that she would cherish in her heart. She recalled that day with peculiar contemplation...

When the time came for baby Mary to be dedicated at the Temple, Milcah sent messenger after messenger to her brother, Amos. He never responded. Milcah was deeply troubled by her brother's overwhelming grief, which prevented him from recognizing the precious gift that his child was. She and Kohath took matters into their own hands and personally brought Mary for her dedication, ensuring it was done in accordance with their Jewish customs.

While the neighbors took care of baby Rachel and young Samuel, Kohath and Milcah made the short journey to Jerusalem from Bethany. The breeze carried a slight chill, causing Milcah to wrap her mantel tighter around her body. She bundled the two-month-old snugly in warm blankets.

To Milcah's surprise, Mary displayed a remarkable level of tranquility for a baby as young as she was. Her own six-month-old Rachel was prone to bursts of crying, but Mary was quiet and undemanding. Falling in love with the child came effortlessly to Milcah as she cradled their peaceful sleeping form.

When they arrived at the Temple, Kohath and Milcah stood in the long line of parents waiting to dedicate their newborn children. According to their traditions and beliefs, all firstborn children who opened the womb belonged to the Lord Yahweh. It was this ritual of dedication that purchased them back from Him by offering a sacrifice. Rachel and Kohath brought with them an unblemished lamb.

A cold breeze swept through the Temple as they waited their turn in the long procession of new parents. A disturbance caught everyone's attention at the front of the line. As if a switch had been flipped, the atmosphere around Milcah underwent a sudden change, leaving her on edge.

"What is it, Husband?" she asked as Kohath stood tall, trying to peer over the heads of the families in front of them.

"It looks like a young family dedicating their son is causing some sort of commotion on the altar. An older man is holding the child up. Hold on, he is about to speak," Kohath reported to her.

The old man's voice resonated through the Temple as everything else fell silent. "Now you are releasing Your servant, Master, according to Your Word, in peace; for my eyes have seen Your salvation, which You have prepared before the face of all peoples; a light for revelation to the nations, and the glory of Your people Israel."[5]

"Did he say salvation?" Milcah asked.

"He did." Kohath was in awe, as was everyone standing around them.

---

[5] Luke 2:29-32

"Could this be..." Milcah began, words failing her as she pondered the implication of what might be happening.

"Wait, there is another. An old woman is coming toward them." Kohath's voice brimmed with excitement as he described the unexpected turn of events. "The Priest looks perturbed. This is definitely unusual."

The old woman's voice resonated with the same force and authority as the man who had spoken only moments before. Milcah could see that the old woman lifted the child high into the air toward heaven.

The woman's voice resonated like thunder through the Temple. "Yahweh's Spirit will rest on Him: the Spirit of wisdom and understanding, the Spirit of counsel and might, the Spirit of knowledge and of the fear of Yahweh. His delight will be in the fear of Yahweh. He will not judge by the sight of His eyes, neither decide by the hearing of His ears; but with righteousness He will judge the poor, and decide with equity for the humble of the earth."[6]

"Is she proclaiming what I think she is?" Milcah asked her husband, gripping his forearm.

"Yes, she is. That child they are dedicating is being heralded as the Messiah," Kohath declared, breathless. He kept his voice down. Even a hint like this was dangerous if the wrong ears heard it.

"Our Messiah," Milcah sighed. The baby Mary stirred in her arms, cooing in response. Milcah looked down at her. "That's right, little Mary. Wouldn't you like to see the Messiah? Could it be true?"

"It could be," Kohath said, a cloud of doubt moving into his heart. "Only time will tell. It's strange."

"What is strange?" Milcah asked him.

"The couple looks so poor, so young. I never imagined our

---

[6] Isaiah 11:1-4

Messiah coming like that. I always thought He would be born of a prominent family." Kohath was a reasonable, practical man. Sometimes that got in the way of his faith. "He is supposed to be a warrior—a man set up to defeat the Romans and set us free. How can a child of humble birth do that?"

"I don't know, Husband, but with Yahweh all things are possible."

Milcah didn't want Kohath's sudden reservations to dampen her enthusiasm. As the crowd moved, she pushed forward, determined to catch a glimpse of this potential Messiah. By the time they reached the dedication altar, He was nowhere to be seen.

The old woman was still speaking of the child. As she stood there, a small crowd formed around her, hanging on her every word. Milcah could see a lightness and energy emanating from her, despite her age. When the old woman locked eyes with Milcah, she excused herself from the crowd and came over to where Kohath and Milcah stood waiting their turn.

"I am Anna. May I see your child?" Anna asked her.

"This is my niece." Milcah stretched Mary out toward the old woman. "Her mother died in childbirth."

"Ahh, this is Magda!" Anna took her from Milcah's arms.

"Her name is Mary," Milcah said, irritated that the old woman would assume such a thing, yet curious about the name.

"Her father named her Mary because he sees her as bringing a sea of bitterness and sorrow into his life. But this child is destined to be a tower that rises out of the sea of bitterness and sorrow. She shall be called Magda. She was delivered here, in the Temple. I know this as truth." The old woman nodded to Milcah and Kohath.

"You were here when Mary, I mean Magda, was born?"

"I was," Anna replied. "She was life out of death. It was an honor to serve the Lord by receiving her that was brought forth in the power of love."

Milcah took the baby back from Anna's outstretched arms. "I will watch over her as best I can," Milcah told Anna.

"Life out of death is her destiny. You needn't worry, my dear. Love's power overcomes the darkness. This child's heart has been spoken for." Anna smiled before walking away.

"Well, that settles it, then," Kohath muttered.

"Settles what?" Milcah looked at her husband.

"That woman is crazy! Forget what I said about the Messiah. I'm sure she was making it all up, just like she did with this baby." Kohath shook his head in disbelief.

"Kohath! I liked her. I think we should dedicate her as Magda. The name suits her. I believe Anna. Why would she lie about something like that?"

Milcah was confident in her understanding of everything that had just transpired. She would not let her husband's doubts infect the holiness and reverence she felt about what they experienced.

"She is your family. You can name her what you would like." Kohath kissed Milcah on the forehead. "I merely want to get back home."

When their time came, they dedicated Magda by sacrificing a lamb, buying her back, and redeeming her for the Lord.

• • •

Belial was distraught with rage. His black heart was an inferno of seething dark energy. Why had he not been able to prevent the couple from taking the child to the Temple? Once inside the sacred space, he and his cohorts could not see anything that happened. A divine shield had been erected around the proceedings, ensuring that no evil force could infiltrate. Belial didn't like not knowing what was going on with his target. His power rested solely in his ability to read the signs. He watched behaviors, determined weaknesses, and used circumstances to his advantage in order to take down his prey. If they were out of his sight, he didn't know what he was up against.

The Captain of Shadow paced back and forth. The dedication was taking too long. It was unusual. He only hoped the couple would talk about it so that he could surmise what happened while they were there.

Belial's obsession with the female child grew stronger by the day. He usually left children to his less powerful cohorts because they were easy to practice on in order to hone their skills for the more challenging adult targets. Curiously, the desire to personally feast on this daughter of Eve consumed him. He wondered what it was in her that evoked such passionate hatred.

Belial calmed by reminding himself that the plan was unfolding exactly as he wanted it to regarding Amos. Discontent had given full power to Despair who led the man in a downward spiral. Belial's greatest power—the power of shadow, the power to blind the faithful—was almost ready to take root. They had to make sure that the ground of Amos's heart was fallow and ready to be replanted.

Once he was blinded to the truth, the man could be led in any direction they chose to lead him. But Amos's child was the object of evil's true desire. Belial would not be satisfied unless he had that female child! The demon's obsession had taken hold of him, leaving him unable to focus on anything else.

When the couple exited the Temple, Belial hovered around them. He got as close as he could, but the woman's faith was strong, keeping him at bay. The man's protection over the child prevented Belial from getting close to the object of his desire, and he hated him for it. He would have liked to target Kohath, too, but that was not the territory he was given at this juncture in the battle. Once the child was out from under Kohath's headship, she would be easier to access. It was only a matter of time.

The one thing Belial could decipher from their conversation was that the couple dedicated her as Magda. That was the child's name now. The name meant a tower. Towers were prone to collapse. He couldn't wait. He would start by making sure the foundation was shaky. Even if this family started to build her up, she would easily topple if the foundation was not secure.

Thinking of her father, Amos, and her dead mother, Belial knew that the foundation for this child's life was only sand. He smiled before taking flight. The Captain of Shadow went to engage some of the servants of the Evil One that still lurked in Zophos, awaiting their instructions.

• • •

Magda reached the milestone of being fully weaned by the time she turned two years old. Milcah always had a lingering sense of unease, knowing that one day she would have to give Magda back to her brother. She was now expecting her third child. Still, Milcah was sad to be saying goodbye to Magda. The child was a delight.

She was soft of spirit with a gentleness and inquisitive nature that drew people in. Milcah could see that Magda was going to possess a beauty that surpassed that of ordinary women. Hers was a beauty befitting a princess of heaven. At two years old, her brown hair glistened in the sun, her eyes sparkled with golden flecks amidst the brown and her fingers were long and slender. Her beauty was truly breathtaking, with a radiant glow that illuminated every room. Magda's heart was full of light that made people see something beyond the physical. If Milcah could recognize that in her at two years old, she wondered what kind of woman Magda would turn out to be.

"Where are we going, Aunt Milcah?" Magda asked in her precocious little voice.

"We are taking you to your father, Magda. He is awaiting your arrival. You have a beautiful home in Magdala." Milcah finished packing the little girl's things.

"Magdala," Magda repeated after her. "Like my name."

"Yes, exactly like your name because that is where you are from," Milcah told her, deciding she was too young to know the extent of the meaning behind her name.

Once they finished packing their things, Milcah took Magda back to Magdala with a caravan that left at first light. Kohath remained behind with the children. Milcah was glad that she had not told him about being with child because he would have insisted on taking Magda home himself. The thought of finally reuniting with her brother after two years of silence filled Milcah with a mix of excitement and nervousness. She worried about him and was a little angry at him for his absence during the formative years of Magda's life. How was the child supposed to adjust to a man she didn't even know?

Upon their arrival in Magdala, Milcah's disappointment was palpable as she observed the dismal state of affairs. Her former home was in disrepair. Her brother had not worked, was living off the inheritance and, apparently, had taken up drinking.

"Amos!" Milcah walked through the empty estate, stepping over discarded trash and brushing away cobwebs. She pulled back the thick curtains covering the windows in an effort to bring light into the darkness of the space.

"Amos!" Milcah's irritation was growing stronger with each passing moment. She could see the fear on Magda's face.

"I don't like it here, Aunt Milcah. Can we go home now?" Magda said, gripping Milcah's long tunic.

"It will be alright, Magda. Let's just find your father." Milcah tried to stay calm, but the more she saw, the more she realized that she wasn't going to be able to leave Magda behind.

As she looked out into the garden, she noticed Amos amidst the sea of weeds. Milcah took Magda by the hand and led her outside.

"Amos!" she yelled, startling him.

"What? How did you get in?" Amos looked at her, his eyes filled with contempt.

His disheveled appearance contrasted with the piercing darkness in his eyes. Milcah shivered. She had never seen her brother this way. He held a cup in his hand.

"What is going on? This isn't like you. Please Amos, your daughter is here. She has come to live with you." Milcah could think of no way to reason with her brother.

"I have no daughter," Amos spat on the ground. "Go away!"

"Amos, listen, we can help you. We can…"

"I said GET OUT!" Amos threw the cup at Magda, hitting her in the head.

Tears streamed down the Magda's face, her cries becoming louder and more desperate. Milcah picked her up and ran out of the dirty house, tripping over some trash that was on the floor. They both grimaced, their injuries evident as they struggled to move forward. Milcah immediately worried about the child inside her womb. In an effort to protect Magda, Milcah had let her stomach take the force of the fall. It hurt.

"Are you alright?" Milcah asked the crying child.

"My head hurts." Magda touched the bloodied spot where the cup hit her.

"It will be fine, Magda. We will tend to it when we get home." Milcah tried to stand. Her ankle had twisted. Her abdomen hurt.

"You hurt," Magda said to Milcah.

"Help me walk if you can, Magda. We need to catch the last caravan leaving for Bethany. We must hurry."

Milcah did her best to suppress the pain. She hobbled to the place where caravans had set up for their travels. It was still early enough that they could make it back to Bethany just after nightfall. The journey would be difficult, fraught with pain, but Milcah was determined. The longing for home consumed her thoughts, driving her need to return.

"Are we going home, Aunt Milcah?" Magda asked, stifling her tears.

Milcah gently lifted her onto the cart, accepting the kind offer from one of the members of the caravan. "Yes we are, Magda. We are going to push through the pain and get home no matter what. Do you understand?"

"Yes, Aunt Milcah. Push through the pain and get home no matter what," Magda echoed.

*L*ANGUISHING

She who has borne seven languishes. She has given up the spirit.
Her sun has gone down while it was yet day.
She has been disappointed and confounded.
I will deliver their residue to the sword before their enemies,"
says Yahweh.
Jeremiah 15:9

CHAPTER SIX

Seeing that Milcah's condition worsened over the course of the journey, their companions on the caravan took Magda and Milcah directly to the dwelling in Bethany so that they wouldn't have to walk. Kohath rushed outside when he saw his wife, pale and perspiring, on top of the oxcart.

"What happened?" he exclaimed.

"I fell, Kohath. I tripped." Milcah tried to get up.

Kohath lifted her from the cart easily, cradling her small frame with his strong arms. He looked at the bloodstain on Magda's forehead. Questions began forming in his mind.

"Thank you, neighbors, for seeing to my wife's welfare. I can repay you. Just let me get her settled in," Kohath offered.

"No payment necessary, neighbor. We are happy to help. My wife and I are newly married. We are moving to Damascus. I know how worried you must be." The compassionate man looked lovingly at his young wife. "I can't imagine if anything happened to her. I pray Yahweh's favor over you both. My name is Ananias."

Kohath bowed slightly. "Thank you, Ananias. I know that

you were sent by the Holy One to protect my wife. Thank you."

"Yes, we are commissioned by the Lord to protect our wives and children, are we not?" Ananias patted Kohath on the shoulder before departing.

Kohath moved toward the house with Milcah but stopped when he realized the child had not followed.

Magda lingered there, silent and unsure. Kohath turned around, ready to scold her for her hesitation...and a thousand other things that rumbled like thunder through his mind, looking for a release.

Ananias's empathetic expression made Kohath bite his tongue. "Don't be afraid, little one," he said to her. "Trust in the Lord and all will turn out well. Love conquers fear."

"Love conquers," Magda repeated, her eyes sparkling with an innocence that pricked Kohath's former fury with a sense of guilt. None of this was the child's fault. So, why was the urge to blame her so strong within him?

"That's right. Shalom." Ananias returned to his seat next to his wife on the oxcart. "If I ever have a daughter, my wife, I will protect her with my life," he promised to his new bride.

Kohath let out a deep sigh, shifting his blame toward Amos instead of the child.

Magda watched them drive away. "Love conquers," she whispered over and over again.

"Let's go," he yelled at her.

Magda hurried her little feet and went into the house after him.

As the days went by, Kohath reluctantly called for the physician's assistance. Milcah was not doing well at all. For reasons he didn't want to express, Kohath's wrestling match with blame shifted once again toward Magda. Why was this child here? She was supposed to be with her father. The child was not his responsibility.

"My lord." The physician exited the room where Milcah lay

resting. "Your wife will be fine in a few days."

"Thank you. That is a relief." Kohath wiped his perspiring brow.

"But I'm afraid the child was lost."

"The child?" Kohath felt a jumble of thoughts and emotions, his confusion overpowering his ability to think clearly.

"Did you not know that your wife was with child?" the physician asked him. "I was not able to save the baby. Her fall was too severe. I am sorry."

Anger seethed within Kohath. His jaw clenched and fists tightened. Why had Milcah not told him about the child?

Magda came in from outside. Kohath instinctively took his pent up rage out on her. He grabbed her by the shoulders and set her down hard in front of him. He didn't care that she started to cry.

"What happened in Magdala?" Without breaking eye contact, he stared directly at Magda.

Trembling with fear, Magda's breath became shallow and her body grew tense. Remorse mingling with misunderstanding had her in its clutches. She tried to hold back her tears, but her trembling lip betrayed her toddler emotions.

"Answer me!" Kohath raised his voice, demanding answers that he knew she probably couldn't give him, even as precocious as she was.

"Aunt Milcah fell on her belly, Uncle." Magda started crying harder. "The man threw a cup at me, cutting my head. We ran away from him and she fell."

"Was she carrying you?" Kohath asked her, surprised by her detailed account of the event.

Magda nodded, tears streaming down her face.

"You lazy child!" Kohath mumbled as he walked away. He went to go check on his wife.

Magda stayed on the bench, her trembled cries following Kohath down the hall, turning his thoughts in a perplexing appeal toward compassion. She was only a toddler. She didn't understand what was happening. Why was he so mad at her? The child loved her Aunt Milcah like a mother. She didn't want to hurt her. She wasn't to blame. Yet, Kohath's heart refused to extend grace to the child.

• • •

Belial's absence from Amos and his child's life was longer than expected. Upon his return to Zophos, Lucifer made his way to the Captains, eager to catch up on their latest endeavors.

"After roaming to and fro among the inhabitants of the earth, I need to inform you that the Messiah is among them." Lucifer roared.

Transforming into a formidable dragon, he unfurled his massive wings and unleashed a scorching blast of wrathful fire. His prophesied enemy forced him to alter his approach in the battle against Yahweh's image-bearers, causing him to reevaluate his tactics.

The Captains of the evil realm all gasped, displaying their greed for increased power to take down their ultimate enemy and destroy the prophecy that good would overcome evil. It was a preposterous notion!

"I stirred up King Herod to destroy all male children under two born in Bethlehem. The plan failed. The Creator managed to get the boy out, somehow. We will have to bide our time. I need all forces in place. Focus the attack on the land of Judah. Belial, take down as many religious leaders with spiritual blindness as you can. I don't want them recognizing their Messiah when He comes to them." Lucifer spat fire.

"As you wish, Master. I am currently working with Amos and the child," Belial reported.

"A child? Why are you concerned with a child? We have greater ground to cover. We must take down the sons of Israel before the Messiah comes into His power." Lucifer growled low, altering his form into that of a dark wolf with green eyes.

"There is something about this child, Master. She is like no other for one so young." Belial defended the claim on his obsession.

"Show me," Lucifer commanded him.

The two arrived at the dwelling in Bethany while Magda was crying on the bench, alone and unprotected. Lucifer lurked near her, sniffing, examining, probing. Her distressed state pleased him, as much as an evil one could be pleased. He was not normally concerned with the children, leaving them as prey for lesser demons was his usual tactic, but Belial was right. There was something different about this one. She reminded Lucifer greatly of Eve. She was strong in her image-bearing potential of the mother of all creation. He loathed the beauty he already saw in one so young.

"She has been marked, chosen for something," Lucifer informed Belial, curious as to what he was sensing but not able to see in her. "Spare nothing to take her down. Make sure that she is not worthy of being chosen for anything. I give you all power and authority of Sheol to do what you must. I want this one in Zophos with us."

"Possession, Master?" Belial had not even imagined taking it that far with this child. The thought of it intoxicated his evil desires.

"Yes, bring her to me. There is something in her that speaks of the power of the Creator. I want it thwarted and destroyed. Do you hear me? Your own skin is on the line for this!" Lucifer turned ravenously toward Belial.

"It will be done as you wish, Great One." Belial trembled before Lucifer, bowing his bat-like form until they both turned to dust and disappeared.

Fear consumed Belial after his encounter with Lucifer. He would have to concentrate on getting the girl out from under her aunt and uncle's protection. He read the signs of the times. In the years that he was gone, the child had been weaned. Unfortunately, his team had done too good a job on Amos, making him unfit as a father. Belial would have to back off of her father and bring him back to a level of tolerance if he was to get the child away from Milcah. His own success had backfired on him.

At least, he could use Kohath's blame for the recent tragedy to his advantage. Belial called in Blame and Deception.

"Yes, Captain, we are here," Blame uttered.

"The man, Kohath, is already blaming the child for the death of his baby. Press it to our advantage. And you, Deception, flame his embers of the belief that the child is a curse until it takes root and grows like a weed in his mind." Belial gave his orders.

"As you wish, Captain," Deception answered. With wings as thin as membranes, the two demons transformed into slithering lizards and raced towards Bethany from Zophos.

• • •

Milcah was up and about in a few days, just as the physician predicted. She spent a lot of time at her loom, letting the lulling rhythmic motion soothe her aching heart. She carried the immense pain of losing her child, but she hid it well, not wanting to compound Kohath's anguish over Magda remaining with them. Why was he so insistent on returning her to Amos?

Milcah was at the loom when her husband came in from the field. She sensed his agitation even before he said anything.

"How goes the work today, my husband?" Milcah asked tentatively.

"That child keeps distracting Samuel. She needs to go, Milcah. She is your brother's responsibility, not ours." Kohath gritted his teeth. She knew him well enough to know he struggled to rein in his temper and keep his emotions in check.

"Please, Kohath. My brother is not well. I fear for Magda's safety with him. I don't know what has gotten into Amos. He is not the same." Milcah fretted often over her brother.

"He is cursed, Milcah. I want nothing to do with it. The child goes. That is my final decision. Make other arrangements." Kohath stormed out.

Milcah found the conflict between them unsettling. Prior to Magda's arrival, they had been enjoying a better rapport with each other. As Milcah sighed, a sense of weariness settled over her. What was she to do?

Kohath kept silent on the matter for the next few days, but Milcah knew he would not wait forever. She had to take matters into her own hands. Magda was nearly three, so she couldn't be much help to anyone yet. The child possessed an exceptional level of intelligence. Perhaps the woman, Anna, would be able to tutor her in the ways of the Lord. Milcah thought the idea was worth a try.

She waited until Kohath had gone out to the fields for the day. Milcah took Rachel and Magda with her to Jerusalem in search of the prophetess, Anna. It didn't take long for her to find the old woman. Anna still spoke of the Messiah to anyone who would listen as she sat on the porch of the Temple.

"Anna?" Milcah inquired of her.

"Ahh, my sweet child Magda has grown into such beauty that proves she is a daughter of Eve." Anna was delighted to see the child.

"You remember us?" Milcah couldn't help but feel a surge of relief at Anna's recognition.

"Of course," Anna replied. "How can I help you?"

"I was wondering if Magda could come to stay with you during the days. Perhaps you could teach her about Yahweh. I know she is young, but she is very smart." Milcah tried not to sound desperate. "I could pay you a small fee if you like."

"No fee is necessary. I will watch over the child for the time given me," Anna said, sadness coming into her eyes. "You will find a way to bring her here each morning, then?"

"Yes, I will find a way," Milcah said, letting the tension in her shoulders dissipate. "Thank you, Anna."

"It will be my pleasure." Anna looked at Magda. "I will teach you about the One who loves you, Magda."

"Alright," Magda smiled.

Kohath reluctantly accepted the arrangement, though his displeasure was evident. It was a compromise that would make his wife content for a while. He did not want to add to her sadness of heart by pushing his own agenda, even though he knew that he had no intention of keeping the child around for long if he could find another way to rid his family of her.

Magda joined a neighboring family each morning as they made their way to Jerusalem. The men worked in the Temple and were happy to take Magda with them, along with some of the young boys learning the Torah.

Kohath went with them on Samuel's first day. He quietly observed as Anna took Magda under her wings like a mother hen with her chicks.

"Shalom, Magda," Anna greeted the child. "Our first lesson today is about loving Yahweh."

"Loving Yahweh," Magda repeated.

Anna took the toddler to the porch. She sat her on a stool, letting her listen while Anna spoke the prophecy of the One to come and claim the children who belonged to Yahweh. Though she was merely a toddler, Anna treated Magda with the respect of someone who understood on some spiritual level the truth being taught. The child was quiet and submissive, listening intently, repeating the things that took root in her little heart. If only Kohath could ignore the deep sense of distrust he had concerning Amos's child. It was so contrary to how Anna treated her.

Anna spoke clearly one morning in the coolness of a winter frost. The Temple was silent, with only the faint echoes of footsteps as most people chose to stay home, sensing the ominous chill in the air. Magda was older, both in age and in spirit. The stones of the Temple were as familiar to her as her own skin, since she had spent every day of the last two years sitting among them.

Anna's voice was stronger than the chill in the air. "For to us a child is born. To us a Son is given; and the government will be on His shoulders. His name will be called Wonderful Counselor, Mighty God, Everlasting Father, Prince of Peace. Of the increase of His government and of peace there shall be no end, on David's throne, and on His kingdom, to establish it, and to uphold it with justice and with righteousness from that time on, even forever. The zeal of Yahweh will perform this,"[7] Anna proclaimed.

"The zeal of Yahweh will perform this," Magda repeated to herself.

Anna coughed. The old woman shivered uncontrollably as a bone-chilling coldness seeped into her very core. Her voice faltered. "I have set Yahweh always before me. Because He is at my right hand, I shall not be moved. Therefore my heart is glad, and my tongue rejoices. My body shall also dwell in safety. For You will not leave my soul in Sheol."[8]

Without warning, Anna collapsed on the portico. Magda rushed to her side.

"Anna," she cried, kneeling down next to the old woman.

"Remember this, child. Their drink offerings of blood I will not offer, nor take their names on my lips. Yahweh assigned my portion and my cup. He made my lot secure."[9] Anna fell back, her eyes closing. "Say it, child."

"Their drink offerings of blood I will not offer nor take their names on my lips," Magda repeated, tears streaming down from her little eyes.

---

[7] Isaiah 9:6-7
[8] Psalm 16:8-10
[9] Psalm 16:4-5

"Say it again," Anna breathed out.

"I will not take their names on my lips nor..." Magda felt Anna's body go limp.

A Temple guard came over. "What have you done?"

He back-handed Magda hard, causing her to fall from the force of the slap. Several other guards came over to help with Anna.

In the fray of mourning the loss of the prophetess, Anna, Magda got lost in the shuffle. She walked back to her dwelling in Bethany alone and unprotected.

CHAPTER SEVEN

Milcah hummed while she worked at her loom. She was expecting another child. As she thought about the promise of a new life, a feeling of pure joy washed over her, like a refreshing splash of cool water on a hot summer day. When Magda walked in unaccompanied, she was surprised to see her all alone.

"Child, did you walk back from Jerusalem all by yourself?" Milcah got up from her loom.

"Anna died," Magda said. Tear stains marked her face, evidence of her emotional turmoil.

"What? She died? What happened?" Milcah wrapped her arms around Magda. This news was not good.

"She just fell and died," Magda cried.

Milcah put her hand on her belly instinctively, remembering that her last fall had cost a life.

"Don't worry, Magda. It will be alright. I know that you miss Anna. She is with the Lord now. We must be happy for her."

Magda nodded her head, her brows furrowing in confusion, but her willingness to cooperate remained unchanged. Milcah would have to keep Magda out of Kohath's way so that he wouldn't send her back to Amos. Once he found out about the new child on the way, Milcah feared he wouldn't care what happened to Magda. She was determined to keep the news from her husband as long as she could.

Unfortunately, within the month, Milcah began getting sick every morning. She had not had to deal with sickness during her other pregnancies, so this both surprised and worried her. She was fixing Kohath his breakfast one morning when she fainted. Kohath was quick to catch her in his arms. He laid her on the sleeping mat. When Milcah woke a few minutes later, she couldn't remember what happened.

Kohath was standing over her. "Are you with child, Milcah?" he asked tenderly.

Milcah could not lie directly to him. She nodded.

"How long have you been sick? Should we be worried?" Kohath asked her.

"No, it is normal for some women. I was blessed not to have it with our first two." Milcah smiled, still feeling a bit light-headed.

"Blessed," Kohath muttered.

Milcah could tell where her husband's thoughts were going.

"Magda would be a great help to me around here. She could…"

Kohath held up his hand. "The matter is closed. I will not discuss it." With that, he walked out.

Milcah had a sick feeling in her stomach that had nothing to do with her pregnancy.

By month's end, when the last of the harvest was in, Kohath packed Magda up with her things and took her to Magdala under great protest from his wife. He was unmoved by her pleas, determined to protect his unborn child from the imagined curse he thought Magda brought upon his family.

Magda remained submissive to his decision. The way she bit her lip, he could tell she was determined not to shed her tears. He should have been impressed by her marked maturity.

She kept muttering something under her breath. "No matter how painful, we will make the journey home."

Kohath battled against the niggling guilt as he took Magda away from the one place she had known as home.

When they arrived in Magdala, Kohath found Amos. Though he was distressed by the state of the man's affairs in Magdala, there was nothing Kohath could do about it. He had his own family to consider and protect. Though he once held the highest respect for Amos, Kohath found himself disgusted by the man in his current condition.

"Amos," Kohath yelled to wake him from his stupor. "Your child is here. It is her birthday. I have shouldered your responsibility for five years! Five years! Do you hear me?"

Amos stared at Kohath with a blank expression on his face. "I hear you. You are releasing her to my care?"

"She has always been yours to care for, Amos. Get yourself together. Do it for Elisheva." Kohath tried to reason with him as a man.

The sound of his wife's name caused Amos to shudder. It had probably been a long time since he heard it. Kohath studied Amos as he looked at the girl standing before him, afraid and sorrowful. Hers was a beauty reflective of that which her mother possessed. She looked a lot like Elisheva. Amos visibly trembled before them.

"I will hire someone to watch out for her. You have my word." Amos stood on shaky legs.

"Your sister will be pleased to hear that. Please come to Bethany with her once in a while. My wife has grown very fond of your daughter. She is expecting our third child, so she is unable to travel. I am asking you to bring Magda to us for visits." Kohath spoke slowly, wanting to make sure that Amos understood him.

"Magda?" Amos questioned him.

"That is her name," Kohath replied, his tone extremely frustrated.

"Let me walk you out," Amos said, acting normal for the first time in years.

Magda stood in the dirty front room of what looked like a nice home at one time. She dared not move, afraid of tripping over something. Despite the time of day, the darkness in the atmosphere was so thick that it felt like night. The dwelling was dimly lit, with only a faint glimmer of light seeping through the cracks. Magda didn't like it. Fear consumed her as she looked around. As she entered the room, a strange sensation washed over her, making her feel as though someone else was present. She heard strange hissing noises.

With determination in her eyes, Magda decided to run, her breathing becoming more rhythmic with each stride. She ran as far away from the hissing noises as she could. She got outside of the dwelling and found herself in a garden. Hidden beneath a thick layer of tangled, invasive weeds, the ground was crawling with all kinds of insects. Magda wove her way through the grounds until she got to an open space.

The thought of being there filled her with an overwhelming sense of dread. She wanted to go back to Bethany. She wanted to return to the only home she had ever known. Magda cried, silently and subdued. There was no one to help her, not now. She was alone with a man everyone told her was her father. Even Magda could tell that he didn't want her.

• • •

Belial stood firm, unwavering under the intense scrutiny of Lucifer. The Evil One was teaching him the value of patience. It was a trait contrary to the nature of demons, but it proved to be a formidable weapon in the war against the heavenly host. Belial hated it. As creatures that existed outside of the confines of time,

Belial had to work within it.

"You must use the human's weaknesses against them. This requires watching and waiting for opportune times. The most effective of you will gather the information necessary to make the most strategic and successful battle plans. Read the signs of the times. Use circumstances to your advantage. All of this requires waiting and watching. If you rush ahead too fast, you will lose your prey. They will become aware of you and flee." Lucifer had summoned his captains once again. His teaching and infusion of power became more frequent as the unrest grew within him.

Belial could tell that the presence of the Messiah in the world increased the wrath of the Evil One. To know the Son of Yahweh was among the humans, but not know which human form was His, created a great disturbance in the forest of Zophos.

With his lessons over, Belial returned to the business at hand. His practiced patience had finally paid off. Though it was excruciating to let the days, months, and years pass, Magda was finally out from under the protection of her uncle. They had lifted their oppression of Amos, letting the man gain some semblance of order back in his life so that he would look capable enough to handle the child when she was brought back to him.

Belial carefully selected someone to care for Magda, ensuring they would be loyal to Zophos. He set influencing demons to steer Amos in the direction of one of the idolaters living in Magdala.

Belial was so excited over the idea that his patience had paid off that he reacted hastily to the access now granted him. He stood next to Magda while she was alone in the big house. He stroked her hair with his talons, longing to consume everything that was good in her. To him, she looked as tempting as a lavish banquet.

With a discerning nature, the child quickly picked up on subtle nuances in their surroundings. She heard his hissing thoughts and ran from him. Belial would have to be more cunning. Over time, the carefully planted seeds of faith within her had taken root and blossomed, filling her with a deep sense of

EMBER AMONG ASHES

spirituality. They would need to be destroyed before they turned into something impossible to fight against. He forced himself to back off from her, deciding to take a more subtle approach to her downfall. His raging desire to devour her was new to him. He had consumed other life forces, claiming their souls for eternity in Sheol, but this was a different desire. He felt as if wounding her and stealing her soul would be a direct assault on the Holy One Himself. What was she chosen for?

• • •

Magda spent her first night in Magdala crying herself to sleep on a dirty floor in an upper room. When she woke up in the morning, she was covered in dirt and grime. She was also hungry, having had nothing to eat since she left Bethany. When Magda left the room she was assigned, she heard voices on the bottom level.

"I have need of someone to clean the place up and watch after a child. The girl is five. She seems like no trouble." Amos spoke to a foreign woman.

"I will live here, then?" she asked. "You are not expecting a concubine?"

"No, no, nothing like that," Amos said.

"Alright. I will keep the child away from you and make this place livable again. My wages are what we discussed. My religion is my own."

"Yes, of course. I will not interfere." Amos paid her in silver coins.

"Where is the child?"

"She is...Oh, there she is," Amos said, spotting Magda on the stairs.

The foreign woman went over to her. She looked her up and down. "You are dirty. This will not do. Come with me." She grabbed Magda and yanked her by the arm.

Magda squealed in pain, but no one paid attention to her. The woman dragged her as far as a stream located a short walk from the property. She roughly ripped off Magda's tunic and pushed her into the frigid stream. Magda's tears mingled with the cold water. She washed as best she could, ashamed to be naked in front of the woman she didn't know.

"Get out now," the woman yelled at her. Magda left the water. "This will not do. It is dirty. Do you have other clothes?"

Magda nodded, shivering as she covered herself with her arms. We will put something clean on. The woman walked Magda back to the house. Magda felt ashamed and humiliated. They went up to her room, where Magda pulled out a fresh tunic she brought from Bethany. She quickly slipped it on.

"You will call me Jezebel," the woman informed her. "You will do as I say without question or you will receive punishment."

Magda nodded. She spent the rest of the day taking orders from Jezebel. They unpacked the woman's things and cleaned up the room assigned to her. Magda was not allowed to speak unless spoken to. The days passed by in the same manner, one falling into another.

Magda became numb to her own emotions by the time another year of her life passed. The place she lived in was livable and comfortable, but it was not home. The woman in charge of her made Magda care for the idols that were now set up around the estate.

In the center of the garden, the Asherah pole, crafted from ivory, towered above everything else. Magda was to rub oils on it weekly. A golden statue of Baal with his goat-like head and thick horns stood in the main foyer. It was six feet tall, the body of it taking on the form of a man but with claws for his feet. This one Magda found particularly frightening, especially at night when he appeared real and alive to her.

Finally, there was Molech. His image was an altar that stood three feet high. It was made of silver and consisted of a dog-like head with open jaws awaiting something to devour when the offering was placed upon it. Jezebel had told Magda that this was a small replica of the very large altar that stood on the plains of Megiddo where her people would sacrifice to him in secret under the cover of night. She never told Magda what kinds of sacrifices the false god demanded.

Magda, though young, was well aware that these were the false gods Anna had cautioned her about. Magda didn't like them, but she did as she was told, living the life of a servant instead of the princess and beloved child of her father that she was meant to be.

CHAPTER EIGHT

B elial was beside himself with raging desire. It was rumored that Lucifer was going to institute a great feast. There had not been one in a thousand years. It was a unique opportunity for the captains to move up in rank. Of those who brought victims to the feast, some were chosen to devour the human hearts themselves in order to claim the image-bearer's souls for the Evil One. It was a wicked delight, one that was usually reserved solely for Lucifer. Once a millennium, Lucifer would share his power with the captains, increasing their effectiveness. The captain who brought the purest soul received great power and authority, becoming a ruler over territories or nations.

Belial knew that his prey would be a most desirous object for this event. He had never before been as obsessed with devouring a human as he was with this one. He hated Magda with a vengeance. He could almost taste the sweet delectability of her purity and goodness.

"Captain, what are your orders?" Discontent had been waiting for Belial to tell him the battle plan.

Belial came out of his pondering. "Summon to me Greed. We will start there. I want no mistakes on this one. We will assault the child with everything we have in order to ensure her demise."

"At your will, Captain." Discontent slithered away.

Belial knew his next move would need to involve his servant, Jezebel. She had been masterfully placed in the estate of Magdala. The only child of a temple prostitute in Thyatira, the woman was a vessel of evil from the beginning. She craved power and united herself easily with the forces of darkness. She would be instrumental in setting the stage for Belial's access to the child.

Belial landed softly as Jezebel knelt before the statue of Baal. He looked at the human effort to display the radiant glory of the Evil One and laughed at their failure.

"These beings will never fully understand the malevolent beauty of the darkness," he thought to himself. Belial folded his bat-like wings, getting close to the servant of evil, Jezebel.

"Bring the child to me," he whispered to her. "Servant of the dark one, you will be highly favored if you have her drink of the blood. Make her offer it to me," Belial hissed.

Jezebel stirred. She heard the voice. She was overcome with rapturous desire to have been noticed and favored by the dark one.

"I obey you, my Master," she said, looking with awe and lust upon the statue of Baal.

· · ·

Magda could tell that Jezebel enjoyed the power she wielded in the household. The foreigner exerted more and more influence over Amos. The man did whatever Jezebel suggested. Magda quickly learned it was better not to cross her. Jezebel's violent temper was easily triggered, bringing both physical and emotional pain to Magda. She missed her Aunt Milcah and the life she once had in Bethany. It felt as if it was so very long ago.

Magda was spreading the oil on the Asherah pole when

Jezebel found her. Magda jumped at the onslaught of her presence. The woman's quiet and calculated approaches kept Magda in a perpetual state of edginess.

"When you are finished, join me in the foyer," Jezebel commanded her.

"As you wish, Mistress." Magda replied as she knew she was expected, but she did not want to join Jezebel in the foyer where the statue of Baal stood.

Magda took her time, hoping that Jezebel would forget about her. Lost in her thoughts, Magda didn't hear the woman walk up behind her again.

"That is enough!" Jezebel yelled, snatching the towel from Magda's hand. She dragged Magda by the arm into the foyer.

Magda's heart raced as fear coursed through her veins. The beast's eyes were boring into her. There were candles lit all around on the floor next to its claw-like feet. Jezebel tore Magda's headscarf off her.

"On your knees!" Jezebel pushed Magda's body down.

Magda tried to cover herself with her arms, but Jezebel made her leave them at her side. Trembling, Magda's whole body quivered with frightening anticipation. She closed her eyes, so she didn't have to look at the horrible image that glared at her.

"Drink this!" Jezebel touched a cold goblet to Magda's lips.

Magda did as she was told. The thick liquid made her choke. Jezebel forced it into her throat, not removing the goblet until she was satisfied. Magda had no idea what it was, but it made her feel sick inside.

"Now, kiss the feet!" Jezebel pushed Magda forward.

Before Magda could kiss the feet of Baal, she vomited all over the golden image. She heard Jezebel's gasp right before she felt the hardness of the woman's grip yank her backward. She watched Jezebel bowing and wiping the mess up with Magda's headscarf.

Magda swiftly made her escape, disappearing into the shadows. She ran to her room where she had hidden another tunic and headscarf which Jezebel knew nothing about. Magda wiped the sticky liquid that crusted on her lips. The back of her hand was stained red. She quickly dressed and ran outside to the stream.

Magda bent down to wash the stain off her hand. She scooped some water up to her mouth, swirling it around before spitting it out. Magda sat down on a rock and pulled her knees up to her chest. She was still afraid.

"Shalom," a peculiar young girl said.

Magda jumped back in surprise, her heart pounding in her chest. She hadn't seen anyone when she got to the stream. The young girl just appeared out of nowhere.

"Shalom," Magda replied, noting the blackness of the girl's eyes. She was not very pretty.

"Are you alone too?" the mysterious girl asked.

Magda nodded. She didn't like being alone. She had been alone for so long now that she could hardly remember what life in Bethany had been like. She wished that she could go visit her Aunt Milcah and see her new baby.

Tears streamed down the girl's face as she began to sob uncontrollably. Her face twisted into an unattractive grimace. Magda didn't know what to do. The girl made her uncomfortable.

"What is the matter?" Magda asked her.

"I want the rock you are sitting on," the girl sobbed. "You took the best spot for yourself."

"Here." Magda stood up. She would do anything to keep the girl from crying her ugly cries. "Take it."

"Thank you," the girl said, smiling, her tears vanishing as if they had never been there. She sat on Magda's rock. "What is your name?"

"I am Magda. And what do they call you?" Magda was trying to be polite, but she really wanted to be left alone. She didn't like the girl.

The girl began crying again. "I don't have a name," she said. "I was abandoned by my family. I have no place to live. I am alone."

"You don't have a name?" Magda asked, curious.

"No. And I don't have a place to live!" The girl buried her head in her hands.

Magda paused, not knowing what to say. A faint echo of Anna's voice arose in Magda's heart—a reminder of her teaching long ago. She tried to make out the holy words that were surfacing in her mind, but she couldn't hear them clearly. Was it something about not taking their names on her lips?

Magda became distracted by the girl's voluminous sobs. Maybe the girl could help her share the load of chores. "Well, you could stay with us," Magda offered.

"I don't want to stay with 'us'," the girl sobbed. "I want to live with someone. I want to be where I am wanted."

Magda hesitated. She didn't know what to say, but she didn't like the idea of the girl being alone.

"You can live with me," Magda declared.

Suddenly, the atmosphere around them became charged with tension. A gray veil fell over the land, obscuring Magda's view. When the girl looked up at her, Magda thought that she wasn't so bad looking after all. She appeared quite friendly. How nice it would be to have a friend.

"I would love to live in you," the girl declared. "I only wish I had a name. I can't live in you without a name."

"How about if I call you," Magda hesitated. Had the girl said that she was going to live *in* her and not *with* her? That was strange.

"Yes, dear Magda. What is my name?" the demon disguised as a girl hissed, tired of the delay when he was so close to the invasion.

"I will name you Haavah," Magda said to her unknown destruction.

"Haavah," the demon repeated. With that, he leapt off the rock and took up residency inside Magda's mind.

Magda was bewildered when she stood up. She must have fallen off the rock and hit her head. She remembered a girl, but there was no girl. It must have been a dream. Magda walked back toward the estate. She felt different, strange. Everything looked gray around her. The colors of Magdala had dulled. Even the sky above her was gray.

When Magda walked into the foyer, Jezebel was gone. The statue of Baal stood tall, clean, and menacing. Magda looked at it, but it didn't scare her anymore. In fact, she found it rather intriguing. He looked like a god who could protect her. Magda wanted protection. In fact, she wanted a lot of things.

• • •

Belial felt a rush of gratitude as he realized he now had unrestricted access to Magda. Once Greed was invited in and given a name, his power over Magda had begun to unfold. Belial could now use Greed to take a look into the soul of the one he so longed to devour.

There was a formidable force around Magda's heart that Belial had not seen in another. No matter, he would take her down patiently. Greed was only the beginning. They would scratch through whatever it was that surrounded the girl's heart.

Haavah took the form of a worm at the command of his captain. He wormed his way into Magda's mind, controlling her desires in order to set the stage and prepare the place for the others who were waiting to make her their home.

CHAPTER NINE

Magda quickly placed the floorboard back in place. She had created a secret place in her room where she could hide her treasures. It was so much fun to take things that belonged to other people. It wasn't hard either. Magda would often sneak out when Jezebel was busy worshipping her gods. Around the village, the people of Magdala knew her now as the daughter of Amos, heir of the big estate on the hill.

She was treated kindly and with respect. It was easy to take what she wanted from these people. Sometimes Magda would manipulate it out of them. Other times, she would easily take it when they were not looking.

Magda admired the silver bangle that she took out of the secret hiding place in the floor. She had gone into the market and met a woman just traveling through Magdala on her way to the Temple. The woman was undeniably beautiful, with her flawless complexion and radiant smile. Her wrists dazzled with an assortment of bracelets and bangles. Magda couldn't resist the allure of the silver bangle that jangled enticingly from the woman's wrist.

Magda made sure the woman saw her crying. Just as she suspected, the woman was moved with compassion and came to investigate the cause of Magda's distress.

"What is wrong, child?" the woman asked her. "Are you lost?"

"Yes," Magda lied. "I can't find my father. He left me with the caravan because he owes some debts. He said I had to stay here to pay them off, but the man is mean to me. He said he will do terrible things to get his money back." Magda cried and trembled for effect.

"That is horrible," the woman said to her. "Here, let me give you some money so you can pay the man."

"No," Magda said. "He will just beat me for stealing. Perhaps if you gave me that silver bangle…" Magda paused, looking at the woman with teary eyes. "I could tell him it once belonged to my mother and he might accept it as payment."

The woman looked tenderly at the bangle. It obviously meant something to her, making Magda want it even more.

The woman sighed heavily. "Well, alright. But hurry, I don't want my husband to see me giving this to you."

"Thank you, kind lady," Magda said before disappearing with her treasure.

Magda smiled at the memory. It was fun to treasure hunt. Her imaginary friend, Haavah, had such great ideas for how to have fun. Magda didn't feel alone when she was talking to Haavah in her head.

"Remember the time we took the sacred bowl?" Haavah's cackle filled the air, a sinister sound that sent chills down her spine.

"I remember," Magda responded. "You pointed out the priests making their way to the synagogue for morning prayers. I was as quick as lightning. When the cart was going by, I easily slipped over to the back, reached in and grabbed the holy relic."

"I thought sure you would get caught," Haavah remarked.

"But I didn't, did I? It was fun to take it right out from under their noses. Stupid priests! If they had all the power of Yahweh, how could they not see me coming?" Magda declared boastfully.

"*Right, they are stupid.*" Haavah laughed a hideous laugh. "*Put the bangle back. Jezebel is coming,*" Haavah told her.

Magda quickly stashed the bangle. Jezebel stormed into her room.

"What are you doing? There are chores to be done!" Jezebel lifted Magda up by the arm.

"I'm going," Magda replied, descending the stairs as quickly as she could.

Magda barely saw Amos throughout the course of a day. When he came to her in the garden, she was frightened. Magda stood before him, silent.

"We are taking a trip to Bethany. We leave in the morning. You will be packed and ready," Amos informed her.

Magda nodded. She watched him turn to go. Something inside of her inaudibly cried out to her father, silencing Haavah and enlightening the gray world around her for just a moment. Sadly, the man did not hear his daughter's silent plea.

Magda was packing a few things when Haavah finally returned. The heaviness of the presence stifled the light that fought to remain inside Magda.

"*I have a friend who wants to meet you,*" Haavah said to her.

"I already have you. Why do I need more friends?" Magda replied, irritated.

"*There is always room for more. Don't you want more, Magda?*" Haavah enticed her. "*I am not enough. Besides, you will like him. He comes from the same place I do.*"

"I don't even know where you are from," Magda said. "I thought you were from my imagination."

"*No, silly girl. I am from Zophos,*" Haavah informed her.

"Zophos? I don't know where that is. I have never heard of it," Magda replied.

"*You will meet a boy on your way to Bethany. Invite him to be your friend, Magda, just like you did me. We will have such fun together. An important girl like you needs more friends, doesn't she?"* Haavah enticed her, setting the groundwork for Pride to take up residency.

Magda rode in the back of the cart while Amos took the reins up at the front. Jezebel was all too eager to see them go. Magda wondered what the woman had planned for the estate during the month that she and Amos vacated the property.

When they stopped for a meal at one of the villages along the way, Magda waited with the cart while Amos went to inquire about a matter in the local tavern. A young boy was walking toward her, a stick in his hand. He was very handsome.

"Shalom," he said to her.

"Shalom," Magda replied, smoothing her hair.

"You are very beautiful," the boy said. "You must be someone of great importance. You look like a princess."

"No," Magda replied, shy and reserved.

"I don't believe you," the boy said. "I am of regal birth myself, and I recognize royalty when I see it. I am very careful about who I allow to be my friends."

Magda watched as the boy circled her, perusing her with his careful eye. Finally, he spoke.

"I choose you to be my friend on one condition," the boy said.

"What condition?" Magda asked him, thrilled to be chosen.

"You tell me my name. If you get it right, I will be yours." The disguised demon settled himself in front of her, waiting.

"Your name," Magda said, wanting desperately to get it right. She wanted more friends, just like Haavah suggested. "I say your name is Gevah."

"Well said, my dear friend." The boy dissolved like small dust particles right before Magda's eyes. She inhaled them on a breeze that blew them toward her.

Magda then realized that this must have been the friend that Haavah was talking about because she now heard the boy's voice inside her head along with Haavah. The world around her grew darker.

"You shouldn't ride in the back like some servant girl," Gevah said to her. *"Get in the front before the man comes back. What kind of father has he been? You deserve better than him."*

Magda agreed. She was sitting in the front of the cart when Amos returned. His breath was rancid with the smell of alcohol. He said nothing to her as he climbed up beside her and snapped the reins so that they would continue their journey to Bethany.

When they arrived, Milcah ran out to greet them, a baby in her arms. "My brother, how I have missed you both."

"I am not staying," Amos replied. "I have business in Damascus. I thought you might want to see the girl." He nodded in Magda's direction.

Kohath and their children were behind Milcah. Amos got down from the cart. Magda waited for someone to help her down. Gevah told her that she was the one who should be waited on. It was Milcah who came over to help her niece descend from the cart.

"Magda, my darling. You are so beautiful." Milcah ran her hands over Magda's long brown hair.

"Yes, I am," Magda replied. She could see the shocked look on Milcah's face, but the woman refrained from scolding her.

"Come inside," Kohath offered. "We have a meal prepared."

They all went inside. Magda sat herself at the head of the table until Kohath roughly removed her. She was not happy about it, but Magda decided not to make a fuss.

"The children sit over there!" Her uncle pointed to a small table in another room.

"Hmmph," Magda retorted. "I deserve better than this," she mumbled.

Rachel, her cousin, was utterly spellbound by her presence. Samuel, too, was captivated, but his fascination took a different form. He was an adolescent now. The toddler, Rebecca, was a bother. Milcah kept the baby, whose name was Naboth, with her at the head table.

"You are so pretty," Rachel said to Magda. "I wish I was as pretty as you."

"Well, you aren't, so don't fret about it," Magda said, silencing the girl.

"You aren't very nice," little Rebecca said out loud.

"I am too important to be nice," Magda said to her, hotly.

Samuel merely stared at her, not saying anything. Milcah set the food down on the table in front of the children. Magda started to grab some of the bread first until Milcah stopped her.

"We say our prayers first, Magda. Don't you remember?" With a creased brow, Milcah communicated her displeasure.

Magda removed her hand from the bread basket. The mention of prayers made her blood boil with anger. What a useless waste of time. She watched as the other children bowed their heads and closed their eyes. Kohath stood up, raising the basket of bread which was on their table. Samuel did the same for the bread on the table set up for the children.

"I will give thanks to Yahweh according to His righteousness, and will sing praise to the Name of Yahweh Most High."[10] Kohath uttered the blessing over the meal.

Magda shuddered at the mention of Yahweh's Name. She could feel the departure of her companions because the light became brighter in the room. It was then that Magda recognized the increased level of darkness which Gevah's presence brought to her life.

During the meal, while the family talked of Yahweh and the recent events at the Temple, Magda felt more like herself than she had for months. She wondered about the shadows that haunted her, making her feel as if she was a part of the darkness.

When it came time to take rest for the evening, Magda sensed

[10] Psalm 7:17

Haavah's presence once again. She lay down upon her sleeping mat, but Haavah refused to let her sleep.

"That brush and comb set would be nice to add to our treasures," Haavah said to her.

"They belong to my cousin," Magda replied, weakly fighting the demonic influence.

"Yes, but she is not worthy like you are," Gevah piped in. *"She is not of royal blood. She isn't even half as pretty as you. What does a girl like that need a brush and comb for?"*

"Come dear one, it would be so easy to take it. You could just hide it outside until you leave to go back to Magdala. They will never suspect you," Haavah said to her.

"Alright, but then I must get sleep," Magda said to them.

She snuck around in the dark while everyone else slumbered. She marveled at how her eyes adjusted effortlessly to the darkness. It was as if the darkness was clearer to her than the daytime. During the day, there was a filter to her sight that didn't allow her to see things as they were.

Magda took the brush and comb from the spot where Rachel had left them. Fortunately, because her cousin did not put them back where they belonged, it would be easy to pretend that they were lost. Magda crept outside as quietly as she could. The exhilaration of the heist thrilled her. She found the animal enclosure where the oxcart was housed. Magda wrapped the comb and brush in an old cloth and hid them in the corner of the cart where they would be safe until she had to return to Magdala.

Magda easily crept back into the house, unseen. She lay down upon her mat, eager to get the promised sleep that Haavah and Gevah agreed to once she did their bidding.

• • •

Belial waited for Greed and Pride to report. He was eager to know their progress. Now that Magda was back under the protection of her uncle, Belial did not have access to her. He would have to wait until she was back in Magdala for the next phase of his plan to unfold. Since Greed and Pride were inhabitants by her own request, they were able to slip under the protective covering of the head of the family in Bethany.

"She is doing our bidding, Captain," Gevah reported.

"And the groundwork for jealousy? Is that being set?" Belial asked them.

"Yes, Captain. We are preparing her well for you. Any news on the timing of the feast?" Haavah asked the Captain of Shadow.

"No, not yet. We must be prepared. But, you must also be patient. The best battle plans are stretched out over time," Belial instructed his servants. "Let her grow under your influence. She will be more a daughter of darkness than we can now fathom. Slow and patient, we will devour her, scratching at her heart until it is exposed and ready for me to devour it."

"As you wish, Captain." Gevah bowed before him.

Belial fluttered his black wings in a proud display of prominence.

CHAPTER TEN

After being with her family in Bethany for one week, Magda was ready to go back to Magdala. The good people surrounding her unsettled her on a deep level. They reverenced Yahweh and talked about Him often, making Magda extremely uncomfortable. Every time the Name was mentioned, her new friends, Haavah and Gevah, departed from her, leaving her to feel alone and confused.

It was the Sabbath meal that caused Magda a serious conflict of soul. The meal had been meticulously arranged on the sturdy acacia wood table. Kohath stood to begin the prayers while Milcah lit the candles. Every candle that was lit felt like a burn upon Magda's skin.

"Blessed are You, Adonai our God, Ruler of the universe, who has made us holy through God's commandments, and commanded us to light the Sabbath candles," Kohath uttered.

Magda inadvertently groaned out loud. Everyone looked at her, but she did not realize she made a sound. Milcah stopped lighting the candles. When no one said anything and Magda remained quiet, they continued. Kohath went over to where the children sat. He placed his hand on each of their heads as he pronounced a blessing over them.

"May Yahweh bless you and protect you. May Yahweh shine upon you and be gracious to you. May Yahweh always be with you and grant you peace."[11]

When Kohath came to Magda, she ducked away from his hand, rolling to the floor in convulsing spasms. Milcah was by her side, instantly. She rubbed the girl's head.

"It's alright, Magda. You're alright." Her voice carried a warmth and genuine concern as she spoke.

Magda sat up, unsure of what had just happened. Kohath looked at her, disgusted by her lack of respect for the Sabbath rituals.

Kohath lifted the goblet of wine set on the table. "Blessed are You, Adonai our God, Ruler of the universe who creates the fruit of the vine."

Magda began shaking violently. Milcah continued rubbing her back. "Are you sick, child?" she asked her, concerned.

Magda's eyes rolled back in her head. She fell over, losing consciousness just as Kohath said the final blessing of Shabbat. "Blessed are You, Adonai our God, Ruler of the universe, who causes bread to come forth from the earth."

• • •

Magda was with Haavah and Gevah. It was dark, extremely dark, where she was, but they gave her the power to see clearly.

"We will protect you, Magda. Trust in us," Haavah said to her in a sweet child-like voice.

"Yes, you are different from them, Magda. You deserve to be worshiped. You are special." Gevah led her deeper into the darkness.

"Where are we going?" Magda asked them, afraid and

---

[11] Numbers 6:25

unsure.

"We are going to show you where we are from. We are taking you to the forest of Zophos," Gevah said to her.

Magda hesitated. She didn't want to go to the forest of Zophos. "Wait, I'm not sure that…"

"Magda, darling. Come on, wake up," the voice of Milcah reached into Magda's darkness. *"Adonai, I praise Your power, Lord. Rescue this child. Bring her back to us. Yahweh, we call on You."*

As Milcah prayed over her, Magda was being pulled back toward the light and out of the clutches of Gevah and Haavah. She opened her eyes to see the entire family standing over her.

"Thank God," Milcah cried, hugging Magda to her chest. "You are sick, child. Come and get some rest."

"She isn't sick, Milcah," Kohath muttered to his wife. "She has a demon. Can't you see that?"

"How can you say such a thing, Husband? She is our niece." Milcah's determination to protect Magda from false accusations stroked Magda's troubled heart. How could she be possessed by demons? Not that it mattered if Milcah didn't believe it. Belial was glad about that.

Belial spat on the ground. "What happened? Did I not tell you to be patient with her?"

"Yes, Captain. We thought she would come willingly. We thought you would be pleased to have her early." Haavah groveled before Belial.

"You were wrong! I have a plan in place. I want assurance that she will come without reservation into the forest. We can leave no opening for her to escape. You will not beckon her here again without permission. Do I make myself clear?" Belial's fangs were dripping with foaming rage.

"Yes, Captain." The two minor demons spoke in unison before departing.

Belial wanted to press his advantage. Milcah's disbelief regarding the possession could be used as a catalyst to empower his battle plan. As long as the aunt suspected nothing was amiss, Magda would soon return to Magdala. Belial would keep a more watchful eye on her there, making sure that there were no more trips arranged for Bethany.

Meanwhile, to keep himself amused and preoccupied, Belial called upon the Captain of Fornication. Belial shared his dominion over the servant, Jezebel, who turned the estate of Magdala into a place of worship to Baal. She filled every room with men and women eager to please both themselves and their god. It turned quite a profit for her as well, since most were willing to provide an offering of silver and gold. Jezebel was surprised how fast word traveled about her shrine to Baal. Travelers came from all over to participate in the worship services offered. Her one problem was figuring out how to continue once Amos returned with his daughter.

$$\bullet \; \bullet \; \bullet$$

The month was almost up, and Amos would be returning from his business in Damascus. Milcah took another hidden opportunity to pray over Magda while she slept. She had no idea how powerfully her prayers protected the child, offering Magda a sweet sleep devoid of the nightmares of darkness. Milcah worried about her husband's suspicions, but wanted to believe the best about her niece. She was such a beautiful girl, so full of potential and promise. *"Lord, don't let her fall to the side of evil,"* Milcah prayed while she stroked Magda's hair.

In that moment, a thought occurred to Milcah. Just around the time that Magda arrived, Rachel's precious hairbrush and comb set, a cherished gift from Milcah's mother, vanished without a trace. Milcah was suspicious that Magda was the one who had stolen them. She hated that she thought that, but she followed the promptings that led her straight to the wagon stored in the animal enclosures. Sure enough, the brush and comb set were hidden inside a cloth in the corner of the wagon.

Milcah bowed her head, disappointed that Magda would steal from her own cousin. She took the brush and comb back inside, determined to speak with Magda about it in the morning.

At first light, Magda awoke from her sweet sleep. Though she didn't like being in Bethany, Magda enjoyed the restful sleep it offered her. She hadn't had strange thoughts in the night during the whole time she was with her aunt and uncle.

"Magda, may I speak with you?" Milcah asked her when she realized she was awake.

Magda went to see her aunt. She noticed the brush and comb in her hands.

"This does not belong to you. How come it was in the cart?" Milcah asked her.

Magda merely shrugged. Her aunt's demeanor irritated her, making her feel on edge. Why did Rachel deserve such nice things and she didn't?

"These were an heirloom from my mother. They belong to Rachel. I'm sorry that you feel like you must have them, but they are not yours to take. Stealing is a sin, Magda. We don't steal. Yahweh would not approve. Don't put distance between you and the Lord by doing such things." Milcah tried to teach Magda what little she could.

Magda said nothing in reply. The thought that Rachel had better things than her left her seething with anger. Milcah looked at Magda sadly, waiting for her to engage in conversation. When she said nothing, Milcah let her go.

"You can go, but don't steal anymore," Milcah warned her.

Magda was glad when Amos returned. She knew that he would see to it that they left by evening. He hated being at Milcah's place even more than she did. The man looked old and worn out. Magda packed her things, still fuming that she had to leave the brush and comb set behind.

"I will get my own brush and comb set," Magda thought to

herself. *"And it will be better than yours, Rachel. Just wait and see. I will have better things than you."*

Magda didn't even thank her aunt and uncle, nor did she say goodbye to her cousins. She sat in the cart, not looking back at Bethany as Amos drove her toward Magdala. Once they crested the hill and were out of sight of Milcah and her family, Gevah and Haavah returned to comfort Magda.

"You did well, pretty one," Gevah said to her. *"Don't worry about the brush and comb. We will make sure that you have plenty of nice things. You deserve it, don't you?"*

"Yes," Magda said. "How dare they treat me like that!"

"How dare they!" Haavah agreed.

When they arrived back in Magdala, Jezebel greeted them warmly. She immediately noticed the difference in Magda's demeanor. It put her a little on edge. Magda felt something had changed inside the estate, but she didn't know what. Amos was oblivious, as usual. He went off somewhere to drink himself into a stupor.

"The Asherah needs tending to," Jezebel said to Magda.

"Do it yourself!" Magda replied. "I am not your servant. I am mistress of this house."

Outraged by her outburst, Jezebel's face turned red with anger. She lashed out at her with such a beating that it knocked Magda unconscious.

Jezebel locked her in her room, having installed locks on all of the doors in the estate while Amos and Magda were gone.

Magda woke to hear strange sounds coming from the room next door. It was loud. When she tried to leave her room, she realized that the door was securely locked. The door handle wouldn't budge. It sounded as though there were people in the house. Fear gripped Magda's heart. She curled up in the corner, wondering what to do.

"Don't worry, Magda," Gevah's soothing voice calmed her. *"They are worshiping Baal. You don't have to be afraid."*

"Worshiping Baal? Here? But why?" Magda asked.

"You are mistress of a very important place, Magda. You should be proud to have such a dedicated shrine to Baal in your home. It is natural that people want to worship. Eventually, when you are older, you can be part of the worship too. Then, they will pay you what they now pay Jezebel," Haavah said to her, preparing the door of Magda's heart for the entry of another.

"That's right. You are the mistress of this place, not Jezebel. She is taking what is yours. She has no right to it. Why should she have better things than you? Just like your cousin Rachel. They don't deserve them, do they?" Gevah suggested.

"No," Magda replied. "I want what they have."

"Patience, child. You must wait. You are not yet old enough. Give it time and we will help you get what you deserve," Gevah said to her.

"Alright, I will wait. But I want to have power, too," Magda spoke into the darkness.

"Power you will have, my child," the demons said in unison.

Months later, Magda was out tending to the Asherah pole when a woman wearing a blue toga came to her. She was breathtaking and beautiful. Magda was drawn to her immediately.

"Shalom," the woman said. "I see that you are a worshiper of Asherah. She is the mother goddess. I am her servant. I was sent to see if you would like to have what I have."

"What do you have?" Magda asked her.

"Anything you want," the woman replied.

Magda wanted her beauty, her apparent wealth. She wanted to be her.

"Yes," Magda replied.

"I ask only one thing in return," the woman said. "I need a place to live."

"You can live with me," Magda replied. "There is plenty of room."

"As you wish, child. I will live in you. What would you call me then?" the woman smiled at her.

"I could call you my lady," Magda suggested.

"No," the woman hissed. "What name would you give me?"

"I will name you Qanah." Magda made the pronouncement.

The woman began to dance around Magda. She made her laugh and then disappeared. It didn't take long for Magda to hear the melodic voice in her head belonging to Qanah.

"Look at that woman, Jezebel. She has everything that belongs to you. Just wait until you grow in age and beauty. She will be sorry she took what was rightfully yours," Qanah said to her, stirring up envy and jealousy within Magda's heart and mind.

CHAPTER ELEVEN

Magda grew in beauty and maturity. By the time she was an adolescent, she had grown accustomed to her constant companions, Haavah, Gevah and Qanah. As they grew more powerful within her, Magda felt herself slipping away. Goodness became an eclipsed shadow of something that no longer felt real.

Memories of her life in Bethany, of the innocence of childhood, drifted away on forgotten strands of memories she no longer had access to.

The relationship between Magda and Jezebel altered over the years. Magda let the woman control Amos, but she rebelled against Jezebel's authority over her, especially regarding duties Magda did not feel warranted her position as rightful heir of the household. Gevah constantly reminded Magda that she was going to be in charge, eventually. As a result, Magda's workload was reduced. With her newfound free time, she indulged in leisurely activities.

Magda resented being locked up during Jezebel's worship services to Baal. Though she didn't approve of the woman's use of the house for these things, she agreed to keep quiet about it as long as Jezebel did not lock her up anymore.

On one particular night, Magda was unaware of the worship service going on. Her sleep was deep, as was usual. Her thoughts in the night were dark and foreboding.

Magda dreamed she was running through a black forest. The air was thick with the stench of death. She had only a thin gossamer gown on. The air was frigid, sending a shiver down her spine. Something was after her.

Magda couldn't see where she was going. Frantically, she scanned her surroundings, desperately searching for an escape route. She wanted to be rescued. There were voices all around her, pressing, hissing. They sounded familiar, yet different. She sensed that Haavah, Gevah, and Qanah were hiding in the trees, looking for her, calling out to her. Their voices were not warm and friendly. They were threatening and raspy.

Magda caught a glimpse of them. Haavah was a worm-like creature dripping with refuse. Gevah was a feathery creature as black as the night. Qanah was a green lizard with a long red tongue.

Magda ran from them. They chased after her along with four other foul creatures. The further Magda ran from them, the deeper she traveled into the darkness. With each step, her feet sank deeper into the soft, muddy ground. There were skulls, human skulls all around, littering the ground. Magda could barely move.

The darkness sucked her in. She pushed, remembering words from her childhood: "No matter the pain, Magda, we will push through until we get home."

Home—where was that? Magda forced her eyes to look. Home—the thought of it touched her heart, allowing her to see differently. In an attempt to concentrate, Magda widened her eyes and took a deep breath, trying to clear her mind. There was something shimmering in the distance. She lifted one leg and then another, pushing through the pain. She needed to get to the small source of light.

A sharp, tearing sensation coursed through Magda's back. She screamed in agony. The pain was the catalyst that she needed to jump out of the pit she was in. Once on dry ground again, Magda sprinted toward the sliver of light. As she got closer, she recognized a stone from the Temple. It was huge enough to shield her. The cornerstone stood tall, a symbol of strength and stability. She knew she had to get to it so she would be safe.

Startled, Magda awoke with a gasp, her breath coming in short, quick bursts. She could feel the sweat trickling down her forehead, her body craving hydration.

It was the third time she had such a dream. Unaware of the time, Magda arose from her sleeping mat, desiring something to quench her thirst. She crept down the stairs, making her way to the cooking area. Passing by the statue of Baal, Magda shivered. She could have sworn the eyes on the fierce-looking statue moved. While she had grown accustomed to its presence in the daytime, at night, it was something else entirely.

She made haste to get to the cooking area, but something stopped her. In the depths of the shadows, a mysterious man lurked. He grabbed her and pulled her to himself, tearing at her as if his hands had talons. Magda screamed. The man's forcefulness pinned her down.

Jezebel must have heard her because she was there in an instant. She pulled the man off of Magda with ease.

"This one is not part of the worship, you fool!" Jezebel hissed, looking more menacing in the darkness of night than she did during the day. "She is the master's daughter. You will pay for the defilement."

"I'm sorry," the man stammered. "I didn't know. I'm sorry."

Magda did her best to cover herself. She ran back up the stairs, Jezebel's conversation with the man reaching her ears before she locked herself in her room.

"You should have known better. You are going to cause trouble," Jezebel scolded, sounding upset and intrigued by what he had done, or almost did.

"She is so beautiful. I would pay handsomely..." the man began.

"Bite your tongue. She is not yet of age," Jezebel spat at him before kicking him out.

Magda didn't sleep the rest of the night. The assault by the man bothered her greatly.

"*Come now, child. Don't worry,*" Qanah's voice soothed her. "*Your beauty is unmatched. It is a good thing that men want you. You are getting older. Look at how women envy your beauty and men desire it.*"

"I know, but he hurt me," Magda protested.

"*You are strong, Magda,*" Gevah said to her. "*Nothing can hurt you. You are in full control.*"

"*Yes,*" Haavah agreed. "*You should be a part of what goes on in this house. You are the one to whom the profits belong. You should be the one making money.*"

"I don't know how to," Magda began to cry. "I don't want to."

"*Hush now, child,*" Qanah said to her. "*We will let you sleep. Just remember that there is plenty of room for more. We have given you much power. You can have everything you want.*"

"Alright," Magda said, feeling sleepy all of a sudden. It was so strange how her imaginary friends could manipulate her physical senses by a mere suggestion.

When Magda awoke, she had forgotten the events of the night before, including her perpetual dream. She went about her day as usual until something unexpected happened. Jezebel was rushing around the place, turning things over and acting frantic.

"What is wrong?" Magda yelled at her.

"Wrong? Everything is wrong. Your father is not getting well. News has reached Bethany of his demise. Now your aunt and uncle are coming here to tend to him. They have barely survived the illness sweeping through these parts and now they are coming here, bringing it with them!" Jezebel was furious.

The news didn't please Magda, either. She could tell that Jezebel sensed her time was short. As soon as Milcah arrived to stake her claim on the estate in Magdala, Jezebel would be out.

"She is going to try to take what is rightfully yours, Magda," Qanah suggested.

"You must stay strong," Gevah hissed.

"We will help you fight," Haavah agreed.

Jezebel went into another room. Magda went to the place where Jezebel kept Amos locked up. It was open. She silently moved inside. The man was snoring loudly. He looked and smelled awful. He probably hadn't bathed in weeks. His body was frail, merely skin and bones. Magda was beginning to feel compassion in her heart when she became distracted by a voice in the room.

"Shalom," the woman said to her. She was old, hunched over, and had no teeth.

"Shalom." Magda wondered where she came from.

The woman looked at her with intense eyes. "You are the most beautiful of women," she said to her. "You are perfectly formed. There is no flaw in you."

Magda delighted in the appraisal. Her companions all agreed in their own voices inside of her.

"Where are you going? Who are you?" Magda asked the woman.

"I have come here to serve you, lady of astonishing beauty." The woman bowed before Magda.

"To serve me? How?" Magda asked.

"You are worthy to be served," Gevah said.

"I only wish to live with you and do your bidding, sweet mistress." The old woman remained bowed.

"Alright, you can live with me," Magda said to her. "What is your name?"

"Whatever your majesty wishes will be my name. I am yours to command." The demon looked at Magda, awaiting the naming which would give him the power to enter her.

"I will call you Chalaq," Magda said to her.

The woman arose, taking Magda by the hand. She became a shadow that moved directly into Magda. Immediately, Magda could feel a shift happening within her. The four companions were becoming more formidable with every challenge they faced. Her will was no longer her own. She could feel it draining out of her.

Jezebel came back in with ointments. "I am calling a physician to tend to him until she gets here."

"When is she coming?" Magda questioned her.

"I don't know, a few months. They are getting their affairs in order in Bethany. The messenger informed us that one of the little ones is still sick, so it depends on whether or not they wait for him to get better." Jezebel was rubbing ointment on Amos's forehead.

"Very well," Magda said. She turned to go, but Jezebel grabbed her by the arm.

"We must work together, Magda dear. If we are to save the estate for you, we need to be prepared." Jezebel led her into the other room while Amos slept.

"What exactly did you have in mind, Jezebel?" Magda asserted her authority over the woman even though she was only in her teen years.

"You are extremely beautiful. You know that," Jezebel said to her. "We could take advantage of that."

"*Your beauty is a commodity to be shared with others,*" Chalaq said to her. "*You could profit from it.*"

"*Think of all that could be gained if you use your beauty and desirability against those trying to harm you,*" Haavah said to her.

"*Yes, we could definitely join in Jezebel's efforts. Why hire other women to perform worship services when you can do them yourself?*"

Qanah's voice was loud.

The demons all began talking at once. Magda couldn't concentrate. They were urging her, enticing her, pulling her into a vortex that she didn't have the strength to resist. Magda had nothing to cling to. The four evil spirits swirled in a cacophony of frenzied chaos until Magda relented.

"Alright, Alright, I will do it," Magda yelled, putting her hands over her head. Finally, they were quiet.

"Do what?" Jezebel asked her. "You will join me in the worship services, then?"

"Join you? No, I will take control of them. All of them. The profits we will share evenly." Magda spoke with the authority of those dwelling within her. Her body was that of an adolescent, but her mannerisms were that of a woman.

Jezebel was a bit frightened by the authority coming from this girl. "As you wish, Mistress," she said. "There will be a service in a few days. Will you be ready?"

"I will be," Magda lied.

Once she got back to her room, the voices started clamoring for her attention again. Magda sobbed. "I don't know what to do. I don't want to do this."

"Now there, my child. You needn't worry. Have we ever let you down? There is one who will be sent to help you. Trust him." Chalaq comforted her with empty words. *"You are the most desirous of women. It will come easy to you."*

Later that evening, Magda walked down to the stream. The constant chatter of her companions was making her anxious. She dipped into the water, letting the coolness wash over her. When she came up to the surface, a man stared at her from the opposite shore. She had not noticed him there before. Magda grew afraid and ashamed. She glanced at her tunic laying on the rock not too far from her.

"Shalom," the man said. "How is the water?"

"It is cold," Magda answered him, nervous.

"Don't be afraid, Magda. I am a friend."

"Who are you?" Magda asked him, experiencing the boldness that Gevah was giving her.

"What name would you give me if I came to live in you? I could protect you, you know."

"Protect me, how?" Magda asked, intrigued by his offer.

"By helping you to get what you want from men. I can't help you from a distance, though."

The man's smile was warm and friendly. He was not unattractive for a man. "Well, I..."

"Magda dear, look at how vulnerable you are," Haavah hissed. *"You need protection."*

"Don't turn down an offer such as this," Gevah said to her. *"You may get hurt if you do."*

"I'm waiting on you, my lady." The man bowed slightly. "My name?"

"I will call you Nechosheth," Magda proclaimed, helpless to drown out the voices that hissed inside of her.

The man turned into a water snake and slithered over to where Magda was standing in the water. He swirled around her, touching her body until he disappeared, taking up his residency inside of her mind. The thoughts that swirled in her head were unclean and obtrusive. Magda became aware of herself as a woman in ways that she had not before. She was no longer afraid of the worship service. She was looking forward to it.

• • •

Belial enjoyed the slow conquer of his prey. With five demons now powerfully controlling her, Magda was losing herself completely to the darkness. The night of the first worship service Magda was participating in, Belial was there. He made sure to invade the man that was first to be chosen to indoctrinate her to the sacred act of the worship of Baal. It had never been sweeter to him to coexist in a human body before. He could sense the fear that was fighting against the spirit of lust which controlled Magda for the moment. Belial relished the oppression. Yet, there was something that troubled Belial. There was light in her yet. Her heart was unscathed. Surely, they should have wounded her heart by now. How was it that Magda's heart remained untouched?

Belial exited the man when it was over. Another was waiting for his turn. In all, Magda would allow five to worship Baal that night. All five demons were keeping her subdued with sounds and noises so that she would not resist.

Belial waited for the report from his troops. "Well, how is it that her heart is still beyond our reach?"

"We are gaining a lot of ground, Captain," Pride informed him. "She listens to us with much less resistance."

"She has enjoyed the worship services," Lust offered. "I have made sure of that. She no longer desires purity."

"She hungers for power and wealth," Greed said.

"I need more. I need access to her heart before we lead her to Zophos. You all know that! We are running out of time. It has been months since Amos took sick. His sister is bound to show up sooner or later. We need to make sure that her husband does not offer protection again, restricting our access." Belial pondered his concerns before his servants.

"The man Kohath is weak, Captain. The sickness stole his strength. We can use that against him should he arrive," Vanity explained to the Captain.

"Keep the man, Amos, alive. If he dies, the estate will belong to Kohath. In the meantime, strengthen Magda with confusion and chaos. Make a way for Anger to come in. Keep her preoccupied with the men. Make sure she is well known in the area so that her reputation soils her. I want to make sure there is little chance of her being worthy of any destiny that the Creator had planned for her," Belial cackled.

"At your command, Captain," the five demons said in unison

before going back to be with their possession.

CHAPTER TWELVE

Within six months, they made twice as much profit as Jezebel had made in the years prior to Magda taking over the worship services. Her popularity and reputation brought worshipers from far away. The true essence of who she was slipped further into a shell buried deep inside her. Her *friends* took care of her. They didn't just live inside her. They lived for her. Magda's existence had been restricted to moments, her mind no longer capable of forming memories. Everything was a reaction to her circumstances.

As Magda slept peacefully, she was abruptly awakened by the sensation of a hand making contact with her bare shoulder. She rolled over and opened her eyes. As she woke up, she found a man kneeling beside her sleeping mat, his presence both alarming and mysterious.

"Worship is over. Come back in two nights," Magda said.

"I am not here to worship. I am a friend looking for a place to live."

Magda was so subdued by the others that there was no strength left in her to resist another occupation. "You can live with me," she replied robotically.

"What would you call me?" the demon asked, already changing into his spider-like form.

"I name you Kaas," Magda said, yawning with indifference. More strength. She needed more. Haavah's influence intertwined with the thoughts in her mind.

The demon smothered her body with his many legs until he disappeared inside of her entirely. Magda slipped back into sleep. Images of taking revenge on all those who hurt her played across her mind. Magda wanted to hurt others the way they had hurt her. She wanted to cause them pain. A rush of invincibility coursed through her veins.

When Milcah finally showed up with her family months later, Magda could feel the anticipation of a change in the air. Jezebel was the first to rush into Magda's room. It was mid-afternoon, but Magda slept during the day, preferring to be awake at night. The light bothered her, making her skin crawl as if being perpetually burned.

"Magda, they are here!" Jezebel shook her.

"Who is here?" Magda rolled over. Filled with anger, she had the sudden urge to pounce on Jezebel for disturbing her sleep. Under Kaas's influence, Magda pondered the sweet satisfaction of taking revenge on this woman who caused her so much misery as a child. It would be so easy to end her threats and make her beg for mercy.

"Mercy is for the weak," Kaas whispered.

"Your Aunt is here with her family. We had no warning. I thought they would send a messenger." Jezebel's brows furrowed and her lips pursed, revealing her inner turmoil.

"Alright, calm down, woman. I'll get up!" Magda slowly stirred from her slumber, stretching her limbs as she reluctantly rose from the bed. When the sunlight touched her skin, she cringed in disgust. After she dressed, she went down the stairs.

Just as Milcah crossed the threshold, a refreshing breeze

brushed against Magda's face, carrying the scent of what Magda used to call home. Her five children followed behind her. Magda's eyes were immediately drawn to her cousin, Samuel. Since their last encounter, Samuel had undergone a remarkable change and had become a fully grown man. His handsome appearance captivated Magda. She embraced the lude thoughts the demons put in her head as she perused her cousin's features.

Milcah's eyes glared when she saw the golden statue of Baal in the foyer.

"What is the meaning of this? Kohath," Milcah yelled.

"Aunt Milcah, so nice to see you." Magda tried to redirect her attention.

"Magda, what is this? Get it out of here now! It is an abomination to Yahweh." There was a visible restlessness in Milcah's demeanor as she fidgeted and tapped her foot impatiently.

The Name of the Lord burned Magda on the inside. She didn't like it. Who did Milcah think she was to come in here and start making demands?

Jezebel came around the corner. She halted when she saw the look on Milcah's face. Kohath entered the foyer as well. Though the man looked weak, there was no mistaking the fury on his face.

"Pack your things and get out!" Kohath yelled with authority. "In the Name of the Lord, Yahweh, I command you to leave. This house is a dwelling for the Lord Most High."

His words scorched Magda's soul, leaving a lingering ache, as if flames erupted from his mouth. The demons inside of her were relentless, their incessant scratching and tormenting causing her immense pain. They lost their ability to communicate using words. Kohath's authoritative faith immediately cast a protective cocoon of light around the estate. The statue of Baal toppled over, smashing into pieces.

Frightened, Jezebel ran upstairs, her footfalls leaving a thundering echo. Magda wanted to run too, but she could not move. She struggled to lift her feet, but they were glued to the spot, making it impossible to get away. Her tongue stuck to the roof of her mouth. Within seconds, she fell down, teetering on the edge of consciousness.

Milcah's arms came around Magda. She took her upstairs to rest while Kohath went to check on Amos. Magda knew what her uncle would find. The master of the estate was in poor health. Magda feigned being unconscious so Milcah would return downstairs. Free from her aunt's clutches, Magda watched from the top of the stairs. She saw Jezebel close the door behind her, leaving with two satchels and whatever else she could fit in her arms.

Milcah and her family spent the next few days ridding the place of all the idols. When strange men showed up to worship Baal, they were sent away. Overwhelmed by the deteriorating conditions in Magdala, Milcah did not hide her discomfort. Magda struggled to be in her presence. The demons hated this family. With them around, their influence lessened. Magda started to feel a bit more in control. She wasn't sure if that was a good thing. Without her friends, she could not survive the horrors of the world.

A physician looked in on Magda and Amos. Both were resting fine, no visible signs of anything serious. Magda drifted in and out of sleep, awaking mostly in the evening. She crept downstairs while everyone was asleep. She felt sick, weak. How long could she endure this invasion?

• • •

Belial was in a rage. "How could we lose control when we were so close?"

"We still have access to her, Captain. She only needs to call on us and we can re-enter beneath the protective covering," Anger reminded him.

"Yes, but will she? If she doesn't say your names, all of your names, we will lose ground!" Belial paced the forest floor, angered that he could no longer access her through the worshipers of Baal.

"I have confidence that she will call to us, Captain," Pride said at the end of a long hiss.

"How long has it been?" Belial asked them.

"Only a few days. But, she is not fully conscious yet. She teeters at the edge, sleeping and waking periodically. We put her in a deep stupor after the frenzy. It was too much for her mind, so we shut it down," Lust informed him.

"Very well, we will wait. But I want a full report once access is regained." Belial stretched his bat-like wings.

"Of course," the six demons uttered in unison.

• • •

Magda couldn't figure out where she was. The dwelling was unfamiliar. Even in the dark, it was brighter. There was a holy book on the table. She longed to reach out and touch it, but fear held her back. The feeling of being out of place washed over her, leaving her with a deep sense of loneliness.

Magda went out into the garden. Even the Asherah pole was gone. The weeds were meticulously uprooted, leaving the ground bare and tidy. The immaculate cleanliness of the space stirred up a sense of unease in Magda. The fountain was filled with clear, refreshing water.

Magda felt a wave of nausea building up in her stomach. She found that place unbearable, and the thought of staying there any longer was unbearable. With only the moonlight guiding her, she sprinted into the pitch-black darkness. She made her way to the stream, stripped off her tunic, and walked into the water. She looked over at the opposite shore. It was empty. She felt empty.

"Where are you, my friends? I feel your nearness, but I can't hear you. Kaas?"

"*I'm with you, Mistress,*" Anger replied. "*I will help you get revenge.*"

"Nechosheth?"

"*I am with you, Mistress,*" Lust replied. "*I will help you fulfill desire.*"

"Chalaq?"

"*I am with you, Mistress,*" Vanity replied. "*I will flatter you and serve you.*"

"Qanah?"

"*I am with you, Mistress,*" Envy replied. "*I will show you what you are missing.*"

"Gevah?"

"*I am with you, Mistress,*" Pride replied. "*I will give you confidence to do what you must.*"

"Haavah?"

"*I am with you, Mistress,*" Greed replied. "*I will help you take what is rightfully yours.*"

Without any warning, they all started talking simultaneously, creating a jumble of voices. Magda was quite used to the noise. It made her feel complete, less afraid. In the midst of such dire circumstances, they rallied together, each one sharing their own insights and suggestions on how she should proceed.

Their power was so overwhelming that Magda couldn't resist being subdued by it. She relinquished control and allowed them to take charge. When she emerged from the water, she suddenly became aware of a man standing nearby, who had gone unnoticed before. She wondered if he was real. When the voices quieted, she assumed that he was. He looked strong and commanding. Something about him reminded Magda of a bat.

Magda moved toward him, hesitating. The man's regal countenance drew her and repulsed her concurrently.

"Are you the one who lets men worship Baal?" he asked her. "There are no services tonight, but we can go back to the house," Magda began, forgetting that Baal had been removed from the premises.

"No," the man hissed, coming toward her. "Can we not

worship here in the water?"

Magda went back to the water, the man following her. The worship experience was intense and satisfying. The man left quickly when it was over. Belial exited his body, fulfilled of his own need to be near his prey once again.

When the family woke up the next morning, Magda heard the voices. The air filled with the sounds of laughter and prayer drifting up from downstairs. The unsettling feeling made her feel physically ill. The demons woke her, frenzied and agitated. They were all fervently vying for power, their voices clamoring in a chaotic chorus.

Magda went downstairs rapidly, barely covering herself with a thin robe. "What is all this noise?" she hissed at them.

Samuel looked at her, and then turned away, ashamed. Kohath did the same. He took the kids into the other room. Milcah approached Magda.

"My dear, you must put some clothes on," Milcah said to her.

"Don't tell me what to do," Magda said to her harshly. "You come here and disrupt my home and expect me to be nice. This is my home, not yours! You had no right to throw out my servant. You get out, Milcah. You get out!"

"Don't talk to my wife like that!" Kohath leveled her with a threatening gaze that made Magda want to laugh. She had not even seen him enter the room.

"Kohath!' Milcah gasped. "Don't."

"She has a demon, Milcah. I mean it. I don't want that thing near my family. Get her out or lock her up. We will not risk her cursed form inflicting more harm on our family." Kohath stormed away.

The demons inside of Magda gnawed at her, causing an unrelenting internal pain. Their encounter with Kohath was a jarring experience, leaving them feeling unsettled and deeply upset.

"I would never harm your precious family, Aunt Milcah,"

Chalaq spoke through her. Magda retreated into the shadows of her own mind, unable to grasp at the light.

"I know," Milcah replied. "He is just upset. You must get dressed."

"Of course, let me make myself presentable," Chalaq said, using Magda's voice.

"Fix yourself up and come down for the morning meal." Milcah helped Magda to her feet.

Magda went to her room, confused that she wasn't able to hold the conversation for herself. It frightened her.

"Don't be afraid. We are helping you, remember?" Haavah spoke to her.

Magda knew she couldn't stay in that house for much longer. She went to her secret treasure spot, where she kept the money she had saved from the worship services over the last six months. It would be enough for her to get out of the house and start a life for herself somewhere else.

Magda lifted up the loose board. She peered inside the space that held her treasures, but it was empty; completely and utterly devoid of everything she had collected over the years.

"Jezebel," she spat, the demons echoing her frustration or fueling it. "Betrayed!"

"We will get her back. She will get what she has coming," the six demons hissed, furious that one of their own betrayed them.

CHAPTER THIRTEEN

Magda was forced to live as best she could under the current circumstances. Jezebel's betrayal locked her into a fate that was unforeseen. With no resources, Magda had no choice but to stay confined to the estate at Magdala. The demons harassed her constantly, not liking their new environment under Kohath's headship.

The months passed by, Magda losing more and more control. She barely did the talking anymore. Her angry outbursts, sudden convulsions and unpredictable rages had the entire family on edge. All went according to plan.

When Kohath died after a short illness, the protective covering was lifted. The demons settled down and Belial was intoxicated with renewed zeal for access to his prey.

Milcah had customarily locked Magda in her room at night at Kohath's request. Now that he was gone, and she was grieving, the room remained unlocked. Milcah prayed often, trying to assuage the burden of her grief.

Unable to sleep, Magda felt enticed to go to the stream where Belial manipulated another man to assert his authority over his prey. No matter how much he tried, he couldn't break through the barriers guarding her heart, and it infuriated him.

• • •

When Amos died a little over a year later, Milcah was even more distraught. Alone in her grief over the loss of her brother, Milcah became troubled that Magda was unmoved by the death of her father.

"Magda, are you not grieving?" Milcah asked her.

"Why would I grieve? The man was nothing to me," Pride replied.

With each passing day, the distance between Milcah and Magda seemed to widen. Late one winter evening, Milcah got up in the middle of the night because she couldn't sleep. The grief of losing both husband and brother was often too much for her. She was in charge of the estate at Magdala until Magda came of age. Her niece's unpredictable temperament puzzled her, leaving her curious and troubled. Her husband's accusation that she had a demon caused Milcah to have doubts about Magda's relationship with the Lord. Magda never prayed with them or participated in the religious observances.

Milcah went to look in on each of her children as they slept. When she got to Magda's room, the girl was gone. Milcah's brow furrowed with concern. Where could she have gone off to in the middle of the night? She searched the property but could not find her. Milcah waited and paced the floor. When Magda snuck in through the garden, Milcah caught her by surprise.

"Magda!" Milcah whispered.

Magda jumped out of her skin, scratching at her arms as if something clawed at her from the inside.

"Where have you been?" Milcah inquired.

"None of your business," Pride spat at her.

"Have you been with a man?" Milcah asked her, sure that Magda was doing things she shouldn't be. She had heard about her sordid reputation. Milcah didn't want to believe the rumors, but what choice did she have now?

"What is it to you?" Greed hissed.

"Magda, why do you sin against Yahweh? When you sin, you make yourself an enemy of God," Milcah pleaded with her.

"We are enemies of God!" All six demons voiced their outrage with a guttural cry that frightened Milcah.

Magda ran upstairs and slammed the door. Milcah had no more doubts about Magda having a demon. In fact, she was sure that there was more than one. Milcah went up after her niece and locked the door. She needed a plan. She needed to protect her family against demonic attack.

.

In the years that followed, Milcah kept Magda locked up. Priests came and went, trying to exert authority over the evil occupants. The more they tried, the stronger the demons became. With no way to release their powers, the demons raged against Magda. Being captive was not conducive to their plan. Belial's rage intensified as he realized he could no longer have his prey in the way he craved the most.

Magda barely slept. She spent her nights curled up in a corner, listening to the bickering, restless demons inside of her. They were pent up, confined. They enticed her to do things to herself that hurt her. She scratched at her arms, pulled out her hair and cut her feet on shards of pottery. She screamed in agony, foaming at the mouth and tearing at the walls.

When Milcah brought in another priest to pray for her, she found Magda in a pool of blood. The Priest left and a physician came. He bound up Magda's wounds.

Milcah let Magda come downstairs for the first time in years. She felt terribly guilty for leaving the girl locked up, but she didn't know what else to do. She was afraid of her niece. Magda seemed subdued in her current disheveled state, so Milcah let down her guard.

"Come on, now. Have something to eat," Milcah said to her.

Magda nibbled on the food offered. She hadn't tasted anything in years. She wondered where the rest of the family was.

"I know that it has been a while since you were down here. A lot has changed in that time. Samuel is married with two children. Rachel is married as well. She lives in Bethany."

Magda didn't reply. She stared blankly at Milcah, not quite understanding her. Magda pulled out strands of her matted hair.

"Rebecca has gone to apprentice as a midwife. Your two youngest cousins are studying the Torah under a rabbi in the Temple in Jerusalem. Rachel's husband is a rabbi. He has great connections. He is a good man. Do you want to get married someday, Magda?" Milcah asked her, coaxing her out of her demonic imprisonment.

Married—the word stirred something inside of Magda. What was that feeling, that longing? The demons reacted to it violently. They began convulsing her. Milcah helped Magda through it by holding her gently and praying over her. When it was over, she gave her niece some water. They sat quietly until a knock at the door startled them both.

Milcah went to see who it was. Magda could hear delighted voices and laughter. She heard a man's voice. He sounded authoritative and clean. The demons arose with a vengeance. No man was going to exert authority over Magda again, not after they had gained so much ground. Time was running out. They had to make more progress or their captain was going to demote them.

Magda's body trembled with an overwhelming rage. Strengthened and infuriated, she went to the foyer where Rachel and her new husband had shown up unexpectedly for a surprise visit. Magda took one look at the man, Eleazar, and was on him in a heartbeat.

She tore at him with the strength of ten men. The women screamed, feeding the frenzy of the demonic attack. When it was over, Eleazar lay in a bloodied heap, unconscious and maimed.

Magda stepped back. She saw the horror on Milcah's face, as well as Rachel's. She looked at the bloodied heap of a man on the floor. Regret and sorrow tried to force their way through the evil stronghold, but the demons were too robust. Magda was forced to run, her heart pounding in her chest. She left the estate at Magdala behind her and kept running until her freshly bandaged feet were raw and bleeding once again.

Magda came upon a woman selling goods in a small village on the outskirts of Magdala. She beckoned Magda over. Holding up a black cloak, she stretched it out to her.

"I have no money," Magda told her.

"I will give it to you if you only let me have a place to live and give me a name," Despair said.

Magda took the cloak. "You can live with us. You will be named Massah."

The woman became the cloak that Magda wrapped around herself. She melted into her easily and without resistance. Magda's sobs echoed through the room as she started to cry. She wandered the streets looking for food until darkness fell upon the land. It had been so long since she had been outside. Belial was eager to be with her once again. He easily lured a Roman soldier to where Magda was hiding.

"What are you doing here?" the soldier asked her. "Shouldn't you be in the house of ill repute with the other girls?"

"I am hungry," Magda said.

"So am I," Belial answered through the man. "I can give you food. What will you give me?"

"I have nothing," Despair replied through her.

The Roman lifted her to her feet. "Come with me."

He led her to the garrison that was not too far away from the village. He fed her a nice meal before exacting his payment, satisfying his lust. Magda survived in this manner for months until the Roman soldiers moved out to answer a battle call.

She wandered the streets once again. The villagers knew she

had demons. Most stayed away from her. One night, hungry and with no money, Magda went to the house of ill repute. It came as a shock to her when she discovered Jezebel was in charge.

The demons strengthened her, determined to take their revenge. Magda enjoyed the shocked look on Jezebel's face when she recognized her.

"My lady, Magda," Jezebel stammered. "I didn't expect to see you."

"You mean after you stole my money?" Anger seethed.

"I didn't steal it. Only borrowed. Look, you can help me here. We do good business. Even more once you clean yourself up." Jezebel groveled.

Magda relished her position of authority. She took Jezebel up on her offer. It took a few months for her to heal and get back to being presentable. Once she was, Magda earned her money back over the years that followed. With the demons now focused on Jezebel's misery instead of her own, Magda regained her former beauty. With each passing day, her reputation continued to gain momentum. Though people knew she had demons, it didn't stop the men from coming to her. Magda retreated further and further into darkness with the help of Despair.

When Lucifer issued the timing of the feast, the demons made haste to finish their work of revenge.

"It is time to take what rightfully belonged to you," Greed hissed.

"Take the money. Set the curtain on fire and leave. Everyone is asleep," Anger commanded her.

Magda did exactly as she was told. She walked out of the fire, money in hand, and disappeared into the night. Only ashes remained where the house of ill-repute once stood. Out of the ashes, a silhouetted bat-like figure rose up and dissolved into the darkness.

CHAPTER FOURTEEN

Belial's rage burned hot against the seven demons. They had not prepared Magda's heart for the feast. They were running out of time. Belial had no other options. Unlike the other captains, he had used all his forces on this one woman. He had no choice but to lure her into Zophos when the time came. He could not show up to Lucifer's millennial feast with nothing.

"Why have you not given me an opening to her heart?" Belial bellowed. "Access to the soul is only granted through the heart! You all know that. You will suffer consequences for this failure!"

"Captain, what if we bind her heart? She will be less resistant if her heart is bound," Greed offered as a solution.

"Perhaps the Great One himself can overcome the barrier that keeps her heart. Would he not be delighted by such a challenge?" Vanity suggested.

"That just might work," Belial considered. "What is the current situation?"

"Jezebel crumbled under her destructive forces. She is back on the streets. She has money to take care of herself," Lust offered.

"Strip her of everything she has," Belial said. "Turn on her until she has nothing but spare her life. Bind her heart and bring her to the forest when I tell you it is time. She needs to believe that there is nowhere else to turn."

"At your command, Captain," the seven demons hissed.

• • •

Magda walked the streets, leaving the village behind her. The money bag was heavy. She had only her black cloak and the tunic she wore beneath it. Magda delighted herself with thoughts of buying new clothing. She walked in the darkness until her feet ached. The night was quiet, with only the occasional hoot of an owl breaking the silence. The peaceful silence was interrupted by a sudden clamor of internal voices vying for her attention.

The demons were in an uproar. Magda dropped to her knees and covered her ears. The tormentors continued to hurt her from within, reopening old wounds.

"Stop," Magda yelled. "Stop!"

"We won't stop, you wicked woman!" The voices were all speaking as one, echoing one after another.

"You are a sinful woman — an enemy of Yahweh."

"No one would want you!"

"Look at what you've done. You are defiled! You are trash. You are worthless!"

"Leave me alone!" Magda pleaded, even as she succumbed to their accusations.

"Disgusting. Shameful. Horrible. You hurt people. You are a child of darkness!"

Magda's heart raced as she started sprinting, desperate to distance herself from them. They only got louder in her head. Magda couldn't even see in the darkness anymore. They were clouding her vision. She ran until a group of Roman soldiers on night patrol caught her, just as the demons had wanted.

Magda tried to fight, but the demons stripped her of any power to resist the lustful violence of the men. When they were done with her, she had nothing but her black cloak to cover herself with. A sense of loss washed over her as she realized her money had been stolen.

"That is all you are good for," the demons chuckled.

"No one sees you. No one protects you. You are no longer beautiful."

Magda found herself back on the streets of Magdala. The condemning voices were so loud that she could hear nothing around her. Her *friends* turned into enemies.

She was frantic, searching for quiet but unable to find any. Magda ate scraps just to survive, but it had been years since she actually tasted food. She didn't want to live, but the demons kept her alive. Their power had completely enslaved her, leaving her helpless.

After months of being shunned by the community, Magda hid herself in a cave by the stream. She snuck out at night in order to find scraps to eat.

One day, the religious leaders found her and dragged her into the center square of the village. They intended to stone her, but the demons empowered her with the strength to fight them off. The sounds of groans and cries filled the air as Magda retreated back into her cave, leaving several men wounded in her wake. They left her alone after that.

One night, as Magda scrounged in the dark for a morsel of food, the demons quieted down. Magda was taken aback by the eerie silence that filled her. She looked up into the sky. It was almost dawn. She would have to make her way back to the cave soon.

"Dear sweet Magda," the demons hissed. *"Are we not your friends? Have we not protected you?"*

"I thought you were my friends, but..." Magda spoke softly.

"We don't hold your sins against you like Yahweh does. Come with us. This is no life for you. We can offer you protection and the glory that you deserve." The demons enticed her as one voice.

"Come with you where?" Magda asked.

"*Come to Zophos – where we are from. There is someone waiting to meet you,*" the demons said.

"Who? Who is waiting to meet me? Where is Zophos?" Magda asked.

"*Zophos is not of this world. It is a beautiful kingdom where you will be part of a great feast,*" the demons said to her. "*You must be starving, are you not?*"

"I am hungry, but I'm not sure what for," Magda replied.

"*Will you let us show you into Zophos?*" the demons asked, knowing that they needed her consent before they took her to the Captain.

Magda hesitated. She looked up into the sky. The bright morning star was emerging, bringing a flicker of light against the dark sky like an ember among a landscape of ash.

"*What are you waiting for?*" The demons were irritated. Their time was running out. "*Are you going to come with us or not?*"

Magda's eyes were fixed on the light from the morning star until clouds formed and she could no longer see it.

"Alright, I will come with you to Zophos."

The demons seized Magda and made her writhe in agony until she lost consciousness and crumpled to the ground.

• • •

Magda found herself in a darkness so thick she could feel the weight of it pressing in on her. She was in some sort of forest. Fear consumed her as she trembled uncontrollably. She was alone, but she felt more like herself than she had in years. Magda began walking, searching for a way out. As she continued walking, a strange feeling crept up her spine, as if someone watched her from behind. She knew she was being chased.

She ran deeper into the dark forest of Zophos. The terrain looked familiar. She remembered it from a dream she had long ago. As she ran, she tried to remember the dream. There was something she was looking for. Her path was illuminated by a flickering ember of light, guiding her towards an unknown destination. Where the light was coming from, Magda wasn't sure. She believed it originated from her own body. Had the morning star become a part of her?

She pushed on, even as her sense of the evil presence gaining on her increased. As she listened intently, she could make out the sound of deep, rhythmic breathing. She had to keep running. She had to get away.

When Magda fell into a pit of mud, her progress was slowed. She couldn't lift her feet. She looked to her left — skulls dotted the landscape. Magda looked up ahead and caught a glimpse of a vibrant light that reminded her of the morning star. She wanted to reach it.

"Push through the pain until you get home!" Her Aunt Milcah's words gave her strength. Magda pushed, even though it hurt. She freed herself from the pit and ran toward the ember of light. She recognized the cornerstone immediately. It was the massive Temple rock, just as she had envisioned it in her dream. Magda leapt for it just as something scratched at her back, tearing her flesh. She clung to the rock with both hands.

Flames leapt up around her, blocking her in, surrounding her. The heat was so intense that it seemed to radiate, making it almost unbearable to breathe. Magda could see the figure of a dragon illuminated in front of her. A bat-like creature was by its side. The flames were rising higher and closer to her. The menacing creatures could not approach her. She knew that her safety depended on remaining attached to the rock. The enemy of her soul was using the heat to try to get her to let go.

"How dare you bring her here, Belial!" Lucifer bellowed. His rage increasing his size. "She is sealed. Did you not recognize that? These particular image-bearers are only meant for destruction, not for the feast."

Lucifer ripped the wings off Belial. The demon spoke in a

trembling voice. "I thought you could break through it, Master. I thought it would be a most delectable treat for you. Her heart is bound with seven chains. We have made good sport of her. She cannot be of value to the Creator now." Belial tried to regain his standing with the Evil One.

"You have put this place at risk. She brings light. She is a threat to us!" Lucifer paced, breathing his fiery breath to increase the intensity of the flames. "If we could get her off the rock, I might be able to consume her with flame."

"Where did the rock come from?" Belial asked, licking the wounds inflicted on him where his wings once had been.

"Are you a fool? The rock was placed here for her by Him! That is why she is dangerous. He gave her a refuge here in the dark, in our domain. It means something, but I don't know what. He wouldn't enter my house, would He?" Lucifer pondered his own agitated thoughts. "His time has not yet come. He can't just…"

They turned at the sound of horse hooves fast approaching. Magda looked up toward the sound. Her skin was burning. She tried to hang on, but it was getting more difficult as the heat intensified around her. The moisture from her perspiration was making it challenging to hold on to the cornerstone. Magda looked up when she heard the sound of rushing wind and saw the bright light coming toward them.

Her eyes took in the figure of a man riding a white horse. He stopped and dismounted where the ring of fire began. Magda had never seen such radiant glory before. He was the morning star. All in the dark forest could sense His authority looming over them. The man looked at her with such love in His eyes that Magda regained strength to hold on.

"You have no dominion here, Son of God! Your time has not yet come!" Lucifer breathed out his threat, but he kept his distance from Him.

"All authority has been given to Me in heaven and on earth," the Son of God declared.

"She is a sinner, condemned by Your own Law, Yeshua of Nazareth," Lucifer argued.

"Her heart is sealed. This one is mine! You have no right to her." His words pierced the Evil One, causing him to step backward.

Yeshua looked at Magda. "Mary," He whispered. "Come to me."

Belial made one final effort to thwart the failure of his battle plan. The Captain of Shadow put himself between the Son of God and the woman he had attempted to prey on. Yeshua lifted His hand toward the beast and imprisoned Belial in a cloud. There was an increased frenzy in the trees surrounding them as the demons became frightened by the powerful presence of light in their dark forest.

"Mary." Yeshua extended His hand toward her. "Walk through the fire. You will not be burned if you keep your eyes on Me."

Trusting Him, Magda slid off the stone. She stepped into the fiery flames and walked toward the One who called her by name. With each step she took, the flames were extinguished, leaving only ashes on the forest floor. Magda placed her trembling hand into His. She was so ashamed of her defilement in the face of such glory. She knelt down before Him, her Lord, her Savior, her Redeemer.

Yeshua lifted her by the chin until she stood to her feet before Him. "Identify them to me," He said to her, not masking His authority.

She knew, without explanation, that He was referring to the demons she had named and invited into her life. Magda bowed her head, overcome with guilt, knowing her own weakness and willingness contributed to the powers of evil that dominated her.

"Mary," Yeshua lifted her chin once again. "Identify them to me."

Magda took a deep breath. "Haavah," she said.

"Haavah," Yeshua repeated.

Magda heard a shriek from up above and felt a snap of release in her heart. It hurt her at first, but then it relieved a built up pressure inside of her. Magda tried to turn her head to look at the trees where she heard the terrible shriek, but Yeshua held her face firmly in His hands.

"Keep your focus on me, Mary," He said to her.

"Gevah," Magda said.

"Gevah," He repeated with thunderous authority. The same thing happened as before.

With every beat, Magda could sense the chains that had bound her heart for so long gradually unraveling. "Qanah," she said.

"Qanah," He repeated.

Magda noticed the beautiful color of His eyes because her own were starting to clear.

"Chalaq," Magda pronounced.

"Chalaq," Yeshua declared, sending the demon into oblivion.

Magda was beginning to feel empowered as her heart was being set free.

"Nechosheth," she said.

"Nechosheth," Yeshua repeated.

"Kaas," Magda confessed before Him.

"Kaas." Yeshua destroyed the demon with His word.

"Massah," Magda said the last name louder than the rest.

"Massah," Yeshua declared, pulling Magda toward Himself as the last chain was broken.

Magda fell into His arms, overcome with the power of love now surging through her entire being. Her heart was one with His. The seal was His seal. She had always belonged to the Holy One.

"Your Father in heaven protects you, beloved. I have loved you with an everlasting love. Nothing can separate you from My love," Yeshua declared, His flaming eyes looking at the Evil One.

Yeshua lifted Magda and placed her on the white stallion. They turned to leave the forest, but the Evil One issued a command of attack. Magda watched as Yeshua turned on Lucifer.

"You are right when you say that My time has not yet come." Yeshua lifted His hand toward heaven. A sword appeared in His hand. He pointed it toward the flames, absorbing every last one until His sword became a flaming weapon. With it, He turned on the army of darkness. "You will have your hour, but it is not yet upon us. I will be back to fight you. You will not take what is rightfully Mine."

The demon army backed off at His Word. They had no authority over Him. Magda feared Him with awesome wonder.

"You can't possibly take the sin of them all upon Yourself. It won't work. They are not worth saving!" Lucifer bellowed as he breathed fire in rage and frustration.

Yeshua took His flaming sword and stabbed it into the ground of the dark forest as if in triumph. The flaming sword turned into a rugged cross.

• • •

Magda came back to consciousness, feeling pain and soreness all over her body. She opened her eyes. The bright light of the sun shocked her sight, which had become accustomed to the darkness. As she looked up, a dark silhouette of a man loomed over her. She couldn't make out His face.

"Mary," He said to her. His voice was warm and inviting. She recognized it from her dream, or was it a dream?

Magda felt released from the power of the demons. She took the man's outstretched hand and let Him help her stand. When her eyes adjusted, she recognized Him from the dark forest—her Rescuer.

"Yeshua," she said to Him, falling at His feet. "Let me live with You, my Lord. I love You and only You."

"First, you must go with one of my followers to a man named John. I will meet up with you again. Do not fear." Yeshua kissed her on the forehead.

"As You wish," she replied.

Yeshua took her to a man named Nathan. "This is Magda, Nathan. She is one of us now. I need you to take her to John."

"Yes, Lord. I will do as You wish," Nathan said obediently.

"Would Joanna be permitted to come as well?"

"Yes," Yeshua said. He looked at Magda. "Mary, you can trust Nathan and Joanna. They have been with Me and will speak to you of many things. Listen to them until we meet again, beloved."

"I will, Lord." Magda wrapped her arms around Him in a tight embrace, causing Him to burst into laughter. The sound of His laughter brought light and new life to her heart.

PART TWO

The Defeat

CHAPTER FIFTEEN

agda went with Joanna and Nathan. They joined up with a caravan making its way to Aenon, the place where the man, John, was baptizing by the Jordan River. Yeshua left them, heading in the opposite direction with a handful of men. Hopeful anticipation filled Magda's thoughts as she longed for another encounter with Him. Her heart felt heavy at the prospect of separation.

"First, let us get you something to wear." Joanna smiled at Magda, making her suddenly aware of her frightful appearance.

Her threadbare clothes draped loosely on her frail frame, a stark reminder of her impoverished state. Her tunic hung in tatters, revealing patches of bare skin. The black cloak was dirty and stained with grime. Her arms were scarred and bruised. Magda's cheeks felt hot with embarrassment.

"Come on," Joanna urged her. "I have some things with me."

Joanna began pawing through some clothes on the back of a cart. Magda stood silently aware of herself and her shame, though she saw no accusation in Joanna's eyes.

"Let's see. How about this one? The blue would look nice on you." Joanna held a blue linen tunic up.

"It's too nice," Magda said. "I have no money to pay you."

"Magda, we share things. This was among some discarded items in the palace. It once was worn by someone of royal standing, I'm sure," Joanna said to her, still holding out the beautiful tunic.

"The palace?" Magda questioned.

"I work in Herod's palace," Joanna said to her. "I am a servant there. I was given leave to come visit my brother, Nathan. He just started following this Rabbi named Yeshua. I had to see for myself."

"He is a Rabbi?" Magda asked, realizing how little she knew about the One who saved her.

"Yes, He is not well known yet, but I believe He is someone great," Joanna said.

The woman's words left Magda wondering in silence, her mind racing to make sense of it all. Was it not known that this was the Son of God, the Messiah they had been waiting for?

"Come, you can change in here." Joanna led her to a small dwelling. "They are friends of ours who let us lodge with them last night," she explained.

Magda took the tunic and went into the small room. She shut the door behind her and hung the new garment on the wall where a hook protruded. She looked at it glistening in the sunlight. The color reminded her of the radiant color of Yeshua's eyes when He rescued her out of the dark forest. Had He actually done that or did she just imagine it?

Magda recalled what Joanna said to her about the clothing. How could she even think of putting on a royal garment? She was not worthy. As she glanced at her body, she couldn't help but notice the stains and scratches that covered her. She felt ashamed and dirty. Even if she washed the outside, how could the inside of her ever be clean again?

Magda's heart was open for the first time since her childhood, but her mind was not yet free. The demons had left a web of lies that clung to her thoughts with a stickiness she thought she would never wash off.

Magda had no choice. She couldn't continue traveling with these good people dressed in the rags she wore. She let the black cloak fall to the floor. When it hit the ground, the entire garment turned to ash. The sight left Magda mesmerized, unable to tear her eyes away. A breeze wafted in through the window, whipping up the ashes until they disappeared from sight.

"If only it were that easy," Magda sighed.

She let her battered tunic fall to the floor before stepping into the blue linen garment presented to her. The softness of the fabric along with the radiance of the color made her feel beautiful, if only for a moment. A vision from her past came through her heart and into her mind...

Anna had been teaching in the Temple, standing by the stone pillar when she said, "I will greatly rejoice in Yahweh! My soul will be joyful in my God; for He has clothed me with the garments of salvation. He has covered me with the robe of righteousness, as a bridegroom decks himself with a garland, and as a bride adorns herself with her jewels."[12]

Anna — it had been years since Magda thought about her. The memory of her death brought sorrow to Magda's heart. She smoothed the blue fabric over the brokenness of her body.

"Garments of salvation," she whispered. "A bridegroom," her heart pondered what that might mean for someone like her.

"How does it go in there?" Joanna asked from outside.

"I am coming out," Magda answered.

With a gentle push, she opened the door and was greeted by a creaking sound. She hesitated, her eyes darting nervously

---

[12] Isaiah 61:10

around the room. When she stepped out and saw Joanna's face, Magda felt her cheeks flush with embarrassment.

"Magda, that looks stunning on you," Joanna exclaimed. "Don't worry, we will stop somewhere and have a chance to get cleaned up. For now, though, Nathan is waiting for us."

"Alright," Magda said.

Joanna said goodbye to the nice couple that offered them lodging. Magda wondered how she had never really seen the kindness within people before. The shadows of darkness had blinded her to all that was good in the world.

Nathan, Joanna, and Magda traveled most of the day. Nathan talked excitedly of the rumors swirling around Yeshua of Nazareth.

"Some say that He might be the Messiah," Nathan said. "But, He has not declared it Himself. Right now, He is only teaching."

"The men with Him, are they followers like you or students?" Joanna asked her brother.

"I think they have been designated His disciples," Nathan answered her. "They are an interesting group. The seven of them are so different. They are not the kind of men rabbis usually decide to teach. But then, He isn't an ordinary rabbi."

"That is the truth, Brother." Joanna smiled. "Will you join up with Him again?"

"I believe that I will if I am given the chance. How long can you stay with me until you have to get back to the palace?"

"I only have another week and then I will be missed." Joanna sighed. "Chuza is missing me as well, I'm sure. He won't like the idea of his wife following the teaching of a new Rabbi who isn't under the covering of the Sanhedrin."

"What is the Sanhedrin?" Magda asked them.

"Were you not raised here in Israel?" Joanna asked her.

Magda flushed red, embarrassed at her obvious ignorance.

"I'm sorry, Magda," Joanna said, putting her arm around her as they walked. "I meant nothing by it."

"I was not taught the ways of our people," Magda said. "I was…" She hesitated, unsure if she should tell them about the demons. What if they abandoned her or were afraid of her?

"You were possessed by demons," Nathan said, matter-of-factly, no hint of judgment in his voice.

"How did you know?" Magda asked them, surprised and relieved at the same time. She didn't want to bear the burden of such a secret. She didn't think she had the strength to.

"We were there, Magda," Joanna said. "We were there when Yeshua cast them out."

"Cast them out? What do you mean?" Magda thought the whole experience had been a dream. How had they seen what happened?

"We came upon you in the early morning," Nathan said. "We had been traveling with such urgency to get to Magdala. Yeshua had a purpose. He knew exactly where you were. He went over to you and held you in His arms. You were unconscious at first."

"He put His hand on your forehead." Joanna picked up the story. "You opened your eyes and began to mumble. The voice that came out of you didn't belong to a woman. It was a demon's voice."

"We were all scared," Nathan said. "People from the village came to us and yelled at us to get away from you because you had the strength to kill and destroy. They called you Magda."

"Yeshua was unmoved by their warnings. He held you and said your name." Joanna smiled. "He called you Mary. You reached for Him when He did that."

Magda remembered the rescue in the forest. Though it played out differently in the spiritual realm, there was an earthly scene she had been unaware of. "Then what happened?" she asked them.

"He called the demons by name, one by one, and rebuked them—all seven of them!" Joanna shuddered. "How horrible it must have been for you, Magda."

Magda's emotions overwhelmed her, and tears started to flow uncontrollably. She walked in silence, letting her tears of gratitude wash the remnant of ash still clinging to her face.

"He set you down gently because you were unconscious again," Nathan said. "Within moments, though, you opened your eyes, and He helped you to stand."

"Yes, He did," Magda said to them. "He gave me strength to stand."

The caravan stopped for the night in a small village. Joanna made camp for them after showing Magda where she could wash up. One of the homes that generously hosted the caravan had a cistern, offering a refreshing oasis in the arid surroundings. The wealthy home had a standing basin behind an enclosure where Magda could wash her body. The water felt cool as it removed the dirt and dust that had caked on her skin. When she slipped back into the blue linen tunic, Magda felt like a new creation.

CHAPTER SIXTEEN

When darkness engulfed the land, Magda became frightened. She felt exposed to the shadows. She wasn't used to not being able to see clearly in the dark. The noises from the land startled her. Every sound was amplified in her ears. The world had never felt so alive before.

Though cleansed by the washing, Magda still felt dirty on the inside. She lingered on the outside of the group, not used to being around people. Joanna was busy and didn't notice Magda at first. Accustomed to traveling, Joanna knew exactly what to do. Magda watched her gather wood, start a fire and prepare a meal all by herself. Magda felt a deep sense of shame at her lack of skills.

Related to the property owner, the caravan leader had several members lodge inside the house. Magda observed this new world she was invited into. It was a world of generosity and kindness that she had only known once a long time ago when she lived with her aunt and uncle as a young child. Yet, she had taken it for granted back then. She even hurt the ones she should have loved. Magda cringed when she remembered taking her cousin's brush and comb heirlooms.

"Here, you need to eat," Joanna said to her, handing her a

bowl of something hot. "It's lentil soup, my specialty."

Magda took the bowl. It smelled good. When was the last time she actually smelled something? When was the last time she ate a meal? Magda put a spoonful in her mouth. Her taste came alive, warming her on the inside as she swallowed. She couldn't believe how good the nourishment was.

"Joanna, this is so good!" Magda licked her lips, crying. "I have never tasted anything this good before."

"Aww, Magda. Don't cry. It really isn't that great. My brother always makes fun of my cooking. It keeps up our strength, though." Joanna patted Magda on the shoulder before going to serve others.

Magda enjoyed every bite of the lentil soup. She didn't want the sensation to end. It amazed her how much better she felt with real food in her stomach.

Magda stayed away from the fire. She didn't like being close to it because she remembered the fire in the dark forest of Zophos that almost consumed her. Perhaps that was her destiny. Perhaps she was meant to be consumed by fire. Her thoughts proceeded in a downward spiral toward guilt and shame. She felt heavy with regret as she thought about all the people she hurt. She was reminded of the fire that she started which took Jezebel's life. Magda didn't deserve to be spared.

Sorrowful, Magda slipped inside the tent which Joanna had set up for them. She crawled into the sleeping mat and covered herself with a thin blanket. The night air was cool, but the tent covering protected her against it. Magda watched the shadows made from the flames dancing on the canvas walls. With each passing moment, fear consumed her. She tried to keep her eyes closed so she could fall asleep, but every time someone outside laughed or raised the volume of their voice, it startled her. Shadows danced and taunted her, making her doubt her freedom.

Yeshua's strong, authoritative voice met her in the dark. *"Her heart is sealed. This one is Mine. You have no right to her,"* He had proclaimed to Lucifer. *"All authority in heaven and on earth is given to Me."*

Even the memory of His voice calmed her. "Mary," she sat up, sure she heard Him in the tent. There was no one there. Magda lay back down. The way He said her name — it was with such love and... and...What was it? Magda let her mind stay focused on the sound of Yeshua's voice saying her name and proclaiming that her heart was His. She knew she loved Him, the Lord. She wondered if anyone else would understand, especially if they didn't know who He really was.

Once she turned her focus away from the shadows and onto the memory of Yeshua, Magda got the sleep that replenished her body with a rest she had not experienced since she was a child.

When she woke up in the morning, the first thought to cross her mind were the words she remembered Anna teaching. *"But let all those who take refuge in You rejoice. Let them always shout for joy, because You defend them. Let them also who love Your Name be joyful in You."* 13

Magda rolled over, drinking in the sunlight. "Love Your Name," she whispered. "Your Name, Yeshua."

Magda got up, determined to figure out how to be more helpful. She watched Joanna and did her best to copy what she did. Magda rolled up the sleeping mats, folded the tent covering, and helped to load the carts. They were on the road traveling after taking a morning meal together. The curds Joanna offered her tasted as good as the lentil soup the night before. Magda's body absorbed the strength the nourishment offered her.

"You are so quiet during our meal prayers, Magda," Joanna said to her. "Do they upset you?"

"Not anymore," Magda said. "They used to, back when..."

Joanna nodded in understanding.

"I guess I am just embarrassed because I don't know

---

13 Psalm 5:11

anything. I can't join in with you because I don't know what to say." Magda looked down.

"That's alright, Magda. Yeshua is a teacher. He will teach you everything you need to know. In the meantime, I would be happy to help you learn some of our prayers." Joanna linked her arm into Magda's. "Let's see, the first one I think I will teach you is this: 'I will give thanks to Yahweh with my whole heart. I will tell of all Your marvelous works.'"[14]

"I will give thanks to Yahweh with my whole heart. I will tell of all Your marvelous works." Magda repeated the holy words. "Who would ever listen to my crazy story?" Magda laughed, aptly applying the Scripture.

"Don't be so hard on yourself, Magda," Joanna said to her. "We all have a destiny that the Lord has mapped out for us. Every step along the journey is ordained by Him."

"I can't imagine that He would have a destiny for someone who strayed so far into enemy territory, Joanna." Magda sighed. "I might have had a destiny once, but I turned from that path and I don't think it can be found again."

"I think you're wrong, Magda." Joanna spoke with confidence. "Yeshua knew exactly where you were and He went to get you. That means something — something greater than you can imagine, I'm sure. I only hope I'm around to watch your destiny unfold."

Joanna skipped forward when she saw Nathan motion to her. Magda admired the woman's joyous demeanor. She wondered about what she said. Was there truly a destiny that awaited her in the Kingdom of God?

They finally arrived in Aenon by late afternoon. They broke off from the caravan, making their way toward the shores of the great Jordan River. Magda, exhausted from the long trip, dragged herself wearily to her destination. She had never done so much

---

[14] Psalm 9:1

walking. Her feet hurt. Her toes ached. Her back was sore.

There was a camp set up along the shore of the Jordan River. Magda looked at the large body of water, feeling the coolness of the air coming off it. The river, while not visually stunning, commanded attention with its sheer size and power.

Magda helped Nathan and Joanna find a spot for them to join the crowd. Only a few were there as lodgers. The rest had only come for the day. Magda wondered what the spectacle was all about. Why had so many people flocked to the Jordan?

The three of them settled in. Nathan left to go look for some people he and Joanna might know.

"Why are all these people here?" Magda asked Joanna.

"They have come to see the prophet, John," Joanna said.

"Prophet?" Magda questioned her.

"A man sent from Yahweh with a message," Joanna explained.

"Sent from Yahweh? Like the Messiah," Magda said, confused.

"No, the Messiah is different. A Prophet is just a messenger. The Messiah is the Deliverer, the Son," Joanna told her.

"What is John's message?" Magda asked.

"Come on," Joanna took her by the hand and helped her to her feet, "let's go see."

Joanna and Magda walked along the throng of people. The sun dipped low in the sky. Several in the crowd were already dispersing to go back from where they came. When they came up over a small hill, Magda had a clearer view of the river. In the midst of it, there stood a man, accompanied by another.

"That's John." Joanna pointed to the man dipping the other man into the water.

His appearance startled Magda, with his tall stature and a rugged beard that added a touch of mystery to his presence. He was wild looking, strong and had strange hair that stuck out in all directions. He wore a very odd garment around his robust body.

Easily up to the task of lifting bodies out of the waters of the Jordan, Magda wondered why he was doing it.

There were still some people standing along the hillside. Magda looked around at the crowd. One man appeared out of place. He wore elaborate robes and a large headdress on his head. He stood off to the side by himself. The rest of the people looked like people of meager means, regular people who were just trying to get through life. The man that caught Magda's eye looked like someone important.

"Who is that?" Magda asked Joanna.

Joanna looked to where Magda's eyes were focused. "Oh, that is one of the Pharisees, the religious leaders that rule in the Temple," Joanna explained. "I think that one's name is Eleazar. He had a horrible accident or something. They say he is cursed by Yahweh. Poor man."

Magda's eyes widened in shock, her face turning pale. She felt sick. She could see the disfigurement now. When the man turned to walk away, she noticed he had a limp. Overcome with grief and sorrow for what she had done to that poor man, her cousin's husband, Magda ran back to the tent. Joanna followed.

"Magda, what is wrong?" Joanna asked, concerned.

"Nothing, go away, Joanna. I am not a good woman," Magda cried.

"None of us is good, Magda," Joanna said soothingly. "We are all sinful."

"Not like me. I have done horrible things," Magda sobbed. "It was me that hurt that man. He didn't deserve any of it. Now, his life is ruined because of me. He is deemed cursed when it is me who is the cursed one."

"Magda, you have been delivered. You are not cursed. Yahweh is writing a master story with everyone's life. We don't always know His purposes. We just have to trust Him." Joanna rubbed Magda's back.

"I don't know why I'm here, Joanna," Magda said. "I don't

deserve to live."

"Alright, our next lesson is this: 'Don't remember the sins of my youth, nor my transgressions. Remember me according to Your loving kindness, for Your goodness' sake, Yahweh,'"[15] Joanna told her. "Come on now, say it with me. Both of them."

"I don't want to," Magda sobbed.

"I won't take no for an answer, Magda," Joanna said. "Sit up and tell me what you know. Speak the truth and let go of the lies."

Magda sat up, wiped her eyes and drew her own strength from Joanna's joy. "I will give thanks to Yahweh with my whole heart. I will tell of all Your marvelous works."[16]

"Good, good," Joanna encouraged.

Magda appreciated the praise. "Don't remember the sins of my youth, nor my transgressions. Remember me according to Your loving kindness, for Your goodness' sake, Yahweh."

"Magda, that is very good. I am amazed that you can recall the Scriptures so easily. You have a very good memory. It took me a long time to remember what was taught to me," Joanna praised her.

Magda felt a little better. She kept repeating the two truths that Joanna had taught her. It calmed her mind whenever her thoughts strayed into the sticky web of lies that wound her up with unsettling emotions.

The three new-comers to John's camp were invited to come near to the fires and partake of the evening meal. The campers made a meal of fish and leeks. They shared bread, dates and nuts. Magda thought the food tasted amazing. The man, John, did not eat the meal with them.

"He doesn't eat with you?" Magda asked one of John's followers.

"He eats only locust and wild honey," the man answered,

---

[15] Psalm 25:7
[16] Psalm 9:1

noticing her for the first time. "I am Joab."

"Nathan," Nathan answered him. "This is my sister, Joanna, and our friend, Magda."

"Nice to have you with us," Joab said to them. "How did you hear about John?"

"We were sent here by Yeshua," Nathan informed him.

"Ahh, Yeshua. John said of Him that He was the Lamb of God sent to take away the sins of the world," Joab said. "I was here when He was baptized."

"Yeshua was baptized by John?" Joanna asked.

"Yes, it was to fulfill all righteousness," Joab said. "It was unlike any other baptism we have ever done here."

John walked up and joined the circle, startling them all. "He came to me from Galilee." When John spoke, everyone and everything grew quiet. Even the crickets stopped chirping, the fire stopped crackling.

Magda saw the intensity of John's eyes as he continued to speak. "'Behold', I said, 'the Lamb of God, who takes away the sin of the world! This is He of whom I said, 'After me comes a man who is preferred before me, for He was before me.' I didn't know Him, but for this reason I came baptizing in water: that He would be revealed to Israel." John took a deep breath before continuing,

"I have seen the Spirit descending like a dove out of heaven, and it remained on Him. I didn't recognize Him, but He who sent me to baptize in water, He said to me, 'On whomever you will see the Spirit descending, and remaining on Him, the same is He who baptizes in the Holy Spirit.' I have seen, and have testified that this, that Yeshua, is the Son of God."[17]

Everyone was silent in awe of the proclamation. The holiness of the atmosphere captured them all, including Magda, whose heart clung to the truth she already knew.

---

[17] John 1:29-34

*O*VERCOMING

He who overcomes will be arrayed in white garments, and I will in no way blot his name out of the book of life, and I will confess his name before my Father, and before his angels.
Revelation 3:5

CHAPTER SEVENTEEN

It was a restless night for Magda. Her mind worked hard to absorb the truth that her heart hungered for. She didn't doubt John's proclamation that Yeshua was the Son of God. She did doubt that she was worthy of His love. Yet, she yearned for it with a passion that consumed her. Why had He sent her here to the prophet John?

Magda rolled over on her sleeping mat. Joanna's rhythmic breathing against the soothing sounds of the Jordan River bothered her when it should have lulled her to sleep. Since she wasn't able to find rest, Magda crept out of the tent. The moon was full, casting a shimmering light on the surface of the water. She walked barefoot to the shoreline.

The coolness of the baptismal waters tickled her toes. Magda was mesmerized by the dazzling beams of light as they danced upon the gently swaying waves. It was as if the water was responsive to the breath of God infusing the night breeze. Magda wondered if her soul was capable of responding to God's love.

She was thankful for the moon's glow piercing the darkness. At one time, the night had been a part of her, the darkness her place of comfort. It was the fear of perpetual darkness that haunted her, as she longed to exist in a realm of everlasting light.

Her heart raced as a rustling noise from behind sent shivers down her spine. A dark figure emerged from the brush that bordered the shore.

"Having trouble sleeping?" John asked her.

Magda was relieved when she realized it was the prophet.

"Yes, I am," she admitted, shyly.

John stood by her side on the shores of the Jordan at night. He silently admired the water and the fullness of the moon. As the prophet looked up into the sky, Magda followed his gaze. She saw wisps of clouds slowly drifting by.

"He gave us a light to govern the night because we were not meant to dwell in darkness," John instructed her. "The Holy Word tells us that in the beginning there was evening and there was morning, the first day.[18] Why do you think our Lord, the Creator of all things, began the day with the dark of evening?"

Magda wasn't sure if he was addressing her with the question or not. Regardless, she had no idea how to answer him. She stood uncomfortably silent, waiting.

John turned his gaze toward her. "The darkness comes before the light. Even when a child is born, it comes from the darkness into the light of this world. How much greater will be our birth into the light of heaven?"

Magda wanted so desperately to grasp the deep meaning of the man's words, but she felt as if a mist hindered her mind from absorbing an abiding truth. Once again, she looked up at the full moon, its light blocked by the faint clouds. It didn't mean it wasn't still there.

"I don't understand the meaning of the baptisms that you do," Magda admitted to John.

He looked at her tenderly. "The Kingdom of heaven is at

---

[18] Genesis 1:5

hand. People must turn away from the darkness in order to see the light. He has come to set the captives free." John sighed heavily. "People love the darkness. They remain blinded to the light unless they confess."

"Confess?" Magda asked.

"Admit the wrong, name the captive, reveal the behavior that led them to the darkness in the first place. Only then can a soul be truly free to live in the light." John's eyes reflected the light from the moon in power and intensity as the power of an invisible night wind whisked them away.

Magda looked at this man, wondering if he could see the darkness that left stains upon her soul. Yet, there was no condemnation in John's eyes.

"What is the stronger force Mary of Magdala, darkness or light?" John asked her.

"The darkness feels stronger," Magda lamented.

"Yet, look at the moon that shines above us. It is smaller than all the darkness that surrounds us, but its light penetrates all of it. The darkness cannot overcome it. It becomes the backdrop for it. The flame of a single candle can light up the darkness of a tomb." John paused, letting his words sink in. "What is the stronger emotion, love or hate?"

Words from her childhood echoed in Magda's heart. "Love conquers all," she recited.

"Love. The commandments are anchored on this power. 'Love the Lord Your God with all your heart, soul, mind and strength. Love your neighbor as yourself.'[19] To live in the light is to live a life of love. Love does not fear punishment because all is open to the light."

John's eyes met Magda's, and she couldn't help but feel a flutter of excitement in the core of her being. Hope. Was there hope for someone like her?

---

[19] Matthew 22:37

"The baptism I offer is a cleansing, a stripping away of the darkness of sin through confession that brings everything deep inside your soul out into the light."

Magda wanted the cleansing that John spoke of. Yeshua had rescued her from the pit of Zophos, where her soul languished beneath the suffocating shadow of death.

For some reason, she still had not overcome the power of the darkness that blackened her on the inside. Magda looked up at the moon penetrating the darkness as it reflected the light of the sun that she could not presently see. A gray cloud returned, moving across it, blocking the light temporarily. Magda shivered.

"The shadow of death may block the light for a time, but it does not defeat it. Sometimes, Magda, the light of love shines from within more powerfully than you could ever have imagined." John turned to go back to wherever it was that he slept.

Magda watched him dissolve into the shadows just as the cloud finished its pass over the moon. The beautiful light dazzled her once more. Due to the contrast of the recent darkness, the light appeared even brighter than before the cloud's shadowy presence.

Magda closed her eyes, listening to the sounds of the water as it lapped the shore at her feet. She recalled the powerful emotion that drew her to Yeshua when He first appeared to her in the dark forest.

With love as her protection, she fearlessly navigated through the blazing inferno of demonic possession. Pulled by love, she found herself irresistibly drawn towards Her savior's side. Love, a gentle whisper that awakened her spirit, captured her soul. The concept of love still held a powerful and mysterious allure for her. The mystery didn't frighten her anymore. Instead, it challenged her to solve it by submitting to its fullness.

When Magda woke the next morning, she was more refreshed than she expected to be. The group of followers made a morning meal while the sun crested the horizon. The chill of the night was quickly replaced by the promise of a warm day.

Magda joined the others, and the smell of burning wood filled the air as they gathered around the fire. The sound of satisfied munching filled the air as everyone eagerly devoured the food that had been prepared.

The conversation was more subdued in the sleepiness of the morning. Magda took her plate down to a large boulder that was nestled in the shrubbery just off the shoreline. She was still feeling contemplative from her encounter with John during the night.

Gradually, a handful of individuals started making their way into the camp. The day was slowly coming to life as pilgrims flocked to hear John preach and contemplate baptism.

Magda watched the expressions on their faces. Some were skeptical, but most were eager, even hopeful. She thought about what John said—*people loved the darkness*. She wondered if that was true about her.

The crowd quickly multiplied, filling the space in no time. Magda had barely finished her meal when the first group of travelers sat down in anticipation of John's message. The prophet did not depart from his purpose.

"Repent," John called out. "The Kingdom of heaven is at hand. Be cleansed in the waters of confession."

Magda watched as a few people responded joyously to the call. John waited for them, waist-deep in the water. When they came to him, he took them by the hand, spoke words only they could hear, and dipped them into the waters until they were completely submerged.

Magda continued as a spectator while several people entered into the freedom John opened to them. She let her mind wander into imagining Yeshua's baptism, which John had described in great detail that first night she was in the camp. Her mind pictured the scene depicting a voice from heaven declaring Yeshua as God's Son, in whom He was well pleased. She was lost in her imagination when a voice startled her.

"Would you like more?" the man, Joab, asked her.

Magda tried to hide her surprise at his appearance.

"Oh, thank you. I am alright," she answered.

"You haven't eaten much," Joab said. He looked a bit concerned. "I hope it wasn't my cooking."

"No," Magda smiled. "I was merely lost in thought, imagining what Yeshua's baptism must have been like."

Joab sat down next to Magda and looked out into the waters of the Jordan. Silence enveloped him as he appeared lost in remembrance of the event he had been privileged to witness.

"It was a holy moment," Joab began. "I will never forget it. His was a baptism of identification, not cleansing. It was different than all the other baptisms I had witnessed. There was a battle waging between the forces of light and darkness. I could feel it begin the moment He came up out of the waters."

"What do you mean, a battle?" Magda asked him.

"I can't really explain it," Joab replied. "I heard from one of His disciples that after He was baptized, He was led into the wilderness for forty days and nights. It was during this time that He was tempted by Satan, himself."[20]

"Tempted?" Magda's eyes widened in shock. How could Yeshua be tempted?

"Yes," Joab said. "He entered the battle with Satan because He was now identified to the forces of evil. They knew who He was. They were not going to sit idly by and let the prophecy be fulfilled unchallenged."

"What prophecy?" Magda asked him.

Joab looked at her quizzically. The realization of her ignorance made Magda's face turn red with embarrassment. There were things her people knew that she had never been taught. Joab's face showed no sign of contempt, but Magda held her lack of education against herself.

"In the beginning of the Torah," Joab explained as if he were

---

[20] Luke 4:1-13

teaching a child, yet his voice was compassionate, not judgmental. "The book of Genesis tells us that when Adam and Eve sinned because of Satan's temptation, Yahweh pronounced the judgment on all three of them. The man would have to work the ground. The woman would have pain in childbirth. And Satan would be thwarted by the offspring of the woman. Yahweh said, 'I will put hostility between you and the woman, and between your offspring and her offspring. He will bruise your head, and you will bruise his heel.'[21] That is the prophecy—the Messiah would bruise the head of evil. He will overcome the darkness with the light, I believe. Of course, no one knows exactly how He will accomplish this."

Magda let the memory of Yeshua's deliverance in the forest of Zophos flood her mind. She remembered the flaming sword with which He absorbed the fires of the evil one. She also recalled how He stabbed it into the ground as if claiming the land. Then the same flaming sword turned into an image of a cross. What did it all mean?

"Are you alright?" Joab asked her.

"Yes, I'm sorry." Magda smiled at Joab. "His ways are hard to understand, aren't they?"

"Yes, they are, Magda. But, He is good." Joab took her plate, leaving her with her contemplative thoughts.

Magda realized as she watched the young man, Joab, walk away that he never once looked at her like most men from her past. In fact, none of the men here looked at her the way she was used to being looked at by men. There was freedom in the way the people in the camp expressed their masculine and feminine image-bearing potential. Magda found it refreshing to see how they interacted with each other, like a close-knit family bound by a love she had never experienced before.

Watching the others work together, take care of one another,

---

[21] Genesis 3:15

and share the provisions made Magda wonder what it would have been like to grow up in a family with siblings.

CHAPTER EIGHTEEN

John's voice echoed from the middle of the Jordan. "The people who walked in darkness have seen a great light. Those who lived in the land of the shadow of death, on them the light has shined."[22]

Magda let the powerful words sink into the marrow of her soul. She was no stranger to the shadow of death. She couldn't help but wonder if that was where she truly belonged. When she looked up toward the heavens, all she could see were the gray clouds of the shadow of death over her. After everything she had done and everything she was, how could Magda be considered one of these people? Wouldn't her very presence taint them? What would they think if they knew what she was? Magda still had so much to learn.

At midday, the sun shared its warmth with the inhabitants of the land. Magda found relief from the heat by wandering off toward the trees dotting the landscape not far from where everyone had set up camp. She was surprised when Joanna found

---

[22] Isaiah 9:2

her. Magda still wasn't used to people looking out for her. She watched Joanna approach her, touched by the woman's concern for her well-being. A memory from long ago surfaced in Magda's mind, reminding her of the prophetess, Anna. The old woman had looked out for Magda when no one else would. She had taught her some things, ever patient with the minimal understanding of a young child.

Magda thought about the last words that Anna spoke to her. She hadn't remembered them in all these years. What was it that she recited as Anna took her last breath? Magda closed her eyes, trying hard to recall the memory before Joanna's presence interrupted her. She could feel the cold stone of the Temple. She remembered the pillars that surrounded her and the cornerstone that she leaned against — the very stone that reminded her of the rock she clung to in the dark forest of Zophos.

Magda was instantly transported to a different time and place as Anna's voice echoed in her memory...

"Remember this, child. 'Their drink offerings of blood I will not offer, nor take their names on my lips. Yahweh assigned my portion and my cup. You made my lot secure.'" [23]

Magda opened her eyes, horrified at the memory as she scanned the years that had passed after that moment. She drank the blood of the offerings to Baal. She took the names of the demons on her own lips. Despite that, Yahweh had sent His Son to rescue her, making her lot secure by providing a cornerstone to cling to in the middle of darkness. Gratitude overwhelmed Magda, filling her heart to the brim. Stifling the tears at the realization of her iniquity, Magda tried to hide her emotions when Joanna walked up.

"Where have you been?" Joanna asked her, a worried expression on her face.

"Just trying to escape the heat," Magda replied, turning her

---

[23] Psalm 16:4-5

face slightly away in an effort to regain her composure.

"Come to the water, Magda. It is very refreshing," Joanna encouraged her companion. When Magda did not move, Joanna sat down next to her in the shade. "What troubles you, my friend?"

"I'm not exactly sure," Magda admitted. "I don't feel like I belong."

Joanna's brow creased in thoughtful consideration for the right words. "I saw the way Yeshua looked at you, Magda. He knows you. He chose you for something. You don't belong because of anything you did or didn't do. You belong because He drew you to Himself. I wish you could see that."

"Then why did He send me away? Why did He send me here? Why couldn't I stay with Him?" Magda let out her pent up frustration.

"One thing I know after following Him is that there is purpose in what He does. Trust Him, Magda, even if you can't trust yourself," Joanna counseled her. The silence between them grew as heavy as the heat pushing into the land. "I will be leaving at first light tomorrow." Joanna announced it with trepidation in her voice.

"Leaving? Why?" Magda asked, suddenly frightened by the prospect of change.

"I need to get back to the palace before my absence is noted. I think you should remain here with my brother." Joanna put her arm around Magda. "There is still something for you here. You will know when you find it."

Magda grew intensely nervous. She didn't want her new friend to leave. She didn't want to remain in the camp with John and his followers if Joanna didn't stay. "Why can't I go with you?" Magda asked her.

"Where would you go?" Joanna said. "Your place isn't to serve in the palace, I am sure of that."

"How can you be sure, Joanna? I need something. I have

nowhere to go, no purpose for my life. I...I don't belong anywhere." Magda let the tears fall silently, ashamed at the part she played in letting darkness into her life and heart.

"You will figure it out, Magda. Don't give up. Open your heart to listen and learn. I have already seen you make so much progress," Joanna encouraged her. "Come on, let's go listen to John. He has quite a crowd gathered. Some of the Pharisees are back, too. It is much cooler next to the water."

Joanna stood up and extended her hand to Magda. Magda accepted it. The women found a place near the waters of the Jordan River. A cool breeze washed over them, fighting the heat that wanted to burn their exposed skin.

Magda enjoyed listening to John. His words were powerfully truthful. She watched the prophet's gaze as he turned toward the Pharisees standing at a distance. The man, Eleazar, was in the crowd of religious leaders. She could see the arrogant expressions on the men's faces change to a look of worry when they realized John was going to speak directly to them. John bent down into the water. He brought up smooth river stones with his hands and held them up high as he spoke.

"You offspring of vipers, who warned you to flee from the wrath to come? Therefore, produce fruit worthy of repentance! Don't think to yourselves, 'We have Abraham for our father,' for I tell you that God is able to raise up children to Abraham from these stones. Even now the ax lies at the root of the trees. Therefore, every tree that doesn't produce good fruit is cut down, and cast into the fire."[24] John's eyes were filled with holy rage.

Magda's mind hung on the idea of producing good fruit that would not be cast into the fire. She was wondering what the teaching meant when Nathan and Joab came to sit with her and Joanna. The men were laughing to themselves.

"That should send them on their way," Joab snickered. "They

[24] Matthew 3:7-10

never stay long once John addresses them directly."

"So, they have come before?" Nathan asked.

"Yes," Joab replied. "Several times. They are looking for the Messiah, trying to convince themselves that John is not Him. Yet, they don't really want to find Him, I believe."

"What does John mean by the phrase, produce good fruit?" Magda inquired.

Joab looked at Magda with tender eyes, obvious in their desire to teach. "I have heard this teaching before. Let me see if I can remember correctly." Joab paused, looking up into the sky.

Magda saw the look of recognition when it donned on the man's enthusiastic face.

"Now I remember where I heard the teaching," Joab said. "My friends, Andrew and John, who now follow Yeshua, told this to me when I went to see them recently. It is one of Yeshua's teachings. 'By their fruits you will know them. Do you gather grapes from thorns, or figs from thistles? Even so, every good tree produces good fruit; but the corrupt tree produces evil fruit. A good tree can't produce evil fruit, neither can a corrupt tree produce good fruit. Every tree that doesn't grow good fruit is cut down, and thrown into the fire.'[25] The teaching was powerful to me, that's why I remembered it."

"What if you aren't a good tree?" Magda asked innocently. "What if you are corrupt?"

"What makes you think you are corrupt, Magda?" Nathan asked her.

Magda looked down at the dirt, mad at herself for opening up to these men. Nathan seemed to read her thoughts. "You know, even Eve was tempted by Satan."[26]

Joab added, "Yeshua was, too.[27] It didn't make Him evil. John

---

[25] Matthew 7:16-19

[26] Genesis 3:1-7

[27] Matthew 4:1-11

is baptizing people so they can be cleansed, turned away from the corruption that came through Adam's sin. We all bear evil fruit unless we let the goodness of Yahweh back into our hearts."

"The woman, Eve, was deceived," Nathan said. "You can turn away from the deception that drew you in, Magda."

"How?" Magda asked.

"Confess in the waters of baptism and be cleansed. He has offered you freedom. Now, you must accept it. Don't waste years wandering in the wilderness like our ancestors did. You are not a slave to darkness anymore." Nathan took her hand. "We are your family now."

Magda appreciated the kindness of these people. Though she knew she would miss Joanna, Magda finally agreed with her friend that there was something more for her to learn among John and his followers. She was determined to stay until she sensed it was her time to leave.

The departure was difficult. Magda wondered if she would see Joanna again. It felt like she was just beginning to connect with people, only to have to be parted from them. She watched with sadness as the woman who had become her friend disappeared with a group of travelers heading toward Herod's palace.

The first few hours after Joanna left, Magda regretted staying. She was alone and uncomfortable without her companion. As was her custom, Magda sat on the rock a few feet from the shoreline so she could watch the people being baptized and listen to John's teaching. Absorbed in everything she was learning from John's powerful words, Magda didn't remember to get herself food during the midday meal. She was surprised when an older man appeared with a plate of fish, nuts and pomegranates.

"Joab asked me to bring this to you. He noticed that you did not eat," the old man said. "My name is Pascal."

"Shalom, Pascal. I am Magda." Magda took the plate from the man's hands. "Thank you for bringing me this."

"May I sit?" Pascal asked her politely.

"Of course," Magda said, already warming to the man's company. She didn't know why she liked him so easily. He had a gentleness about him that drew her in and put her at ease.

"He is a good teacher," Pascal observed of John.

"Yes. How long have you been following him?" Magda inquired.

"Since the beginning. I knew his parents. I was delivering my sheep to the Temple the day that John's father was visited by an angel. I was just a boy then," Pascal said to her.

"John's father was visited by an angel?" Magdas curiosity was piqued, captivated by what he suggested.

"Yes, I am surprised you hadn't heard the story already." Pascal's eyes delighted at the prospect of a new hearer to one of his favorite tales. "Zechariah, John's father, was chosen to perform the priestly duties on the most holy of days — the Day of Atonement. When he went into the Holy of Holies, he was met with an angel who promised him that a child would be born to them in their old age. Zechariah doubted the angel, so he was struck with loss of speech."[28]

"John's father couldn't talk?" Such a punishment surprised Magda.

"Only for the duration of the pregnancy. Imagine, this man who now speaks relentlessly of the coming Kingdom had a father whose discipline included loss of speech." Pascal chuckled. "Our Lord knows what He is doing and I believe He has a sense of humor."

"So, Zechariah doubted the angel and lost his voice until after John was born?" Magda asked him.

"Yes, he regained his voice when he made it known that the child's name was to be John. The angel had informed Zechariah of the child's name. He also told him that the child would turn many of the children of Israel to the Lord, their God. And, that he would

---

[28] Luke 1:1-25

go before Him in the spirit and power of Elijah to turn the hearts of the fathers to the children, and the disobedient to the wisdom of the just; to make ready a people prepared for the Lord."[29]

"That is what John does. He prepares the people for the Lord," Magda confirmed. "John told me once that people loved the darkness. What do you think he meant by that?"

Pascal rubbed his chin, contemplating Magda's question. "When I was a shepherd, I loved my sheep and knew them all by name. Yet, there were some that had such a stubborn disposition that I would have to continually discipline them in order to keep them safe. They continuously wanted to leave the protective territory of my presence so they could wander off where they didn't belong. It always led to danger. I suppose people are like that. We want our own way more than we want the way of the Lord. We wander out of His loving protection and then wonder why we find ourselves in danger. For some reason, people are drawn to the darkness."

"I don't like the dark," Magda sighed. "It frightens me."

"I used to be afraid of the dark, too. Being a shepherd was lonely at times, but especially at night when I couldn't see the danger clearly. I was always grateful for the light of a full moon or the dazzling glimmer of stars against the dark canopy of the heavens. It reminded me that Yahweh provides light in the midst of darkness. Especially that one glorious night when everything in my world changed." Pascal looked up toward the puffy clouds overhead. He closed his eyes, a smile sweetening his face.

"What happened to you, Pascal?" Magda wanted to know caused the change in the man's countenance. Pascal didn't even open his eyes when he started to retell the story.

"It was chilled that dark night. I was staying in the field, keeping watch by night over the flock. I was afraid because it was so dark when suddenly, an angel of the Lord appeared, and the

---

[29] Luke 1:16-17

glory of the Lord shone around me and my companions. We were more terrified of the light that was shining than we had been of the darkness. The angel spoke to us, 'Do not be afraid, for behold, I bring you good news of great joy which will be to all the people. For there is born to you today, in David's city, a Savior, who is Christ the Lord. This is the sign to you: you will find a baby wrapped in strips of cloth, lying in a feeding trough.'"

Pascal shuddered with remembrance. "I had no doubt. I believed everything the heavenly creature said. I knew that the true light had come into the world. I fell down like a dead man. I was powerfully exposed and humiliated in front of such perfection."

"You felt unworthy?" Magda could relate to Pascal's story.

The man nodded, opening his eyes to look at her. "Suddenly, there was with the angel a multitude of the heavenly army praising God, and singing, 'Glory to God in the highest, on earth peace, good will toward those on whom Yahweh's favor rests.' I wanted the favor of the Lord so badly. Yet, in the moment I was fully aware of my own iniquity. When the angels went away from us into the sky, we decided to go to Bethlehem to investigate the wonder of the Lord."[30]

"You saw the baby?" Magda asked in wonder.

"I did. And I worshiped Him. It was the most incredible experience of my life. I knew I would never be the same again," Pascal admitted to her.

"Why do you follow John?" Magda asked him.

"Though our Messiah moves among us, there are those who will not see Him. They are blinded to the light of the Lord's love. After that visit to Bethlehem, I continued watching my sheep. I tended the flocks destined for sacrifice at the Temple. I worked for a family that lived in Bethany. They hired us to pasture the sheep for them." Pascal's tone of voice turned agitated. "I quickly

---

[30] Luke 2:8-15

learned that the Temple authorities are corrupt – loving the darkness, as you have said. They exchanged the unblemished lambs required for sacrifice for the blemished lambs, charging people for the exchange. It was more about making money than it was about sacrificing for the Lord."

"What did you do?" Magda was upset at the news, troubled that even those who proclaimed to honor God behaved in a way that didn't.

"I tried to expose their evil deeds. When I did, I lost everything. There was a man, Simon of Kerioth, who was in charge of the treasury. He made sure that I never shepherded again. I was fortunate that he didn't make me a slave. They levied debts on me from unseen fines that I couldn't pay. My only choice was to give up my entire herd." A single tear slipped from Pascal's eye and fell into his beard.

"That must have been extremely difficult for you," Magda put her hand on Pascal's shoulder.

"I didn't know what to do. I felt as though I lost my identity. I didn't belong anywhere. I had actually forgotten the majesty of that moment so many years ago when I was privileged to see the Messiah shortly after He made His entry into the world. It took me a while, but I remembered that I had been chosen. I came here to find the path Yahweh wants revealed to me," Pascal said to her.

Magda let the words that Pascal spoke penetrate her own heart. Guilt overwhelmed her as she realized how she had taken for granted all that Yeshua had done for her. She had an experience similar to Pascal's, yet she questioned her belonging. She didn't trust His power over her own iniquity.

Magda watched as another person came up out of the water, a smile of freedom on the person's face. She knew what she was about to do. The waters of the Jordan beckoned her.

CHAPTER NINETEEN

Gray clouds rolled in like animals stampeding before a threatening predator. Magda felt them before she could see them. As fat raindrops bathed the land, the scorching heat of the day was instantly replaced by a refreshing coolness. Pascal stood up abruptly, extending his hand to help Magda.

"We must take cover," Pascal said, looking up into the sky. "This one looks like it will hit us hard."

To prevent Magda from slipping, Pascal tightly grasped her hand. His arthritic fingers were remarkably soft. As they ran toward the center of the camp, the sounds of their hurried breaths filled the air. Additional tents were being erected for the travelers to shelter in while the unforeseen storm played itself out. Nathan called out to them.

"Magda, Pascal, come in here, quick!" Nathan went to help them.

The thick downpour had turned the surroundings into a disheveled, sodden mess. As she walked through the mud, she could feel its slippery texture beneath her feet. The challenge not to slip required intense focus.

Once beneath the protective canopy, Magda took her long, brown hair and squeezed out the excess water. She was surprised at how wet she got in such a short amount of time. Pascal was vigorously shaking his tunic, trying to get rid of the excess water.

"These surprise storms are great for the crops, but they sure wreak havoc on everything else," Pascal laughed. "It does feel good after the heat of the day, though, doesn't it?"

"It does," Magda agreed.

She found herself drawn to the charm and wisdom of the older man. His kind and gentle nature was mirrored in his deep, dark brown eyes. He reminded Magda of Anna. The prophetess had the same depth in her eyes that this old shepherd had.

Pascal and Magda sat with Nathan and Joab in the tent. Despite the rain hitting them at an angle, they decided to keep the tent flaps open in order to take in the scenic view of the river.

To Magda's astonishment, John remained in the water, refusing to leave. Instead, the prophet raised his arms towards the sky, allowing the plump raindrops to cascade over his entire body like heavenly tears descending upon him. Magda had never seen such an expression of joy on anyone's face before.

"He is worshiping Yahweh," Joab announced quietly. "I have never seen anyone worship the Holy One like John does. Sometimes, I wish I could see what he sees or feel what he feels."

"Worship?" Magda questioned, scarred by what that word had meant to her in the past.

"I suspect he is thanking Yahweh for the rain, the water, the gift of life that it brings. John sees His hand in everything. He told me once that the rains are drops of heaven, baptizing the land in preparation for harvest. Even a storm doesn't thwart John," Joab said, respectfully.

"I like that," Magda said. "I like thinking of the rain as drops of heaven."

"It isn't unlike the manna that Yahweh dropped from heaven when our people wandered the wilderness," Nathan pondered. "I hadn't really thought of it that way, either. "

"What is manna?" Magda asked.

Pascal answered her. "Manna was bread sent from heaven, wafers that tasted like honey and could be made into cakes. Yahweh supplied it each and every day of the forty years that our people wandered the wilderness after being freed from four hundred years of slavery in Egypt. Every day, except on the Sabbath, when they rested." Pascal's voice was full of awe. "Even then, the Lord provided enough for them to gather the day before so that they would not have to go hungry on the Sabbath."[31]

"Even then, the people complained and grumbled," Nathan added, his mouth tipping up into an awkward smile.[32]

"They grumbled when the Lord sent them bread?" Magda inquired, shocked that anyone would not be grateful for heaven's provision.

"Yes, it didn't taste good. They got tired of eating it every day," Joab added.

"Just like sheep that go astray. We all want our own way over the way of the Lord," Pascal sadly said.

Magda furrowed her brow, deep in thought, as she tried to make sense of the men's conversation. She observed John, his figure standing tall and proud in the middle of the Jordan River, expressing gratitude for the wondrous blessings bestowed upon him by the Lord. He was alone in his reverent praise, but it didn't matter to John.

Magda looked at all the people huddled in the tents, seeking shelter from the rain instead of worshiping within it. She wondered if they were missing something by hiding themselves away from the cleansing waters sent from heaven.

As Magda reflected, she realized that she had been avoiding the freedom that Yeshua had intended for her at the river. She

---

[31] Exodus 16:1-36
[32] Numbers 11:4-10

couldn't simply sit there and let the storm keep her from her destiny. Like the fire in Zophos, she needed to walk through the storm.

Magda arose from the place where she sat. She stepped out into the pelting rain. Carefully and methodically placing her feet in the slippery mud, she took one step after another until she reached the edge of the Jordan River. The scent of fresh water filled her nostrils as she approached the flowing river.

As she waded into the water, she could feel the coolness enveloping her ankles. With her face tilted to the sky, Magda could feel a gentle breeze brushing against her cheeks in the undercurrent of the storm. The gray clouds were departing, revealing the unmatched hue of the heavens at dusk. Day was giving way to night, making the space in between beautifully breathtaking.

Magda could feel the river lapping at her feet. She felt the soaking of the drops of heaven on her skin. Raising her arms according to John's example, Magda was grateful for the gift of freedom. The overwhelming power of holiness beckoned her into its embrace as she entered.

"Lord," she prayed in her heart, "I am unworthy, yet You saved me from the darkness. I drank the blood offered to idols, Yahweh. I gave in to the desires of the flesh. I wanted more — more money, more power. I took life that wasn't mine to take. I gave the demons power over me with names."

Magda fell to her knees, the muddy waters of the Jordan River coming up to her waist. Her hot tears mingled with the cool baptismal waters. "I let them lead me into the darkness. Bring me back to the light, Lord. Keep me by Your power alone. My heart is only ashes. I ask You for a new heart because You are faithful to rescue me. Is there anything in me worth saving?"

When Magda opened her eyes, John was looking at her. She stood slowly, the tears coming faster than the rain. She entered into the deep where John waited with open arms. There was an unspoken understanding in the way he gazed at her, as if words were unnecessary. There was a palpable touch of divinity in that moment, an inexplicable feeling that they both shared.

John embraced her, placing his strong hand on her back while securing her with her own prayerfully postured hands. She willingly let go, falling back into the waters of the Jordan River. The immersion pulled her into a space she had never been before. Time stood still. Magda could hear the rhythm of her heart in her ears. She could feel the weightless gravity of the water's buoyancy holding her up…

She felt as if she was being lifted higher and higher until she saw the gray clouds beneath her feet. She had risen above the shadow of death. She looked down on death and up into the light of the Kingdom. A glorious staircase stretched out before her. She could feel the invitation in her heart—an invitation to something more, something that would satisfy every desire. Placing her hand upon the banister, Magda stepped off the cloud of death's shadow and placed herself onto the staircase of life. Her reflection in the shimmering pearl finish of the stairs was blurred. She couldn't see herself. She was unfinished. Magda heard His voice from above.

"I have placed in your heart of ash an ember of love that will burn brightly for the glory of My Kingdom, beloved. Come to Me. I have never left you nor forsaken you. I am your Father in heaven."

Magda saw Yeshua standing at the top of the staircase, His hand stretched toward her. He was dressed in royal robes. His eyes flashed fire that united with her own heart, setting ablaze an intense love that she knew would never leave her or let her go.

Magda came up out of the waters of the Jordan River burning with a passion that engulfed her guilt, shame, and sin. She wanted nothing more of her old self. She knew in her heart that she belonged with Him, her soul had been chosen by Yahweh. It was her decision how she would respond to that.

She was determined to follow Yeshua faithfully, no matter where He led her. Her heart was no longer open to the powers of darkness because the light of love had been lit. The ember, hidden among the ashes, had finally been ignited into a roaring flame of faith.

VICTORIOUS

But thanks be to God, who gives us the victory
through our Lord Jesus Christ.
1 Corinthians 15:57

CHAPTER TWENTY

W hen Magda's feet left the waters of the Jordan River and touched the wet sand, the rain mysteriously stopped. She looked up into the twilight sky, gratitude flooding her heart for the glimpse of heaven given to her while she was immersed beneath the water. The sun bowed reverently behind the horizon, kissing the world goodnight with a dazzling display of color before it rose again the next morning, vanquishing the darkness that was almost upon them.

Pascal hurriedly stepped outside to meet Magda, a warm, aged smile spreading across his face.

"Here," he said. "I brought this for you. I borrowed it from one of the other women. You will need to dry off. She said you could have this tunic."

Touched by the man's tenderness, Magda took the gray tunic from his hands. "Thank you, Pascal. You are like a brother to me." Magda was going to hug the man, but she didn't want to get him wet.

Once she dried off and dressed in her new tunic, Magda rejoined the men. Seated by the fire, they savored the flavors of their evening meal, the flickering flames casting a comforting glow. As Pascal handed Magda a plate, she could smell the delicious aroma of the meal. Joab filled it with an assortment of delicious food, from fresh fruits to savory meats.

Magda nibbled on the morsels given her while she watched the flames dance before her. The heat felt good against the chill of the night air. The sight of the dancing flames captivated Magda, revealing a beauty she had never noticed before. Nor had she realized its potential for good. She had been afraid of fire ever since her encounter with it in Zophos. Sitting before the fire now, she saw it as another gift from her Creator.

Why did the forces of darkness persist in corrupting divine gifts and twisting them into abominations?

Magda shivered as old memories of her past trickled from her mind and brushed her heart, attempting to infect her with feelings of shame again. She angled herself away from those shadows and toward the light of what she would be in the future, not what she had been in the past.

John sat down in the circle of people warming themselves while they ate. He had his own plate of exotic-looking food, and he gingerly savored a small piece. No one dared ask him what it was. Magda raised her gaze to meet the prophet's intense stare. His gaze broke through normal barriers, exposing her to his scrutiny. She saw recognition in his eyes of the holy moments they shared in the Jordan River that afternoon. She wondered if her baptism was different from the other ones that John had performed. When John nodded in her direction, she had the uncanny feeling that the man could read her thoughts.

When John cleared his throat, the quiet whispering ceased. An air of anticipation filled outside the tent as everyone leaned in to catch what he was about to say.

"Jacob went out from Beersheba, and went toward Haran. He came to a certain place, and stayed there all night, because the sun had set. He took one of the stones of the place, put it under his head, and lay down in that place to sleep. He dreamed. A stairway set upon the earth, and its top reached to heaven. Jacob witnessed the angels of God ascending and descending on it. Yahweh stood above it, and said, 'I am Yahweh, the God of Abraham your father, and the God of Isaac.'[33] The Lord called to Jacob in Bethel. He revealed Himself to Israel in a vision of the night. Who knows how Jacob responded?"

Though John was testing everyone, Magda knew the lesson was especially for her. The knowledge that John had been aware of everything that had happened while she was submerged in the waters of the Jordan awed her.

"Jacob was afraid," Joab replied. "He set up a stone and made it a pillar. He vowed that if the Lord took care of him, Jacob would make Yahweh his God."[34]

"Some respond to the Lord's invitation with fear. How blessed are those who respond with love," John finished, looking directly into Magda's eyes, though she felt as if he was seeing her heart.

The moment John walked away from the group, a collective effort to clean up commenced. Magda's enthusiasm to help was palpable as she eagerly volunteered for any task, hoping her lack of skills would not be a hindrance. She had learned a lot by watching Joanna. Taking the dishes from the men, she joined the group outside the tent, where the sound of running water and the smell of soap filled the air, as she eagerly absorbed the knowledge she had been deprived of as a child. Jezebel had her engaged in chores that solely revolved around tending to and maintaining the idols in her home when she was a child.

In the days that followed, Magda learned how to set up tents, assist with cooking, mend a torn garment and start a fire. Joab had left the camp to go visit his cousin, Andrew, who once followed

---

[33] Genesis 28:10-13
[34] Genesis 18:18-22

John. Though Magda still missed her friend, Joanna, the men in the camp were becoming like brothers to her. She found herself comfortable in the predominantly male society in which she now lived.

John's daily teaching of the Word of the Lord fed her heart. Magda was amazed at how the Scriptures resonated deeply within her soul when she heard them. Though she didn't always understand everything being spoken, she treasured the truth in her heart, knowing that the meaning would be revealed at a later time.

One morning, John was speaking to his followers before the crowd descended on them for the day. Magda couldn't help but notice the sad expression on the prophet's face as he spoke.

"Abraham rose early in the morning, and saddled his donkey, and took two of his young men with him, and Isaac his son." John sighed heavily. "His Son," he repeated the phrase before continuing.

"Abraham split the wood for the burnt offering, rose up, and went to the place of which God had told him. On the third day Abraham lifted up his eyes, and saw the place far off. Abraham said to his young men, 'Stay here with the donkey. The boy and I will worship, and come back to you.' Abraham took the wood of the burnt offering and laid it on Isaac, his son. He took in his hand the fire and the knife. Isaac spoke to Abraham, his father, and said, 'My father?' He said, 'Here I am, my son.' Isaac said, 'Here is the fire and the wood, but where is the lamb for a burnt offering?' Abraham said, 'God will provide himself the lamb for a burnt offering, my son.'"[35]

Magda thought she saw a glimmer of tears forming in John's eyes. His face was tightly drawn, betraying the emotions he had been holding back.

John finished, almost in a whisper. "Yahweh will provide the

---

[35] Genesis 22:3-8

lamb."

"Do you speak of the Lamb of God who takes away the sin of the world?" Nathan asked out loud.

John looked at Nathan before he set his gaze on Magda. He got up without replying. Magda was left bewildered by the exchange, her heart heavy with thoughts and questions.

The sound of footsteps echoed as pilgrims started to arrive at the river. Over the last few days, the crowds coming to John grew smaller and smaller. Among the people walking into the camp were Joab and two others who had gone with him to fetch supplies for the group. The men did not look happy upon their return. Magda went out to help put away the provisions.

When she neared the donkey, she could feel the agitation between the men. Magda sensed that they had been arguing about something.

"Is everything alright?" Magda asked Joab.

He turned around, as if noticing her for the first time. "I'm sorry, Magda. I didn't know you were there," Joab said without answering her question.

"I'm going to speak to John." One of the other men spoke to Joab directly, his eyes narrowed.

"Don't bother him about this." Joab grabbed the man's arm forcefully. "It isn't important."

"It matters to me, Joab, even if it doesn't matter to you!" The man strode away.

When Magda took the provisions to the tent where they kept the supplies, she couldn't help but overhear the conversation between the returning men and John. As Magda placed things in the designated baskets, they stood together just outside the space, not really keeping their voices down.

"Rabbi," said one of the men, his tone of voice lined with anger, "He who was with you beyond the Jordan, to whom you have testified, the same baptizes, and everyone is coming to

Him."[36]

Magda knew the man was talking about Yeshua. The ones who left must have seen Him.

John answered without reacting to the man's subtle hint of offense. "A man can receive nothing, unless it has been given him from heaven. You yourselves testify that I said, 'I am not the Christ,' but, 'I have been sent before Him.' He who has the bride is the bridegroom; but the friend of the bridegroom, who stands and hears Him, rejoices greatly because of the bridegroom's voice. This, my joy, therefore is made full. He must increase, but I must decrease."[37]

John's voice was devoid of any trace of jealousy, frustration, or pride. The prophet's presence resonated with an undeniable sense of divine purpose, leaving Magda with no doubt that he was on a mission to reveal the Messiah. She could hear the joy that satisfied John's heart even as she sensed that his mission was almost complete.

"Rabbi, how can you become less? Your teaching is necessary for the people," Joab said in defense of the one he followed.

"The wedding will take place. He will take His bride and the bridegroom's friend will have finished his work." John's voice was strong, confident. "Where is He now?"

"They are in Capernaum," Joab offered. "He has a lot of followers now. Twelve of His disciples are always with Him. Andrew is there. The sons of Zebedee, James and John, are among them."

"As it should be," John said. "They believed me when I told them He was the lamb of God."

Magda was overcome with the desire to join Yeshua. *"Come to me."* She heard His voice echo in her heart and in the air above the tent. The moment had arrived for her departure. How she was

---

[36] John 3:26
[37] John 3:27-30

going to get to Capernaum, she had no idea.

Magda went back to the area where they were preparing the morning meal. She started the fire, perfectly adept at striking the flint in such a way as to get a spark on the first try. Everyone was amazed at how fast she picked up the skill.

"I can see that something is bothering you," Pascal noted as Magda laid the fish on the open flame.

"I want to go to Capernaum. I need to be there, Pascal. I feel called by the Lord to be with Yeshua and His followers." Magda wasn't sure what the man would say to her bold statement. She knew how much Pascal enjoyed being among the followers of John. She would miss him very much.

Pascal was silent for some time before replying. "I am from Capernaum," he said to her. "I ran away from there when I was a young shepherd. Perhaps it is time that I return and make amends for my wrongdoing."

"Amends? What could you possibly have done, Pascal?" Magda was surprised by the man's admission.

"I have changed my ways since then, Magda. I am glad you did not know me when I was a thieving youth." Pascal rubbed his chin. "I got myself into a lot of trouble. The life of a shepherd is not an easy one. Sometimes, I wanted things that others had. I was not wise enough to trust in the Lord for my provisions. In a way, I was not unlike the Priests of the Temple that took everything I had to put more coins in their own pockets."

"We all have strayed like sheep, as a wise shepherd once taught me." Magda put her hand on Pascal's shoulder.

"I can take you into Capernaum if you would like the company," Pascal offered. "Though I am not sure what kind of reception we will get once we arrive. There are people in that village that have not forgiven me."

"Yes, I am sure that there are people in my own village who have not forgiven me either," Magda admitted. "In fact, there are a lot of people who might remember me very differently than the woman I am now before you, Pascal."

"Well, it sounds like we will make ideal traveling companions," Pascal said, the corners of his mouth tipping upward. "Shall we prepare to leave at first light?"

"That sounds like a good idea," Magda said, a little unsure about the change, but driven by the warm ember of faith in her heart.

CHAPTER TWENTY-ONE

Preparing to leave was harder than Magda thought it would be. To her, the camp of John the Baptist was more than just a place to stay; it had become a home, with the people becoming her brothers and sisters. Magda was grateful now more than ever for Pascal's company on the journey. The sun had just peaked over the horizon, marking the beginning of something new. Magda set to work packing a satchel with provisions for their travels.

"Are you almost ready?" Pascal appeared at the opening of the tent. He had a traveling satchel of his own. He also carried an acacia wood staff.

Catching Magda's lingering gaze, he explained, "My staff. I used it for many things when I was a shepherd. It is useful for both balance and protection. I made it myself when I was only ten. Acacia wood isn't easy to come by, either. The trees are covered in thorns."

Magda grinned at him, admiring the craftsmanship of the tall wooden stick.

"I am ready," she said with a confidence that felt as thin as mountain air. What if she made a mistake? "Can we say goodbye to John?"

"Of course." Pascal went to look for the prophet.

Magda found Joab and Nathan first. "I am going to Capernaum with Pascal," Magda said to them, giving them both a hug. "You have been so kind. Thank you for teaching me all that you know."

The two looked at one another before looking back at her. They didn't seem surprised that she was leaving.

"We will miss you, Magda," Nathan said. "I will be sure to tell Joanna where you have gone."

"Please, tell her that I hope to see her again." Magda turned to Joab. "Thank you, Joab, for everything."

"Go in peace, Magda. May your destiny be revealed to you in His timing." Joab squeezed her hand. "I am glad to have met you."

Magda had never experienced this kind of relationship with men before. The brotherly love was hard for her to leave behind. She wondered if she would ever experience that kind of bond again. Pascal motioned to her when she moved past the tents. He was with John.

"Magda," John said to her. "The Lord will honor your obedience. Do not be afraid. Do not resist His invitation."

Magda merely nodded, words escaping her in the power of John's proclamation over her.

Pascal and Magda moved toward the rising sun. It wasn't easy, but Magda fought the urge to look back. She remembered Joab's words of wisdom in her heart. *"If you keep looking back at where you have been, you will never get to where you are going."*

With each step, she had to carefully navigate the unsteady terrain, making the walk even more difficult. By the time they arrived in Salim at midday, Magda was relieved to find rest and refreshment in one of the local establishments. Attentive to her needs, Pascal was not oblivious to how tired Magda felt. Being an older man, she didn't doubt that he felt it too. He reached out to Jacob, a caravan owner based in Shechem, and made arrangements for their journey. The two of them would travel with the merchant as far as Tiberius. They would be safer in a large group, especially at night when they had to make camp.

"Magda." Pascal found her rubbing her blistered feet. "That doesn't look good," he said, resting against his staff.

"I will be fine. My feet are not used to covering such distances." Magda resisted speaking the truth about the pain inflicted by her injuries. She didn't want to discontinue their quest to find Yeshua and His followers.

"Let me see if I can get you something to soothe your pain," Pascal informed her. Reaching into his satchel, Pascal pulled out an alabaster flask of sacred ointment.

"What is that?" Magda asked, biting the inside of her cheek as the pain radiated from her feet to her calves.

"It is a healing ointment I used for my sheep. I invented it myself. It would help them when they were wounded. It was especially good for their hooves when they were infected by a deeply lodged thorn."

"Here, my lord. I can do that for you." A young woman with brownish-golden hair appeared at Pascal's side. He offered her an appreciative smile.

Pascal turned to Magda and spoke in a reassuring tone. "You will be relieved to know that I have made arrangements for us. This is Jacob's wife, Leah. Jacob is the caravan owner that we are going to travel with."

Immediately, the young woman took a cloth and soaked it with the special ointment Pascal handed her. She then gave the soaked cloth to Magda.

While the woman tended to Magda's wounded feet, Pascal set off to gather a few additional supplies.

"This ointment smells good. Did he tell you what was in it?" Leah asked. "Hopefully, it will reduce the swelling and soothe the blisters."

"No, Pascal only said it was his own recipe that he used when he shepherded his sheep. It helped to heal their wounds faster," Magda said, wiping her feet carefully.

Despite the pain, she felt an immediate sense of relief as the promised healing started to soothe her.

"Thank you," Magda said to Leah. "I appreciate your kindness."

"Here," Leah offered her a new pair of sandals. "You look like the same size as I am. These haven't been worn and they will probably be more comfortable than what you are wearing now."

"I'm sorry," Magda apologized. "I haven't any money."

"Don't worry about that. Consider it a gift," Leah said, her beautiful smile haunted by buried pain. "You have a long way to go, according to Pascal. These shoes would be more beneficial to you than to me right now."

Pascal returned, worry creasing the wrinkles on his forehead even more. "Are you able to walk to the caravan? Jacob said you can ride with him for a while in the cart. At least until your feet are feeling better. He doesn't want anyone to slow him down."

"Yes, of course," Magda said, standing to her feet. "Goodbye Leah. It was nice to meet you."

"And you, Magda," Leah said, the haunted expression hinting at a story Magda sensed she could relate to. "I hope you find healing."

Pascal guided Magda towards the cart, where a visibly annoyed man impatiently awaited their arrival by tapping his sandaled foot hard against the packed dirt. Without introductions, the caravan leader barked his instructions. "We need to get moving."

Magda observed the frenzy of activity, as people hurriedly found their positions. Both demanding and impatient, Jacob was not one to tolerate delays. He looked at Magda with an interest that he quickly stifled. She had known men like him. If not for her injured feet, she would have walked rather than ride with Jacob.

Throughout the rest of the long day, there was an unbroken silence between the two as they continued their journey. That suited Magda just fine.

As they settled down for the night, Magda's tense shoulders finally relaxed, relieved to have a safe place to rest. Pascal had made friends among the other members of the caravan, settling in with the young men for the night. The women welcomed Magda into their tent. Away from Jacob, Magda's spirits lifted, grateful for the escape. He may have said nothing to her, but his countenance wasn't exactly a comforting one. She could tell that the others felt the same. No one dared speak openly about him, though. Fear lingered in the camp, its presence palpable to Magda, though its source remained a mystery.

The evening meal was ritualistic and unsatisfying. Jacob had strange customs of blessings and prayers that sounded lofty but only served to exalt him, not the Lord. Magda couldn't help but recognize the contrast between how Jacob conducted a meal in the wilderness with how John and his followers had. There was a heartfelt worship and love in the camp by the Jordan that was non-existent in this group of people who followed a man who seemed to make more of himself than he did of Yahweh.

Fortunately, at the quick pace of the caravan, they arrived in Tiberius the next afternoon. Magda and Pascal parted ways with the caravan, eager to put distance between themselves and the strange man, Jacob.

Magda's feet had healed completely so she and Pascal traveled the rest of the distance to Capernaum on foot. They were relieved to have the opportunity to openly share their skepticism and uncertainty about the members of Jacob's caravan.

"That man was very peculiar," Magda said to Pascal. "He said all the right words. He acted as if he knew the Lord, but something was missing."

"Yes, you are right about that," Pascal agreed, shaking his

head. "One thing I have learned over the years is that people can look right on the outside, but inside they are not at all what they appear to be."

"Yes," Magda said. "That's it. Jacob looked like he was devoted to Yahweh, but I think he was more interested in himself than the Lord."

"You have been given the gift of great insight, Magda," Pascal observed. "I pray that our Lord shows you how to use it well."

Finally reaching their destination brought a tremendous sense of relief to the both of them. They were on the outskirts of Capernaum when their path was obstructed by a Roman patrol.

"Halt!" One of the Roman soldiers yelled out to them.

He rode up with two others on horses, kicking up the dust on the road. Magda coughed when the man dismounted. As she walked through the cloud of dust, she could taste its foulness on her tongue.

"What is your business out here alone on the road?" the Roman asked Pascal before looking at Magda. When his eyes fell on her, she could see the hunger in his gaze. It took all of her strength not to tremble as a shiver of unease trickled down her spine.

"We are..." Pascal began before he was cut off.

"Wait! I know you." The man moved toward Magda. Sensuously, he gently grazed her arm with his fingertips. "You have grown into a very beautiful woman. You were barely a child when I..."

Magda knew what he meant without him finishing the sentence. Her face flushed. Her discomfort intensified as soon as the man's touch grazed her skin. Like a relentless ghost, her past haunted her every step. The three Roman soldiers were armed. She was afraid for Pascal. The other two soldiers were dismounting their horses as well, all three circling them like vultures.

"Help us, Lord," Magda prayed in her heart. *"Help us."*

Magda had barely finished the silent words of prayer when she heard another horse in the distance coming toward them.

"Take your hands off her!" Pascal stepped toward the Roman soldier, inserting his staff between the man and Magda.

The Roman moved swiftly. He knocked the staff to the ground and pulled Magda even closer to him, pressing against her body.

"What are you going to do about it, old man?" The three soldiers laughed and began dragging Magda away from Pascal.

The horse she had heard suddenly rode up on them. Magda couldn't see because of the brightness of the sun, but she heard a strong, commanding voice.

"What is going on here?"

The soldiers released Magda. "Nothing, Centurion. This man threatened us. We were taking them in for questioning. They look like zealots."

"They don't look like zealots to me," the Centurion remarked. "It looks as though you three have too much time on your hands if you are hassling innocent travelers."

"This one is not innocent, Abner. I assure you of that," the first soldier said, rubbing his hand down Magda's arm.

"That's enough! Unhand the woman and get back to your post." The Centurion sounded angry. "And if you dare address me with such insolence again, I will report you."

"As you wish, Centurion," the three soldiers said in unison. They mounted their horses and rode away.

"Are you alright?" The Centurion dismounted his horse. "Are you hurt?"

"I am alright," Magda said, a wave of nausea curling tight in the pit of her stomach. "Thank you for your kindness, Centurion. We are simply passing through."

"I am sorry about that. My men don't know how to behave in front of beautiful women. Here," he said, turning to Pascal, "you best take this for protection."

Pascal took the dagger the Centurion offered him. "Thank you, Centurion," he paused, swallowing hard, "but I…"

"Please, call me Abner. And, I insist you take it or I will just have to escort you both to where you are going and that might make things more difficult for both of us."

Pascal laughed, admiration flickering in his old eyes. The confrontation frightened Pascal. It probably brought up things in his past that he wanted to forget as much as Magda did.

"You are right about that, Abner. Thank you for the protection. I will be sure to use it for that purpose alone."

"I have no doubt." Abner mounted his horse. "Safe travels, my friends."

"And you as well," Pascal said as the Centurion rode off. He stared curiously after the Roman.

Pascal turned toward the strained expression on Magda's face. He pressed a hand to his forehead.

"You see, people are not always what they seem, are they, Magda?"

"No, Pascal. I suppose not."

"A Roman came to our rescue. I never thought I would live to see the day," Pascal chuckled.

The encounter unnerved Magda. She had forgotten that even though she was no longer looking at what she had been, others would not be so quick to forget.

Magda hoped that they would not encounter any more triggers that would force her to confront the painful memories of her past. When they finally crossed the border into Capernaum, the throng of people moving about overwhelmed her with a fear of being recognized.

The warm afternoon sun beat down on her skin. The dust still clung to Magda's skin, making her uncomfortable. To her horror, Magda recognized two of the religious leaders, elders from Magdala. She wondered what they were doing there in Capernaum, hopeful that they would not notice her. Magda drew the hood of her cloak up over her head despite the heat of the day. Looking at her sideways, Pascal was quick to notice.

He wove a way through the crowd that would not intersect the path of the religious men making a way through the crowded streets. He managed to keep himself and Magda on the other side of a cart laden with goods. It hid them both well from the men moving in the same direction on the opposite side of the street.

Unfortunately, the cart and donkey that provided them cover as they moved became agitated by a slithering snake and took off running, dropping the contents of the cart along the cobblestone street. As the people in the crowd shoved and pushed their way around in an effort to pick up the wares, Magda and Pascal were thrust straight into the path of the men they were attempting to avoid.

Magda bumped into a man she didn't know, but she could tell from his robes that he was a prominent man, probably a Pharisee. The man stared her down. She recognized the desire in his black eyes as she stood before him, feeling exposed.

"I am sorry, my lord. Please excuse me," Magda stuttered.

Her face flushed red as the other two men from Magdala obviously recognized her. A look of disgust registered on their faces. Magda felt the heat of their judgment and shame. She inadvertently made eye contact with the one elder she knew more intimately than the man would ever dare to admit.

Pascal helped Magda up after she slipped on the spilled contents of a broken jar of olive oil. Magda heard the whispers of the elders as they informed the prominent Pharisee who she was.

"Simon, she is an unclean woman. A sinner of ill-repute, worshiper of Baal and one who prostituted herself," the elder informed the Pharisee, whose eyes still lingered on her female form.

"She was the ruin of her family in Magdala. Her father had been a good man," the other one said. "Come, let us hurry if we are to travel with the others out of this cursed area. You are eager, no doubt, to check on the new property you acquired."

The men moved away quickly. Magda knew that Pascal's ears caught every word they uttered. She was afraid to look into the shepherd's face. Yet, he did not let go of her arm as he continued to help her navigate the chaotic crowd. Once they escaped the fray, Pascal found a quiet step for Magda to sit on and catch her breath.

"You look worn out. Are you alright?" Pascal asked her, no hint of judgment in his voice.

"I am fine," Magda replied. "I knew those men from a life I had hoped to forget, just like the Romans. My past is ever before me, Pascal."

"My dear Magda, we cannot forget where we came from. We can only set our sight firmly on where we are going without looking back, no matter what attempts to distract us." Pascal comforted her with his wise counsel. "You are not what you once were, regardless of how those blind men see you."

"Thank you, Pascal," Magda replied, grateful for the man's company.

"I'm going to find us something to eat. You stay here." Pascal disappeared around the corner, entering back into the craziness of the crowd.

Magda closed her eyes. She was fighting back tears, fighting the cloak of shame that was being thrust upon her.

"Lord," she silently prayed. *"You are my Deliverer. You have cleansed me. Help me not to succumb to the opinions of others. Grant me the power to see myself only as You define me. Lead me to Yeshua, Lord God."*

Magda smelled the bread before she opened her eyes. Pascal stood before her with a soft roll, freshly baked and glazed with olive oil. She hadn't realized how hungry she was until the bread was right before her.

"That smells delicious." Magda took the offering from Pascal's hand.

"It tastes even better," he smiled, his mouth full.

Once the two of them filled their empty stomachs, they began walking once again. It was nearly dusk. The sky was tinged with a blue-gray hue as the stars came out one by one, scarring the canopy of darkness with holes of illumination.

"We should probably ask some people if they know anything," Pascal suggested.

Magda nodded in response. The idea of talking to people was not enticing, but she knew it was necessary. Two young women approached from the opposite direction. They looked friendly enough.

"Shalom," Magda greeted.

"Shalom," the women replied.

"We are looking for a man named Yeshua. Would you happen to know where He might be? We were told He came to Capernaum." Magda felt overwhelmed by the vastness of the territory they were now searching, making her quest seem impossible.

"I think He moved on," one young woman said. "He was here a few days ago. We heard Him speaking about John the Baptizer. I think the Rabbi went on to Nain."

Frustration filled Magda as she realized they had missed the opportunity to meet Yeshua and His disciples. The trip to Nain would take another day and a half, at least. She hoped they were not too late to find Him.

"Do you know when they left?" Pascal asked the women, sensing Magda's disappointment.

"Only this morning," one answered. "We were sad to see them go, but the religious leaders practically shoved Him away."

"Why?" Magda inquired.

"They don't understand His teaching," the woman said. An awe-struck look illuminated her face. "He teaches with such power and authority. He told us so many things. 'Be merciful, even as your Father is also merciful. Don't judge; and you won't be judged. Don't condemn, and you won't be condemned. Set free, and you will be set free. Give, and it will be given to you: good measure, pressed down, shaken together, and running over, will be given to you. For with the same measure you measure, it will be measured back to you.'[38] His way is not like that of the religious rulers."

"No," the other woman interjected. "His way is different. He offers freedom."

"Thank you for your help," Magda told them, graciously. "May the favor of the Lord follow you both."

With that, the women departed company with Pascal and Magda.

"We can catch up with the last caravan that just left Capernaum," Pascal suggested. "There was an oxcart with an open space that would make the journey easier on your blistered feet."

"Are you sure, Pascal? You must be weary from traveling," Magda said. "I know that you have business here in Capernaum."

"I am as eager to catch up with Him as you are, my friend." Pascal took her by the arm, rushing toward the departing caravan, eager to cover some distance in the last hour of daylight.

---

[38] Luke 6:36-38

CHAPTER TWENTY-TWO

The group of travelers made camp when it became too dark to keep moving. Magda welcomed the rest. She was weary physically from traveling and emotionally from her encounters with the past. The memory of John's teachings resurfaced. *No matter the chaos around her, she could always find solace in worshiping the Lord with gratitude.*

Picturing John standing in the middle of the Jordan while everyone else took cover from the fat raindrops falling from heaven, Magda smiled to herself. She found a comfortable spot beneath the open sky and closed her eyes, listening to the chirping of night insects and feeling the soft grass beneath her. A bundle of clothes cradled her head while a borrowed cloak shielded her from the coolness of the night. Magda let her mind review the recent days of traversing a lot of ground.

"Lord, thank You for the people You send me. Pascal has been a wonderful companion. His very presence has been a source of protection. Thank You for the Centurion who chased away those men who desired evil in their hearts. Thank You for that sweet woman, Leah, who mended my feet so I could walk where You are sending me. Thank You for the

many things that I have learned over these past weeks. Truly, I am a different woman now. I can cook, set up tents, walk long distances, tend to wounds, and enjoy the company of men as if they were my brothers."

Magda paused in her worshipful remembrance, awe-struck at all that had transpired in such a short amount of time. She couldn't help but wonder if she was being prepared for something more. There was no longer any doubt in her mind about Yeshua's intentions in sending her to John. He had not been trying to distance himself from her sordid reputation.

Magda finished her prayer. *"Use all that You have taught me for Your glory, Lord."*

With a deep breath, Magda let her eyelids fall shut. Her mind lingered on the image of Yeshua rescuing her in the forest of Zophos, claiming the ground with a flaming sword that turned into a cross of crucifixion. What did it all mean? Why was that image imprinted so deeply on her heart?

Sleep came so slowly that Magda feared it wouldn't come at all. Her eyes fluttered between open and closed, marveling at the twinkling stars because her ears convinced her that things stalked her in the darkness. She wasn't alone. She constantly reminded herself of that. Pascal's soft snores provided just enough auditory distraction that she believed the assurances she whispered to her heart.

As Magda opened her eyes at first light, she could feel a newfound sense of refreshment and renewal. Pascal pulled a few of their left-over provisions from his satchel. The figs were too ripe to eat. He and Magda would have to make do with nuts and the unleavened bread.

The caravan departed before the sun had fully emerged. They moved along quickly, increasing the pace during the early morning hours because it wasn't as hot.

The group arrived at the gates of Nain that very afternoon. Pascal thanked the man in charge of the caravan with a generous contribution before parting ways with them. He and Magda entered Nain only to notice a large crowd in the center of the village. The air was filled with a cacophony of lamenters and mourners, their voices intertwining in a chaotic symphony. Magda could see a body wrapped in grave clothes being carried along on a flat board. A woman dressed in black, crying and holding her head, laboriously walked beside it.

"What is going on here?" Pascal asked one of the on-lookers.

"The widow's son has died," the man replied with sadness. "He was her only child."

"Pascal! Look!" Magda tugged his arm. She saw Yeshua in the crowd on the other side of where they were standing.

"Is that Yeshua?" Pascal asked her.

"Yes, that's Him!" Magda said, excitedly. "We can't get to Him. The crowd is too large."

The multitude surged like an incoming tide, wedging itself between Magda and her destination.

"Wait, He is coming this way," Pascal said, able to see above the crowd because he was taller than Magda.

Magda and Pascal watched as Yeshua and His disciples pushed their way through the multitude to the place where the widow and her dead son were. Magda's attention was drawn to a gathering of religious leaders, intentionally keeping their distance from the dead body to uphold their sanctity. When Magda recognized Simon, the Pharisee they had encountered in Capernaum, a wave of dismay washed over her.

Magda turned her eyes back to Yeshua. He not only entered the space where the widow was, He actually touched the bier that carried her dead son. Magda could hear His voice echo above the crowd. His actions left everyone in disbelief as he fearlessly reached out and touched the dead body.

Even from a distance, she could clearly perceive the depth of compassion in Yeshua's eyes. She heard the tenderness of His voice. "Don't cry," He said aloud to the widow.

Don't be afraid. That was what he had said to her.

Yeshua placed both hands on the bier. "Young man, I tell you, Arise!"[39]

Time stood still, bowing to the authority in His voice. Everyone in the crowd gasped and stepped back as the dead man sat up. Yeshua unwrapped the grave clothes and placed the man's hand in his mother's.

Frenzy consumed the multitude, their restless energy filling the air. Everyone moved about, shrieking at the miracle. Magda looked over at the religious leaders who were still standing on the platform overlooking the entire scene. The Pharisee she knew as Simon had a sinister look on his face. Unlike Simon, who remained composed, the rest of them were seething with anger and outrage. When Magda looked back, Yeshua and His disciples were gone.

"Pascal, they disappeared! Where did He go?" Magda was furious at herself for taking her eyes off Yeshua for even one second. Had she lost her chance to find Him?

"Come on," Pascal said. "Let's try to follow if we can. Maybe we will catch up with them."

The two of them pushed and shoved their way through the chaotic scene. The miracle left some people ecstatic with joy. Others were skeptical, calling it a work of Beelzebub. Magda hated hearing the name. She shivered at the work of darkness she sensed around her. Tensions were escalating in the dispute between the people, as tempers flared and arguments grew more intense. No wonder Yeshua disappeared from the crowd.

"The religious leaders are trying to arrest Him because He is a charlatan, this Yeshua of Nazareth!" One man was yelling at another. "Nothing important comes out of Nazareth."

"How can you say that after what you just witnessed? He raised someone from the dead. He heals the blind. He makes the lame walk. What other proof do you need?" A younger man

---

[39] Luke 7:11-15

argued in defense of Yeshua.

"He is working with Satan!" the first man said.

The voices grew faint as Magda and Pascal distanced themselves, leaving the rest of the argument unheard. In her heart, Magda felt sad for the people's blindness. She knew for certain who Yeshua was. She had forgotten that others did not see Him even when He stood right in front of them. When the crowd thinned out, Magda and Pascal found themselves in an alleyway.

"We lost them," Magda said in a defeated tone of voice.

"Don't give up, Magda. We have come this far. They haven't left Nain," Pascal encouraged her.

"How do you know?"

"Because they were coming from that direction," Pascal pointed to the gate, "which means that they just entered the city. We can ask around and find out where they are lodging for the night."

Pascal took Magda's arm. "Let's go see if we can find some place to get food. I have a few coins left, but the rest of our food is gone."

Exiting the alleyway, Pascal and Magda were startled by the clattering of hooves as two horses came into view, blocking their path. The Roman soldiers they had met before in their travels were now in Nain.

"Well, look what we have here." The soldiers both quickly dismounted.

Magda was glad there were only two of them. She hoped the third would not show up. The first man grabbed her with a firm grip, forcefully pulling her towards him.

"You won't have the protection of the Centurion this time, woman," the man hissed in her ear.

The other soldier went after Pascal. The sound of Pascal's staff hitting the ground and rolling away told Magda that the other soldier had Pascal subdued.

Magda wondered why the road was deserted as the Roman

pulled her back into the alleyway. She could hear Pascal struggle with the other soldier. She feared for him. The Roman ripped her cloak and tore at her tunic. Magda felt sick as the man held her by the throat. Before he could do anything more, Pascal was there. His dagger was already bloody.

"Leave her alone," Pascal warned.

The Roman turned around fast, knocking the dagger out of Pascal's hand. The weapon slid along the cobblestones a few feet before coming to a stop. It met with the obstacle of Pascal's alabaster flask of ointment which had fallen out of the satchel attached to the old shepherd's waist.

The two men struggled on the ground. Magda didn't know what to do. Pascal reached out and fingered the dagger. Grabbing it, he plunged it into the Roman's side, but it wasn't deep enough. The dagger fell to the ground with a clang. The Roman slipped his own hand inside his garment and stabbed Pascal with a long, curved knife. Magda screamed in horror as the blood spilled quickly on the cobblestones.

The scene was suddenly disrupted by the presence of the Pharisees Magda had previously spotted. They came around the corner, obviously surprised to see the display in the alley. The Roman soldier stood up, sheathed his knife and ran out of the alley, kicking the alabaster flask so that it rolled until it stopped at Magda's feet. Magda could hear the soldier helping his companion up on the horse before they rode away. She picked up the ointment and rushed to Pascal's side, completely forgetting about her ripped clothing.

"Pascal! Pascal!" Magda shook him. "Are you alright?"

The religious men continued to fix their eyes on her, their steadfast stares causing her unease. Simon did nothing to hide his desire as he stared at her, drinking in the sight of her exposed flesh. The other men looked away.

"Help me," Magda pleaded. "He needs help."

"And how would you pay me for that help?" Simon spoke with

his lewd look.

Magda wondered if the man spoke it out loud or if she was only hearing his thoughts because the other men did not respond to what Simon had said.

"This is an outrage. Let's get out of here," the other Pharisees both insisted, pulling Simon away.

Magda turned back to Pascal. "Pascal! Pascal!" She rubbed his face with her hands. "Talk to me. Please."

Pascal opened his eyes. The pool of blood soaked into Magda's ripped tunic. Magda unstopped the flask of ointment. Pascal put his hand over hers, placing the stopper back on the flask with the little strength he had left.

"Go in peace, Magda. He calls to you as He now calls to me. I have brought you here. I am a shepherd returning the Master's sheep to the fold. Find Yeshua. He is Your protector now. Take this with you," he said, breathlessly, referring to the alabaster flask of ointment.

With that, Pascal closed his eyes, a look of sweet contentment on his face. "No," Magda cried. "No, Pascal, you can't give your life for me. I need you here. I'm sorry. I'm so sorry."

Magda didn't know how long she remained in that position, covering the dead body of her protective shepherd. His last words were ones she would never forget. When two people came down the alleyway, the woman was by her side in an instant.

"Are you in need of help?" she asked. "Barnabas, help me."

A man came over. Magda felt his strong hands lifting her off of Pascal's body. "It looks like he is dead," Barnabas announced.

The woman helped Magda to her feet. "Come, we can help you. My name is Jerusha. This is my brother, Barnabas."

Magda's hands were shaking uncontrollably. Her clothes were torn. She was cold and soaked in blood. Jerusha covered her with her own cloak.

"Brother, would you see to this?" Jerusha asked, nodding toward the body of Pascal. "I will take her back to the dwelling to get cleaned up."

"Yes, I will take care of it," Barnabas promised.

Magda let Jerusha lead her to a humble dwelling not far from where they had been. Once inside, Magda had a chance to wash up, put on fresh clothes, and fix her hair. She was still in shock from the recent occurrence, but the freshening up helped her to get over her stupor. When she went back into the main area of the dwelling, Jerusha had fixed a meal for them.

"Well, you look much better," Jerusha said when Magda emerged.

"Thank you for letting me use your room. Thank you for these clothes." Magda could hear the hollowness in her own voice.

"I am sorry for the loss of your friend," Jerusha said. "May I ask your name?"

"I'm sorry. My name is Magda."

"We are glad to help you, Magda. Please sit down and eat." Jerusha had barely finished her sentence when Barnabas walked through the door.

"My brother, that took you a while," Jerusha said.

"Yes, the man who caused all the commotion earlier today, Yeshua, has been summoned to Simon's house." Barnabas relayed the information. "There was another issue with the crowd that delayed the authorities from helping me."

"I don't like that Pharisee, Simon. He should just go back to the Temple treasury where he belongs. I don't know why he has to keep acquiring land and property. What does he need with a dwelling in Nain? The man already has more wealth than anyone could possibly spend in a lifetime." Jerusha's voice was tinged with irritation.

"Did you say Yeshua?" Magda asked, life coming back into her voice at the resurrection of her mission.

"Yes, He was here earlier. He raised a widow's son from the dead," Barnabas said to her.

"I was there." Grief gained purpose as excitement to resume

what she had started with Pascal resurfaced. "Where is Simon's house?"

"You aren't going there, are you?" Jerusha asked her.

"I have to. I have been looking for Yeshua, traveling a long distance to find Him," Magda said, remembering Pascal's final instructions to her.

"Simon's newly acquired property is two streets over in the upper section. It is a large house with a red awning outside of it. I can go with you, if you like," Barnabas offered.

"No, you have both done enough already. I will find it. Thank you very much for your kindness." Magda hugged them both, energy now surging through her body. "Oh, I almost forgot."

Magda went back to the area where she had left her satchel and the alabaster flask of ointment. She was surprised that the delicate container had not smashed during the turbulence that claimed Pascal's life. She placed it gently inside the satchel with her other meager belongings.

"Are you sure you want to go alone?" Jerusha asked her. "The sun is about to set."

"Yes, I am sure, Jerusha. Twilight is my favorite time of day." Magda smiled at her before setting off beneath the gray-blue sky. She looked up just as a single star poked its way into the pending darkness.

"Thank you, Yahweh, for giving me the shepherd Pascal to bring me here safely," Magda prayed.

She walked quickly according to the directions that Barnabas had given her. When she spotted the dwelling, her heart raced. She felt His presence even without seeing Him with her eyes. Despite not being invited, she felt an irresistible pull towards the gathering.

Magda stepped beneath the red awning and across the threshold with hesitant steps. Her eyes scanned the room, taking in the sight of a bunch of men sitting down at the table enjoying a meal. Yeshua was there, reclining on a cushion with His bare feet exposed behind Him. He looked up when Magda entered. The smile in His twilight eyes unraveled her soul in an instant. Everything else in the room disappeared from Magda's perception. She could only see Him.

Magda rushed toward Him. She fell at His feet, overcome with grateful adoration. The tears cascaded down her cheeks like a waterfall washing over His feet. She knelt before Love Himself. Her Lord in the flesh who rescued her from darkness and married her to the light. He made her the beloved of the Holy. He claimed her heart with the flaming sword of victory. He ignited the ember of love He put there until it consumed the ashes of her past with a fiery passion of faithful devotion that lifted her high above the shadows of death.

Magda kissed His feet in worshipful adoration, tasting the salty tears with which she anointed Him. Trembling, she began to wipe His feet with the hair that had fallen loose around her shoulders. Was there any expression of devotion that could match the immensity of the love He offered her? Did her soul even possess the capacity to receive all that He willingly gave?

She realized the answer was *no*. The divine love would flow like the river Jordan between them as He supplied what she could pour out—an incorruptible love that brought her beneath the protective banner of His authority. Magda was no longer exposed and vulnerable to the dominion of darkness because she was a bride of Christ, her Redeemer, her Savior, her Lord and King. She looked up, seeing Him as He was when He stood at the top of the staircase to heaven, beckoning her to come to Him.

He reached out to her, wiping the tear stains off her face with His tender hands. When Magda looked back down at His feet, she caught a shimmer of unseen scars. She removed the alabaster flask of ointment from her satchel, overcome by the urge to minister to His future pain. She carefully rubbed the healing balm on the tops of His feet where none but her could see the scars that were His destiny.

The holiness of the moment was shattered by the hushed whispers that suddenly filled the air around Magda. It was Simon's voice echoing in her ears, instantly recognizable. Yet, she was sure he was not speaking out loud, even though she heard his words in her head.

"This man, if he were a prophet, would have perceived who and what kind of woman this is who touches him, that she is a sinner."[40]

Yeshua looked up, obviously hearing the same thing Magda did, though no one else appeared to have heard it.

"Simon, I have something to tell you." Yeshua looked directly at the man, startling Simon.

Simon replied, darkness in his eyes. "Teacher, say on."[41]

Yeshua's voice was clear. "A certain lender had two debtors. The one owed five hundred denarii, and the other fifty. When they couldn't pay, he forgave them both. Which of them therefore will love him most?"

Simon answered, "He, I suppose, to whom he forgave the most."

Yeshua said to him, "You have judged correctly."[42]

Yeshua placed His hand protectively on Magda's head while speaking to Simon. "Do you see this woman? I entered into your house, and you gave Me no water for My feet, but she has wet My feet with her tears, and wiped them with the hair of her head. You gave Me no kiss, but she, since the time I came in, has not ceased to kiss My feet. You didn't anoint My head with oil, but she has anointed My feet with ointment. Therefore I tell you, her sins, which are many, are forgiven, for she loved much. But to whoever little is forgiven, the same loves little." Yeshua cupped Magda's face in His hands, "Your sins are forgiven."[43]

---

[40] Luke 7:39

[41] Luke 7:40

[42] Luke 7:41-43

[43] Luke 7:44-48

Magda could feel the hatred rise in Simon's heart without even looking at the man. Simon kept quiet, seething at the public rebuke in front of his guests. Magda remained silent at Yeshua's feet as the meal commenced.

Pascal's voice echoed in her heart with his parting words. *He is your protector now.*

When she looked around the room, she was astonished to see light radiating from Yeshua reflected in all but one of His followers. A young man with a strong resemblance to their host, Simon, sat in the corner, shrouded by the same grayish hue that canopied the forest of Zophos.

CHAPTER TWENTY-THREE

Magda easily fell into rhythm with Yeshua and His group of followers. Thanks to the preparation she had received in John's camp, she felt well-equipped for whatever challenges awaited her. Looking at Yeshua, she knew without a doubt that His plans always had a purpose beyond what people could recognize in the moment. She loved being with Him. In His presence she felt complete, satisfied, and empowered to be who she was destined to be.

Magda served the men with the devotion of a full heart. The group left Nain the morning after their meal at Simon's. They were on their way to Bethany, tracing the path that Yeshua often walked when He visited this family that He had known since childhood. When the sun disappeared below the horizon, the travelers knew it was time to halt their journey and set up camp. Magda quickly lit two fires and helped the disciple, John, prepare the food.

"You are good with fire," John said to her.

Magda smiled at the compliment and laughed a little to herself. "I suppose I am. I learned how to start fires when I was in

John's camp at the River Jordan. Fire once terrified me."

Memories of her time in the forest of Zophos flooded Magda's mind, and she could vividly recall the sensation of fear mingling with helplessness as flames licked up around her. Shaking off the soul tremble, she shook her head.

"I see it differently now. What the enemy attempts to use for destruction, Yahweh can use it for our good."

"Your words are full of wisdom, Magda. Fire brings the light into the darkness and I can see that you have learned to master it well." John squeezed her shoulder. Taking the cooked fish off the open flame, he went to distribute it to the others.

Magda appreciated the quick and deep connection she had with her new family of disciples. Though she missed those she had befriended during her time at the Jordan, she knew that this was where she belonged.

After a comfortable night sleeping beneath a dark canopy dusted with illuminating stars, Yeshua and His followers packed their things and began walking again. Magda was grateful that she could keep up with the men's quicker pace. Throughout her journey with Pascal, her body had become accustomed to the demands of the rugged terrain. No more blisters hindered her forward momentum.

The intrusion of the memory made Magda choke back tears of grief which she had not yet expressed fully. She missed her friend, who called himself her shepherd. Truly, Pascal accomplished his mission and would have been glad to see her now among the disciples of Yeshua.

Yeshua came up beside her, sensing her distress. His nearness was an instant comfort to Magda. Being within the fullness of divine love lifted her soul in ways she couldn't begin to describe with words.

Yeshua spoke softly to her. "If anyone desires to come after Me, let him deny himself, take up his cross, and follow Me. For whoever desires to save his life will lose it, but whoever will lose his life for My sake, the same will save it.[44] Your friend did well to see you here safely, Mary. His destiny was fulfilled."

Yeshua's voice filled with warmth and tenderness as he called her Mary, and Magda couldn't help but feel a sense of belonging. It was a name no one else used. She remembered being told as a child that it was a name her father chose for her—a name that meant bitter sorrow, a constant reminder of the pain he carried.

They had not traveled too far from Nain when word arrived via messenger that Peter's mother-in-law was sick. Their route took an immediate detour, and the group quickened their pace as they redirected towards Bethsaida.

They arrived back in Capernaum at dusk, finding lodging in a home near the synagogue since it was the Sabbath. The man hosting them was a former fishing partner of Peter's. Magda helped the man's wife prepare the Sabbath meal.

"How is business for you, Naftali?" Peter asked the man.

"It is great now that I own your boat too!" The jovial man laughed and patted Peter on the shoulder. "Has your 'fishing for men' been profitable?"

Magda sensed Peter's discomfort and unhappiness from his pinched expression as he endured the mocking. She and Naftali's wife, Susanna, brought the meal in to the men so they could break the growing tension in the room.

"My husband doesn't see past the prospect of making money," Susanna whispered to Magda. "He seeks power and blessing from Yahweh, nothing more."

Magda heard the sadness in the woman's voice. Susanna's observation also alerted Magda to the fact that the woman recognized there was something different about Yeshua and His followers. Watching Susanna, Magda wondered how difficult it would be to be married to someone who didn't share the same beliefs and convictions as she did.

---

[44] Luke 9:23-24

The group enjoyed the Sabbath meal, lighting the candles and saying the prayers together. Yeshua led them through the same prayers Magda had heard Jacob, the caravan leader, use when she traveled with him. There was a huge difference in the depth and scope of the words as they came forth from Yeshua's lips with the power of life and truth as opposed to the ritualistic sense of duty with which Jacob had led his group in prayer.

The more time Magda spent with Yeshua, the deeper her bond with Him became. The ember of love within her heart had been stirred, igniting a flame of faithful devotion that radiated warmth, dispelling the darkness that had once consumed her soul. The moment she entered His presence, a comforting, radiant light dispelled the darkness within her spirit, offering a shield of divine protection.

When the new day began, Yeshua left for the synagogue before any of them knew He was gone.

"Where is Yeshua?" Peter asked, stretching his arms over his head as he yawned.

"He left before sunrise," Naftali answered him. "He mentioned something about going to the synagogue. Though it was way too early for that."

"He usually gets up before dawn to go pray," Peter retorted. "He probably did that first. I'm going to join Him at the synagogue."

"I'll come with you," John replied.

The others all nodded their affirmation. Magda put her things together, intending to follow the men to the synagogue. Unexpectedly, Susanna appeared beside her, holding a travel satchel in her hands.

"I want to come with you," Susanna said to Magda. "I asked Naftali, and he said I could go. He is going to be gone for a month anyway, on business. I don't want to be alone here."

"I would love your company," Magda smiled, hugging her new friend.

When the group came upon the synagogue, Yeshua was already teaching. They could hear His voice from afar, carried on the wind, as if the wind itself was an instrument designed to amplify the voice of the Lord. The crowd was so large that they couldn't push through to get inside the stone building.

"He speaks with such authority," one man said. "I have not heard of such teaching before."

Magda heard the astonishment in the man's voice. Without warning, Magda's entire body chilled. She sensed something dark, even though the sun shone brightly above them.

Turning around, Magda noticed a man moving toward the crowd. A deep, dark hue surrounded his body, creating an aura of intensity. His eyes were hollow. Magda knew instantly that this was an emissary of Zophos. She trembled as the man neared. No one else appeared affected by what she saw.

The man locked eyes with her. The magnetic force of evil seemed to have a hold on Magda, making it impossible for her to look away from the man's captivating gaze. Right before her eyes, the man transformed into a bat-like creature with long talons and fierce green eyes. He came toward her with a forceful desire that sucked the light out of her very soul.

"You are unclean," he hissed.

Magda, alone, could hear him. She was unaware of the crowd around her now, locked into the demon's gaze as he pulled her toward himself.

Magda stood her ground, trying hard not to move toward the force tugging at her. The demon lost his focus and turned toward a penetrating light that appeared as suddenly as the first star did when night took over the land.

The demon cried out in a loud voice that reminded Magda of how it felt to be scratched on the inside of her soul.

"Ah! what have we to do with You, Jesus of Nazareth? Have You come to destroy us? I know who You are: the Holy One of

God!"[45]

Yeshua rebuked him, saying, "Be silent, and come out of him!" When the demon had thrown the man down in the middle of the crowd, he came out of him, having done him no harm.[46]

Magda watched as the bat-like creature dissolved into the darkness that no one in the crowd saw. Weakness overcame her, leaving her feeling completely drained of strength. Yeshua was by her side, linking His arm with hers to hold her up. The disciples gently lifted the freed man off the ground, supporting him as he regained his balance.

Magda heard the whispers of the crowd. "What is this word? For with authority and power He commands the unclean spirits, and they come out!"[47]

"What is your name?" Yeshua asked the free man standing in front of Him.

"Lord, my name is Manasseh." The man bowed before Yeshua.

"Go in peace, Manasseh. Do not give the enemy a foothold. Remain in the light." Yeshua kept his hold on Magda as He led her out of the crowd.

When they found a quiet place to rest, Yeshua handed Magda His wineskin, and she took a long, refreshing sip. He turned toward the disciples, who were unusually quiet amongst themselves. The atmosphere was thick with fear, affecting each and every person.

Yeshua broke the formidable silence. "I saw Satan having fallen like lightning from heaven. Behold, I give you authority to tread on serpents and scorpions, and over all the power of the enemy. Nothing will in any way hurt you. Nevertheless, don't rejoice in this, that the spirits are subject to you, but rejoice that

---

[45] Luke 4:33-34

[46] Luke 4:35

[47] Luke 4:36

your names are written in heaven."[48]

His words brought comfort to Magda who was still shaken by the familiar experience. While the others took a meal, Yeshua sat beside Magda, talking to her quietly.

"You will see many things, Mary—things that others do not see. Don't be afraid. I am with you. I will not leave you. The demons are subject to you, just like the fire you once were afraid of is now mastered by your hands." Yeshua squeezed her hand. "Eat. We will begin our journey again at sundown."

Magda ate the food He offered her, finding replenishment more from His words than from the meal.

Several people from the surrounding area heard about Yeshua's display at the synagogue that morning. Their serene hideaway in the hills was abruptly interrupted by an insatiable sense of inquisitiveness in the local community.

When the sun set behind the hills, all those who had sick relatives with various diseases brought them to Yeshua. He laid His hands on every one of them, and healed them. Demons also came out of many, crying out with vehemence that identified Him. "You are the Christ, the Son of God!"

Rebuking them, He didn't allow them to speak, because they knew that He was the Christ.[49]

Magda took in the scene like a frightened animal. She stood back, overwhelmed by the darkness she saw in several of the people coming to Yeshua. Most were being dragged against their will by caring family members.

One woman was engulfed by a flaming dragon that hissed and spit fire at Yeshua. He laid hands on her forehead and the fiery demon was snuffed out. Another man appeared entwined with a snake-like demon that had its fangs completely embedded in the man's skull. Magda could hardly watch as Yeshua

---

[48] Luke 10:18-20
[49] Luke 4:40-41

approached the man. She heard the demon's blasphemous, foul words, even though no one else in the crowd could. Yeshua was unmoved by the verbal onslaught. He merely laid His hand on the man, His touch burning the demon to ash.

Even though she wasn't directly involved in their healing, Magda still felt emotionally exhausted from the experience. The other disciples couldn't contain their excitement as they witnessed the immense power and authority displayed by Yeshua. Magda felt weakened each time they brushed up against emissaries from Zophos.

"Are you alright?" Susanna asked her.

"I'm just tired," Magda lied. "The day has been long."

They walked well into the night. The light of a full moon guided them along the road to Bethsaida. They stopped a short distance from the village, seeking a moment of respite. They chose to enter Peter's home as soon as the first light of day appeared.

When the group arrived, Peter's mother-in-law was not doing well. She was in bed with a high fever. It had been days since the woman fell ill.

Yeshua wasted no time. He went toward the fragile woman, stood over her and rebuked the fever, which left her instantly upon His command. The room was filled with an overwhelming sense of joy, as everyone celebrated together.

Magda couldn't believe how effortlessly Yeshua performed his healing miracles. Without fanfare, He showcased His power, never expecting extravagant shows of gratitude in response.

As soon as Peter's mother-in-law woke up, she showered them with hospitality that would rival the treatment of a king. Magda could tell that Peter enjoyed the comfort of his home. He laughed and seemed more at ease than he had ever been. She could tell that it was hard for the man to follow Yeshua while leaving the life he once knew.

It suddenly dawned on her that they all had that in common. Every single person following Yeshua had left a life that they once knew. They dropped an identity that they were comfortable with, embarking on a grand adventure that led them to an unknown destiny. The risks were great. What was the reward?

It was everything Magda couldn't begin to put into words because she didn't fully understand the true answer to that question.

As they left Peter's house, they found themselves surrounded by a multitude of people in a deserted place outside Bethsaida. Again, they brought several of their sick to be healed. Yeshua's heart swelled with compassion as he looked at the crowd. He welcomed them, and spoke to them of Yahweh's Kingdom. He cured those who needed healing.

When the day wore away, Bartholomew approached Him with a suggestion. "Send the multitude away, that they may go into the surrounding villages and farms, and lodge, and get food, for we are here in a deserted place."

Yeshua's reply was quick to come. "You, My disciples, give them something to eat."

Andrew, standing nearby, laughed to himself. "We have no more than five loaves and two fish, unless we should go and buy food for all these people."

By now, there were about five thousand men in the deserted area with them. Magda felt a surge of anxiety as she contemplated how to feed such a large crowd. She agreed with Andrew and Bartholomew that they should send the people away.

Yeshua addressed His disciples without a hint of apprehension in HIs voice. "Make them sit down in groups of about fifty each."

Both Magda and Susanna helped with the task of settling the people in groups of fifty. Magda thought it a strange task, but she had learned not to question Yeshua's instructions. Yeshua took the five loaves and the two fish. Looking up to the sky, He blessed them, broke them, and gave them to the disciples to set before the multitude.

Magda and Susanna helped serve as well. The atmosphere dripped with the holiness and power of the miracle. The food didn't stop coming. It miraculously appeared as they went back to Yeshua for what they needed. The entire crowd ate and were all filled. The disciples gathered up twelve baskets of broken pieces that were left over.[50]

When Magda sat down next to Susanna with her own bread and fish, she was tingling with excitement in the electrified environment of heaven's provision. She remembered the story of manna coming down from heaven in the wilderness.

"Who is He?" Susanna asked, astonished and in awe.

"He is the Son of God, our Messiah," Magda answered, a deep love giving authority to her voiced proclamation.

---

[50] Luke 9:10-17

CHAPTER TWENTY-FOUR

After spending the night in Peter's dwelling, Magda awoke to the warmth of the sun's beams as it crested the hills surrounding Bethsaida. The window was open to the east, providing Magda with a perfect view of the glorious light as it overtook the darkness of the night before.

When she went out of the sleeping area to the main room, she noticed that most of the men were already gone.

"Where is everyone?" Magda asked Peter's wife.

"Yeshua left hours before sunrise for His prayers," she answered. "The others are preparing a boat for your travels. You can find them on the shore. They are waiting for you and Susanna."

"Thank you," Magda replied. "I will go wake her."

"I have some food for you to take with you as well," Peter's wife said.

Magda and Susanna left with a bundle of food that Peter's wife and mother-in-law prepared for the group. The women must have been up most of the night making sure the travelers would have enough to last them until they arrived in Bethany.

When Magda looked at the boat Peter secured for them, she felt a sense of hesitation wash over her. She had never been on a boat before. Her heart raced as she felt an unexpected wave of fear wash over her at the sight of the sea. Though the waters of the Sea of Galilee were a clearer blue, aptly reflecting the sky above them, their mysterious depth frightened Magda.

"Are you coming?" Susanna asked her when Magda stood frozen on the shoreline.

Magda nodded her head, stifling the insecurity in her heart. Her feet wouldn't move. She was feeling frustrated at her own weakness when the others who had been preparing the boat fixed their gaze on something behind her. She turned around. Yeshua was coming toward them. His eyes locked onto Magda's, and a knowing smile spread across his face.

He strode up to her, linked His arm in hers and began walking alongside her toward the boat. "Don't be afraid, Mary. Grow your faith. Trust in Me."

His words alone comforted her once again. His touch strengthened her. Magda boarded the boat along with the other followers of Yeshua, thankful that her fear bowed to the authority of the One she loved.

Once on the open sea, Magda couldn't help but smile as the water sprayed her face, the wind tousled her hair, and glimpses of fish swam beneath the surface. There was an entire world hidden beneath the waters of the Sea of Galilee that Magda knew nothing about. She looked up toward the sky, realizing that there was an entire spiritual world in the heavens that Yahweh privileged her to glimpse, even though it frightened her.

The group ate their meal as they traveled across the open sea. They arrived on the other shore by late afternoon. The terrain looked familiar to Magda. Peter and the rest of the men secured the boat, unpacking everything.

Magda walked up to the grassy knoll just beyond where they landed. She recognized the village immediately and her blood ran cold. This was the place where she and Jezebel had once been in business together. Only a few miles away were the ashes of a burned down house of ill-repute. Further still were remnants of a life she once lived in Magdala.

"Don't be afraid, Mary. Grow your faith. Trust in Me," Yeshua whispered in her ear as He walked up beside her.

Magda trembled as the group made their way into the village she wanted so much to forget. Puzzled, she questioned Yeshua's motives for leading her to this peculiar place. She feared what the others would think if they knew all of her horrible secrets.

"What is bothering you, Magda?" Susanna asked her as they walked. "You look sick."

"I don't feel well, Susanna. This place holds horrible memories from my past," Magda admitted.

"I'm sorry, my friend. Hopefully, we will just be moving through quickly." Susanna was at a loss for words that would comfort Magda.

As they arrived at the ruins of the place where Magda once worked, a wave of nausea washed over her. Yeshua sent the men out to gather food for the group. The village was quiet, mostly deserted. Yeshua remained with Magda and Susanna.

Magda's thoughts were casting ugly shadows on the landscape of her mind. She remembered what she was, opening a door to her past that was better left shut. How could she have done what she did? How could Yahweh forgive her?

Yeshua's voice silenced her questions.

"If a kingdom is divided against itself, that kingdom cannot stand. If a house is divided against itself, that house cannot stand. If Satan has risen up against himself, and is divided, he can't stand, but has an end. No one can enter into the house of the strong man to plunder, unless he first binds the strong man; and then he will plunder his house."[51] Yeshua spoke into her thoughts,

---

[51] Mark 3:24-27

closing the door to condemnation. "I sense your struggle. Let go of the shame, Mary. In these ashes, do you not recognize the reason I came?"

"My Lord," Magda cried, clinging to His cloak. "Let me not fall into the shadows again. Forgive me my weaknesses. Turn me away from the dark."

"Perfect love casts out fear, Mary. There is no punishment for those who truly believe. Love has set you free." Yeshua lifted her from her knees and wiped the tears from her face. "You have repented. Now, go in peace because you have been forgiven. Freely forgive others in the power of love, my child. Look again at what once was," Yeshua commanded her.

When Magda turned around to look at the ashes of the house of ill-repute, she realized that it was no longer an ash heap. Before her was a beautiful field of wild flowers growing beneath the light of the sun. The beauty of the spot was absolutely breathtaking. Confused, Magda looked back at Yeshua.

"Do not become so blinded by your past, Mary, that you do not see what is," Yeshua taught her. "There is beauty from ashes if you have the faith to behold it."

Magda hugged Him tight, her tears wetting the cloak He wore. He held her close, assuring her with the strength of His embrace. Magda never wanted to let go. The sound of Susanna's sobs served as a stark reminder that they were not the only ones present.

"I'm sorry," Magda said, releasing her Savior.

"No, I'm sorry, too," Susanna said. "There are so many things that I am grateful to be forgiven of, too."

The others arrived with provisions, breaking the private teaching the women had with Yeshua. Magda couldn't contain her excitement when she saw another woman joining them.

"Joanna!" Magda ran toward her friend.

"Magda!" Joanna exclaimed. "I was so excited when I saw Peter and John. I knew that you would be close by."

"Is Nathan with you?" Magda asked.

"No, he is still with John the Baptizer." Joanna answered with a smile on her face.

Magda introduced Joanna to Susanna. The women got to know one another over the meal that the group ate in the field of glorious wild flowers that colored the landscape.

Twilight was nearly upon them when Yeshua arose, informing the group of their travel plans.

"We go to Magdala," He said with authority.

Magda trembled. She knew this was Yeshua's way of growing her faith, testing her forgiveness. Her Aunt Milcah still resided in the house Magda once knew as her home. Magda looked up into Yeshua's face. He nodded to her. She knew, without words, that He intended for them to stay at her estate in Magdala.

The walk from the village on the outskirts of Magdala to her estate wasn't terribly long, but it felt as though she was walking through mud. Magda could feel the inner turmoil weighing her down. It was one thing to forget about your past, to put it behind you and look forward. It was entirely another thing to walk in the way of forgiveness and let the past be undone before your very eyes. Would Milcah forgive her? Would her cousin Rachel?

They had every reason to throw her out. Her Uncle Kohath had been right about Magda. She was cursed, and she brought trouble upon her own family. They suffered from her own choices.

Fear consumed Magda, making her tremble. She turned her thoughts toward Yeshua. He had never led her astray before. He knew what He was doing even if she did not understand it. Magda watched Him walking confidently up ahead of her. She followed Him now, not her own desires. She belonged to Him, not to anyone else's expectations. Love's footsteps guided her path, eliminating any need for fear. Yeshua was her protection now.

"Lord, help me to see what is in front of me now, not through the

filter of my past shame," Magda prayed silently.

Yeshua turned around when she looked at Him. He nodded His approval to her, giving her confidence that her prayer was heard.

As they turned the corner, Magda's eyes widened in awe at the stunning view of her grand estate in Magdala. The property exuded an air of elegance and sophistication, thanks to its impeccable maintenance. Trees flourished. The grounds were clean. People were bustling about, creating a whirlwind of activity in the place.

Magda looked up at the twilight sky, watching the changing hues as the sun sunk back into the horizon, giving way to night once again. As the bluish gray filter fell over the land, the property of her estate stood out, glowing against the encroaching darkness.

Everyone waited for her to be the first to enter the courtyard. Magda willed her resistant feet forward. She went up to the large oak door and knocked. A servant answered.

"Yes," she said politely. "Are you here to inquire about a child?"

"A child?" Magda asked, confused. "I'm sorry. I thought this was the residence of Milcah and Kohath."

"It is Milcah's, Mistress. I do not know of a Kohath. This is Milcah's orphanage." The woman looked at Magda quizzically as she noticed the rest of the large group with her.

"I am Milcah's niece, Magda. Would you inform her that I am here?" Magda said to the woman.

"Magda!" the servant exclaimed. "Yes. Yes. Please come in. Milcah informed the entire staff that if a woman by that name ever came here, she was to be escorted in immediately. Come in."

Magda teared up at the display of love that her aunt showed her even after all that she had done.

The servant graciously escorted the entire group inside. The place was immaculate. Milcah had been busy reconstructing the entire dwelling from its fallen estate of darkness to its current position of light in the world. The foyer, which once housed a statue of Baal, now glistened with white walls, candles, and evening sun shining through because of an added window. The garden was thriving with plants that consisted of a grapevine, a fig tree, and an olive tree. Blooming flowers brought color to an area once dominated by decaying weeds.

Children were playing, their laughter carrying on the breeze, bringing life to a place where there had once only been death. Magda was so deeply moved that words failed to capture her emotions. The physical dwelling of her past was a perfect reflection of what had happened spiritually in her heart. She looked at Yeshua. He smiled at her, their exchange reflective of the intimacy they now shared.

"Magda, is that you?" Milcah came in from outside, a babe in her arms. When she set her eyes on Magda, Milcah burst into tears. The servant quickly took the baby from the Mistress of the house.

"Aunt Milcah, I'm so sorry. Please forgive me," Magda cried, overcome with the power of gracious love that flowed from this woman.

"Oh, my darling Magda, that was done a long time ago. How I have waited for you to return home!" With a tight embrace, Milcah and Magda shed tears of joy and forgiveness.

When they finally broke their long-awaited embrace, Magda wiped her face and came to her senses.

"Aunt Milcah, I want to introduce you to my new family. This is Yeshua and His disciples," Magda said to her.

Milcah's eyes went wide. "I have heard about You."

Yeshua stepped close, taking Milcah by the hand. Magda saw the recognition in Milcah's eyes before she fell to her knees, bowing before Yeshua.

"My Lord," Milcah whispered. "Please, stay as long as You like."

"Daughter, your faith is commendable. You have done well with what you have been given," Yeshua said to her.

Milcah ordered the servants to prepare space for the large group. There were twelve children currently housed with her as well. The evening meal was full of life and laughter. Magda was exhausted from the joy of the small feast which Milcah had prepared. The two women were able to catch up on everything that had happened over the years.

The mention of her uncle Kohath's death saddened Magda. She couldn't believe she had forgotten. She was also troubled that Milcah's daughter, Rachel, had distanced herself from her mother at the command of her husband, Eleazar.

"You must be careful, Magda," Milcah whispered to her. "The leaders in the Temple are determined to silence Yeshua. I have heard rumors. Eleazar threatened me that if he ever heard of my association with Yeshua, he would have me arrested."

"Arrested? Why would he do that?" Magda's face twisted with indignation at the mere suggestion.

"He is obsessed with making a name for himself. He is trying to win the favor of those in power despite his disfigurement," Milcah told Magda.

Magda looked down, her heart heavy with the memory of the disfigurement she had inflicted upon the man. "I'm sorry, Milcah, I don't want to add to your troubles."

"My dear, Magda. That man, Eleazar, was disfigured long before you attacked him. You only made visible on the outside what was already lying dormant in his heart." Milcah patted her on the shoulder.

Magda hadn't thought of it, nor saw it that way before. She looked at her Aunt Milcah as she went about serving the children and the new guests she had for the evening.

"*Lord,*" Magda prayed in her heart. "*Thank You for such a woman of faith being in my life all along. I never saw it before. I never appreciated it. May Your mighty blessings fall upon her as she seeks to be a fragrant blossom in this once dead place."*

When Magda looked up from her prayer, she fixed her eyes on Yeshua. He smiled in response. Feeling renewed and released from the shackles of her past, Magda rose to help the other women clean up from the evening meal.

Once the chores were done, the group went out to the courtyard. Magda took out her flint and struck the spark that ignited the wood. The open fire served to warm the chill of the night air as they sang the Psalms of David.

Magda closed her eyes, the voices of the children in song calming her heart with praise. *"Give thanks to Yahweh, for He is good; for His loving kindness endures forever. To Him who alone does great wonders; for His loving kindness endures forever: To Him who by understanding made the heavens; for His loving kindness endures forever: To Him who spread out the earth above the waters; for His loving kindness endures forever: To Him who made the great lights; for His loving kindness endures forever."*[52]

When the singing ended, the children eagerly surrounded Yeshua, their eyes filled with adoration and excitement. Magda was surprised when the disciples tried to keep them away, assuming Yeshua was tired from the day's travels.

Yeshua spoke up when He overheard Peter rebuking one of the boys. "Allow the little children, and don't forbid them to come to Me; for the Kingdom of Heaven belongs to ones like these."[53]

Peter and the others sat back down. The children all nestled themselves at Yeshua's feet. Two sat on His lap. The adults took the outer rim of the circle surrounding the Rabbi as He was about to teach.

Yeshua let out a long breath. "Most certainly I tell you that you who have followed Me, in the regeneration when the Son of Man will sit on the throne of His glory, you also will sit on twelve

---

[52] Psalm 136:1, 4-7
[53] Matthew 19:14

thrones, judging the twelve tribes of Israel. Everyone who has left houses, or brothers, or sisters, or father, or mother, or wife, or children, or lands, for My Name's sake, will receive one hundred times, and will inherit eternal life. But many will be last who are first; and first who are last."[54]

Despite the fact that His teaching was completely contrary to that of the Pharisees, not a single adult had the courage to ask Him any questions. On the other hand, the children eagerly embraced His words, believing them wholeheartedly.

Magda helped her aunt put the children into their beds that night. She held two little boys by the hand and led them up the stairs to the room where they slept. The slightly older boy had sandy brown hair and deep brown eyes. His skin glistened with a sun-kissed bronze hue. His facial features showed the promise of a handsome man in the future. The younger one had dark, curly hair and green eyes. He was ordinary in appearance and a bit on the timid side. Apollos, the older child, spoke with a confident, clear voice. While Agabus, the younger child, had a bit of a stutter.

"Miss Magda," Agabus said, squeezing her hand when they entered the dark room where the boys slept. "I'm af...aff...afraid of the dark."

Agabus clung to Magda's knees. Apollos let go of Magda's hand, proclaiming, "I'm not afraid of the dark. I can actually see better in the dark," the boy said proudly.

Magda recalled the days when she, too, could see better in the dark. She quickly lit another candle on the wall sconce. The two boys clamored onto their sleeping mats.

"It is good not to be afraid of the dark, Apollos," Magda said to the boys. "But you must never get used to seeing in the dark. Always search for the light. Do you understand?"

Both boys nodded to her. Though she wasn't sure they understood the deeper meaning, she hoped that she sparked an

---

[54] Matthew 19:28-30

ember within each of their hearts that would protect them from a life of spiritual blindness.

"We have nothing to fear of the dark," Magda said, ruffling Agabus's hair. "Just remember that you are children of the light. The light is where you need to be. Stay in the light, boys. Promise?"

"Promise!" the boys said in unison.

When Magda returned to the foyer where Milcah was settling things with her servants before dismissing them for the night, she waited to talk to her aunt.

"I just said goodnight to Apollos and Agabus. They are adorable little boys," Magda commented.

"They are," Milcah replied. "A sad story for those two. They came to me after a ship-wreck. They were sailing from Alexandria with their families when they hit a storm. Everyone was lost except those two boys. I took them in so that they would be spared the slave trade. I was able to intercept them before they went to auction."

"How long ago was that?" Magda asked her.

"About a year now. They are both doing much better. It was difficult at first. Grief can be overwhelming and dark." Milcah shook her head. "My brother succumbed to the darkness of it. I was determined to spare these little boys in an effort to fight the fate that I knew awaited them if I didn't."

"You have done an incredible job, Aunt Milcah. The boys are well-learned." Magda complimented her aunt, in awe of her generous spirit and intuitive nature.

"Apollos will be fifteen in a few months. He could have left here, but he wants to stay until the Lord tells him what to do next. Agabus, at ten, is still a bit frightened. He didn't have the maturity that Apollos had to process the tragedy. The boy has dreams of bats and winged creatures with long talons taking down the ship that they sailed on. He tells me that they are still after Apollos. Some nights, I have a real tough time calming Agabus down."

With a tinge of sadness and a trace of frustration in her voice, Milcah told Magda the details of the boy's lives.

Magda felt a profound empathy for the boys and their struggles. She knew it well. Agabus had been given a glimpse into the forest of Zophos like she had and would never be the same. Apollos must have a divine destiny that threatened the evil one.

"Perhaps, try reading Scripture over Agabus every night, Aunt Milcah. I think it would help." Magda offered her advice.

Milcah looked at her niece, love in her eyes. "I will do that, Magda. I have some scrolls that Kohath left me. They were a gift from a woman named Tirzah who cared for us in Bethany. Tirzah presented them to us when our family was too sick to go to synagogue or the Temple. Her husband had been a scribe in the Temple. He left her a widow when she was still young with three children to care for."

They remained two days with Milcah in the orphanage. Yeshua blessed the children there, healing the few who were sick and transforming one little girl who had been crippled in her feet. Milcah was overjoyed by this particular blessing for the crippled girl. Now, it would make it easier for the girl to find her place in the world because she had been made whole again.

Magda was curiously sad to leave the estate. As she stood upon the threshold that had so graciously welcomed them a few days before, Yeshua's transformative teaching once again astonished her. Truly, He brought light to the dark places of her past so that the haunting memories no longer shackled her with shadows of what once was. Now, she saw things as they were — redeemed and used by Yahweh for good in the world.

CHAPTER TWENTY-FIVE

The journey to Bethany was longer than Magda had anticipated. They stopped in villages along the way. Yeshua healed the sick, cured the lame, and even made a blind man see again. The miracles were astounding, but it was the power of the love with which He performed them that touched Magda deeply.

Joanna had to return to the palace. Susanna went back to her home as well so that the two women would not have to travel alone. Magda was sad to see them go but grateful that Yeshua's mother had joined the group of followers after they went through Nazareth.

The travelers stopped in Bethphage on the Sabbath. The day was humid. Everyone was edgy and tired. Once again, the disciples were caught up in a dispute over their rankings, their voices growing louder with each passing moment. Magda could tell that Yeshua didn't like their topic of conversation. When Yeshua got up to go preach in the synagogue, the conversation ceased. Everyone followed Him.

Yeshua stepped into the synagogue, a hushed reverence

tickled the atmosphere. There was a man there whose hand was withered.The religious leaders were present, their robes flowing as they moved. Many from Jerusalem had heard that Yeshua was in Bethphage and came to see Him. Their gazes fixated on Him with the unwavering focus of hawks ready to swoop down and seize their prey. It was the same look which she had seen on the faces of religious men witnessing John the Baptizer at the Jordan.

Magda sensed their malignant intentions as they watched. They wondered if Yeshua was going to heal on the Sabbath. If He did, they would be quick to accuse Him.[55]

Yeshua called to the man who had his hand withered, "Stand up."[56]

The man obeyed, his trembling visible even from Magda's distant spot in the women's section. Yeshua's mother stood right beside Magda, fidgeting with anticipation over what was going to happen next.

Yeshua stepped up to the bimah where the customary teaching usually took place. He spoke directly to the religious authorities. "Is it lawful on the Sabbath day to do good, or to do harm? To save a life, or to kill?"[57]

Magda closed her eyes. The sensation of dark shadows sent from Zophos descended upon her, sending a shiver down her spine. The religious leaders were silent, ready to be stirred up. Unbeknownst to them, those hunting Yeshua were prey to the emissaries of Zophos. Their own souls barricaded them from the truth in a way that left them exposed to the deceptive lies.

Yeshua looked around at them all with great intent. His eyes were filled with anger, being grieved at the hardening of their hearts, because it left them vulnerable to deadly forces.

Yeshua spoke to the man with the infirmity. "Stretch out your

---

[55] Mark 3:2

[56] Mark 3:3

[57] Mark 3:4

hand."[58]

The trembling man stretched it out, and his hand was restored as healthy as the other. He bowed in grateful adoration toward Yeshua, further inciting the religious leaders.[59]

When the religious leaders went out of the synagogue, Magda heard the cackles of the demons inciting them to conspired anger. She suddenly feared for Yeshua's safety. Over and over, she heard the hissing whispers. *"Destroy Him! Destroy Him!"*

When she opened her eyes and looked at Yeshua, He was unmoved by it all, as if He expected it. As her eyes locked with His only briefly, she heard His voice in her heart. *"Don't be afraid, Mary."*

Everywhere they went, the crowd following them swelled. Some were there out of curiosity, some out of desperation and some because they wanted what He offered. Yeshua knew the intentions of every heart coming after Him. He would not let them go unexposed.

On their way out of Bethphage, a certain man addressed Yeshua. "I want to follow You wherever You go, Lord."

Yeshua looked intently at the man, having placed His hand on the man's shoulder. "The foxes have holes, and the birds of the sky have nests, but the Son of Man has no place to lay His head."[60]

The man abruptly turned away from Yeshua, obviously unwilling to give up the comforts of a warm home and soft bed.

When they came upon a lonely traveler who walked along the road, sad and dejected, Yeshua approached him. "Follow me!" Yeshua invited the man.

The man looked at Yeshua. Magda sensed the grip of the grief on the man's heart. She closed her eyes and saw a hovering cloud of gray shackles attached to the man. Up above, in realms unseen

---

[58] Mark 3:5
[59] Mark 3:5-6
[60] Luke 9:57-58

by the naked eye, sat a dragon-like creature. It exploited the man's weakness by making links in the chains that bound him.

The man answered Yeshua, "Lord, allow me first to go and bury my father."

Yeshua said to him, "Leave the dead to bury their own dead, but you go and announce Yahweh's Kingdom."[61]

Magda saw the demon holding the man with shackles of grief shriek in horror. At Yeshua's command, the chains shattered with a resounding crack. The man's eyes brightened, and he joined the crowd, following Him.

Another traveler they encountered approached them and said, "I want to follow You, Lord, but first allow me to say goodbye to those who are at my house."

Yeshua answered him, "No one, having put his hand to the plow, and looking back, is fit for Yeshua's Kingdom."[62]

Magda resonated with that truth, feeling a deep sadness as the man arrogantly walked away, visibly hurt by the rebuke.

They finally arrived in Bethany as night fell on the land once again. Magda thought the home was quaint and welcoming. The nice dwelling nestled into the shadow of the Mount of Olives. The property was not as large as her estate in Magdala, but it was not entirely modest, either.

She followed Yeshua, who was obviously familiar with the family that dwelt there and eager to see them again. Once inside the dwelling, Yeshua made the introductions. Magda remained behind in the crowd, feeling a little out of place. She was pensive about what she felt and witnessed in Bethphage.

"This is Mary, but we call her Magda." Magda heard her name and stepped forward. She smiled at the other woman named Mary, but she immediately felt the coldness in the young woman's greeting. She also thought she saw fear in her eyes.

---

[61] Luke 9:59-60

[62] Luke 9:61-62

"And, of course, you know my mother." Yeshua pulled His mother forward too.

The young woman named Mary hugged Yeshua's mother with obvious warmth, making Magda feel even more out of place.

Yeshua quickly took charge, comfortable in this setting that was unfamiliar to everyone else. The disciples took seats around the low table. John sat next to Yeshua. Peter sat across from Him, just as they usually did when they sat around the open campfires. The others filtered in around the table in their familiar positions. Fortunately, their seating arrangement made Magda feel more comfortable too, and added to her a sense of belonging to this family of followers.

It was around the time for the evening meal. Magda sat next to Yeshua's mother near the table. The young woman, Mary, sat at Yeshua's feet, obviously enraptured by His voice. Magda smiled to herself, relating to the young woman's heart. She sat quietly, listening to the sounds around her. The chatter of the men as they waited for something to eat settled Magda's soul as well.

"Lord, what teaching would you have us learn?" Andrew asked loudly so that the others would stop talking.

The other sister, Martha, brought them food. She hurried back and forth into the cooking area, bringing cheeses, dates, and nuts. Magda observed the woman's abrupt demeanor and heard her sigh, suggesting that she was bothered by the presence of a large group of people in her home. Magda wanted so much to connect with these women who were obviously important to Yeshua. He looked at each of them with such powerful love. She hoped that the Lord would give her a chance to know this family.

Yeshua bowed his head, leading them all in prayer. *"Father, let Your Name be glorified as You provide for us all that we need daily."*

"Help me find a way to connect with these women, Lord. Tell me what I need to do," Magda prayed silently.

When the prayer ended, Yeshua began teaching.

"A man's foes will be those of his own household. He who

loves father or mother more than Me is not worthy of Me; and he who loves son or daughter more than Me isn't worthy of Me. He who doesn't take his cross and follow after Me, isn't worthy of Me."[63]

Magda pondered the deeper meaning of love that Yeshua presented in His teaching. His was a love that sacrificed, gave, and suffered. He called people to a love that was difficult to understand. Magda knew well what it was like to live in a household where your own father was a foe. She knew what it felt like to be alone, even when you were surrounded by people.

The meal was enjoyable, but Magda couldn't help but feel the strained atmosphere between the two sisters. Magda remained quiet and reserved, not knowing what to say to the women, Mary and Martha. Because they were important to Yeshua, Magda was extremely uncomfortable in their presence. They were such good people. She didn't know if she feared getting to know them more than she feared them getting to know her.

Before settling in for the night, Yeshua caught Magda by surprise. He took her by the arm as she came out of the cooking area, covered in wetness from the dishes.

"Tell them what you know, Mary. Tell them what you have seen. Share your story," Yeshua commanded her with love ringing in His voice.

He left before she could even reply.

Magda felt refreshed in the morning. Her sleep had been comfortable. She was up before everyone — everyone except Yeshua, who was already gone to pray somewhere undisturbed. Magda set out some food and drink, having familiarized herself with the cooking area as she helped with chores the night before. She was humming when the young woman, Mary, came downstairs.

Magda noticed her, but Mary didn't say anything to her.

---

[63] Matthew 10:36-38

Determined to follow through on Yeshua's command despite her discomfort, Magda went after Mary. The young woman was out by the animal enclosure, picking up watering jars. Magda took a deep breath.

"Mary!" Magda called out to her. "May I join you?"

The young woman turned around. "Of course," Mary stuttered a bit, fear in her voice.

They walked in silence for a little while. Magda felt an overwhelming sense of unease as she struggled to find the right words to begin a conversation with this woman. She could tell that Mary kept glancing at her from time to time. Magda wondered what she was thinking.

Magda's soft voice finally broke the silence. "How long have you known the Lord?" she asked.

Mary hesitated before answering. "Well, I met Him when I was a child—right here in this meadow, actually." Mary smiled at the memory.

"Really?" Magda said. "Would you tell me the story?"

Mary relayed the story of her first meeting with Yeshua on her tenth birthday. Listening to Mary's story had calmed Magda's restless heart until the two women comfortably conversed like old friends. When they got down to the creek, they filled the water jars and sat down to rest.

The silence wasn't uncomfortable between them anymore. Magda listened to the soothing sounds of life all around them. The flowing water, the singing birds, and the hum of hidden insects was a symphony of worship.

"What about you, Magda? How long have you known Yeshua...I mean, the Lord?" Mary asked her.

Magda smiled, her expression filled with humility. "Not long, actually. But it feels as though it has been a lifetime. I was dead before I met Him. He gave me my life back."

Mary looked confused by Magda's words. A soft smile curled Magda's lips as she gratefully recalled being rescued from the forest of Zophos. She wondered how she could possibly explain that to anyone. She had never even tried before.

"This probably doesn't make sense to you, but He changed me. He changes people, Mary." Magda looked into Mary's eyes with such intent that it almost frightened the young woman. "I wasn't well. My own family shunned me. There was a darkness that pulled me down every time I reached for the light. I heard voices in my head shouting all the time. I never knew quiet. I would get crazy and throw myself into rivers bigger than this creek, or even into open fire. I attacked people. I wandered the streets at night, not able to defend myself against the wiles of men. I was fierce and violent against those who didn't deserve it, but weak and helpless against those who wished me harm." Magda rubbed her arms, turning her gaze to the ground.

Mary listened, obviously stunned by Magda's story. Mary kept silent. After a few moments, Magda continued.

"I lived with seven demons, Mary. I knew them each by their wicked voices. It was rare for me to have a single moment of control. When my father took ill, his sister, Milcah, came to help out. I did horrible things to her family. I even attacked her son-in-law so violently that he neared death." Magda paused, trembling.

"I know about Eleazar," Mary admitted. "My sister, Martha was very fond of him."

Magda looked at Mary with shame in her eyes. "I'm sorry. I wished death for myself, but it wouldn't come. I tried cutting myself with broken pieces of clay jars, but I could never make the cuts deep enough. They only hurt me without killing me. The people in the village were afraid of me. No one came near me until that day — that miraculous day!" The dark look reflected on Mary's face departed. Magda sighed, looking at her hands.

Magda looked into Mary's eyes again. "He came to me right there in the village square that day. I was sitting in a crumpled heap. I hadn't bathed in days. My hair was matted down. I had ripped my flesh with a broken piece of pottery." She looked at her arms, touching the skin with her fingers. "On the ground before me, I saw a shadow approach. The voices ceased. For the first time, there was quiet inside of me. I looked up into the face of Adonai. There was so much light! He reached out and touched me. He touched me! Do you even know what it's like to be touched after decades of never feeling tenderness from another human hand?" Tears filled Magda's eyes. She turned her face to the sky. "His eyes—looking into them was like..."

"Looking into the sky at dusk," Mary interrupted. She was completely drawn into Magda's story.

"Yes," Magda smiled, delighted they could share seeing Him the same way. "He lifted my chin with his fingers and drew me to my feet with one hand. I could feel His power surging through me, cleansing me, purifying me. I can't explain it, but..." she drew in a breath, "I became the woman I was supposed to be in that instant." The tears spilled over the floodgates of her eyes. "The noose that was choking the life out of my soul was cut the moment His hand brushed my cheek. It was like I had been falling endlessly into the darkness until I was caught up in the hands of Yahweh, who lifted me to the light. The demons were gone. I was free to come out of the abyss." Magda sighed. "I know this sounds crazy, but it's what happened to me. I never want to leave His side. He called out the life that was buried inside of me. He is life!"

Mary was silent, but not in a judgmental way. The strong bond of belief between them reassured Magda that their relationship would transcend mere friendship.

When Mary and Magda returned with the water, Martha made them each a plate of food. The others had left to go into the surrounding villages for the day.

"Thank you, Martha," Magda said politely. "You have done so much for us. Your home is lovely."

Martha nodded, hesitant. Magda wanted to break down the barrier between them.

"Thank you for helping my sister fetch the water for the animals." Martha spoke uncomfortably.

"I understand that your family is close to Eleazar's family," Magda timidly offered, deciding a direct approach might be better with Martha.

"Yes," Martha replied, looking uncertain, even skeptical.

There was a long pause before Magda continued. "I am so sorry for what happened to Eleazar. He is a good man. He didn't deserve the attack."

Martha was silent, obviously struggling to bury her emotions. Magda could sense the woman's anger. She felt compelled to explain.

"I was imprisoned by darkness, Martha." Magda began her confession. "I feel strongly that I must share this with you. I'm sorry if I make you uncomfortable." Magda searched for permission in Martha's eyes.

Martha nodded to her, relating to Magda's confession of being imprisoned by darkness. Magda sensed her curiosity.

"Demons haunted me since I was a child. I saw monsters in the dark. I feared the night. I'm not sure when the first demon took me, but I know I was very young." Magda fought against tearful emotion.

"Demons?" Martha sounded unnerved. "There were more than one?"

"Seven, actually. I knew them by names which I do not utter anymore. I was blinded by lies that I believed to be true. Lies that made me do things which I didn't want to do." Magda sighed heavily with the weight of remembrance. "I attacked good people, like Eleazar, while bad people were allowed to harm my body. I know this sounds crazy and doesn't make sense. The power of the deception was so strong. I felt unworthy. I felt like I was responsible for the bad things. I thought I was cursed."

Captivated by every word, Martha's mouth hung open slightly. She remained silent while Magda continued.

"The good things that I wanted to do, I was powerless to do, Martha. I was imprisoned. I couldn't see. The blindness made me scared. There isn't any control in the dark. You can't see where to go. It's impossible to find the way. I was so lost." Magda wiped tears from her eyes before they fell. "Then everything changed the moment I heard my name called. It was Yeshua. He called to me from the dark place where I was lost. I heard Him and responded. I knew He came to get me out."

Martha nodded, urging her to go on. Magda sensed a connection to her.

"Yeshua touched me, Martha. He touched me physically, yes, but it was so much more. Not a single person had touched me with love in years. When I felt His hand on my face, the demons inside me trembled. For the first time, I felt their fear, and it wasn't my own. His authority entered me, casting them out by the light of His truth. He spoke truth by speaking my name over the names of all the demons holding me captive. I could see. My eyes were opened. I left the darkness behind me." Magda exhaled with forceful gratitude.

"That is amazing, Magda," Martha said. "I can't imagine what that must have been like for you." Martha looked at her with admiration replacing the suspicion.

"I have a lot of regrets over things that happened while I was imprisoned, but I no longer want to be captive to the lies that tell me I am cursed or unworthy or responsible for bad things. It's different now. Sin has no hold on me. Yeshua has taught me that His love is forgiveness. Love holds no record of wrongs. Love rejoices in truth. The grace He offers truly sets people free."

Magda spoke with awe and wonder. Her entire countenance changed. "When we were in the Synagogue, He read from the Scriptures as if He wrote them Himself. He is the Word made flesh, I believe."

"What Scripture did He read?" Martha asked.

"I wish you could hear from His own voice, Martha. He read

from Isaiah," Magda said.

Yeshua entered the cooking area, startling both women. His voice resonating with authority, He completed what they had started. "The Lord Yahweh's Spirit is on Me; because Yahweh has anointed Me to preach good news to the humble. He has sent Me to bind up the broken hearted, to proclaim liberty to the captives, and release to those who are bound."

He touched Martha's shoulder before continuing, "To proclaim the year of Yahweh's favor, and the day of vengeance of our God; to comfort all who mourn; to provide for those who mourn in Zion, to give to them a garland for ashes, the oil of joy for mourning, the garment of praise for the spirit of heaviness; that they may be called trees of righteousness, the planting of Yahweh, that He may be glorified."[64]

Magda went outside, drained and exhausted. The pouring out of her story was not easy, but it offered her a connection with these women who already played an important role in Yeshua's life. She saw them now as sisters, not merely friends.

"Thank You, Adonai," Magda prayed. *"Let me pour out everything so that You may be glorified. Give me strength, Lord. I have much to learn."*

---

[64] Isaiah 61:1-3

CHAPTER TWENTY-SIX

After they left Bethany, the group continued to move around from village to village preaching the good news of the Kingdom of heaven. Magda longed for the cozy familiarity of Martha and Mary's home in Bethany. She understood why Yeshua frequently visited there. She could sense the deep-rooted bond he had with that family, as if it was etched into heaven itself. It moved her to ponder what it would have been like to live an uninterrupted life.

Remembering some of the things Mary shared with her about the difficulties of growing up without her parents made Magda realize that no one truly lived life uninterrupted. Mary and Martha grew up knowing the love of their parents, but having that love separated from them by death. Magda grew up not knowing the love of her father because grief had stolen it from her. Death's sting was as pervasive as a deeply embedded thorn resulting from a hastily picked rose.

Magda walked along, her steps slow and deliberate, lost in her own pensive world. Beside her, Yeshua's mother walked in silence, their synchronized steps creating a peaceful rhythm.

Magda was so preoccupied that she didn't notice when Yeshua came up alongside them. His voice penetrated her deep thoughts.

"The thief only comes to steal, kill, and destroy. I came that they may have life, and may have it abundantly."[65] Yeshua looked into Magda's eyes with such sweet compassion that she let the tears flow freely.

She realized what a gift the banner of His love was over her. Because she was under the protection of His love, Magda felt safe enough to expose her own heart to these women who knew Him so well. Magda felt an unbreakable bond between herself, Mary, and Martha, as if they were connected by an invisible thread forged with divine weaving. She missed them even more than she missed Joanna and Susanna. Having no siblings of her own, the sensation of the deeper connection was unfamiliar to Magda. It was a gift from Yeshua.

When they came into the region surrounding Magdala, several of the Pharisees from Nazareth and the surrounding villages came to see Yeshua. They kept their distance but would stop and listen whenever He preached in the open. Having been invited by a local family, Yeshua was beginning to teach in their courtyard when several people crowded around them, making it difficult to move.

Magda noticed several sick people, some lame, some blind, and some with evil spirits attached to them. She also recognized two familiar faces. Joab and Nathan were pushing their way through the multitude to get to Yeshua. With a sense of purpose, Magda joined them, the sound of her footsteps crunching on the ground.

"Joab! Nathan," she yelled over the din of the crowd. "Come this way."

The men followed her outstretched finger, their eyes scanning the direction she indicated. The path went around a building on

---

[65] John 10:10

the outside of the property. Magda opened the gate so that they could come inside. She hugged them both, glad to see them. She hadn't noticed the third man with them.

"What are you doing here?" Magda asked. Startled, Magda's eyes widened as she noticed the third person standing there, causing her to gasp in disbelief. "Apollos? What are you doing here? What are you doing with them?"

"Magda, you make it sound like a bad thing," Joab snorted.

"Were we such a poor influence on you?" Nathan teased her.

"No, no. I'm sorry. It's just that Apollos is so young. I didn't know he left Magdala." Magda explained her outburst, eyes darting between the three men.

"I didn't leave Magdala," Apollos corrected. "I was called by the Lord to go see John the Baptizer. And I am glad that I did, too."

"Does Milcah know where you are?" Magda asked, motherly concern etching her voice.

"I told her before I left, but she didn't want me to go. I had to." Apollos still had the confident voice that Magda admired in one so young.

"He was the last person John baptized," Nathan said, sadly. He hiccuped a breath as if he wanted to say more, but couldn't.

"Last person?" Magda questioned, arching a brow.

The three men looked at one another, then back at her.

"John has been arrested. Herod imprisoned him. He sent us here to Yeshua. He has questions." Joab explained the tragedy, his expression stretched tight with resignation.

A wave of terror washed over Magda, leaving her paralyzed with fear. Her stomach hurt at the news—John, imprisoned. How could that be? What could be done?

"Let's get you to Yeshua. He'll know what to do," Magda said, wishing her stomach wasn't doing somersaults.

With determination, they pushed through the tightly packed crowd, feeling the heat and pressure of bodies all around them.

Yeshua was healing the sick, giving sight to the blind, and casting the demons out with His voice. The four of them watched, marveling with the rest of the crowd.

Yeshua looked up, noticing John's disciples. Joab stepped forward, invited by Yeshua's gaze.

Joab bowed. "John sent me with a message: 'Are You the one who is coming, or should we look for another?'"[66]

Yeshua answered them, "Go and tell John the things which you have seen and heard: that the blind receive their sight, the lame walk, the lepers are cleansed, the deaf hear, the dead are raised up, and the poor have good news preached to them. Blessed is he who finds no occasion for stumbling in Me."[67]

With determination, Magda was about to speak up and deliver the news to Yeshua that John had been imprisoned. He silenced her before she even got the words out.

"He is where he needs to be for now," Yeshua's voice rang in her heart like a tolling bell of divine assurance.

She wondered if Joab and Nathan had heard it as well, considering their sudden departure. Magda followed them out.

"Where are you going?" she asked them, the settled feeling Yeshua offered her dissipating like dew beneath the afternoon sun.

"We will go report to John," Joab said, lips pulled into a tight line.

"Apollos, what about you?" Magda asked, concerned for the boy's safety.

"I need to be with John's disciples, Magda. They are my family now," Apollos said to her, confident but not arrogant.

"Alright, but please be careful, Apollos." Magda hugged the three of them.

"I will stay in the light just like you told me," Apollos

---

[66] Luke 7:19
[67] Luke 7:22-23

whispered in her ear.

As Magda watched them walk away, she could hear the rustle of their footsteps on the gravel path. She remembered John's words. *"He must become more while I become less,"* the prophet had said, understanding his mission.

With John's messengers gone, Yeshua began to tell the multitudes about John the Baptizer.

"What did you go out into the wilderness to see? A reed shaken by the wind? But what did you go out to see? A man clothed in soft clothing? Behold, those who are gorgeously dressed, and live delicately, are in kings' courts. But what did you go out to see? A prophet? Yes, I tell you, and much more than a prophet. This is he of whom it is written, 'Behold, I send my messenger before you, who will prepare your way.' For I tell you, among those who are born of women there is not a greater prophet than John the Baptizer, yet he who is least in God's Kingdom is greater than he."[68]

When all the people and the tax collectors heard this, they declared God to be just, having been baptized with John's baptism. But the Pharisees, standing far off away from the crowd, rejected the teaching, not being baptized by John themselves.[69]

Magda could feel their piercing stares, like daggers against her skin. If they imprisoned John, what could they possibly do to Yeshua? What *would* they do? Magda felt the forces of Zophos closing in, gaining strength. Old fears loomed on the horizon of her soul. She wanted to be stronger, reminding herself that faith anchored her no matter what was coming. Her one task was to keep her focus on Him.

Yeshua, unafraid, pushed His way through the healed people. He went close to the religious leaders standing on the periphery. They took a step back when He approached.

---

[68] Luke 7:24-28
[69] Luke 7:29-30

Yeshua did not speak to them. He only looked at them with intensity in His eyes that obviously penetrated their souls. Magda could see them shifting their weight, uncomfortable.

Finally, one of them was brave enough to break the silence. "By what authority do You do these things? Who gave You this authority?"

Yeshua answered them, "I also will ask you one question, which if you tell Me, I likewise will tell you by what authority I do these things. The baptism of John, where was it from — from heaven or from men?"[70]

Magda heard their thoughts as they reasoned among themselves. *"If we say, 'From heaven,' He will ask us, 'Why then did you not believe him?' But if we say, 'From men,' we fear the multitude, for all hold John as a prophet."*

They answered Yeshua, saying, "We don't know."[71]

Yeshua said to them, "Neither will I tell you by what authority I do these things." He turned away and faced the crowd. "But what do you think? A man had two sons, and he came to the first, and said, 'Son, go work today in my vineyard.' He answered, 'I will not,' but afterward he changed his mind, and went. He came to the second, and said the same thing. He answered, 'I go, sir,' but he didn't go. Which of the two did the will of his father?"[72] Yeshua now set His gaze on the Pharisees.

The men hesitated, their discomfort evident as they shuffled before providing an answer.

"The first." One of them spoke harshly.

Yeshua said to them, a force in His voice that Magda had not heard before, "Most certainly I tell you that the tax collectors and the prostitutes are entering into God's Kingdom before you. John came to you in the way of righteousness, and you didn't believe

---

[70] Matthew 21:23-24

[71] Matthew 21:25-27

[72] Matthew 21:27-31

him, but the tax collectors and the prostitutes believed him. When you saw it, you didn't even repent afterward, that you might believe him."[73]

Magda felt the force of the furious unspoken response the religious leaders had. Oppressive clouds darkened the spiritual atmosphere, choking the light of Magda's heart momentarily. As they departed, the darkness seemed to dissipate, yet Magda sensed its lingering presence, casting an ominous aura over the territory.

The crowd dispersed as evening came upon them. Yeshua and His followers lodged at the house where He had been invited to speak.

The group left in the morning at first light. They were in Magdala by mid-afternoon. Milcah welcomed them gladly. She prepared an extravagant meal. Magda couldn't believe her eyes when she realized that there were four additional children in the orphanage since they last visited.

"I saw Apollos," Magda told Milcah.

"You did? Is he alright?" Milcah sounded concerned. "I knew he would go sooner or later. He is of age. But, I enjoyed having him around. There was something special about that boy."

"Yes, there is. He is with John the Baptizer's disciples. They will take good care of him and teach him well. He was the last person John baptized before he was arrested." Magda's heart still ached at the news. She wondered why Yeshua wouldn't do anything to rescue him from prison.

"Apollos is a strong man. He is smart. He will learn a lot. I will pray that the Lord uses him for greater things," Milcah said.

They didn't remain long at Milcah's. Yeshua wanted to leave just as the sun was setting. Magda found it peculiar that He wanted to travel at such a late hour, with the darkness already settling in. Peter made the boat ready so they could sail across the

---

[73] Matthew 21:31-32

Sea of Galilee.

Magda stood in awe as she watched the light slowly descend below the horizon, painting the sky with vibrant hues. Pink, purple, and golden hues painted the sky and reflected off the water. Before darkness took over, there was a final burst of brilliant light that illuminated everything.

Yeshua had fallen asleep in the front of the boat. A big windstorm arose, and the waves beat into the boat, so much that the boat filled with water. Magda was as afraid as the other disciples. They feared for their lives.

Yeshua remained asleep on a cushion, completely at peace in the rocking boat. The disciples woke Him up.

John and Peter, frantic, told Him, "Teacher, don't You care that we are dying?"[74]

Yeshua smiled as He awoke. He stood up and rebuked the wind, speaking to the sea, "Peace! Be still!" His voice sounded like thunder. The wind ceased, and there was a great calm.

Yeshua said to them, "Why are you so afraid? How is it that you have no faith?"[75]

Fear engulfed them all.

Thomas spoke up. "Who then is this, that even the wind and the sea obey Him?"[76]

Magda feared the growing power of the forces of evil to instill doubt and fear in the hearts of Yeshua's own followers more than she feared the elements which obeyed His every command.

They landed on shore within moments of the storm being stilled. They had arrived in the territory of the Gergesenes. Magda was the first to notice the two people possessed by demons coming toward them as the group exited the boat. The absence of light created an eerie atmosphere, as if the darkness had a weight

---

[74] Mark 4:37-38

[75] Mark 4:39-40

[76] Mark 4:41

of its own. The night sky was completely dark, without a single sliver of moonlight. Magda's sharp gaze immediately honed in on the demonic forms, their presence unmistakable. The sense of empowerment emboldened the creatures of Zophos. The men they possessed came out of the tombs, exceedingly fierce. People trying to make their way home before nightfall had been detained, unable to pass by them.[77]

The emissaries of Zophos cried out when they saw Yeshua. He looked at them, approaching them without fear. The demons spoke in voices so pitched that it hurt Magda's ears. "What do we have to do with You, Yeshua, Son of God? Have you come here to torment us before the time?"[78]

Though she heard the fear in them, she could also feel their increased power. A distance from where they had landed, there was a herd of pigs feasting on their meal. Magda could hear the swine even though she couldn't see them. They were merely dark shadows on the cover of night.

The demons begged Yeshua, saying, "If You cast us out, permit us to go away into the herd of pigs."[79]

With great force Yeshua commanded the demons, "Go!"[80]

They came out and went into the herd of pigs. The whole herd of pigs rushed down the cliff into the sea, and died in the water.

Magda's ears perked up at the rhythmic splashes echoing from the water. The possessed men were dazed and confused. Magda went to minister to them immediately. She gave them clean clothes, which they had in the boat, as well as some wine and bread. The disciples had made a fire to warm and give light.

The people who had been detained went away into the

---

[77] Mark 8:28
[78] Matthew 8:29
[79] Matthew 8:31
[80] Matthew 8:32

village, and told everything, including what happened to those who were possessed with demons.[81]

It wasn't long before several of the elders of the village came to Yeshua, asking Him to leave their territory.[82] Magda could tell they were frightened of Him. She didn't like the foreboding feeling that surfaced in her heart as the powers of darkness seemed to be gaining ground over the land of Yahweh's very own people.

Yeshua led them away from the area, proclaiming that their next destination was Jerusalem.

---

[81] Matthew 8:38
[82] Matthew 8:34

CHAPTER TWENTY-SEVEN

Magda fell asleep beneath the stars. The visit to Jerusalem had taxed her soul. Yeshua directly challenged the authorities. Magda had seen the demons that were somehow invited into the sacred space through the religious leaders. How they gained that ground, she had no idea. Shadows of wolves, dragons, and serpents hung over several of the Pharisees who confronted Yeshua. They had an arrogant power that frightened Magda. She wondered at the time why Yeshua was not fighting them more forcefully. Why was He not driving them out?

As Magda fell into the abyss of sleep, her mind swirled with strange thoughts—memories of the forest of Zophos. She was there, hearing the plot of the evil one, yet she was protected and unseen by their eyes.

• • •

"Do it," the evil one hissed. He appeared like a dragon in Magda's nightmare.

"Yes, Great One," the demon replied. "We are in position. He is fearful of losing power. We have gained much ground. The Baptizer will be silenced."

Magda looked up. The canopy of gray clouds shadowing the landscape of Zophos moved in formation. A giant spider appeared, spinning a web that fell over the land of Judea. Magda watched in her night vision as the demonic creature descended from the lair of Zophos into the waters of the Jordan. John the Baptizer stood in the midst of the waters, his arms outstretched, his hands lifted to the heavens in worship. Magda tried to call out to him, to warn him, but her voice was mute in this realm.

She watched in horror as the spider covered the sky, blocking John from the glimpse of heaven that was drawing him in. A serpent slithered in the water beneath John's feet. Still, the Baptizer worshiped.

Infuriated that they could not induce fear in the man, the spider spun its web around John. The serpent curled around the Baptizer's body while the spider affixed itself to John's head. In one swift motion, John's head was in the spider's fangs while his body was being dragged away by the serpent.

Magda fell to her knees in the dream. She couldn't breathe. She heard a thud like the sound of an ax. She covered her ears when the shrieks of victory assaulted her, knowing they came from the forest of Zophos.

• • •

Magda awoke suddenly, her heart racing, her forehead perspiring. She didn't know what the dream meant, but she couldn't quell the terrible feeling it left her with. She got up to walk in the darkness of the night. The shrieks of delight from the forest of Zophos still rang in her head.

They traveled relentlessly, preaching the good news of the Kingdom of Heaven. Magda wasn't sure if she was exhausted from the journey or the oppression she could feel because of the encroaching darkness. Everywhere they went, the opposition grew. Yeshua's words were thought-provoking, causing many to question their beliefs. The harder His teaching became, the more disgruntled were His listeners. Several turned back from following Him after hearing His words for themselves.

The storm of emotions Magda had weathered left her feeling utterly drained and fatigued. The crowds would gather, stretching as far as the eye could see, filling her with hope that people would embrace and follow their Messiah. Then, the clouds of deceit would roll in, casting shadows over the hearts of many so that they quickly fell away from listening.

The group was camping in the wilderness on the outskirts of Nazareth. Yeshua had been gone all night long, praying on the hillside. When He returned at dawn, the disciples were stirring awake. Magda had already started a fire.

Yeshua called His disciples even before the morning meal. A crowd had already gathered. People from all over Judea were coming to hear Him speak. Yeshua took the twelve men, Peter, Andrew, James, John, Philip, Bartholomew, Matthew, Thomas, James, Simon, Judas the son of James, and Judas Iscariot. He set them before the crowd. In the hearing of the multitude, Yeshua designated these twelve men apostles. Those who had dedicated themselves to following Him were now going to be sent out by Him.[83]

Magda couldn't help but wonder about the intention behind the assigned positions given to the men. She wondered if the men were ready. In Yeshua's eyes, she detected a newfound depth, something she had yet to see. She sensed He was distributing His power to these twelve men in a way He had not done before. Magda couldn't help but wonder why. Why now? What was changing? Did it have something to do with the power of darkness she could feel all around her?

As Yeshua stepped out onto the open plain, His voice rose

---

[83] Luke 6:14-17

above the din of the crowd. Everyone grew silent as He began to speak. There was an urgency to His message that made Magda's heart ache for something she feared but didn't understand.

Yeshua walked among the twelve apostles who were standing with Him, obviously confused as to what their new designation was going to mean.

"Blessed are you who are poor, God's Kingdom is yours. Blessed are you who hunger now, for you will be filled. Blessed are you who weep now, for you will laugh. Blessed are you when men hate you, and when they exclude and mock you, and throw out your name as evil, for the Son of Man's sake. Rejoice in that day, and leap for joy, for behold, your reward is great in heaven, for their fathers did the same thing to the prophets."[84]

The apostles shifted uneasily beneath His blessing. Magda was a bit disturbed by the words as well. The calling sounded difficult. Out of the corner of her eye, she could see some of the religious leaders on the periphery of the crowd. They were mocking His teaching because what He spoke did not align with their concept of Yahweh's blessing people. Yahweh blessed the rich and healthy. The respectable and powerful had earned Yahweh's favor in their sight. Yeshua spoke of a blessing that was completely opposite of that notion.

Yeshua set His gaze upon those standing far off. The religious leaders, now uneasy, fidgeted while He spoke.

"But woe to you who are rich! For you have received your consolation. Woe to you, you who are full now, for you will be hungry. Woe to you who laugh now, for you will mourn and weep. Woe, when men speak well of you, for their fathers did the same thing to the false prophets."[85]

Some in the crowd sneered at the religious leaders. They loved it when Yeshua put them in their place. Sensing the

---

[84] Luke 6:20-23
[85] Luke 6:24-26

growing arrogance of the crowd, Yeshua next turned toward the people.

"But I tell you who hear: love your enemies, do good to those who hate you, bless those who curse you, and pray for those who mistreat you. To him who strikes you on the cheek, offer also the other; and from him who takes away your cloak, don't withhold your coat also. Give to everyone who asks you, and don't ask him who takes away your goods to give them back again."[86]

Several in the crowd grumbled. Half of them walked away. Magda could hear their murmurings as they departed.

"This man is crazy! His teaching is too hard. What does He expect from us?"

Another said, "Surely, Yahweh is a God of justice. He would not want us to show favor to our enemies. Preposterous!"

With a thinning crowd, Yeshua continued, undeterred. "As you would like people to do to you, do exactly so to them. If you love those who love you, what credit is that to you? For even sinners love those who love them. If you do good to those who do good to you, what credit is that to you? For even sinners do the same. If you lend to those from whom you hope to receive, what credit is that to you? Even sinners lend to sinners, to receive back as much. But love your enemies, and do good, and lend, expecting nothing back; and your reward will be great, and you will be children of the Most High; for He is kind toward the unthankful and evil."[87]

Magda thought about what He said, challenged by His call to love. She knew that in her own strength, she was unable to love those who hurt her, used her, and abandoned her. Yeshua was right. It was easy to love those who loved you. Magda thought of Milcah. She also remembered that Milcah extended love to Magda when no one else would. Milcah took her in when she didn't have

---

[86] Luke 6:27-30
[87] Luke 6:31-35

to. Milcah didn't hold Magda's harmful behavior against her. Her aunt's love was unconditional, just as Yeshua's was. Forgiven of sin, redeemed from the darkness, called to live above the shadows of deceit blanketing the world, how could Magda not love those who were still lost in the dark?

Yeshua and the apostles emerged from the wide open plain. Magda helped Yeshua's mother to prepare a meal for the men. There were a few in the crowd that lingered. Several people had followed Yeshua for quite some time, adding to the provisions for the camp. Though the numbers were dwindling and always changing depending on where they were, Magda appreciated those who generously gave to them.

Magda watched silently as Yeshua sent His apostles out to the surrounding villages. He gave them authority to cast out demons, heal the sick and preach the truth.

"Go to the lost sheep of the house of Israel. As you go, preach, saying, 'The Kingdom of Heaven is at hand!' Heal the sick, cleanse the lepers, and cast out demons. Freely you received, so freely give. Don't take any gold, silver, or brass in your money belts. Take no bag for your journey, neither two coats, nor sandals, nor staff: for the laborer is worthy of his food. Into whatever city or village you enter, find out who in it is worthy, and stay there until you go on. I send you out as sheep among wolves."[88] He commissioned the men.

Magda shivered at the choice of His words, fearful for her brothers, the apostles.

After the apostles left, spreading out in groups of two and three, Yeshua turned to Magda and His mother.

"We will stay in Magdala," He informed them.

Milcah was delighted to see them again. She had taken in new children since their last visitation. In the days that Yeshua, Magda, and His mother lodged with Milcah at the orphanage, Yeshua

[88] Matthew 10:5-11, 16

delighted the children. Magda marveled at how effortlessly they flocked to Him.

After quite a few days, the apostles finally returned. Magda could see the joy and exuberance on all of their faces.

"Lord, even the demons are subject to us in Your Name!"[89] Bartholomew said.

He said to them, "I saw Satan having fallen like lightning from heaven. Behold, I give you authority to tread on serpents and scorpions, and over all the power of the enemy. Nothing will in any way hurt you. Nevertheless, don't rejoice in this, that the spirits are subject to you, but rejoice that your names are written in heaven."[90]

Yeshua rejoiced with His apostles. Magda could see the proud look on His face, filled with love for their obedience. The moment was so joyful that his lesson became somewhat secondary in importance. Yet Magda pondered it in her heart. The power of His love was not defined by conquering evil, but by beckoning those who are destined for the Kingdom of God.

Magda helped Milcah prepare a meal for everyone. The apostles were excitedly sharing everything they heard and witnessed as they preached the good news, healed the sick and cast out the forces of evil. The children were as excited as the disciples to listen to their stories.

Yeshua prayed over them before they began to eat.

"I thank You, O Father, Lord of heaven and earth, that You have hidden these things from the wise and understanding, and revealed them to little children. Yes, Father, for so it was well-pleasing in Your sight."[91]

When they finished the meal, Yeshua made an announcement to the group. "I am going into Nazareth," He said.

[89] Luke 10:17
[90] Luke 10:18-20
[91] Luke 10:21

"Nazareth? But, Lord, they tried to throw you off a cliff. They rejected you,"[92] Magda protested.

Yeshua looked at her. Taking her hand into His own, He said, "Love your enemies and do good."

Magda nodded to Him, aware that even she had trouble internalizing His teaching. "Lord, help me to take what You have said into my heart."

"Your heart is mine, Mary," He spoke over her. "Even when darkness comes, remember that."

Magda was fearful. What did He mean? What darkness awaited her?

Before she could ask Him any questions, Yeshua arose, left the table and went out to pray.

The following morning, she and the apostles packed their belongings and went with Him toward Nazareth. They were on the outskirts of the village when they intercepted a caravan. Magda's face lit up with joy when she spotted both Joanna and Susanna in the midst of the travelers. The women climbed down from the oxcart immediately upon seeing Yeshua. They ran over to them. Magda noticed the strained expressions on their faces as they came closer.

"Lord," Joanna cried. "Oh, Lord."

Joanna fell at Yeshua's feet. He placed His hand on her head. She was too distraught to speak. Magda's heart cracked with wonder at what tragedy had befallen her friend.

Susanna, tears streaming down her face, picked up the dialogue. "John the Baptizer has been killed."

Magda gasped in horror! She almost fell down at the news, but Peter caught her.

"What happened?" Peter asked.

Yeshua helped Joanna to her feet. There was deep compassion in His eyes, but He remained silent.

---

[92] Luke 4:28-30

"Herod was entertaining a lot of men," Joanna explained. "I was serving for Herod's birthday party. All the prominent people were there. They were drunk on wine quickly. It was getting out of hand. Herod wanted Herodias's daughter to dance for them. The men wanted entertainment."

Joanna took a deep breath. Her emotions were still fresh, leaving Magda to determine that the party must have happened recently. She wondered if it was the same evening she had the night vision.

"After Herodias's daughter danced, Herod promised her anything she wanted." Joanna's tears began to fall again. "I was just taking a platter to the main table when the girl grabbed it out of my hand. She told Herod she wanted John the Baptizer's head on the platter."[93]

Joanna sobbed uncontrollably. Yeshua comforted her, pulling her into His embrace. Still, He said nothing.

Joanna stepped back. "The King did it. He beheaded John in the prison. John's head was brought on the platter."[94]

Magda knew her friend's words were true. She recalled the cackles of delight from the evil forest which she had heard that night. Why was darkness gaining such victories? Why was Yeshua silent on the matter?

The heaviness of grief settled upon the apostles, leaving them bewildered as they struggled to understand why these events were happening. Magda remembered the perplexing blessing Yeshua had just spoken over the men. Was this the beginning of the hard way of love?

Before anyone dared ask Yeshua any questions, Yeshua spoke into the heaviness of the void of understanding surrounding His followers.

He said to them, "Most certainly I tell you, there are some

---

[93] Matthew 14:8
[94] Matthew 14:9-11

standing here who will in no way taste death until they see God's Kingdom come with power."[95]

What it meant, they had no idea, but it brought them comfort, nonetheless.

At that moment, a young man who had been traveling with the caravan that brought Joanna and Susanna came running toward them. Magda immediately recognized the powerful demon driving the man. Behind him, she saw a black hue with bat-like wings. The man was running straight at her, not slowing his pace.

Yeshua stepped in front of her, shielding her from the attack. The man got close, but stopped as if slammed into some invisible force. Magda wrinkled her nose as she caught a whiff of the man's overpowering stench. Foam dripped from his mouth, creating a white, frothy mess. His eyes were black as obsidian — empty and void.

"What is your name?" Yeshua held up His hand to the man's chest.

"What have you to do with me, Son of the Most High? Your time has not yet come," the demon hissed through the voice of the man.

"Your name!" Yeshua commanded in a forceful tone of voice.

"Belial," the demon answered. "You think your apostles can contend with our rulers? You think your disciples are a match for our captains?"

"Silence." Yeshua's eyes burned with fire.

"Your forces are weak, Son of God," Belial roared.

"Be gone, Belial. Leave this man alone. You have no authority here," Yeshua said.

The demon pulled itself away from the man like burned skin falling off a victim of fire. The man writhed in pain, collapsing to the ground. Magda saw the look in the demon's eyes as it set its

---

[95] Mark 9:1

sights on her for a moment. Magda felt a sharp pang inside her soul when she saw the familiar gaze he directed towards her, as if an old wound had been freshly opened.

Yeshua spoke forlornly. "The hour of darkness is coming when no one will be able to work. But, take heart, while I am in the world, I am the light of the world."[96]

With the demon gone, the man finally came to himself. Magda helped him up off the ground. His eyes were clear, blue like the sky.

"Come, we can help you," she said.

"What is your name?" Yeshua asked the man.

"I am Zadok," the man replied. "Son of Pascal, the shepherd."

"Pascal?" Magda exclaimed. "He was your father?"

"You knew him?" the young man asked.

"He was my good friend," Magda said, sorrow in her voice.

"Where is he?" Zadok inquired.

Magda swallowed hard. "I'm sorry, Zadok. Your father died protecting me."

Zadok took a step back from Magda. His grief was immediate. "This is too much," Zadok said.

"Come, eat something. We have clothes for you, too. You can get cleaned up." Magda led the man towards the cart.

Just as the group settled, a sudden commotion arose as a stream of people poured out from Nazareth, shattering the tranquility. It looked like a group of elders.

Magda stopped with Zadok. They both turned around to look at the group of men coming toward them. Peter stepped between the approaching group and Yeshua.

"We have no business with You," one of the elders shouted. "You blaspheme the Lord."

"He speaks the Word of God," Peter proclaimed.

"On whose authority?" another elder questioned.

---

[96] John 9:4-5

"On His authority," John answered confidently.

"That is blasphemy," the group of elders proclaimed.

With stones tightly clenched in their hands, the elders of Nazareth unleashed their judgment through a relentless barrage. The apostles shielded Yeshua and the others as they made their way out of the region.

When they finally put enough distance between themselves and Nazareth, the group found a quiet spot to sit and rest. Magda set to work preparing food for the others. She also gave a clean set of clothes to Zadok. The young man went down to a nearby stream to wash and get cleansed.

The recent events took a heavy toll on the travelers. Even Yeshua was silent. The news of John the Baptizer's death, the encounter with the demon, and the rejection from Nazareth all weighed heavily on their minds and emotions.

Even in their own company, the newly appointed apostles remained hushed, their faces etched with seriousness. The rest of the crowd quickly dispersed when the elders showered down their rocks of condemnation. People were becoming wary of their association with Yeshua. Magda felt the weight of the increasing power of darkness.

After the meal, Yeshua took Peter, John, and James and departed for the mountain. No one felt like asking Him where He was going or when He would be back. They just had to trust in His mission, even if they failed to understand it.

Chapter Twenty-Eight

Magda was sitting down with Zadok as the group of weary travelers took the evening meal together. Yeshua, John, Peter, and James had been gone for quite a while. No one knew when they would return. Bartholomew came over to where Magda and Pascal's son were sitting.

"This is for you," he said, handing Magda a staff.

She recognized it immediately. "Pascal's staff! Where did you get it?" she asked Bartholomew.

"That night in Nain. Yeshua sent me to retrieve it after you entered Simon's house. He knew exactly where it was. We have kept it with us ever since," Bartholomew explained. "Before He went up the mountain, He told me it was time to give this to you—that you would know what to do with it."

"Thank you," Magda said, standing and hugging Bartholomew. Magda ran her hands up and down the acacia wood staff. "This means a lot to me."

With a nod, Bartholomew resumed his place at the fire, continuing his meal alongside Andrew and Simon.

"You knew my father well?" Zadok asked her.

"He would want you to have this, Zadok," Magda said, handing the young man his father's staff.

"I doubt that," Zadok replied, bitterness in his voice.

"Why?" Magda inquired, puzzled by the young man's response.

"I think my father was ashamed of me," Zadok said, hanging his head while rubbing the back of his hand along his brow. "He left my mother and I when I was really young. He never married my mother. I was not his legitimate son."

Magda was silent for a moment. Pascal carried a lot of regrets. She didn't think having a son was one of them. Though, she did wonder why he never told her about him.

"I don't think that your father was ashamed of you, Zadok. I think he was ashamed of himself," Magda told the young man whose soulful eyes reminded her of Pascal. "What do you know about him?"

"I know that he got in trouble for stealing. I know that he lost everything. I know that he didn't bother to come back for us."

With a pinched expression, Zadok did a poor job of hiding his bitterness. He firmed his lips, neither agreeing or disagreeing with Magda.

Once the silence settled and Zadok calmed down, he spoke again. "After he left, I was so lost. My mother was heartbroken. She loved him very much. She wasn't able to care for me in her grief."

Magda placed a hand on Zadok's shoulder, surprised at how much she could relate to the young man's story. She waited for him to continue.

"I was sold into servitude. That's when the voices started coming. That's when I had trouble keeping reality separated from the nightmares." Zadok trembled, keeping his eyes on the dancing flames. "I had done well in service to a prominent man. I kept his sheep, just like my father had done. Although my father lost his flocks, I gained everything back."

"Do you know why your father lost his flocks?" Magda asked him, treading carefully on the ground that opened up her own reservoir of grief.

"No, I assumed he sold them for money," Zadok said, a harsh edge to his voice.

"No, Zadok. Everything was taken from Pascal because he knew that the priests were exchanging the blemished lambs for the perfect lambs. They were sacrificing the wrong lambs according to the Law. When your father spoke out against them, they heaved fines on him that he couldn't pay."

The memory of her friend, her shepherd, hit Magda like a wave of grief, leaving her feeling overwhelmed. He should be the one having this conversation with his son. As she locked eyes with Zadok, she couldn't help but notice the familiar twinkle that reminded her of Pascal.

"I didn't know that," Zadok admitted.

"My guess is that your father didn't come back because he didn't want the troubles he was having to fall on you and your mother," Magda said. "He told me a story once about stealing a prominent man's cloak. The man was in charge of the Temple treasury. Pascal noticed a paralyzed man begging outside the Sheep Gate when he went to take the sheep to the Temple. That was the day that your father found out about the priests taking the unblemished lambs from the people and using the blemished lambs for the sacrifice. He was so infuriated that he went to talk to the man, Simon, fearing he couldn't trust the priests."

"This doesn't sound like a good story," Zadok remarked with the same dry humor his father had.

Magda smiled to herself in remembrance of the night on their journey when Pascal shared his story. They had just run into Simon, the Pharisee, after Yeshua raised the widow's son from death. Pascal recognized him immediately, but the man had been too focused on Magda and the frenzied crowd to recognize Pascal.

"Unfortunately, the man, Simon, was more corrupt than the

priests. He was the one who issued heavy fines on your father and issued a demand for his arrest. Your father escaped the Temple guards. On the way out, he grabbed one of Simon's ornate cloaks. As he ran out of the Sheep Gate at twilight, fleeing from the guards, he tossed the cloak to the paralyzed man."

Magda paused, sharing in Zadok's subdued amusement.

"As a shepherd, Pascal knew how cold the nights got. He said he was glad to give the helpless man something to keep warm. He knew his intentions were good, but stealing was still the wrong thing to do. It made him just like the men he was condemning." Magda felt another wave of sorrow hit her as she thought about Pascal. In their short time together, he had cared for her the way she always wanted her father to.

"Didn't they deserve it after what they did to him?" Zadok asked, indignant. "They didn't just steal my father's livelihood. They stole him from his family."

"Yes, they are in the wrong, Zadok. But your father knew that living a life of forgiveness was more powerful than living a life of seeking revenge," Magda explained. "He received the forgiveness he was looking for when he remained with John the Baptizer at the River Jordan. I think, at first he went there to hide, but ultimately, he found his purpose and meaning in life."

A melancholic silence settled comfortably between them, giving space for reflection. That space had a cleansing effect, washing away any emotions that could have turned bitter.

"I wish I could have seen him again," Zadok said. "I wish I could say I'm sorry. I wish that the demon hadn't stolen so much of my own life."

"Your father was on his way to you when he was struck down, Zadok. He was going to come home. He was going to try to find you and your mother again," Magda said, putting a hand on his knee. "He died protecting me. He told me that he was my shepherd and that he fulfilled his mission to bring me to Yeshua. He was not afraid when he died."

Magda's tears came from a place deep within her heart.

Zadok hugged her. "Thank you for telling me. Somehow, being with you makes me feel closer to him."

"What happened to your mother?" Magda asked.

"She died a few years ago," Zadok replied. "I wasn't there for her. I had lost my mind to the demon by that time. Nothing mattered to me. I have the scars to prove it."

Magda's eyes widened as she took in Zadok's arms, which were marked with numerous scratches. "Fortunately, I left my flocks in the care of my friend, Ithai, before I completely lost myself. At least I didn't hurt them. I did care for my sheep."

"I have an ointment for that," Magda said, looking at Zadok's scarred flesh. "It was your father's very own recipe. He used it on his sheep when they were hurt."

Getting up to leave, Magda found her jar of ointment. Miraculously, it was still full even though she had used it on Yeshua's feet all those months ago.

"You know," Zadok said while Magda rubbed the ointment on his arms, "I was so lost when I felt abandoned by my father. I couldn't understand why he left us, why he didn't fight for us. Even though I was young, I remembered how strong and at peace I felt when he was with us. Without him, I didn't know who I was anymore."

Magda listened intently to the young man. With each stroke of the ointment, his scars faded away, leaving behind a renewed sense of hope. What had been defiled could be made new again. Maybe the powers of darkness wouldn't win. Magda was in awe of the miracle but didn't want to interrupt Zadok's story.

"I suppose that is why I was prey to the darkness. I didn't know who I was anymore without my father. I needed him around and he wasn't there. Now, I have to live without him and I don't know how to do that. I think I had hoped that one day I would find him again," Zadok said.

"But he is with you, Zadok. He is a part of you. I hear your father in your voice. I see him in your eyes. You are his representative in this world. I know that he would be proud," Magda assured Zadok.

The young man smiled at her. Looking down at his scars, seeing his clear flesh, Zadok gasped.

"How did you do that?" he asked, astonished. "The scars are gone! I have had them for years."

"It is a miracle, Zadok. It is a gift from Yahweh. You have been made free. Now, figure out what mission you have been sent on. Serve the Lord with all your heart. Remain in the light," Magda instructed him.

"I don't know how," Zadok said.

Magda remembered her confusion after first being set free from the forces of evil.

"You will," she said to Zadok. "Don't be afraid. You will."

Magda and Zadok heard a strange commotion coming from behind them. Getting up, Magda saw the apostles, Bartholomew, and Thomas arguing with some Pharisees. She went closer to see what was going on.

A man had brought his son to them.

"You say you are from God," one of the scribes remarked to Thomas. "Yet, you cannot drive out demons!"

"Is it because you are of the house of Satan?" A Pharisee spat on the ground.

"We are not of Satan!" Bartholomew argued back.

"Our teacher speaks the truth against your lies," Thomas said heatedly.

Magda watched as the grayish hue hovering around the boy took on the form of a hairy wolf with red eyes. Writhing in his father's arms, the boy's fear became palpable. The wolf snatched him hard, pulling the boy to the ground. The boy shrieked in pain as the wolf sunk its teeth into the boy's arm, thrashing his small body all around. It dragged him toward the open fire, but Magda stepped between it and the fire.

"Stop arguing," she yelled at the apostles and Pharisees.

In that moment, Yeshua appeared with John, Peter, and James. He looked different to Magda—more powerful for some reason. Light emanated from Him in ways she had not seen before.

The father of the boy addressed Yeshua. "Teacher, I brought to You my son, who has a mute spirit; and wherever it seizes him, it throws him down, and he foams at the mouth, and grinds his teeth, and wastes away. I asked Your disciples to cast it out, and they weren't able."[97]

Looking around Him, Yeshua said, "Unbelieving generation, how long shall I be with you? How long shall I bear with you? Bring the boy to me."[98]

Bartholomew and Thomas brought the man's son to Yeshua. When the demonic wolf came near to His presence, it convulsed the boy again, attacking furiously. The boy fell on the ground, wallowing and foaming at the mouth.[99] Magda was distraught by the display that only her eyes could see.

Yeshua asked the boy's father, "How long has it been since this has come to him?"

The man replied, "From childhood. Often it has cast him both into the fire and into the water to destroy him. But if You can do anything, have compassion on us, and help us."[100]

Yeshua looked at the man, sympathy in His eyes. "If you can believe...If..." Yeshua paused, placing a hand on the father's shoulder, "all things are possible to him who believes."

Overcome with emotion, the boy's father fell to his knees, weeping, "I believe. Help my unbelief!"[101]

Magda was moved by the father's powerful display of

---

[97] Mark 9:17-18
[98] Mark 9:19
[99] Mark 9:20
[100] Mark 9:21-22
[101] Mark 9:23-24

humility. Everyone in the crowd was silent, watching what Yeshua would do next. Magda witnessed the demonic wolf-spirit release the boy from its mouth at the power of the father's confession. It backed up, as if looking for cover.

Yeshua approached the demon. While He laid hands on the boy, His gaze remained fixed on the piercing eyes of the wolf. His rebuke was powerful and authoritative.

"You mute and deaf spirit, I command you, come out of him, and never enter him again!"[102]

The wolf made one more pass at the boy causing him to cry out and convulse. Yeshua lifted His hand in a quick motion that sent the beast back to Zophos. The boy was as still as a corpse. His breathing was shallow.[103]

The Pharisee standing nearby proclaimed with a note of triumph in his voice, "He is dead."

Yeshua stared silently at the Pharisee before taking the boy by the hand, and raising him up.[104]

"What is his name?" Yeshua asked the father of the boy, giving him back his son.

"Sylvanus," the father replied.

Yeshua knelt down so that He was face to face with the boy.

"Silas, you will have work to do. Listen to your Father. Heed His voice," Yeshua told the child.

With clear eyes and a beautiful smile, Silas nodded his understanding to Yeshua.

The Pharisees and religious leaders turned to walk away. Magda couldn't help but notice that the prominent religious men cast shadows on the ground that resembled wolves.

The group traveled on early the next morning, making their way to Capernaum.

---

[102] Mark 9:25
[103] Mark 9:26
[104] Mark 9:27

"You were gone a long time on the mountain," Magda inquired of James as they were walking along behind the cart of goods they took with them.

"It was quite an experience," James admitted.

"Yeshua seems different," Magda said to him. "Did something happen on the mountain?"

James looked at her, hesitant. "I'm not sure," he began.

Discerning James's thoughts, Magda said to him, "You saw Yeshua as He really is, didn't you?"

A look of astonishment flickered across the disciple's face. "How did you know?"

"I've seen it, too, James. A long time ago. When He rescued me from the darkness," Magda informed the disciple.

James felt free to proceed with telling her what he saw. "His clothing became glistening, exceedingly white, like snow. Elijah and Moses appeared, talking with Yeshua. It was utterly overwhelming. I'm not sure what it means,"[105] James said to her.

"You will in time, James. I'm sure of that," Magda said.

They were just outside of Capernaum when the group stopped abruptly. A gathering of shepherds were taking their flocks to higher pastures, blocking the road they were traveling on. Magda moved up ahead so she could see what was going on. Zadok spotted her and followed her toward the front of the crowd.

Watching the multitude of sheep, Yeshua reached out for Zadok's staff. Leaning on it, He began to teach them. A deep sadness colored Yeshua's eyes and voice.

"I am the Good Shepherd. The Good Shepherd lays down His life for the sheep. He who is a hired hand, and not a shepherd, who doesn't own the sheep, sees the wolf coming, leaves the sheep, and flees. The wolf snatches the sheep, and scatters them. The hired hand flees because he is a hired hand, and doesn't care

---

[105] Mark 9:3-4

for the sheep. I am the Good Shepherd." Yeshua began walking among them, touching each person. The bleating of sheep as they crossed the road lingered on the air.

He continued. "I know My own, and I'm known by My own; even as the Father knows Me, and I know the Father." He looked intently at Magda, touching her on the arm. "I lay down My life for the sheep." He paused before moving on to Peter. "I have other sheep, which are not of this fold. I must bring them also, and they will hear My voice. They will become one flock with one shepherd. Therefore, the Father loves Me, because I lay down My life, that I may take it up again. No one takes it away from Me, but I lay it down by Myself. I have power to lay it down, and I have power to take it up again. I received this commandment from My Father."[106]

His teaching left everyone silently bewildered. The moment was heavy with holiness. Frustration was evident on his face as he struggled to convey the significance of what he was saying to them. A voice broke the power of the silent contemplation.

"Zadok? Zadok, son of Pascal, is that you?" A young shepherd came over toward them.

Zadok pushed out of the group, his eyes and ears straining to recognize the voice and face of the one coming toward him.

"Ithai? Is that you?"

The two young men embraced. "I thought something terrible happened to you," Ithai exclaimed. "I am glad to see that you are well."

Zadok turned toward Yeshua and His followers. "This is Ithai, my brother. We grew up together, that is, when I served his father."

"I have kept Zadok's sheep, awaiting his return," Ithai said.

"You did?" Zadok questioned, looking back toward the herd. "You did! I recognize them."

---

[106] John 10:11-18

Zadok rushed toward the herd that was now making their crossing. Using his shepherd's voice, he called out to his sheep. One by one, Magda looked on as the sheep separated themselves from the others, moving toward the voice of the shepherd they hadn't seen in years.

"The sheep never forget the voice of their own shepherd," Ithai remarked, smiling.

"You speak correctly," Yeshua said to Ithai. "You have done well."

Magda could see the reverence on Ithai's face as he bowed before Yeshua without saying a word in reply. She went over to Zadok, who reveled in his reunion with his sheep. The wooly creatures appeared delighted to see him again.

Zadok looked up at Magda. "I didn't realize how much I missed them," Zadok said.

Watching Zadok with his sheep, Magda realized how hard it must have been for Pascal to be torn away from his own sheep. There was deep love and affection in the shepherd's eyes as he gazed upon his flock.

"Looks like you will be staying with them," Magda remarked.

"I will," Zadok said to her. "But I am so grateful for everything. Yeshua spoke to me while we were walking. He taught me a lot in such a short time. I will remain in the light, fulfilling my calling as a shepherd, to the glory of Yahweh."

"Well, you might need this," Magda said, reaching into her satchel. She handed him the jar of ointment which his own father had made.

"My father gave it to you," Zadok said, not taking it from her hands as the sheep puddled around his ankles.

"He would want you to have it. Heal his sheep. Take good care of them, Zadok. Make your father proud." Magda released the ointment into Zadok's hands.

"I will, Magda. I will." Zadok hugged her goodbye.

Yeshua came over and handed Zadok his father's staff. "With

My authority, I send you out as a shepherd, Zadok son of Pascal. Protect My flock from the wolves."

"Yes, my Lord," Zadok bowed before Yeshua, staff in hand, flock separated unto himself.

CHAPTER TWENTY-NINE

Magda was relieved when they finally arrived in Capernaum. Yeshua had been graciously invited to stay with a warm and welcoming local family. Magda was pleased that they would not have to sleep outside for the duration of their stay in Capernaum.

The family that was hosting them were actually Peter's relatives. Newly married and full of anticipation, the young couple eagerly awaited the teachings of the One they believed was their promised Messiah.

As she lay down that first evening on a comfortable sleeping mat, washed and cleaned with a fresh tunic given to her by the new bride, Magda felt the ache of both heart and body. Her heart ached because of the loss of friends such as John the Baptizer and Pascal. Her body ached because of the weariness from traveling such an arduous journey.

Magda vividly remembered the crackling sound of the evening fire they had gathered around that night. Yeshua looked at her, aware that she was exhausted. She loved the way He understood her even when she said nothing.

He spoke to them all with such powerful love in His voice. "Come to Me, all you who labor and are heavily burdened, and I will give you rest. Take My yoke upon you and learn from Me, for I am gentle and humble in heart; and you will find rest for your souls. For My yoke is easy, and My burden is light."[107]

Even now, the remembrance of those words brought comfort to her aches. Magda closed her eyes, letting the remembrance of His voice play like a sweet lullaby on her mind. Letting go of her worries, Magda quickly slipped into a dream state...

She felt herself wandering in a darkness so thick that she could hardly breathe. As she walked, she felt a heavy burden pulling at her, slowing her down. She looked to see herself shackled, hindered by the weight of heavy chains upon her body. The sound of heavy panting filled the air as she sprinted, feeling the adrenaline pumping through her veins. Something chased her.

Magda tried to run, but she couldn't. When she turned to see what was coming after her, she felt herself being dragged by some unseen force. It bound her to a stake by her shackles.

She stood there, helpless to defend herself. Her eyes adjusted to the dark. She strained her eyes and could make out the silhouettes of the wolves, their sharp fangs visible even from a distance. Frightened, Magda tried to scream out, but her voice was mute.

When she heard the bleating of a lamb, it startled her. Magda turned her head toward the sound. Standing next to her was a lamb so pure and pristine, it seemed to radiate an ethereal glow. Its wool gleamed white like light. Its eyes were the deep color of the sky at twilight.

The lamb stood there, bleating at her, unmoving as the wolves fast approached. Magda was now more horrified over the fate of the lamb than her own fate. She struggled to break her shackles, but was powerless to do so. She wanted so badly to free

---

[107] Matthew 11:28-30

the innocent lamb.

The wolves were so close that she could hear the sound of paws trampling the ground. She saw the green and red glow of their eyes. The stench of their foul breath wafted towards her, making her cringe. Just as the wolves were about to pounce, their attention was diverted by the presence of the small, vulnerable lamb. The lamb stood silent as the wolves descended upon it.

Magda watched in horror as one wolf after another scratched the flesh off the lamb. The lamb fell on its side, silent and submissive. The wool that once adorned its body was now torn to shreds, fluttering in the air like scattered fragments.

The wolves ruthlessly tore apart the lamb's body, greedily feasting on its blood, and relentlessly suffocating it until its final breath. When they were finished, the lamb's carcass hardly resembled a lamb at all.

Satisfied, the wolves moved on, triumphant in their destruction. Magda's shackles fell off, the chains dropped to her feet, and she was freed from the stake that kept her bound. She rushed to the bloodied remnant of the innocent lamb. The rags she wore quickly absorbed the blood, leaving dark stains. There was no life left in the creature.

Magda sobbed uncontrollably, knowing that the wolves had been coming for her, knowing that the lamb died in her place. She stood, her rags soaked in his blood, and cried out to heaven for mercy. She heard the voice of John the Baptizer. "The Lamb of God who takes away the sin of the world!"

Magda bolted upright in her sleeping area. Her heart pounded in her chest, and beads of sweat formed on her forehead once more. Another bad dream! What was happening in the night that she was experiencing such strange visions? Perhaps it was the distant howling of wolves that set her imagination ablaze.

Magda shared none of her night visions with the others. She feared that it was a sign that she was being pulled back into the shadows, back into the forest of Zophos. Yeshua had told her not to be afraid, but recent events, the current atmosphere swirling around them, made her more afraid than she had been in a long time.

The fishing village of Capernaum, with its narrow streets and bustling markets, was filled with a pungent smell that intensified in the humid air. Yeshua had compelled them to go into the center of the village early, as if He was keeping an appointment.

"There is much work to be done today," He said to Magda as she arose that morning.

As usual, He wasn't wrong. Though Magda was still feeling a little worn from the dream of the night before, her spirits were lifted when she saw a familiar face from Bethany. Magda heard Mary call out to John and turned around. When John informed Yeshua, the entire group went toward Mary and the people she had traveled with. Magda could hardly believe that the young woman she thought of as a sister was there in Capernaum.

"Shalom," Yeshua greeted as He walked up to the young man escorting Mary.

"Shalom," the man replied, reservedly.

"This is my friend, Azrael and his wife, Hannah," Mary introduced them.

Yeshua stared at Azrael for a long time, obviously making the young man uncomfortable. Azrael's cheeks turned pink and his brow began to sweat, but he didn't break Yeshua's stare. Magda sensed the oppressive hold hindering the poor man. She could see a deep sorrow in his wife's eyes as well. Her heart broke for them.

Finally, Yeshua ended the excruciating silence. "We will be traveling to Bethany. You are welcome to come with us once your business is completed here."

"Uhhh, thank you, but we have other arrangements." Azrael stammered. Magda noted the defensiveness in his tone.

"I'd like to go, please," Mary spoke up for herself. "Yeshua is a very old family friend. He is dear to Lazarus as well. I know my brother would approve." Mary addressed Azrael with a determination that Magda admired.

"Yes, fine," Azrael said, obviously eager to get out of their presence. "I will send a messenger informing Lazarus. When do you expect to return to Bethany?" He addressed the question to Mary instead of Yeshua.

"We will be there in a few weeks," Yeshua answered, turning aside. "I'm glad you've joined us, Mary. There is much to see."

With that, Azrael hastily grabbed his wife, Hannah, and abruptly departed.

Magda went over to Mary, standing there with her traveling satchel and hugged her. Magda could tell from the wide-eyed expression on Mary's face that she was in awe of the large group accompanying Yeshua. Though Magda had become accustomed to it, she couldn't help but acknowledge how surprising it would be to someone unfamiliar with traveling alongside Him. It might even be somewhat intimidating.

"The group isn't always this large, Mary. They are only here with us in Capernaum. Once we get back on the open road, most of them will return to their homes. I'm so glad you are with us." Magda linked arms with Mary.

With her new friend by her side, Magda felt a renewed sense of excitement for their upcoming travels. Seeing things through Mary's fresh eyes brought delight to Magda's heart.

Mary nodded. "I need to see a merchant here who is selling threads and linen. Do you know where the market is?"

"I know exactly where to take you. Let me see if John can escort us." Magda went to find the disciple.

Just as she was about to explain the situation to John, a sudden commotion grabbed everyone's focus. A shriek in the distance stopped the hustle of the crowd. People were swarming the street, but they quickly cleared a path on either side as if something was about to move through.

A figure, draped in tattered rags, moved with a curious,

laborious shuffle down the center of the street. Magda heard its cries. The sound, pitiful as it was, wrenched her heart.

"Unclean, unclean," came the raspy voice.

The stench of death crashed like a wave in the poor creature's wake. Magda instinctively put her hand over her mouth and nose like everyone else. She still wasn't used to being close to those with leprosy.

Magda couldn't tell if it was a man or a woman as the figure passed by her. The street had emptied because every person gave the creature a wide berth to move through. Most had their backs to the leper. All, except one person.

Magda watched as Yeshua stood His ground right in the middle of the road. Even the disciples had moved to the side. Yeshua was unaffected by the pungent odor. His eyes looked on the leper with love, while everyone else looked away. The leper dragged itself before Him. Magda heard the raspy voice from where she stood.

"Lord, if You want to, You can make me clean."

Yeshua stretched out His hand, touched the creature and said, "I want to. Be made clean."[108]

Magda watched as the rotted skin reformed itself beneath Yeshua's touch. The putrid smell of decay disappeared as the leper's body underwent a remarkable transformation, leaving behind a scent of newfound vitality. Falling at Yeshua's feet, the man worshipped Him with heartfelt gratitude. The momentary silence that followed left the crowd in a state of astonishment before they burst into complaints. Magda could hear the hiss of whispers floating in the air.

Each person returned to what they were doing, unmoved by the miracle. With a strong sense of purpose, the healed man bowed repeatedly, his gestures filled with enthusiasm.

With his leprosy cleansed, the man was restored to the image-

[108] Matthew 8:2-3

bearing potential that had been stolen from him.

Yeshua took the man aside to speak with him privately. "See that you tell nobody; but go, show yourself to the priest, and offer the gift that Moses commanded, as a testimony to them."[109]

Magda and John retraced their steps, making their way back to where Mary anxiously awaited their return. They were all gratefully astonished at what they had just witnessed. Magda set her eyes on Yeshua as He stood at a distance, giving further instruction to the newly reformed man. He radiated life and love.

The three of them stood silent for a moment, trying to absorb the holiness in the atmosphere for just a little longer, but the commotion of the crowd infringed on the sacred space.

Sighing, John spoke first. "I know where you need to go," John whispered, still unwilling to break the holiness of witnessing a miracle.

John continued, "I can take you there. I've told Peter where we are going. We can join them later. I think the man you are seeking is a distance from the market area. I have heard that the man does not own an open booth. Instead, he sells directly from his dwelling."

With that, the three of them left the area where travelers congregated as they either joined or left passing caravans. Mary and Magda let John guide them. Magda appreciated traveling with these men, now designated apostles, who knew how to navigate the land much better than she did.

Shadows concealed the small dwelling tucked away in a secluded section of Capernaum. Magda was taken aback by how effortlessly John managed to find it. The place looked like it had been abandoned for years, with broken windows and overgrown weeds.

They knocked on a door to a mortar hut in the middle of a reed field. The door creaked open, revealing a hunched, elderly

---

[109] Matthew 8:3-4

man.

"Yes?" he croaked loudly.

"We're here to buy some of your goods. Are you a seller of threads and fine linen?" John asked loudly, assuming the man couldn't hear by the way he had yelled when he answered the door.

"Go around back. The materials are there." The man slammed the door.

The three went around to the back, sinking into the muddy surroundings. Magda didn't like the feeling of oozing mud in between her exposed toes. But, the more she tried to step carefully, the more she sunk in the wet soil. There was a small booth in back where wooden containers were stacked. The man appeared from the back door of the hut.

"What are you looking for?" the old man barked.

"I heard you have purple threads and cloths. We would also like blue and other colors if you have it." Mary spoke up with confidence so the man could hear her.

As Magda looked at the short man, she couldn't help but notice his cloudy eyes, as if they were veiled by a thin layer of mist. Curiosity filled her mind as she pondered the extent of his visual perception. Perhaps the man's lack of eyesight was why the area around his hut was so unkempt.

"I have all colors. The finest quality. How much do you want?" The man sounded irritated by their presence, rushing to get rid of them.

Mary bargained with the man. Magda was impressed with the young woman's bargaining skills, particularly her ability to negotiate with a man. Mary held her ground and got the price she wanted. Then, she finalized the details with the man, ensuring that everything would be sent to Bethany with the next caravan.

While Mary was finishing up her business, John and Magda went back around the front. They had heard voices that sounded familiar. Rounding the corner, they were met with the unexpected sight of Yeshua and a handful of companions.

"Where is Mary?" He asked them.

"Come see, Lord," John answered.

Magda and John led Him around the back.

"Is your business concluded?" Yeshua asked Mary.

"Yes, Lord," Mary said, surprised to see Him.

With a focused stare, Yeshua observed the man meticulously preparing Mary's order.

"Ira," He said with power that practically knocked everyone over.

Magda marveled at how Yeshua already knew the man's name because the man had not even introduced himself to them. Turning around, the man named Ira accidentally released his grip on the box, causing it to slip from his hands and hit the ground.

Yeshua walked over to him. The man was suddenly pushed back by an unseen force, causing him to stumble and fall onto one of the boxes. Ira said nothing.

Magda remained rooted to her spot in the mud. The other followers rounded the corner but grew silent as the power of the moment overwhelmed them. Everyone was still.

"Do you want to be made well?" Yeshua asked Ira.

Ira started to cry. "Yes, Lord."

Yeshua touched the man's eyes with His thumbs and then placed His palms over Ira's ears. The silence was deafening. Even the birds ceased their chatter. When Yeshua stepped back, the man stood up straight. His eyes were clear.

"Shalom, my son," Yeshua said, smiling.

"I can hear again," Ira whispered with gratitude through the tears spilling from his clear eyes.

Magda couldn't help but feel invigorated by the contagious joy radiating from the man. With each joyful stride, Ira's muddy embrace marked the disciples, leaving them with a messy reminder of his affection.

Magda soaked up the power of love manifested in the healing

of the blind and deaf. Completely absorbed in heaven's happiness, Magda didn't notice the mud staining her feet as she walked.

The group began the long walk back toward the center of Capernaum after departing Ira's dwelling. The air buzzed with animated conversations as everyone enthusiastically recounted the incredible sights they had witnessed throughout the day.

"I hope I never get used to it," John said. "The miracles. Did you see the way the crowd just acted like nothing happened with the leper? They didn't even acknowledge the cleansed man. They still treated him as if he was unclean."

"People have a hard time recognizing the work of Yahweh in another person," Magda commented sadly.

In the years that she had been following Him, Magda had only grown more aware of the blindness covering people who thought they could see. She knew how easy it was to get used to seeing in the dark, becoming more afraid of the light.

The sound of thundering hooves made them all turn around. A Roman Centurion, accompanied by a small group of men, was rapidly closing in on them. Fear gripped Magda, making her tremble. Were the Romans after Yeshua too?

Yeshua's preaching never failed to ruffle the feathers of the authorities. Magda wondered if the religious leaders had turned Him over to the Romans for some imaginary crime. Magda heard Yeshua's voice in her heart. *Don't be afraid.*

Magda watched Yeshua turn and walk toward the Centurion. The Roman dismounted his horse. Magda couldn't help but notice his strikingly handsome appearance. Then she recognized him. He was the same man who had helped her and Pascal on the road. The Roman's brow was furrowed, deep lines etched across his forehead. He looked extremely upset.

"My name is Abner." There was no hostility in the Roman Centurion's voice.

"Shalom, Abner. What do you want Me to do for you?" Yeshua asked him.

"Lord, my servant lies in the house paralyzed, grievously tormented."

Yeshua said to him, "I will come and heal him."

The Centurion answered, "Lord, I'm not worthy for You to come under my roof. Just say the word, and my servant will be healed. For I am also a man under authority, having under myself soldiers. I tell this one, 'Go,' and he goes; and tell another, 'Come,' and he comes; and tell my servant, 'Do this,' and he does it."[110]

Yeshua's gaze lingered on the man, his interest evident in his eyes. The Roman stood before Him, breathlessly waiting. Yeshua closed his eyes for a moment before re-opening them to address the Centurion.

"Most certainly, I tell you, I haven't found so great a faith, not even in Israel...Go your way. Let it be done for you as you have believed."[111] Yeshua intently looked at Abner with approval in his eyes.

Abner bowed to Him. He glanced in Mary's direction and nodded as if in gratitude. Magda saw the look of utter belief in the Centurion's eyes. The Roman knew that what Yeshua said was truth.

That night, lying on her sleeping mat in the house where they were staying, Magda heard the sweet sound of Yeshua's voice while He said the nightly prayers. With her heart tuned to His, she let the indistinct song of His prayer lull her to sleep. Even in melodic whispers on the wind, Yeshua's voice carried authority.

"Why do the nations rage, and the peoples plot a vain thing? The kings of the earth take a stand, and the rulers take counsel together against Yahweh and against His Anointed, saying, 'Let's break their bonds apart, and cast their cords from us.' He who sits in the heavens will laugh. The Lord will have them in derision. Then He will speak to them in His anger, and terrify them in His wrath: 'Yet I have set My

---

[110] Matthew 8:5-9

[111] Matthew 8:10

King on My holy hill of Zion.' You shall break them with a rod of iron. You shall dash them in pieces like a potter's vessel."[112]

Somehow, Magda knew that the forces of darkness were listening to His song. But, like her, they were surely not understanding.

---

[112] Psalm 2:1-6, 9

CHAPTER THIRTY

T hey joined a caravan on their way back to Bethany. The atmosphere was calm and serene on the Sabbath, as everyone in the village took a well-deserved rest after traveling. Magda followed Yeshua, Peter, Thomas, and James when they got up to leave the shade of the olive trees which the group was reclining beneath. Adjacent to them, a peaceful field spread out, with the sound of gentle wind rustling through the grass. Hunger gnawed at everyone's insides, making them feel weak and desperate for food. Yet no one complained. Provisions were scarcer as the crowds following Yeshua thinned out.

With silent determination, Yeshua led his disciples through the field, their footsteps barely making a sound. The silence was broken only by the sound of Magda's heavy sigh, indicating her deep state of reflection.

She was thinking about her father, Amos. It saddened her that the enemy used grief to steal the ground of Amos's heart, which had once been claimed by love. As Magda pondered, she wondered if her own heart was protected, shielded from vulnerability. The onslaught of sudden doubt concerned her, making her afraid.

Magda watched as Peter, Thomas, and James plucked the heads of grain and ate them.[113] Suddenly, a crowd of religious leaders emerged from the opposite direction and headed towards them.

Magda immediately recognized a familiar face. Eleazar, her cousin's husband, was among the Pharisees who approached Yeshua. Their faces twisted into varying expressions of disgust. Magda couldn't imagine what was wrong. Yeshua wasn't even speaking at the moment.

"Your disciples do what is not lawful to do on the Sabbath."[114] The Pharisee's tone was arrogant and rude.

Yeshua looked at them as if just noticing their presence for the first time. He then glanced over at Peter, Thomas, and James who were guiltily finishing the morsels they had just placed in their mouths.

Magda could tell from the expressions on their faces that the disciples were ashamed of themselves for bringing dishonor to their Rabbi.

As Yeshua stood tall, the gentle breeze rustled through the stalks of the grain fields. He plucked one Himself and held it for a moment. Rather than eat it, He let the grain fall to the ground. He looked at the group of Pharisees.

"Haven't you read what David did when he was hungry, and those who were with him: how he entered into God's house and ate the show bread, which was not lawful for him to eat, nor for those who were with him, but only for the priests?"[115]

The Pharisees fidgeted nervously, their uneasiness palpable. Magda wasn't sure if they were perspiring because of the heavy clothes they wore or because of the power of the words Yeshua

---

[113] Matthew 12:1

[114] Matthew 12:2

[115] Matthew 12:3-4

spoke to them.

He looked intently at them, but none of them said a word in reply.

"Or have you not read in the Law that on the Sabbath day the priests in the temple profane the Sabbath and are guiltless? But I tell you that one greater than the Temple is here. But if you had known what this means, 'I desire mercy, and not sacrifice,' you wouldn't have condemned the guiltless. For the Son of Man is Lord of the Sabbath."[116]

Peter, Thomas, and James let out a sigh of relief. They had not put their teacher in harm's way after all. Magda was amazed at the means by which Yeshua continually redefined the way the religious leaders interpreted the Law that they loved.

As Yeshua walked through the grain field, the gentle whisper of the wind danced through the golden stalks, following eagerly behind him as if ready to carry anything He said a great distance.

Magda followed, wondering how it was that even those who proclaimed to love Yahweh couldn't see fit to love His Son. How was it that those who studied the Law were so easily deceived?

Magda wondered if her love for Him was strong enough to withstand deception. Why was she so afraid lately? Why did the crowds that followed Him ebb and flow?

Sometimes there were a lot of people who seemed enthusiastic about His message, but they didn't stay for long. Why was it so hard for people to believe Him, to love Him?

Without saying a word, Yeshua turned around and looked at her. He stopped walking. Peter, Thomas, and James stopped walking as well. Yeshua took Magda by the hand. They stood at the edge of the field. He turned her around to look at the stalks of grain blowing in the slight breeze.

"Behold, a farmer went out to sow. As he sowed, some seeds fell by the roadside, and the birds came and devoured them.

---

[116] Matthew 12:3-8

Others fell on rocky ground, where they didn't have much soil, and immediately they sprang up, because they had no depth of earth. When the sun had risen, they were scorched. Because they had no root, they withered away. Others fell among thorns. The thorns grew up and choked them. Others fell on good soil and yielded fruit: some one hundred times as much, some sixty, and some thirty. He who has ears to hear, let him hear."[117]

His teaching left Magda in awe, pondering its profound meaning. She could tell that Peter, Thomas, and James were as confused as she was, but they said nothing. The disciples walked ahead at a distance as they made their way back through the field of grain. Yeshua kept in step with Magda.

When they reached the same spot where Yeshua had conversed with the Pharisees, He stopped. Bending down, He picked up the kernel of grain which He had dropped. He held Magda's hand in His own. Opening it, he dropped the kernel of grain into her palm.

Magda's heart ached as she saw the pain in His eyes, piercing her soul. She held her breath, inexplicably frightened.

Yeshua's voice was strained. "Most certainly I tell you, unless a grain of wheat falls into the earth and dies, it remains by itself alone. But if it dies, it bears much fruit. He who loves his life will lose it. He who hates his life in this world will keep it to eternal life."[118]

"Lord," Magda began.

He placed His finger on her lips. "The time is almost near. Don't be afraid, Mary."

With that, He turned and walked away from her. Magda stared at the kernel of grain in her hand. It made tears stream down her face, yet she remained bewildered by her own emotional state.

---

[117] Matthew 13:3-9
[118] John 12:24-25

When they rejoined the group shading themselves beneath the olive trees, Magda heard Peter ask Yeshua what He had meant by the parable He shared with them earlier.

Sighing, Yeshua answered Peter. "When anyone hears the Word of the Kingdom and doesn't understand it, the evil one comes and snatches away that which has been sown in his heart. This is what was sown by the roadside.

"What was sown on the rocky places, this is he who hears the Word and immediately with joy receives it; yet he has no root in himself, but endures for a while. When oppression or persecution arises because of the Word, immediately he stumbles.

"What was sown among the thorns, this is he who hears the Word, but the cares of this age and the deceitfulness of riches choke the Word, and he becomes unfruitful. What was sown on the good ground, this is he who hears the Word and understands it, who most certainly bears fruit and produces, some one hundred times as much, some sixty, and some thirty."[119]

Magda contemplated her Aunt Milcah's unwavering faith, which blossomed and bore abundant fruit. She thought about her father, whose faith was stolen because of the cares of the age. She thought about the Pharisee she knew as Eleazar, who seemed more focused on riches than on the Word of God. She thought about those people who followed Yeshua when He produced miracles of providing food or healing sick ones, but then walked away once they sensed the oppression from the religious leaders. Where was Magda in the story?

There was so much that she didn't understand. She was afraid that she was a prime target for the enemy to steal away her heart.

As the night wore on, Magda found herself unable to find peace, her mind consumed by restlessness. Unable to sleep, she arose in the middle of the night. She went to the edge of the grain

---

[119] Matthew 13:18-23

field. As the moonlight bathed the stalks, they seemed to come alive, glimmering and swaying like a watery illusion. Magda jumped in surprise as Yeshua suddenly appeared by her side. He must have been praying.

"The time is coming, yes, and has now come, that you will be scattered, everyone to his own place, and you will leave Me alone. Yet I am not alone, because the Father is with Me. I have told you these things, that in Me you may have peace. In the world you have trouble; but cheer up! I have overcome the world."[120]

"I sense things that I do not understand," Magda admitted to Him. "You told me not to be afraid, but I am, Lord. I don't know what to do. Help me overcome my doubt. Help me stay rooted in Your love."

"Mary," Yeshua touched her cheek. "There are many things I would like to explain to you, but you are not ready for them now. Peace I leave with you. My peace I give to you; not as the world gives, give I to you. Don't let your heart be troubled, neither let it be fearful. Trust in Me, beloved."[121]

Magda swallowed her tears. Looking into His eyes reminded her of the lamb from her dream.

"I trust You," she said in spite of her own feelings.

"I have fought for you. I have claimed your heart. You are mine," Yeshua said with authority as He wiped the single tear that escaped from Magda's eyes.

The residual power of his touch accompanied by the sweetness of His words lulled Magda to sleep when she returned to her pallet.

Morning seemed to come too soon. Another day of travel. Another step closer to the inevitable storm brewing on the spiritual horizon.

Making their way back to Bethany, Magda was appreciative

---

[120] John 16:32-33
[121] John 14:27

of the company of the other women. Mary, at her young age, exuded an infectious joy that was impossible to resist. Her enthusiasm was contagious as she witnessed the miracles of Yeshua's healing power for the first time. The blind could see, the deaf could hear and the lame could walk. While the young woman, Mary, saw the incredible power of Yeshua's touch, Magda felt the increasing hostility as His popularity increased.

The forces of darkness swirled around them like a noose waiting to be jerked closed. Magda knew that the religious leaders sent spies everywhere Yeshua went. Though these spies tried to remain hidden within the crowds of common people, Magda could sense their evil presence. She immediately recognized the shadows reflective of the forest of Zophos.

After leaving one of the synagogues where Yeshua had taught, Magda felt the warmth of the sun on her face as she walked through the bustling streets. He had preached the good news to men who were not willing or eager to listen. The closer they came to the city of Jerusalem, the more resistant the crowds were. Outside, under the expanse of an open sky, Yeshua taught the multitudes regardless of the threat.

"The Kingdom of Heaven is like a grain of mustard seed which a man took, and sowed in his field, which indeed is smaller than all seeds. But when it is grown, it is greater than the herbs and becomes a tree, so that the birds of the air come and lodge in its branches."[122]

Magda's eyes were fixed on the same men who had expelled Him from the synagogue, as they targeted innocent members of the crowd. They lurked on the edges at first. She could sense their dark motivation. When they moved closer, Yeshua merely looked at them. His one look brought the onslaught of self-defense. The religious leaders were trying to undo the work He had done amongst the people. The prominent men were being used by

---

[122] Matthew 13:31-32

Satan to snatch away the good seed which had been planted in the hearts of many.

"How does this man know letters, having never been educated?" the ruler of the synagogue questioned openly.[123]

With a gentle sigh, Magda closed her eyes, shutting out the world around her. She saw the seeds of doubt being planted in the place where seeds of hope had been sown by Yeshua's own voice. The hearts of many were turning away from the light He offered. It was a troubling sight to witness the leaders of Israel leading the flock astray, betraying the trust of the One who put them in charge. They were wolves disguising themselves as shepherds.

Yeshua replied calmly to their disruptive tactics. "My teaching is not mine, but His who sent me. If anyone desires to do His will, He will know about the teaching, whether it is from God, or if I am speaking from Myself. He who speaks from himself seeks his own glory, but he who seeks the glory of Him who sent Him is true, and no unrighteousness is in Him."[124]

When Yeshua fell silent, Magda opened her eyes and took in her surroundings. He looked out upon the crowd, compassion welling up in His eyes because they were a flock without a shepherd.

Yeshua looked back at the religious leaders, contempt in His expression. "Didn't Moses give you the Law, and yet none of you keeps the Law? Why do you seek to kill Me?"[125]

Shock washed over them as they were confronted with the unexpected exposure of their sinister motives.

"You have a demon! Who seeks to kill you?" The leaders all laughed uncomfortably, but Magda could see that they were rattled.

A division arose in the crowd. People argued among

---

[123] John 7:15
[124] John 7:16-18
[125] John 7:19

themselves. Those that did not have the seeds of hope snatched away by the enemy were being pummeled by the ones that did. Some stood fast, the roots of faith digging deep. Others were persuaded, discarding what had just been planted.

The group following Yeshua decreased in size greatly after each interchange with the religious leaders. They were finally on the outskirts of Bethany when the small group was halted by a battalion of Roman soldiers on their way to Jerusalem. The Roman governor, Pontius Pilate, was returning to Israel after a stay in Rome. The sight of the heavily armed guards flanking him in the procession sent a clear message of his importance and the level of protection he required.

Magda was exceedingly uncomfortable walking in the footsteps of so many Roman soldiers. Her experience with them had not fostered any sense of security in their presence. She and the other women had been talking together about Yeshua's teaching. Because they were not paying close attention, they had inadvertently put distance between themselves and the men.

Magda hoped they would go unnoticed, especially when she recognized some of the officers. She was sure she saw the same man who assaulted Pascal. Her blood boiled. She felt an overwhelming urge to charge at the man and unleash her anger upon him. She hated the Romans! She hated every man that harmed her and used her and shackled her as prey to their lust.

Magda feared for her friends. She wanted to get them to safety. Unfortunately, the women didn't escape the wandering eyes of some of the rougher soldiers.

While the women could still see Yeshua and the disciples up ahead, their brothers in faith were obviously not aware of their current situation. The soldiers moved in on Magda. She had no choice but to step between them and the other women. If an assault was inevitable, it most definitely should fall on her.

"Well, well," the Roman soldier hissed, touching Magda's hair. "You've brought friends this time."

He was close enough so that only Magda heard him. "Leave my friends out of it and I'll give you what you want," Magda said out loud even while she prayed in her heart, *"Help me, Lord!"*

Her prayer was heard immediately, but the answer came in a completely unexpected way. While Magda assumed Yeshua would intervene and save her, to her surprise, the Roman Centurion whom they had met in Capernaum came riding up on his horse.

"What goes on here?" the Centurion yelled.

"Just some stinking Jews getting in the way," the soldier responded. He had been stroking Magda's long hair. He let go of her arm.

"Back to your post, soldiers! We don't have time for this. The governor grows impatient." Abner roared his commands.

The soldiers immediately got back into line with the marching guard. Abner brought his horse closer to the women. "Are you alright?" he asked, leaning toward them.

They nodded. The disciples who had walked on ahead, not noticing what was taking place, had turned around. Yeshua led them back to where the women were standing.

Abner saluted Yeshua after making sure none of the other soldiers were watching. Blessedly, the battalion had made significant progress and was now well ahead.

"My servant is well, Lord. I thank You. He was healed the moment You spoke the word." The awe in Abner's voice was unmistakable.

Yeshua nodded in affirmation. Abner acknowledged Mary and Magda before riding off to catch up with the rest of the battalion. Joanna and Susanna just stood there, too stunned to speak. The idea of a Roman Centurion coming to their rescue was a complete contradiction for all of them.

"How did that man know you?" Joanna asked.

"We met in Capernaum and on the road to Nain," Magda smiled at her. "He is one of the good ones."

"Are there any good Romans?" Susanna laughed.

Magda chided herself for her recent misgivings about Romans. She needed to live in the shadow of the forgiveness that was extended to her by trusting people first and not issuing blanket judgments devoid of love. Magda graciously relayed to Joanna and Susanna the story about Abner's servant being healed when they were in Capernaum. The women stayed close to the rest of the group while they continued toward Bethany.

Magda was as happy as Yeshua when they arrived back in the small village. Though it was not her home, Magda felt a sweet comfort in the dwelling that she didn't feel anywhere else. Young Mary was overjoyed to be reunited with her siblings. Magda loved to witness the bond between the three. She could also tell that Yeshua was especially fond of this family of orphans.

The evening was relaxed and enjoyable. It was nice for Magda to have the opportunity to clean up and eat a good meal. Something about being off the road, settled in next to Yeshua and the other disciples, provided Magda with a peaceful sense of replenishment. There was light in the house of Bethany, which dispelled the darkness surrounding them in the land of Judea. Magda understood why Yeshua always made it a point to stay with Lazarus and his sisters when He passed through the area.

"It is good to see you smile again," Yeshua said to Magda.

"I have felt the heaviness out there, my Lord," Magda replied. "It has wearied my heart to sense the darkness."

"I am the light of the world. He who follows Me will not walk in the darkness, but will have the light of life."[126] Yeshua stood. "I am going to the Mount of Olives."

"Lord, it is almost dark," Magda protested, not wanting Him to leave at such a late hour.

"Yes, that is why I must pray," Yeshua said mysteriously.

Magda watched Him depart. He whispered to John before He

---

[126] John 8:12

exited from the dwelling. The disciples were enjoying one another, eating what was left of the food and drinking the wine. When Lazarus came back inside, the entire atmosphere altered.

It didn't take long for Magda to find out that someone Lazarus and his sisters cared about was very ill. The sun had already set, which meant that traveling to Jerusalem to see their sick friend, a woman named Zhiva, would have to wait until morning.

CHAPTER THIRTY-ONE

Magda awoke to dazzling sunlight streaming through the window of the sleeping area that she shared with Mary and Martha. Joanna and Susanna had already risen. Despite her surprise at sleeping late, Magda was grateful for a restful night's sleep, free from any unsettling dreams. Magda joined the others downstairs. There was a fresh plate of food waiting for her.

"Where is everyone?" Magda asked.

"Yeshua took Mary with Him to Jerusalem. Judas went with them. They left before the sun was fully up," Martha informed her.

"Judas went?" Magda queried.

"Yes," Martha said, an edge to her voice.

"You don't like him?" Magda asked Martha.

"I don't trust him," Martha replied. "But," she sighed. "I trust Yeshua."

Magda had stifled her own concerns regarding Judas during their time together following Yeshua for the very same reasons Martha cited.

"Any news of your friend, Zhiva?"

"Nothing." Martha turned to go back into the cooking area.

"Magda?" Peter came in from outside. "We are all going to Jerusalem. The Rabbi shouldn't be alone, not now anyway."

"We are going to look for Him," John added.

"I want to come with you," Magda said. "We could split up and try to find Him."

"Let's get going. The sun is already high," John said with urgency.

With quick strides, they hastened their journey towards Jerusalem. The path was teeming with people, their voices mingling in a cacophony of different languages and accents. Though they had kept a good pace, they frequently got stuck behind slower caravans.

Magda picked up on the concern that weighed heavily on the disciples' minds. Every man was silent, probably upset that Yeshua would put Himself right in the middle of the lion's den. All of the religious leaders eagerly anticipated a chance to accuse Him, or even worse, condemn Him.

Once they finally arrived inside the city gates, Magda pressed close to the disciples. The city of Jerusalem was alive with a constant flow of people, creating a lively and energetic ambiance. The marketplace was overly crowded. The streets were like a fast-moving river of bodies. The noise made it impossible for them to speak to one another.

Within moments, Magda found herself separated from the disciples. She got lost in the crowd, shuffled off in a direction that she wasn't intending to go. With the crowd pressing around her, Magda squeezed out of the main thoroughfare into an alley so she could get her bearings and catch her breath.

Magda could see the glory of the Temple in the distance. It was beautiful beneath the emerging rays of a newly born sun. She caught her breath at the splendor of it, remembering long-lost memories of being taught by the prophetess Anna as a child.

"Thank You, Lord for teaching me," Magda prayed.

She was about to re-enter the flowing crowd when a strong hand grabbed her, ripping her tunic slightly. When Magda turned around, she stood face to face with the Roman soldier who had killed Pascal. This time, he was alone, and he was not talking. He forced her up against a wall, holding a knife to her throat. Magda didn't struggle. She submitted to her fate, praying in her heart.

"Lord, I know what I was. I know that this man is lost, used by the enemy. Help him to see the light even as he takes what he wants, Lord. Help me forgive him as You have forgiven me. Help me remember who You say I am. The enemy has no dominion over me. I am Yours," Magda smiled.

Inexplicably, the man stepped back. "Why are you smiling?" he roared.

"I'm sorry," Magda said to him. "I forgive you for killing my friend."

"You're sorry?" The man was confused. "You forgive *me*? You?"

"Do you need help?" Magda asked the Roman soldier.

"Do I need help?" he retorted, taking further steps back from her. "Who are you? What is wrong with you?" The Roman was clearly afraid of her.

"I am a child of Yahweh, beloved of Yeshua. I can help you, my lord." Magda looked at him with a love she didn't feel for the man but somehow was able to extend to him.

The man looked horrified. Only, Magda didn't see the man. She saw the demon of lust that held the man captive. It had become disarmed by the power of love. The shield around her as she remembered who she really was proved to be her protection. The Roman soldier said nothing more, but turned and ran down the alleyway, disappearing from her sight.

Once he was gone, the inexplicable calm retreated and Magda felt the full force of a flooding fear over what had just happened. She leaned up against the wall, catching her breath and willing her racing heart to be still. She didn't want to be alone anymore.

Magda pushed her way through the crowd, drawn to the glory of the Temple. When she arrived, she immediately recognized Yeshua. The sunlight covered Him, radiating off His entire being. As Magda looked at Him, she saw the same glory in Him that was in the Temple. He was the glory of the Temple! She knew that as long as she was with Him, near Him, she didn't need to fear the powers of darkness. She made a firm decision to always stay by His side, no matter what. She was His.

He reclined on the steps, wearing His beautiful bluish-gray cloak, teaching a small gathering of people. Young Mary stood off to the side, listening. As soon as Magda entered the area, Yeshua's intense gaze locked onto her, sending a shiver down her spine. She stood there watching Him, unaware of the shadows encroaching.

A group of Pharisees came from behind Magda. As they moved forward, they forcefully pulled a woman along with them. As they passed by her, Magda could feel their indignant ferocity. Their ornate robes flapped like wings as the men walked hurriedly toward where Yeshua was teaching.

The poor woman was barely covered, her undergarments half falling off her body. Magda hurt for her. In this young woman, Magda saw herself. The men threw her down on the ground like refuse. They positioned her in front of Yeshua. Her long brown hair fell around her shoulders, offering her a little bit of cover. Magda felt the poor woman's soul ripping in shame as she lay there exposed before the eyes of these men. She wanted to run to her. She wanted to cover her or take her place.

The religious men, hatred in their eyes, let the prominent Pharisee speak for them.

"Teacher, we found this woman in adultery, in the very act. Now in our Law, Moses commanded us to stone such women.

What then do You say about her?"[127] A short, overweight man with gray hair peeking out from beneath his headdress spoke forcefully to Yeshua.

Magda didn't like the mocking tone the man used when he addressed her Lord as *Teacher*. She knew they were testing Him. She knew they were not interested in the truth. They were only looking for a reason to accuse Him. Fear engulfed Magda as she imagined the authorities closing in on Him, ready to make an arrest. Her gaze fixed upon the young woman and her heart ached. Magda knew there was a story behind this scene. Where was the man? Was he not also to blame?

Magda held her breath. The Law demanded not only the woman's death but also her public humiliation. Yeshua's way was different. What could He do? If He disobeyed the Law, they would arrest Him. If He did what they demanded, all of His teaching about forgiveness would look like hypocrisy.

Magda remembered Yeshua's teaching from their days traveling around the territories of Judea. *The devil was a murderer from the beginning, and doesn't stand in the truth, because there is no truth in him. When he speaks a lie, he speaks on his own; for he is a liar, and the father of lies.* [128]

Magda watched as the web of lies these religious men spun wrapped itself around the light of truth that Yeshua was bringing. She had no idea how He would escape the trap. She wished that the disciples were there with her. Helplessness washed over her, leaving her feeling utterly powerless.

Yeshua didn't respond to the agitated religious leaders at first. He began writing on the stone ground of the Temple in response to their question. Magda watched as His finger touched the stone. She quietly remembered Anna teaching her about the Law of Moses. The words were etched onto stone tablets by the

---

[127] John 8:4-5
[128] John 8:44

divine finger of Yahweh Himself. Magda heard the echo of Moses' words to the people in her heart.

"Yahweh delivered to me the two stone tablets written with God's finger. On them were all the words which Yahweh spoke with you on the mountain out of the middle of the fire in the day of the assembly."[129] Magda was shocked that her mind resurrected the buried memory.

The Pharisees were offended by Yeshua's silence. Their pride would not allow them to enter into the silent teaching He was freely giving them.

"What do You say? Does this woman's sin deserve to be punished?" The old Pharisee in charge kept pestering Yeshua as He continued writing with His finger on the ground.

The exposed woman quietly lay there, trembling, her hands bound behind her back. Magda could see the tears falling from her eyes onto the stone beneath her. She could feel the weight of the shame that buried the woman's soul. Magda watched as the condemned one's tears flowed down the stone pavement, mingling with the Word that Yeshua had written in the dirt.

Once her tears united with His Word, Yeshua straightened up. With the power and authority Magda knew so well, He looked straight into the eyes of the religious leaders, already holding the stones in their hands.

He commanded them, "He who is without sin among you, let him throw the first stone at her."[130]

Magda felt as though she had been punched in the stomach. This couldn't be happening! Why would He condemn this woman when He had freely forgiven her?

Magda swirled on the edge of the cliff of doubt and misunderstanding. She couldn't be witness to this. She couldn't watch as darkness closed in around this woman, sealing her fate.

---

[129] Deuteronomy 9:10
[130] John 8:7

Magda looked at Yeshua, a plea in her eyes. He just looked through her.

Yeshua bent down to continue writing on the stone ground of the Temple. What was she missing? She didn't understand His teaching. Magda could see that His finger now mixed the wet tears flowing from the condemned woman with the dirt on the stone ground, making words. Straining her eyes, Magda thought she read, *"My beloved is mine. I am His."*[131]

A sound startled Magda out of her reverie. Magda turned when she heard the strangest thumping noises. It grew louder and more frequent, like a rainstorm that was just getting started. She watched as the Pharisees dropped their stones, one by one, leaving with looks of conviction etched all over their faces.

Magda understood. Yeshua had done to them what she had done to the Roman soldier. He fought the powers of darkness with light in the unseen realm rather than engage in a battle of words with the men who didn't know they were only pawns in the hands of the great deceiver. For a moment, Magda felt pity for the religious leaders, remembering the shackles of her own deception.

The convicted men vanished. The legacy they left behind consisted of the stones that had fallen from their hands. Magda's eyes fell upon the crumpled woman, awaiting her fate. Yeshua stood up slowly. He moved closer to the young, exposed woman. Magda saw His shadow touch the place where she knelt. The silence wrapped around them, its power filling the space. The holiness of Yeshua surrounded them, creating a shield of protection. The woman looked up. Bending, He merely touched the ropes used to bind her and they fell off, freeing her hands.

"Woman, where are your accusers? Did no one condemn you?"[132] He asked, His words dripping with love.

---

[131] Song of Solomon 2:16
[132] John 8:10

The woman's voice trembled with fear, "No one, Lord."[133]

"Neither do I condemn you. Go your way. From now on, sin no more."[134] He handed her a fresh tunic with which to cover herself. But, Magda knew the more important covering He offered the young woman was His love.

Magda saw young Mary move forward to be by the woman's side. The knowing look on her face told Magda that the accused woman was probably Mary's friend. Before she got to where her friend was, Mary stopped. Magda witnessed it, too. There was a deeper exchange happening between Yeshua and the young woman that neither of them wanted to interrupt. Magda saw the fiery love in Yeshua's eyes as He claimed this woman for His own. Not breaking His gaze, the condemned woman let go of His hands and fell at His feet, dropping the tunic on the ground.

"My Lord!" Her tears fell profusely, wetting Yeshua's feet.

Magda was moved by the scene as it brought up her own very personal memories. She watched the two friends reunite, their tears of joy testifying to the love they had for one another.

Yeshua came over to where Magda stood.

"Teacher," Magda said to Him, tears in her eyes.

"What have you learned, beloved?" He asked her.

Magda's mind went blank. "I have so little understanding, my Lord. Help me with my little faith."

Yeshua touched His hand to her cheek. "You have learned more than you know, beloved. You will need to remember what you have seen and heard. Love is not only a feeling; it is an action, a protection, a gift, and a sacrifice."

"A sacrifice, my Lord?" Magda asked.

"You will understand, beloved," Yeshua told her. "Come with Me."

---

[133] John 8:11
[134] John 8:11

CHAPTER THIRTY-TWO

Yeshua continued teaching in the Temple. Magda remained by His side, fully aware of the hostility brewing while some of the Pharisees watched and listened to Him. As Magda looked upon the faces of the religious leaders lurking on the periphery of where Yeshua stood speaking to the crowd, she could sense the intensity of the battle waging in the unseen realm. Some were more inclined to the light He offered than others. Yet, she sensed their fear in drawing too close. They resisted Him even as their hearts were drawn to Him. Fear once had a strong influence on Magda's heart, and she could still feel its power when she thought about it. Part of her felt pity for those who were blinded by deception.

But there was hope on the horizon. As Magda looked at the religious teachers, she could also discern a look of respect in some of their expressions. It was possible that one day, Israel's leaders would have a revelation, sensing the heavy chains binding their souls. In that day, all would be made right again. Magda longed for the day when all of God's people would recognize and receive the love available through His Son.

The majority, however, wore hatred on their faces as proudly as they donned the ornate robes designating their positions of power and authority. Magda looked at Yeshua, simply dressed, donned with the intricately woven cloak which Mary had made for Him. He was humble and gentle in His attire, yet full of power and authority. The Pharisees, on the other hand, were attired in power and authority, yet were only full of pride and hypocrisy.

Movement caught Magda's eye, breaking her reverie. She followed the dark shadow that suddenly appeared on the ground before her. As she spun around, her heart skipped a beat when she saw Judas unexpectedly come out from inside the Temple, his presence sending a chill down her spine. He appeared flustered and guilty. Upon seeing him, Magda wondered where he had been all day and why he came from the direction of the High Priest's courtyard. His eyes held a troubling darkness that unsettled her. She had never trusted the man, but his current sneaky behavior made her feel even more concerned.

Judas halted abruptly when he spotted Yeshua surrounded by a crowd of people. As Judas made his way through the crowd, looking as if he was trying to escape, he stopped in front of one of the head Pharisees. They exchanged a knowing look which confirmed in Magda's mind Judas's connection with those who were trying to silence Yeshua.

One of the prominent Pharisees stepped forward in front of Yeshua, interrupting Him with a question. The crowd was hushed, hanging on every word of the exchange between the two men.

"Teacher, we know that You are honest, and don't defer to anyone; for You aren't partial to anyone, but truly teach the way of God." The man's tone was one of mocking superiority. "Is it lawful to pay taxes to Caesar, or not? Shall we give, or shall we not give?"[135]

---

[135] Mark 12:15

Yeshua looked right through the man. The silent stare made the overly large Pharisee take a step back. Yeshua's voice was commanding. "Why do you test Me? Bring me a denarius, that I may see it."

Yeshua moved toward the man who promptly gave him a coin. "Whose is this image and inscription?"[136]

"Caesar's," the man replied, having lost his superior tone of voice. He shuffled before Yeshua uncomfortably.

Out of the corner of her eye, Magda saw Judas staring intently at the scene as if anticipating something. There was no respect in the disciple's eyes. Looking at him reminded Magda of looking into the eyes of the wolves in her dream.

Yeshua's voice was calm, unmoved by the continual testing.

"Render to Caesar the things that are Caesar's," Yeshua paused, holding up the coin. "And to God the things that are God's."[137]

Yeshua's words had such power that several people in the crowd gasped in astonishment.

Judas just shook his head and disappeared. As Magda watched him snake his way through the crowd, intending to figure out where he was going, the sight of the other disciples distracted her. Thrilled to see them again, she forcefully maneuvered through the dense crowd. The swelling multitude hindered her progress.

A division arose among the people. Some respected Yeshua, while others hated Him. Few remained neutral after hearing Him teach.

Magda navigated through the tumultuous crowd, her senses overwhelmed by the feeling of bodies brushing against her and the sounds of voices blending in a cacophony of grumbles and complaints. The entire exchange between the religious teachers

---

[136] Mark 12:15-16
[137] Mark 12:16-17

and Yeshua had stirred up everyone who had witnessed the scene. While the restlessness of the crowd filled the air, an epic battle was unfolding in the unseen realm.

As Magda approached, she could make out John's hushed voice as he whispered to Yeshua. Amidst the pressing throng, she broke through and linked her arm with Yeshua's, following John as he led their Rabbi out of the bustling Temple area. Young Mary had maneuvered her way through the people so she could grab hold of Yeshua's cloak, too.

The oppressive atmosphere weighed heavily on Magda, making her shoulders tense and her breathing shallow. She prayed as they walked. *"Thank You, Lord, that I can cling to Him. Let me never let go."*

Exiting the city proved more difficult than they expected due to the multitude of pilgrims entering Jerusalem. They decided to lodge with Mary's friend, Zhiva, for the night.

Once inside Zhiva's dwelling, the large group made themselves at home. The instant Magda met Zhiva, she felt a deep connection and affection for her. She reminded her of long-lost memories of the prophetess, Anna. A young man named Stephen was the center of attention as he told them about the miraculous healing that Yeshua performed for this dear woman who had been so close to death.

Despite the scarcity of provisions, they were relieved to find ample space in the spacious upper room for a good night's sleep. When Magda closed her eyes that night, listening to the breathing sounds of the men she now considered her brothers, she reflected on the events of the past days.

She recalled seeing Yeshua in the Temple that morning, radiating the glory of it as if it belonged to Him, as if it was Him. Magda remembered when she fled through the dark forest of Zophos all those years ago. The cornerstone, like the stones of the Temple, emitted a comforting glow in the darkness, offering her solace and support. It was this cornerstone that kept the enemy at bay. The great deceiver could not get near her as long as she clung to that stone.

When Yeshua had appeared on the horse, she thought that was the moment He saved her. Looking back on it now, she realized that the moment she was saved had already been pre-destined because the cornerstone she ran to was there in the darkness, placed just for her. The cornerstone was as much Him as was the Temple. Magda had a hard time grasping the full meaning, yet the idea that she was known before time began touched her heart with the majesty of love's timeless power.

They returned to Mary's house in Bethany the next day. After resting with their favorite friends for a short time, Yeshua announced that it was time for them to move on again.

"We leave before first light," He said. "We go to Samaria."

Though none of the men said anything, Magda sensed their troubled responses. She wasn't quite sure why they were particularly upset by this new assignment.

Recognizing Magda's perplexed look, John explained it to her. "We usually avoid Samaria, no matter what. The people there hate the Jews."

"Why?" Magda asked. "Surely, He must have His reasons for going there."

"I'm sure that He does, but…" John paused. "Well, if you thought the hostility in the Temple was bad, just wait until we get to Samaria. I can't imagine anyone being open to His message there."

Magda felt defeated before they even got back on the road. Contrary to His custom, Yeshua did not stop along the way. He did not teach nor did He heal the people who were coming to Him. There was a sense of urgency in His stride which Magda had not witnessed before.

When they arrived in the village of Sychar, Yeshua looked fatigued. Their exhaustion was palpable, each member of the group longing for a meal and a chance to rest. Yeshua sat down by a well, resting.

"Go into the village and find provisions," Yeshua told them. "I will wait here. All of you, go."

No one dared argue with Him. Magda followed the disciples as they made their way into the village. The men were all tired and not very agreeable.

"I don't know who He thinks will give us provisions here," Thomas complained.

"These people won't even talk to us," Andrew grumbled. "The Samaritans and Jews just don't mix."

"Why not?" Magda asked.

"They don't accept our ways," Peter said. "They worship on Mount Gerizim instead of at the Temple. They intermarried with Gentiles. They have added to the Word of the Lord with strange traditions."

"I wouldn't even drink out of one of their cups," Thomas said. "Why do we have to get food from them?"

"Isn't the way of Yeshua different?" Magda said softly, not wanting to upset the angry men. "He has brought people together who were once divided. He taught us that the Temple wasn't going to remain standing. He taught us that in the Kingdom of Heaven people will not marry. He taught us that the two most important commandments are to 'love the Lord with all our heart, soul and mind; and to love our neighbor as ourselves.' [138] If we hold to His teaching, then your objections to these people, Samaritans, don't really matter."

Magda's words silenced the men. She was a little surprised herself at what she recalled and applied in the current situation. The disciples were a lot more subdued by the time they entered the village.

By sharing what she had learned, Magda diffused the hostility so that they did not enter the center of Sychar

---

[138] Matthew 22:37-39

predisposed to the judgments of the flesh.

Unfortunately, the people of Sychar only proved the point the disciples had been making. No one wanted to do business with them. The stubbornness of the Samaritans particularly enraged James and John. Magda decided to step in because the men were getting agitated, making matters worse.

"Please," Magda pleaded with a woman in the marketplace. "Would you sell me some bread, fish, and cheese? I will pay your price, no bargaining. We have traveled a long way. We are worn out. Your kindness would be most appreciated."

The woman had kind eyes which responded to the gentleness in Magda's voice. "How much do you need?" she asked.

"Enough for a dozen people," Magda replied.

She completed the transaction while the disciples were still milling around, complaining, and casting judgmental looks at all the merchants. Lost in their own grievances, they remained oblivious to Magda's absence, unable to find a way out of their predicament.

Yeshua's voice rang true in Magda's heart as she looked upon her brothers whom she loved even in their failures. *"Why do you reason among yourselves, you of little faith, 'because you have brought no bread?"*[139]

Magda smiled at the remembrance. *"Lord, our faith is small indeed. We all have much to learn. Help us to grow,"* she prayed.

Magda came up behind James and John, who appeared particularly offended by the lack of hospitality in Sychar.

"I have enough food here," she said. "Shall we go back to the Teacher, now?"

The men looked at the two full baskets Magda was carrying. Peter immediately went to her aid, lifting one onto his shoulder. Andrew took the other. As they made their way back to the well where Yeshua was waiting for them, Magda saw a woman

---

[139] Matthew 16:8

frantically running toward them. She exuded joy and light. Magda was drawn to her immediately. She looked vaguely familiar.

The woman ran right past them as they approached the well. When Magda saw her face, she remembered who she was. It was Leah, the woman from years ago, who helped Magda and Pascal on their travel after leaving John the Baptizer's camp. Leah had ministered lovingly to Magda's wounded feet.

Magda could sense the lingering agitation in the air as she observed the disciples' tense expressions. Now, they were troubled that Yeshua had been talking to a woman while He was alone with her.

"Why was He talking to her?" John whispered. "A Samaritan woman?"

"I don't know," James said.

Upon approaching Yeshua, Andrew told Him about the inhospitality of the people in the village. As they relayed their stories, the disciples all rallied around the remembered offense.

Magda could hear the superiority in their voices. It reminded her of the tone the religious leaders often took when they spoke to Yeshua. It bothered her.

"Lord, do You want us to command fire to come down from the sky and destroy them, just as Elijah did?"[140] James and John asked in unison.

Yeshua looked at them. He turned and rebuked them. "You don't know of what kind of spirit you are. For the Son of Man didn't come to destroy men's lives, but to save them."[141]

The disciples were silent. They recognized their failure at last. Yeshua walked around them, placing His hand on each one's shoulder, giving it a gentle squeeze.

"I have other sheep, which are not of this fold. I must bring them also, and they will hear My voice. They will become one

[140] Luke 9:54
[141] Luke 9:55-56

flock with one shepherd."[142]

Peter broke the silence first. "Rabbi, eat."[143]

Yeshua looked at Peter. "I have food to eat that you know nothing about."[144]

James leaned closer to his brother, John. "Has anyone brought Him something to eat?"[145]

Yeshua looked up into the distance. A crowd was coming toward Him. He smiled, placing His hand on James's shoulder.

"My food is to do the will of Him who sent me and to accomplish His work. Don't you say, 'There are yet four months until the harvest?' Behold, I tell you, lift up your eyes and look at the fields, that they are ripe for harvest already."

Yeshua pointed toward the coming crowd. "He who reaps receives wages and gathers fruit to eternal life; that both he who sows and he who reaps may rejoice together."[146]

The people came to Him. Those who shunned the disciples by their inhospitable nature only hours before were now eager to receive the light offered to them. In all the months of traveling around with Yeshua, Magda had not seen a crowd as eager as this one to listen to His teaching. The people of Sychar not only listened, but they learned.

Magda overheard a man talking to Leah. "Now we believe, not because of your speaking; for we have heard for ourselves, and know that this is indeed the Christ, the Savior of the world."[147]

Yeshua and the disciples remained in Sychar for two more days. The crowd that James and John had wanted to consume with fire were consumed with a fiery faith that had them clinging

---

[142] John 10:16
[143] John 4:31
[144] John 4:32
[145] John 4:33
[146] John 4:34-36
[147] John 4:42

to Yeshua. They didn't want Him to leave. Magda was touched by the ease of their embrace of love's power—a love that broke down dividing walls of hostility. She also greatly enjoyed spending time with Leah.

The woman's story of suffering and trials of faith moved Magda. Her heart filled with joy knowing that Leah would be joining them as they continued their journey to Galilee.

"He is the Messiah," Leah said to Magda, awe in her voice. "How can I not stay with Him? There is nothing for me here."

"I understand," Magda agreed. "I cling to Him with everything that I am."

PART THREE

The War

CHAPTER THIRTY-THREE

Leah and Magda walked together down the dusty road. The bond between them was immediate, both having arrived at Yeshua's side after a long season of suffering. One woman's suffering was physical, the other spiritual.

"How long have you been following Him?" Leah asked Magda.

"I can hardly remember my life before He delivered me," Magda smiled gratefully. "He snatched me out of the clutches of demons."

"Demons?" Leah exclaimed.

"Yes, I suffered much at the hands of evil and the lusts of men. But, through it all, love had been shielding me. I never knew it until I met Him, Shoshana."

"I'm still not used to being called by that name," Leah admitted. "It was the name He gave me."

Magda laughed. "He calls me Mary. Everyone else knows me as Magda."

"There is power in a name," Leah said.

"You speak a profound truth, my friend," Magda remarked,

knowing that a name could be used for good or evil.

"I waited so long for deliverance. I almost gave up. My faith was so weak," Leah admitted shyly.

"He often speaks to the disciples and calls them 'men of little faith,'" Magda laughed. "Yet, there is never condemnation in His voice, only understanding and so much patience. We all have a lot to learn. Every trial, every struggle, every source of pain is a teaching tool, not a punishment."

Leah agreed with her, their conversation making the monotony of travel on foot delightful and engaging. For the rest of the walk, Magda listened to Leah explain everything she learned about the process of growing grapes on the vine. The need to overcome challenges was essential for cultivating the juiciest, ripest fruits.

When they finally approached Galilee, the cool breeze came off the Sea in waves of refreshing welcome. It had been many months since they had been near a large body of water. The olive and tamarisk trees shaded them. Their footsteps left imprints on the ground, revealing a reddish tinge to the soil beneath them. The surroundings were full of life and the promise of spring.

Back in the familiar territory of this region, Magda was relieved. Once again, the many stops along the way made the journey feel excessively long. Yeshua interacted with the multitudes, offering them a chance to follow Him. Most turned down His offer, preferring the riches and comfort of this world rather than the promised inheritance of heaven.

In a serene grove of tamarisk trees, the group found the perfect spot to set up camp for the night. Leah stayed by Magda's side, learning as much as she could about life on the road. Magda was eager to teach her the best way to set up a tent, start the fire, and prepare the food.

It wasn't long before the word had spread that Yeshua, the great healer, was there. People swarmed to the region. The crowd gathering on the shore of the Sea of Galilee increased in size with every passing day. Yeshua urged Peter to bring his boat, the one they had sailed in before.

Yeshua stepped into the boat. Peter pushed out a little way from the shore. Magda heard Yeshua's voice carry strong across the waters like thunder. Was He upset by something?

"Don't think that I came to send peace on the earth. I didn't come to send peace, but a sword. For I came to set a man at odds against his father, and a daughter against her mother, and a daughter-in-law against her mother-in-law."[148]

Yeshua turned His head, looking toward a man at the back of the crowd. "A man's foes will be those of his own household. He who loves father or mother more than Me is not worthy of Me; and he who loves son or daughter more than Me isn't worthy of Me. He who doesn't take his cross and follow after Me, isn't worthy of Me. He who seeks his life will lose it; and he who loses his life for My sake will find it."[149]

The intensity in Yeshua's teaching was one that Magda had not heard before. He sounded agitated, almost forceful, in trying to help people to understand the truth. Was time running out? Magda could feel the pleading authority of the force of His love.

"Help the people respond, Lord. Lead them to open their hearts, not fearing the exposure," Magda joined His mission in prayer. *"Conquer the resistance that lies within the heart of Your people, Lord. Lead them to overcome their grief, pain, and bitterness. Rid them of the misguided notions of who the Messiah should be so that they can see Him as He is. Undo the work of the evil one, Lord."*

When He had finished speaking to the crowd, Peter brought the boat back into shore. While Peter, James, and John moored the boat, Yeshua moved directly toward the young man He had singled out in the crowd. Magda wondered who the young man was. She left Leah with a few tasks to continue setting up camp

---

[148] Matthew 10:34-35
[149] Matthew 10:36-39

while she went to join the disciples and Yeshua.

Yeshua took a solitary walk with the young man. Magda could tell that the man received Yeshua's message. She saw the struggle he experienced in Yeshua's presence written on his face.

Magda found out from John that the young man's name was Matthias. She walked with Peter, James, and John as they followed behind Yeshua and Matthias.

"Who is he?" Magda whispered. "I saw Yeshua singled him out."

"We did too," John whispered. "I'm not sure who he is. I haven't seen him before. Yeshua certainly knows him, though."

"Something about the way Yeshua approached Matthias reminds me of when He approached us, all those years ago, John," James observed, quietly.

When they got closer, the three of them were able to overhear the conversation. Yeshua had paused, giving Matthias a chance to speak.

"I have a message for you from Bethany, Lord. It is urgent." Matthias stammered. "Martha says: 'Lord, behold, he for whom You have great affection is sick.'"

Magda gasped, feeling as if the wind had been knocked out of her. The one for whom He had great affection. Was it Mary? Martha? Lazarus? Magda hurt with worry. They had to do something! She cared about these people. Yeshua loved them.

Magda was equally shocked by Yeshua's lack of response to the man's urgent message. He said nothing. He didn't react. He didn't tell them who it was. He merely looked at Peter. The disciple understood His silent command and took the others back to the crowd on the shore.

"Walk with Me," Yeshua repeated to Matthias.

Matthias followed Him away from the crowd. Magda watched them disappear over the small hillside. She went back to the camp, carrying the burden of the news on her own.

"What's wrong?" Leah asked her immediately.

"I just heard news from a messenger that a friend I care about is terribly sick." Tears welled up in Magda's eyes. "I'm worried." She paused. "No, I'm upset."

"Upset? Why?"

"Because Yeshua doesn't seem to care," Magda replied. "Why aren't we going to them? Why is He spending time with the messenger?"

"He must have His reasons." Leah tried unsuccessfully to encourage her new friend.

Magda looked up from her brewing emotions. Yeshua weaved His way through the camp. Open fires were cooking freshly caught fish. Joanna and Susanna were distributing bread. The disciples were pouring wine. Peter, James, and John were sharing the bad news with the others. Yet, no one dared ask Yeshua about it.

"Shoshana," Yeshua touched Leah's shoulder.

She stood and turned around, smiling at Yeshua. He stepped aside, revealing Matthias. Magda stood with Yeshua.

"A reunion," He whispered to Magda.

"Leah?" Matthias exclaimed. "Leah, is it you?"

Leah's eyes brimmed with tears, her body shaking with sobs. "My brother?" She fell into his arms. "I don't believe it. At last, we are together again."

Matthias hugged her tight. "I thought you were dead. I was told that you..."

"Lies, Matthias," Leah informed him. "They were all lies! We were betrayed by Raman. It was all a plot from the beginning. Now it is time for the deception to end."

The scene touched Magda deeply, leaving a lasting impression on her. The power of sibling love quelled her own storm of emotional disturbance. No matter what happened, Mary, Martha, and Lazarus shared that same powerful love between them.

A woman named Salome joined Leah and Matthias. She was

another friend from Leah's past. Magda spent the remainder of the evening listening to their stories of redemption and reveling in their reunion. She wasn't the only one who had scorch marks from her past.

Everything that happened to them, even though it was difficult and trying, had prepared them all to meet with their Messiah. As Magda listened to how others suffered and overcame the darkness, her own faith was bolstered.

Yeshua did not make haste to return to Bethany. This was troubling not only to Magda but also to the disciples. They all cared about Mary, Martha, and Lazarus.

Magda was serving the morning meal. She poured mulled wine into Andrew's empty cup.

"I don't understand why He does nothing in response to the message," Andrew stated, an edgy concern in his voice.

Yeshua came silently up behind the man, startling them all, even Magda, who had not heard His approach. "This sickness is not to death, but for the glory of God, that God's Son may be glorified by it."[150]

His words held the power to put everyone at ease. Yeshua was in control. If He was not concerned, then the disciples would not be either. For the entire day, the friends of Lazarus, Martha, and Mary put the heaviness of the news behind them.

The following morning, when Yeshua finished His morning prayers, He began packing up the camp.

"Let's go into Judea again."[151] Yeshua announced with authority.

"Rabbi, the Jews were just trying to stone You, and are You going there again?"[152] James asked Him.

Magda followed Yeshua's example and began taking down

---

[150] John 11:4
[151] John 11:7
[152] John 11:8

her own tent. She could still hear the conversation going on between Yeshua and James. The other disciples were gathering around them.

Yeshua replied to James's question. "Aren't there twelve hours of daylight? If a man walks in the day, he doesn't stumble, because he sees the light of this world. But if a man walks in the night, he stumbles, because the light isn't in him."[153]

Confused by His response, no one dared asked Him what He meant.

Yeshua seemed to sense their confusion. "Our friend, Lazarus, has fallen asleep," He said, "but I am going so that I may awake him out of sleep."[154]

"Lord, if he has fallen asleep, he will recover."[155] John spoke up next.

Yeshua placed His hand on John's shoulder. "Lazarus is dead." Every one of them gasped in horror before Yeshua continued. "I am glad for your sakes that I was not there, so that you may believe. Nevertheless, let's go to him."[156]

Yeshua moved to pack up camp as if they were only moving on to preach in another village. The disciples were in shock, confused and troubled at the news of their friend.

Grief hit Magda like a tidal wave, overwhelming her completely. Dead? Lazarus had died? How could Yeshua have let that happen? What were Mary and Martha going through right now? The questions swirled like a storm within her thoughts. She remembered losing Pascal. The wound of deep loss opened again at the news of Lazarus's death.

Grief was not of the light. It was not part of Yahweh's original design. Her heart rebelled against it, but the power of the emotion

---

[153] John 11:9-10

[154] John 11:11

[155] John 11:12

[156] John 11:14-15

was strong. It hurt in ways that Magda couldn't begin to fix. She needed Him. Only He could reach that place inside of her where darkness beckoned. That slippery slope of intense emotion that had claimed her father, taking him down to the abyss, was opening up inside of her. Magda tried to turn herself toward the light.

"I trust You, Lord," she prayed. *"Help me trust You more."*

They made haste toward Bethany. Everyone was silent, processing the impending news in their own way. The journey was arduous, with treacherous terrain and steep emotional inclines. Magda felt as though she was walking through mud to get there. The slowness made time feel like their enemy. There was no hope if Lazarus was already dead. Why did Yeshua not leave sooner? He had told them that He was glad He wasn't there so that they would believe. What did that mean?

Peter and John were moving so fast that they got way ahead of the rest of the followers. Magda saw their tiny silhouettes disappearing toward the village of Bethany.

A while later, Magda saw Martha come running toward them. Magda's heart broke at the hurt look in Martha's eyes. Martha just stared at Yeshua's feet.

"Lord, if You would have been here, my brother wouldn't have died."[157] Her voice trembled.

Yeshua reached out and lifted Martha's chin so that she was looking into His compassionate eyes. In a broken voice, Martha proclaimed her little faith, vanquishing the grip of grief with her statement. "Even now I know that, whatever You ask of Yahweh, Your Father will give You."[158]

Yeshua said to her, "Your brother will rise again."[159]

"I know that he will rise again in the resurrection at the last

---

[157] John 11:21
[158] John 11:21-22
[159] John 11:23

day."[160]

Yeshua took Martha's hands in His own. Looking at her, He proclaimed, "I am the resurrection and the life. He who believes in Me will live, even if he dies. Whoever lives and believes in Me will never die. Do you believe this?"[161]

Magda wept in belief. Resurrection and life, He said. What did it mean? She felt the power of the moment as all darkness trembled around her.

They met up with Mary at the intersection of the path that led to Jerusalem. Her grief was even more intense than her sister's. Mary was vulnerable beneath the weight of her despair. The poor, young woman fell at Yeshua's feet in complete exhaustion. Her voice was barely audible. The sound of Mary exposing her wound broke Magda's heart.

"Lord, if You would have been here, my brother wouldn't have died."[162] Mary sobbed.

A single tear rolled down Yeshua's cheek as He shared her pain. He took Mary by the hand. "Where have you laid him?"[163]

Led by the grieving sisters, the few of them near Yeshua moved toward the tomb. The rest of the crowd followed at a distance. By the time they arrived at Lazarus's resting place, the remainder of the crowd, including the disciples, had caught up to them. Everyone had followed them to the tomb.

Mary and Martha stayed close to Yeshua. Outside the tomb, Yeshua, with power and authority, commanded, "Take away the stone!"[164]

"Lord, by this time there is a stench, for he has been dead four days,"[165] Martha reminded Him.

---

[160] John 11:24

[161] John 11:25-26

[162] John 11:32

[163] John 11:34

[164] John 11:39

[165] John 11:39

Yeshua looked at Martha intently, "Didn't I tell you that if you believed, you would see Yahweh's glory?"[166]

When the stone was rolled away and the stench of death nearly knocked them all over, Yeshua looked into the dusky sky. Magda put her hand up to her nose. Her thoughts had been silenced by her belief in the impossible. Her grief had been vanquished by rising hope. Yeshua prayed to His Father while darkness preyed on the people.

"Father, I thank You that You listened to Me. I know that You always listen to Me, but because of the multitude that stands around I said this, that they may believe that You sent Me." When He finished the prayer, He cried with a loud voice. "Lazarus, come out!"[167]

In moments, Lazarus came out, bound in his grave clothes. Yeshua commanded that the clothes be removed so that Lazarus could be set free.

Awe consumed Magda, leaving her breathless. He was the Resurrection and the life! Love overcame death. Even as the realization of the power hit her, and love took back the ground that grief had tried to claim in her heart, Magda sensed the forces of darkness increasing the intensity of their attack.

Some in the crowd whose allegiance was with the Pharisees grumbled as they left. "What are we doing? This man does many signs. If we leave Him alone like this, everyone will believe in Him, and the Romans will come and take away both our place and our nation. We must inform the authorities."[168]

"We need to call a council," another disgruntled man said. "He must be stopped!"

"*He must be stopped. He must be stopped. He must be stopped,*" Magda heard the incessant hissing from the unseen realm.

---

[166] John 11:40
[167] John 11:41-43
[168] John 11:46-48

EVERLASTING

Angels who didn't keep their first domain,
but deserted their own dwelling place, He has kept in everlasting bonds
under darkness for the judgment of the great day.
Jude 1:6, WEB

Chapter Thirty-Four

In the days and weeks that followed Lazarus's resurrection, Yeshua and His followers traveled the region. Yeshua continued to preach the good news of the Kingdom of Heaven. The only difference now was that He spoke in secret places, avoiding the open areas and synagogues.

One day, they traversed a farmer's land. The pungent smell of freshly turned soil filled the air as the farmer diligently tilled his field. Yeshua took off His sandals and walked through the freshly turned over soil. Magda and the disciples followed His lead. She felt the coldness of the ground squeeze between her toes. The more she walked, the dirtier her feet became. When they were in the middle of the field, Yeshua began teaching them.

"The Kingdom of Heaven is like a man who sowed good seed in his field, but while people slept, his enemy came and sowed weeds also among the wheat, and went away." Yeshua bent down and let the soil run through His fingers, sifting it. "But when the blade sprang up and produced grain, then the weeds appeared also. The servants came and said to him, 'Sir, didn't you sow good seed in your field? Where did these weeds come from?' The farmer replied, 'An enemy has done this.'"[169]

Yeshua stood up. Magda heard the edge in His voice. She saw the troubled expression in His eyes.

He looked at the disciples, letting His gaze linger on James and John. "The servants asked him, 'Do you want us to go and gather up the weeds?' But the farmer said, 'No, lest perhaps while you gather up the weeds, you root up the wheat with them. Let both grow together until the harvest, and in the harvest time I will tell the reapers, 'First, gather up the weeds, and bind them in bundles to burn them; but gather the wheat into my barn.''"[170]

They remained silent. Every one of them felt the weight of the moment. Gradually, the small group of people who had trailed behind them started to disperse.

Peter cleared his throat. "Explain to us the parable of the weeds of the field."[171]

Magda appreciated Peter's humility in asking the Lord for further explanation. She had made her own assumptions about what He meant by the teaching, but she wanted confirmation that her own assessment was correct. Knowing firsthand the underhanded plotting of the evil one, Magda thought this parable had something to do with the forces of darkness in the unseen realm attempting to undermine Yeshua's mission.

The troubled expression that clouded Yeshua's eyes changed to a look of expansive love. He gave them an answer none could truly understand.

"He who sows the good seed is the Son of Man, the field is the world, the good seeds are the children of the Kingdom, and the weeds are the children of the evil one. The enemy who sowed them is the devil. The harvest is the end of the age, and the reapers are angels. As the weeds are gathered up and burned with

---

[169] Matthew 13:24-28
[170] Matthew 13:29-30
[171] Matthew 13:36

fire; so will it be at the end of this age. The Son of Man will send out His angels, and they will gather out of His Kingdom all things that cause stumbling and those who do iniquity, and will cast them into the furnace of fire. There will be weeping and gnashing of teeth. Then the righteous will shine like the sun in the Kingdom of their Father. He who has ears to hear, let him hear."[172]

Magda did her best to quell the rising waves of fear in her heart. She could feel the atmosphere around her perpetually changing. She caught glimpses of a strain in Yeshua's countenance as He preached. He pleaded with the people that He loved, imploring them to follow His way.

As the days turned into weeks, time seemed to slip through their fingers. The animosity from the religious leaders grew, creating an oppression that moved in like a threatening storm. The week before Passover, Yeshua took His disciples back to Bethany. Being in Mary and Martha's home brought a sense of comfort and relief to Magda. Lazarus was delighted to see them all.

"There is a plot against Lazarus's life," Martha informed Magda while she helped her with the preparations for the meal.

"A plot for his life? But why?" Magda's question came out as a protest, her tone laced with disbelief.

"The Sanhedrin is threatened by his testimony," Martha answered. "They want him silenced."

"There is another they want silenced as well," Magda replied, shaking her head.

Magda carried a plate to the table where the disciples and Yeshua were seated. The men were talking amongst themselves, boasting. Magda could tell that their discussion displeased Yeshua. Yet, He remained silent. Magda wondered how those closest to Yeshua could still be so unaware of His displeasure.

Magda passed out some bread. A sweet fragrance suddenly filled the air. She turned to see Mary anointing Yeshua's feet with

---

[172] Matthew 13:37-43

perfume. The scent that filled the air was unlike anything Magda had ever experienced before, pure and enchanting. It immediately transported her to the memory of her vision of heaven's staircase…

Magda had been high above the gray clouds of spiritual darkness. Yeshua stood at the top of the stairs, beckoning to her. She looked into His eyes, seeing a glimmer of her reflection. She couldn't quite make it out. Magda took the first step toward Him, taking her eyes off the dark shadows that were now beneath her feet. She heard Him speak to her heart. "Come away with Me, beloved, where the righteous will shine like the sun in the Kingdom of their Father."

The sound of smashing glass broke Magda's sweet reverie. Startled, she dropped some bread on the floor. She bent over to pick it up, a little dazed at the sudden awareness of her surroundings again. She had no idea what she missed, but the mood around the table had been altered.

Within a few awkward moments, the conversation resumed. Everything went back to normal, or at least to a new normal. Brooding, Judas stared off into the distance, his brow furrowed in deep contemplation. Magda could see the darkness in the man's eyes. She was glad that she couldn't listen to his thoughts. As she looked at Judas, the image of the stain on her feet from that day in the farmer's field flashed in her mind.

When morning came, Yeshua resolutely set out for Jerusalem. His gaze burned with intensity, like a piece of flint sparking a fire. He rode on the donkey which the disciples had brought back from Bethphage. They covered the little creature with cloaks made by Mary's own hand. The sun was shining brightly overhead. The day held the promise of glorious sunshine and clear blue skies.

As they neared the city, a large crowd gathered. People were shouting praises to Yeshua. Several in the crowd bowed to Him, proclaiming Him the coming King.

"Hosanna! Blessed is He who comes in the name of the Lord,

the King of Israel!"[173] The repeated shouts echoed through the crowd.

As the praise subsided, Magda became aware of a lingering echo that filled the air. *"He must be destroyed. He must be destroyed."* The hissing phrase from the bowels of Zophos followed every praise the people shouted.

As Magda looked around at the joy on the faces of the others, she realized that she was the only one who could hear evil's echo.

When they entered the city, the multitude threw down palm branches for Yeshua's colt to walk upon. Even the donkey looked overly joyed to Magda. The beast was proud to be carrying the King. With a firm grip on the rope, Peter guided the animal forward, its hooves clopping softly against the ground.

Yeshua touched the hands that were extended to Him. Magda followed as closely as she could. The more excited the crowd became, the harder it was for her to keep close to Him. Everyone pushed and shoved to glimpse the Messiah.

Magda saw Yeshua dismount the donkey. He walked toward the Temple steps. Magda was close enough to see the troubled expression on His face. She was too far to hear Him, but she knew what He said even if He was not speaking aloud.

"The time has come for the Son of Man to be glorified. Now my soul is troubled. What shall I say? 'Father, save Me from this time?' But I came to this time for this cause. Father, glorify Your Name!"[174]

Did anyone else hear Him? Why were they not responding? Why was Yeshua sitting on the steps?

A thunderous light broke through the unseen gray clouds that veiled the Temple. Magda heard the authoritative voice respond to Yeshua from heaven.

---

[173] John 12:13
[174] John 12:23, 27

"I have both glorified it, and will glorify it again."[175]

Magda looked around. The religious leaders watched like birds of prey on the periphery. The only thing keeping them from interfering was the protection of the people's current adoration. A feeling of fear began to grow inside her, like a gnawing pit in her stomach. Doubt swirled like a tempest. As quickly as it had come, the light from heaven withdrew. Magda was jostled and moved in a direction contrary to where she wanted to be.

"You think you can escape my grasp," a voice hissed.

Magda whipped around. There was no one there. She looked up into the clear blue sky. Without warning, her eyesight dimmed. As she looked up, a blanket of gray clouds stretched across the sky. They were moving in, shielding the people from the sun. Magda wanted to scream out, to tell everyone to run, but no one else seemed to notice what she did.

The once calm atmosphere suddenly turned ominous, filling her surroundings with an unsettling fear. The forest of Zophos was upon them. Magda looked at the landscape. Everything had turned to gray. The vibrant hues of life seemed to fade away as she stood amidst the swirling chaos.

She looked at the people who had become strange ghosts in her eyes. She could see into them. Some had embers that glowed in their hearts. When Yeshua touched them, the flint of His eyes sparked their hearts into flame. Others had black hearts, devoid of life, composed only of ash. They were doused by their own pride, unable to catch the fire of true love.

Magda kept turning in circles. Everywhere she looked, people were exposed to her sight. She saw the unseen realm. Looking toward the religious leaders standing on the periphery, Magda saw their vulture-like forms. Fear ran through her veins as she trembled with anxiety. They were waiting for the signal to attack.

The voices of the people became a distant sound in Magda's

---

[175] John 12:28

ears. Instead, the sounds of evil rose to a volume that hurt. Screeches, howls, and screams assaulted her in a language she didn't understand. Magda was afraid that she was being pulled back into the forest of Zophos. Was she going mad? Was she slipping out of reality?

Magda turned around again, her hands over her ears. She stood face to face with a bat-like creature. His eyes were flaming red. She felt the magnetic pull of his lust. She tried to resist him, to fight him off. Her mind was blank. She couldn't think straight. Was someone touching her? Was she falling?

Magda hit the ground hard. The creature was on her, tearing at her. A bright light suddenly blinded her. She shielded her eyes, heard a thud, and felt the warm blood soaking the ground beneath her arm. She felt no pain. Whose blood was it?

"I am my beloved's and my beloved is mine," Magda whispered before fading into the darkness.

When Magda woke up, she was in a strange place, wearing strange clothes. In the corner, a bloodied sheet concealed what seemed to be a lifeless figure. Magda stood up slowly. She walked toward the covered figure. Hesitating, she followed the compulsion of her curiosity and lifted the sheet. The dead body of the Roman soldier who had taken Pascal's life stared up at her.

Magda jumped back with a shock, fearing she had done something to the man. Her memory of the most recent amount of time was blurry. The door to the shadowed room opened abruptly. A large man walked in. Magda scurried to the opposite corner, looking for something she could use as a weapon.

"It's alright," the man said, placing his hands in the air before her. "I'm not going to hurt you. You know me. I'm Abner, the Centurion. We met in Capernaum."

Once he moved out of the shadow of the open door, Magda's eyes could focus on his features. She recognized him.

"What am I doing here?" she asked, secretly relieved.

"There was trouble in the city on the way to the Temple. I'm not exactly sure what happened, but you were in distress. I saw it from my horse. You were spinning around and around in circles." Abner helped Magda to sit down on the cot.

"I don't really remember what happened," she lied as the memories came back to her. She feared being truthful would make her look like a lunatic.

"I tried to get to you, but the crowd was pressing in around you too hard," Abner said. "Then I saw that man," he pointed to the dead soldier, "approach you. He began assaulting you right there in the middle of the crowd. So, I got off my horse and forced my way through the crowd. He and I fought." Abner paused. "I won."

Magda didn't know what to say. She sat silent, Yeshua's words rising in her heart and mind. *The Son of Man will send out His angels, and they will gather out of His Kingdom all things that cause stumbling and those who do iniquity, and will cast them into the furnace of fire. There will be weeping and gnashing of teeth.*

Abner broke into her silent thoughts. "I picked you up and brought you here. Your clothes were ruined, so I got you something else to wear. I'm sorry that it isn't the customary attire of your own people. This was all that I could find."

"Thank you, Centurion," Magda said. "It is a very fine garment. I like the color blue."

"Please, call me Abner," he said, smiling.

"What is this place?" Magda asked, looking around at the dark and dismal surroundings.

"I'm sorry. I didn't know where else to take you." Abner sighed. "This is the place where we keep the prisoners awaiting sentencing. I haven't figured out what to do about him." Abner glanced over at the dead soldier. "It was unfortunate that it had to end that way. I've had trouble with that one before."

"Yes, so have I," Magda said. "He killed my friend, my guide, when I was in Nain."

Abner looked at Magda, compassion in his eyes. "No wonder

you were frightened to see me. Not all Romans are bad."

"I know that now," Magda said. "You came to my aid before, when I was on the road, traveling from Capernaum. It was that man and two others that stopped me that day. They did not have good intentions."

"I remember now," Abner said. He looked at the sheet covering the dead man. "I suppose justice found Lucius in the end. The only question now is how I'm going to explain this to Rome."

"Was he someone important?" Magda asked.

Abner hesitated, unsure if he should answer her. "He was the grandson of the Emperor. He was trying to prove his worth by disguising himself as a soldier. I never thought it was a good idea. The man didn't like to take orders and never stayed with his patrol."

Magda looked at the ground. "I hope I didn't bring trouble on you, Abner," she said.

"It isn't anything I can't handle," he replied.

Magda noticed a bundle of thorny branches in the corner. It mysteriously drew her attention. She walked over to it. "Why do you keep thorny branches?" she asked Abner.

"They make good deterrents when the prisoners get out of hand," Abner replied.

Magda reached out and touched them with her finger. The sharpness immediately stung, drawing blood.

"Ow," she said. "They are sharp!" She touched her finger to her lips.

"Yes," Abner handed her a cloth. "That is the point."

Magda smiled at his sense of humor.

"Do you happen to know where Yeshua went? Is He alright?" Magda asked.

"Alright?" Abner replied. "The last thing He said before He disappeared was: 'Yet a little while the light is with you. Walk while you have the light, that darkness doesn't overtake you. He who walks in the darkness doesn't know where he is going. While you have the light, believe in the light, that you may become children of light.'[176] His words are powerful."

"Where is He?" Magda asked.

"No one knows," Abner replied. "He just disappeared."

"Disappeared? He can't just disappear. He has to be somewhere." She sounded frantic. "I need to find Him."

Abner graciously led her out of the enclosed room.

Magda made her way through the dark streets of Jerusalem. Abner did not want her to go unescorted, but he was called away on urgent business. To avoid attracting attention in the Roman toga, he had provided her with a cloak to wear.

The city looked different at night. The bustling city of Jerusalem took on a whole new atmosphere at night, leaving Magda in awe of its mystery. Something about the shadows cast by the many torches and the slithering movements of the people as they scurried to their destinations reminded Magda of the forest of Zophos. At night, the city of Jerusalem was prey to the less than honorable intentions of men.

Magda drew her hood up over her head. She did her best to make herself invisible. Unfortunately, she didn't quite know where she was going.

"Help me find my way, Lord," she prayed. *"I am lost. Guide me."*

Magda didn't like being separated from Yeshua. Thoughts of where He might be plagued her mind relentlessly. How was she to find Him? Had He moved on from the city?

A familiar voice caught her attention. Magda looked up. Where was the voice coming from? She saw two men standing beneath the torches, only a few feet away from her. She was at the Temple again. When Magda turned the corner, she recognized Judas. He was heavily cloaked as she was, but she could see his face illuminated by the torch. He was talking to another man she

---

[176] John 12:35-36

didn't recognize. The other man looked important. Magda remained on the other side of the pillar, hidden from their view.

"Malchus, I can't just hand Him over to you. You know that, right?" Judas was saying.

"What do you propose, then? You were the one who offered to help the High Priest," Malchus replied, a little irritated.

"My father arranged that," Judas said. "Just give me some time. I will think of a way," Judas pleaded.

"We are running out of time, Judas. The High Priest wants Him silenced. He will not wait forever, especially now that Passover is upon us." Malchus shifted his weight.

"Please, Malchus, just a couple more days," Judas said.

"Fine, but if you don't do something, we will be coming after you," Malchus said before storming off.

Magda moved quickly so that the man would not see her as he stalked by. Fortunately, Judas slinked off into the night before ever noticing she was there.

Magda did not like what she heard. Was Judas working with the High Priest against Yeshua? Surely, Yeshua must sense this. Why wouldn't He do something? Now more than ever, Magda wanted to find Yeshua. She didn't know where to start.

Tears blurred her vision. She was lost in the city at night. Magda didn't know what to do. She felt as if she was walking in circles. To her utter surprise, she turned a corner and bumped into a man on a horse. Magda jumped back, just about to run away from the Roman when she heard him say her name kindly.

"Magda? Is that you?" the man asked.

Magda turned around and looked up into the face of Matthias, Leah's long-lost brother. "Matthias! I am so glad to see you," Magda almost cried for joy. "I'm lost."

"Here," Matthias extended her a hand. "You can come with me. I am staying with some people we just met here in the city. You will be most welcome."

Magda grabbed hold of Matthias's hand as he helped her up

onto his horse. He brought her to the home of Salome in the upper city. Magda was delighted to be reunited with Leah and Salome, especially since everyone sensed a foreboding in the atmosphere around Jerusalem.

As the night wore on, they couldn't sleep, so they gathered around and shared stories of their most recent adventures, their laughter filling the air. When Magda finally fell asleep, her rest was fitful. She didn't like being parted from Yeshua.

When she closed her eyes, her mind formed images of the thorny branches and dripping blood. She saw the dead body covered with a bloody sheet. She walked in bloody footprints until she reached the body. Lifting up the sheet, she saw Yeshua laying there, not the Roman soldier.

Magda woke with her heart racing and her body shaking. Looking at the sky, she realized that morning was still hours away. She was paralyzed as long as it was night. Yet, even in the powerlessness of the moment, a determination to find Him caught fire within her. She would wait for the sun. And when it arose, she would set out on her mission.

CHAPTER THIRTY-FIVE

It was the day before Passover when Magda finally realized she hadn't checked the one place she knew Yeshua had visited in Jerusalem before. The woman named Zhiva had a dwelling near the marketplace. Yeshua had taken them there not too long ago. Perhaps He went there again.

Magda knocked on the wood door. There was no answer. The place was entirely quiet. After a few moments, Magda heard the shuffling of feet. Zhiva opened the door slowly.

"Yes?" the old woman remarked. "Oh, I know you." The woman's face lit up with recognition. "He told me a beautiful young woman would be stopping by. You are Yeshua's. "

"I am," Magda smiled, appreciating the description.

"Come in. Come in." Zhiva ushered her inside.

Magda stepped across the threshold into Zhiva's dwelling. The solitude of the place was palpable, with no other souls in sight. A sense of disappointment washed over Magda. She had been searching for Yeshua for two days, fearing to leave the city because something in her heart told her to remain in Jerusalem. Was she wrong to trust her instincts?

"Stephen went to get some supplies for Passover. I am here alone for now," Zhiva said. "I usually have some of Joseph's friends from the Temple here for Passover."

"The religious leaders are coming here for Passover?" Magda asked, fear nipping at the edges of her heart. "Don't worry, Miss Zhiva. I won't be staying. I was just looking for Yeshua and His disciples. I have somehow become separated from Him."

"Oh, my dear, you will never be separated from Him. Of that, I am sure. I can see it in His eyes when He looks at you." Zhiva shuffled over toward her cooking area. "Would you like some tea?"

Before Magda could answer, the door flew open. Stephen was carrying large boxes, breathing heavily under the strain. Magda went over to help him.

"Here, let me get that," she offered.

"Thank you, umm?" Stephen said.

"Magda. I am a follower of Yeshua."

"That's right, Magda. I remember now."

They finished bringing in the supplies, stacking them neatly in the cooking area. Stephen was sighing.

"Is something wrong?" Magda asked him.

"All this work for nothing," Stephen said. "I don't have the heart to tell Zhiva."

"Tell Zhiva what, young man? We don't keep secrets." The old woman had impeccable hearing.

Stephen looked at her with deep affection. "It seems that Joseph got called away on urgent business. He won't be taking Passover here. I'm sorry Zhiva. I know how much it means to you. He said he will still pay us for the room, though."

"Well, we will have plenty for the three of us," Zhiva remarked. "You must stay, Miss Magda. I won't hear of you leaving now."

Magda smiled. She didn't want to disappoint the woman, but she really wanted to continue her search for Yeshua. Why did she have to wait to go to Him? Where was He? Magda couldn't stand the separation. She wanted it to be over. She wanted to be with Him again.

A knock on the door surprised the three of them. Stephen went to answer it.

"Yes?" Stephen said, opening the door.

"James! Andrew!" Magda exclaimed upon seeing the men.

"Magda, what are you doing here?" James asked, surprised.

"Come in," Stephen said to the men.

Magda rushed over and hugged Andrew first, then James. She held them tight, tears of joy falling down her cheeks. "I've been looking for you all. Where have you been? I got separated in the crowd the day He came in on the colt," Magda said.

"Yes, we all had been scattered for a bit. Yeshua disappeared." James explained.

"He sent us here now," Andrew interrupted. "He will be here before sundown."

"Here? Why?" Magda asked.

Looking at Zhiva and Stephen, James delivered his message. "The Lord has need of the upper room for Passover. He sent us here. He said that we would find it furnished and ready."[177]

"That you will," Stephen said. "We have plenty of room."

James smiled, a look of relief washing over his face. Magda could tell that he hadn't been sure about this errand that the Lord sent him on.

"Are you alright, James?" Magda asked him.

"I am now," he replied. "The Lord sends us out on these missions and, I admit, sometimes I doubt that it will be as He says it will. My faith is little, Magda. Even after all this time."

---

[177] Mark 14:14-16

"I know, James. I feel the same way," Magda confessed. "Come, let me help you set up for the meal tonight."

The thought of being reunited with Yeshua filled Magda with a renewed sense of energy. She couldn't wait for Him to arrive. Anticipation filled her to the brim, spreading a profound sense of joy throughout her being. They set up the room for Yeshua and the disciples. Candles were lit. Soft light emanated from the sconces mounted on the walls. It was a beautiful space.

When she heard the knock on the door, Magda's heart skipped with delight. Stephen opened the door on Martha and Mary. They had come with Abner, the Centurion. While Magda was happy to see them, she was disappointed that it wasn't yet time for Yeshua's arrival.

The women embraced, chatting comfortably while they worked together preparing the food. Magda was so involved in the task they were doing that she didn't even hear the door open. Yeshua and the other disciples had arrived while Magda busily chopped the sprigs of bitter herbs. Mary and Martha had left the area to work on arranging the table with a few extra items that they brought with them.

Lost in thoughts about the thorny branches while chopping away furiously, Magda sliced her finger. Before she had a chance to react to the pain, Yeshua was beside her. He took her finger in His hand, staunching the blood with radiant pressure. In His presence, Magda was rendered speechless. Her heart was mingled with emotions of joy and sadness, fear and trust, confidence and weakness.

"You always have to rescue me, Lord," Magda said with a trembling voice.

"And I always will," Yeshua replied. "You see the struggle and the agony, Mary. I see in you the reason that I came."

Magda smiled at Him, touching her healed finger to His cheek, resting her hand there until He put His own hand on top of hers. "I don't want to be parted from You again," she whispered.

Yeshua did not reply. He silently looked at her with a love that could not be explained or understood, only received.

The Passover began in the most unusual manner. Yeshua disrobed in front of them all. Everyone was shocked. The silence covered the room. He took the bowl of water, wrapped a towel around His waist and began to wash the disciples' feet.[178]

He started with Peter. "Lord, do You wash my feet?"[179]

"What I am doing you do not understand now, but afterward you will understand."[180] Yeshua replied.

Peter pulled his feet away and said to Him, "You shall never wash my feet."[181]

Yeshua looked Peter in the eye. "If I do not wash you, you have no share with Me."[182]

"Lord, not my feet only but also my hands and my head!"[183] Peter exclaimed, extending not only his feet but his hands as well.

Yeshua laughed slightly. "The one who has bathed does not need to wash, except for his feet, but is completely clean." Yeshua sighed deeply. "And you are clean, but not every one of you."[184]

In that instant, Magda remembered what she had witnessed that night at the Temple. Yeshua knew. He knew that Judas was not clean. Magda wondered what He was going to do about it.

When Yeshua washed Judas's feet in the same manner that He had washed the other disciple's feet, Magda found herself perplexed. Why was Yeshua treating Judas the same when He knew what the man was?

Magda helped Martha and Mary serve the meal. She followed their lead since this was an area in which these two women were

---

[178] John 13:5
[179] John 13:6
[180] John 13:7
[181] John 13:8
[182] John 13:8
[183] John 13:9
[184] John 13:10

experts. Though Magda understood more about hospitality than she ever had before, she still had a lot to learn.

Magda was bringing the unleavened bread into the room when she heard Yeshua talking. "I know whom I have chosen. But the Scripture will be fulfilled, 'He who ate my bread has lifted his heel against me.' I am telling you this now, before it takes place, that when it does take place you may believe that I am He."[185]

Magda didn't like the deep sadness she saw in Yeshua's eyes. Nor did she like the strained tone of His voice. She went back to the cooking area to retrieve more wine. When she returned, the first thing she did was pour the new wine into the silver goblet that Yeshua held out to her. She had seen Him with it before at Martha's house. He always had it on the table, but He had never used it before now.

He was still talking in a voice thick with emotion. "I have earnestly desired to eat this Passover with you before I suffer, for I tell you, I will no longer by any means eat of it until it is fulfilled in Yahweh's Kingdom."[186] He took the silver goblet, lifted it toward heaven and gave thanks.

Magda felt the holiness of the moment. When she looked up, her eyes closed, she saw nothing but clouds moving in. Her heart felt the storm coming. She was afraid.

Yeshua looked around at each of those who followed Him. "Take this, and share it among yourselves, for I tell you, I will not drink at all again from the fruit of the vine, until God's Kingdom comes. This cup is the new covenant in my blood, which is poured out for you."[187]

Magda saw tears welling up in John's eyes as he was the first one to take the cup and drink from it. The twelve men passed the silver goblet around, silent and obediently reverent. Yeshua

[185] John 13:18-19
[186] Luke 22:15-17
[187] Luke 22:17-18, 22

waited for them.

Next, He took the bread, lifted it toward heaven and gave thanks. He broke the bread harshly. Then, He gave it to them, saying, "This is My body which is given for you. Do this in memory of Me."[188]

Yeshua had them pass around the unleavened bread until they had each eaten a piece. The men looked as distraught as Magda felt. What did He mean by saying, *'Do this in memory of Me?'*

Yeshua spoke with a heavy sorrow in His voice as He sat down. "Behold, the hand of him who betrays Me is with Me on the table. The Son of Man indeed goes, as it has been determined, but woe to that man through whom He is betrayed!"[189]

Magda wanted to scream out. She wanted to expose Judas. She wanted to stop the evil man. But, her tongue was stuck to the roof of her mouth. Her feet felt like lead. She was powerless to stop anything. Judas had invited the evil to their sacred space. How could he do that?

When Magda remembered the agreements which she had made with the darkness, she fell to her knees in repentant prayer. She was no better than Judas. She was a betrayer of Yahweh, too. She needed her Rescuer, her Savior. In a similar way to Judas, she felt a sense of powerlessness as she struggled to find a way out.

The men began singing a sweet melodic psalm of the Hillel. The strong emotion in their voices struck a chord in Magda's heart. As they sang, she heard another sound increasing in volume beneath the holy melody. The lyrics of the language she knew, sung by her spiritual brothers, were being drowned out by the unsettling language of Zophos, sung by sinister demons.

The louder they got, the more Magda could make out the words of evil.

---

[188] Luke 22:19
[189] Luke 22:21-22

"We have Him now. Our hour has come. He is ours."

Magda looked up and saw Judas scurry from the room.

Yeshua rose from the table and put on His cloak. The others began packing up quickly, even though they had not quite finished the rituals of the traditional Passover meal.

Yeshua went around touching each man on the shoulder.

"You are those who have continued with Me in My trials. I confer on you a Kingdom, even as my Father conferred on Me, that you may eat and drink at My table in My Kingdom."[190]

Magda couldn't help but feel like He was saying goodbye. She didn't like it. For the first time since she became His follower, she didn't want to hear what He was saying.

When Yeshua got to Peter, He looked at the disciple longer than He had looked at the others. "Simon, behold, Satan asked to have all of you, that he might sift you as wheat, but I prayed for you, that your faith wouldn't fail. Peter, when once you have turned again, establish your brothers."[191]

A look of great fear and concern etched itself on Peter's face. He looked as vulnerable as a child even as he mustered up adult words to speak. "Lord, I am ready to go with You both to prison and to death!"[192]

Yeshua touched the man on the cheek. He looked at Peter with such love and compassion that even Magda felt like crying. "I tell you, Peter, the rooster will by no means crow today until you deny that you know Me three times."[193]

Peter swallowed the tears that were trying to surface. Yet, the shaken disciple said nothing in reply.

Yeshua left the dwelling so quickly that Magda didn't even have time to inform Mary and Martha that they were going. She

---

[190] Luke 22:28-30

[191] Luke 22:31-32

[192] Luke 22:33

[193] Luke 22:34

didn't even know where they were going. All Magda knew was that she wasn't going to let Him out of her sight ever again. The last couple of days searching for Him had been excruciating. She stayed close by as the group pushed their way into the blackness swallowing up Jerusalem.

When Magda got out into the street, the darkness sucked at her soul like a black hole. She caught her breath, feeling the difference in the night. Something was going on that had never taken place before. Magda looked up at the full moon as they walked. The light shone directly on Yeshua as if it were a beam from heaven especially for Him at this hour.

Yeshua spoke while He walked with them. "I will no longer talk much with you, for the ruler of this world is coming. He has no claim on Me, but I do as the Father has commanded Me, so that the world may know that I love the Father."[194]

The disciples didn't say a word. Despite their internal struggles, everyone made an effort to comprehend His message.

Yeshua's voice echoed in the dark void of sound this particular night brought. "This is My commandment, that you love one another as I have loved you. Greater love has no one than this, that someone lay down his life for his friends."[195] He stopped, looking at each of them in the darkness. "Already you are clean because of the Word that I have spoken to you. Abide in Me, and I in you."[196]

When they arrived at the Mount of Olives, they entered into the garden area. Yeshua looked exhausted. Magda had never seen Him so troubled before. She wanted to hold on to Him. She wanted to stop whatever storm was coming even though she couldn't fully see it.

---

[194] John 14:30-31
[195] John 15:12-13
[196] John 15:3-4

"Pray that you don't enter into temptation."[197] He instructed them while the night pressed in around them.

Magda remained with the disciples. They knelt to pray as He had commanded. Yeshua took Peter, James, and John a stone's throw away to pray together. Magda watched as Yeshua went a little further away from them, leaving Peter, James, and John at the foot of a tree.

Even as Magda prayed, she could see the silhouetted figure of her Lord praying in the darkness. The light from the moon still fell like a beam appointed to Him.

"Please Lord," she prayed. *"Don't let anything bad happen. I don't understand what is going on. My faith is too small. Keep me near Him. Teach me how to abide in Him, as He has taught us. Help Him, Yahweh."*

Magda felt a chill in the night air. Her skin tingled. She looked in the distance but couldn't see Yeshua anymore. When she looked up at the moon, a gray cloud covered it north to south. Another gray cloud covered it east to west. Each one was a sliver in shape, making the light of the moon appear blocked by a cross.

Magda remembered her rescue in the forest of Zophos. He had pulled out a sword which turned out to be a cross. What did it all mean? Magda's mind refused to make the connection.

They prayed for what seemed like a long time. Yeshua got up two times to check on Peter, James, and John. The other disciples near Magda had fallen asleep. She was getting drowsy herself, but willed herself to stay awake.

As she tried to pray, Magda's sleepy mind replayed scenes from the past week, mixing things together in a jumbled mess of confusion. She fought it off. He said to pray that she wouldn't be led into temptation. What was coming that would tempt her? Magda dared not tell anyone else of her vulnerability to the powers of darkness.

---

[197] Luke 22:40

"Lord, help me fight the darkness. Help me not to fall into temptation," she prayed as she fell into sleep.

When Yeshua returned, it startled her. "Wake up. The hour has come." He spoke to all of them, raising them up out of their unintended slumber.

The group followed Him into the open area of the garden. Magda could see light from torches coming in the distance. The shadows dancing in the trees reminded her greatly of the forest of Zophos. Magda grabbed John's arm, afraid to try to stand on her own.

Leading the group that approached them was none other than Judas himself. Behind him was a legion of Roman soldiers as well as the Temple guard. Magda recognized the man named Malchus whom she had witnessed Judas talking to earlier that week.

Judas walked right up to Yeshua and kissed Him on the cheek. Trembling with fear, the former disciple could barely stand. Yeshua looked at him, pity in His eyes. "Judas, do you betray the Son of Man with a kiss?"[198]

When no one moved, Yeshua stepped forward. "Whom do you seek?"[199] He asked them.

Malchus answered, "Yeshua of Nazareth."

"I am He," Yeshua answered with the authority of heaven anointing His Words. The soldiers fell back upon hearing Him proclaim who He was.[200]

Peter, full of zeal mixed with desire to defend his Lord, rushed forward with a sword. He cut off Malchus's ear. Magda saw the body part fall to the ground, blood spurting from the man's head as he fell to his knees in utter pain.

Yeshua looked at Peter. "Put your sword into its sheath! Shall

---

[198] Luke 22:48

[199] John 18:4

[200] John 18:6

I not drink the cup that the Father has given Me?"[201]

Yeshua walked over to Malchus. Picking the sliced off ear up from the ground, Yeshua knelt before the man sent to arrest Him and restored him, completely.

Magda was shocked that even in the face of betrayal and the knowledge that these men meant Him harm, Yeshua still chose to heal Malchus. There was no end to the mysterious power of His love.

Yeshua looked at Malchus. "I told you that I am He. So, if you seek Me, let these men go."[202]

Malchus just stared at Yeshua, speechless. When the man didn't move, another soldier came up and arrested Yeshua. They knocked Him to the ground, causing Magda to gasp. They shackled Him and put a bag over His head. Standing Him to His feet roughly, they dragged Him away like a sheep to slaughter.

Magda couldn't breathe. She was choked with fear, doubt, confusion, rage, pain and shock. She was unable to move. Why wasn't she going after Him? Why wasn't she following Him now?

Once Yeshua was out of sight, some of the soldiers came back toward them. Magda looked at the man, Malchus, who still kneeled in disbelief where he was. His hand was on his newly attached ear.

"Come on," John grabbed her by the arm. "We need to get out of here. They're coming back for us, too."

With that, Magda ran into the thick darkness of the night alongside John while the other disciples scattered, each to find his own way apart from the Lord.

---

[201] John 18:10
[202] John 18:8

CHAPTER THIRTY-SIX

Magda remained close to John as they fled. She tripped several times over dead branches that had fallen from the trees. At the edge of the garden, John brought them to a sudden halt. Taking cover behind an olive tree, Magda and the disciple felt the cool shade and the rough texture of the trunk against their backs. After John confirmed that there were no soldiers patrolling, they cautiously made their way across the open space towards Jerusalem. Not even a sliver of moonlight could penetrate the thick clouds, casting everything into pitch-black darkness. They had to tread cautiously, carefully navigating the dark shadows.

John took Magda directly to Zhiva's. Despite the fact that it was the second watch of the night, Stephen opened the door after John knocked only once.

"Something has happened," Stephen whispered. "Come in. Tell us. Where did you all go?"

John was out of breath. He and Magda had been running. They both sat down at the table. Yeshua's mother brought them something to drink.

"Yeshua has been arrested," John breathed out.

"Arrested?" Stephen exclaimed.

"Arrested at night? How is that possible?" Yeshua's mother asked.

"It was Judas," Magda said. "He betrayed Him."

Not a single word was spoken, and silence filled the room. The spiritual impact of the blow was powerful and sent shockwaves through the air. Vibrations of triumph straight from Zophos. This was not what anyone could have expected.

"He will be alright. They can't stop His mission. He was sent by God." Stephen tried to sound confident, but Magda could hear the trepidation in the young man's voice.

"I don't know what is happening," John admitted. "The others didn't come here?"

"No," Zhiva said. "You were the only ones who arrived."

"Where is everyone?" Stephen asked.

"We all scattered," John said, stifling emotions. "We all just left Him."

Magda and John hung their heads, their eyes fixed on the ground in shame. Up until this moment, Magda had never considered the disloyalty of her actions. She merely reacted in the moment. She let fear drive her away from Him. They all did.

"Can we find Him?" Magda asked, self-condemnation as frigid as ice coursing through her veins.

John looked up, thinking. "I have connections with the High Priest. Perhaps I can find out what is going on." John sounded hopeful. He stood up, preparing to leave.

"I'm coming with you," Magda said, wrapping her cloak around her.

"I am, too," Yeshua's mother added. "He is my Son."

No one dared argue with her. The three departed, not even taking time to say goodbye to Stephen and Zhiva.

The atmosphere crackled with tension, making everyone feel uneasy and on edge. When they arrived at the court of the High

Priest, Magda and Yeshua's mother waited outside while John used his connections to find a way inside. Several individuals gathered in the courtyard, alongside Magda and Yeshua's mother. They gathered around the fire, basking in its flickering glow and the cozy heat it provided against the chill in the air.

Yeshua's mother saw some women that she knew, so she went to talk to them. Magda stood alone in the shadows. She could hear some of the rumbling conversation around her.

"They've arrested that charlatan," a man was saying.

"About time," another responded. "He leads the people astray."

Magda moved away from them. She didn't want to hear what they were saying. As she stood in a spot a bit further from the fire, she couldn't help but notice the presence of men she had seen before in the garden. They were among those who had come to arrest Yeshua.

"What are they doing now?" one guard asked the other.

"They are questioning Him. The High Priest called a trial. Members of the Sanhedrin are being brought in to determine the man's fate." The guard answered with no feeling in his voice.

"Isn't it unlawful to have a trial at night?" the other guard questioned.

"The High Priest can do what he wants. I heard him say, 'It is better that one man should die for the people, not that the whole nation should perish.'"[203]

Magda's lungs were burning. Die? Death? It couldn't be! Magda felt like the flame in her heart that had burned bright with love and faith had just been blown out as easily as a candle facing the power of a single breath.

She leaned against the wall, drawing in oxygen as best she could. Magda crumpled to the ground in a posture of prayer. Her mind rebelled against it.

---

[203] John 11:50

"*Lord,*" she breathed out. "*Father, help Your Son. Save Him. Spare Him.*"

The assault of doubt surprised her. "*He is not really God's Son, is He? If He was, why wouldn't He fight back?*"

Magda was on the precipice of accepting the notion when she remembered how Yeshua had saved her from the forest of Zophos. He had a flaming sword that turned into a cross. He told her captors that He would be back.

"He is the Lamb of God, come to take away the sins of this world," Magda retorted to the attack.

The assault of blame came next. "*Why did He leave you? Why has He forsaken you?*"

Magda stood up, her feet a little wobbly. "He is always with me. I abide in Him."

The assault of confusion tried to get at her. "*How can this be the way? How can death be a part of the plan?*"

"He has the power to lay down His life," Magda said in response. "I trust in Him."

The assault of anger lurked around her, whispering thoughts. "*The others left Him. They scattered like unfaithful dogs. They were not true to Him.*"

Magda sighed. "They will be forgiven by the power of His love. They scattered to fulfill the Scripture, just as He said."

Magda could feel the intensity of the spiritual warfare going on around her. She did her best to stand her ground. So tired that her eyelids felt heavy and her body ached with every step, Magda moved toward the fire again. She could feel her strength slipping. Yahweh was protecting her mind as He gave her the answers to the enemy's taunts.

When fear nipped at her, Magda braced herself. "*Where will you go now? Who would take you in? You will be vulnerable again — vulnerable to the powers of darkness. You will go back to the life you once knew.*"

"I am a child of light. I will not live in the darkness. I have been forgiven, cleansed, and redeemed. I have faith in Yahweh," Magda proclaimed under her breath.

The assault of despair went after her. *"You are nothing if He dies. You will be hunted and punished."*

"I am a child of God, beloved of Yeshua. I am my beloved's and my beloved is mine."

Finally, the seventh assault befell her. She recognized the voice of the demon that haunted her, pursued her. *"I will have you. I will thwart your testimony. Your heart is mine to destroy. It always has been."*

"Away from me, Satan! I will have nothing to do with you. I am under the protection of my Father," Magda yelled, falling to her knees.

People nearby stared at her. She remained hidden beneath her cloak, relieved the attack failed — this time!

When John came back outside, he found Yeshua's mother first. Magda could see them in the distance. She used the last reserve of her strength to push through the crowd so she could get to them.

She immediately saw the pain in John's eyes. "He is accused of blasphemy."

The distant echo of sinister laughter hit her heart, stirring up a tempest.

"Blasphemy? But the punishment…" Yeshua's mother began.

"Is death." Magda let the tears fall.

The three of them stayed up all night long, hiding themselves in the crowd of on-lookers. Word had spread about the strange occurrences going on at the Temple. The people coming were more curious than supportive.

John made sure to keep the women updated on the latest developments. Passed back and forth like a pawn, Yeshua was caught in the power struggle between Pilate and Herod, both vying for a way to pass off sentencing Him to death. Pilate was less than sympathetic to the High Priest's cause.

At first light, John took Magda and Yeshua's mother over to the Roman court where they were handling Yeshua's case. The crowd swelled to an uncomfortable size. John did his best to push through people so that Magda and Yeshua's mother could hear what was going on. Despite the odds, they clung to a flicker of hope that Pilate would set Yeshua free.

When they brought Yeshua out, Pilate addressed the crowd. "I find no basis for a charge against Him. But you have a custom, that I should release someone to you at the Passover. Therefore, do you want me to release to you the King of the Jews?"[204]

Magda could feel the forces of evil extending their power over the people. As the sun rose, the crowd seemed oblivious to the deception and darkness creeping in. Several in the crowd shouted until they all took up the chant. "Not this man, but Barabbas!"[205]

Magda wept, knowing that her single voice would not be heard above the clatter. This was evil's hour. What did it mean? How was this going to end?

Pilate released the man, Barabbas. Yet, rather than have Yeshua crucified, he sent Him away to be flogged. Magda went with John and Yeshua's mother to go see the punishment.

"Are you sure?" John asked the women. "This won't be easy to watch."

"I have to be as near to Him as I can," Magda answered John. "I need to, John."

Yeshua's mother nodded in agreement. Both women were already crying, emotions raw and exposed.

When they got to the area where the Romans carried out their wicked punishments, Yeshua was already stripped and shackled to a post. All the goodness that was left in Jerusalem was ripped by the first whip to penetrate Yeshua's skin, revealing bone and

---

[204] John 18:38-39
[205] John 18:40

blood, the price of life's demand. Magda instantly felt sick. She fell to her knees, grabbing her heart, which ached with a stabbing pain from the unseen realm.

As blow after blow fell on His body, she remembered the dream she had about the lamb. It was her that should be there, shackled to that post. It was her defiance of Yahweh that needed to be punished. Magda lifted her head slightly. Her tear-blurred gaze fixated on the river of blood washing over the stone pavement. It was in that moment, the one breathless instant, when Mary of Magdala realized that He, the Son of God, took her punishment upon Himself. *"The Lamb of God who takes away the sin of the world."* She realized the truth of John the Baptizer's proclamation.

Magda stood in the power of the realization, forcing herself to watch. It was the least she could do. Magda was silent as the Roman wolves slaughtered the Lamb. *"I am my Beloved's,"* she sobbed quietly. *"My Beloved is mine."*

When it was over, they dragged Him away, barely alive. Thankfully, a Roman Centurion stepped in to prevent the soldiers from killing Yeshua with their relentless torture.

"What do you think you are doing?" The Centurion yelled. "Pilate said to *flog* Him, not kill Him."

"Our apologies, Centurion Longinus," the soldier wheezed. He was breathless from the physical strain of whipping with the instruments of torture. As Magda looked at the man, she couldn't help but notice his face, which was speckled with Yeshua's blood.

The scene disturbed both John and Yeshua's mother to the same degree. Neither of them spoke a word. John protectively led both women back to the Praetorium, where Pilate would decide Yeshua's fate.

Pushed by the crowd, Magda, John, and Yeshua's mother waited. It felt like such a long time, but Magda had lost all awareness of time now. Where was He? What were they doing to Him? Why was it taking so long? How could He survive such torturous treatment?

Magda's arms and legs felt weak. She swayed back and forth. How long had it been since she had eaten? Her body felt like a foreigner to her. She was stuck between the physical and spiritual realm, not fully belonging to either, not sure if she wanted to be.

When they finally brought Yeshua out, Magda's head started spinning with dizziness. He barely looked human. They had cloaked Him in purple. A crown of thorns sat on His head. Intense pain bore into Magda's own head. She remembered touching the thorns that were kept in the prison. She knew that those thorns were the ones that now caused Her Lord pain. She squeezed her finger where the thorn had pricked her, causing blood to seep out. While chopping the bitter herbs, she accidentally cut the same finger she had injured earlier. Yeshua was there in that moment. He healed her, rescued her. He told her that He would always rescue her.

Magda looked back up at where He stood, this barely recognizable figure that claimed her heart. How could He save her now? She knew He took her place, accepted a punishment designed for her, but what good would that do once He was gone? She wanted to be with Him. She couldn't survive without Him. Without Him, the demons would hunt her again.

"Behold," Pilate silenced the crowd. The governor of the province looked disturbed. "I bring Him out to you, that you may know that I find no basis for a charge against Him."[206]

Before the religious leaders even responded, Magda felt the gray clouds of Zophos moving in. She heard the hissing whispers from the unseen realm, *"Crucify Him! Crucify Him!"*

The High Priest and several members of the Sanhedrin echoed the evil taunt. "Crucify Him!" was their response.[207]

The crowd picked up the chant in agreement.

---

[206] John 19:4

[207] John 19:6

Pilate still tried to fight against the forces of darkness that were closing in. "Take Him yourselves, and crucify Him, for I find no basis for a charge against Him."[208]

The High Priest answered Pilate, but it was another voice that Magda heard prompting the man. "We have a law, and by our law He ought to die, because He made himself the Son of God."[209]

Magda watched Pilate have a private conversation with Yeshua. Even in the midst of facing death, He still had a majesty about Him. Even as He barely looked human, He carried glory. She could see it, even if she didn't understand it. Looking beyond what was right in front of her eyes, Magda knew who He was — her Rescuer, her love.

Pilate faced the religious leaders once more. Before the governor of Judea said anything, the High Priest spoke first, obviously prompted by one who knew Pilate's only weakness.

"If you release this man, you aren't Caesar's friend! Everyone who makes himself a king speaks against Caesar!"[210]

Pilate stepped back, retracted what he was going to say, and stood silent for a moment. He glanced one more time at Yeshua. Pilate said to them, "Shall I crucify your King?"[211]

The chief priests answered in unison with the hideous voices from the unseen realm. "We have no king but Caesar!"[212]

Pilate took a bowl, washed his own hands and declared to the crowd. "I am innocent of the blood of this righteous Man. You see to it."[213]

All the people answered. "May His blood be on us and on our children!"[214]

---

[208] John 19:6

[209] John 19:7

[210] John 19:12

[211] John 19:15

[212] John 19:15

[213] Matthew 27:24

[214] Matthew 27:25

"Very well," Pilate declared, turning his back on Yeshua. "Crucify Him!"

CHAPTER THIRTY-SEVEN

Magda walked barefoot, placing her feet in the bloodied footprints as she followed the shadow of the cross He carried. John knew better than to argue with the women about following Him all the way to Golgotha. Magda wasn't going to leave His side now. She would stay until the end, even if it killed her.

The path stretched out before her, seemingly endless in its length. The journey felt long and exhausting, with every step taking a toll on her weary body. Magda pushed herself forward, ignoring the weakness of her flesh by tapping into an unseen power she didn't know existed within her. Was it faith? Was it love? Was it both?

"What have you learned, Mary?" He had asked her once.

She couldn't answer, not then anyway. Now, what would she say to Him if she had one more chance?

She learned from His life that love was more than an emotional response to another person. Love was action. It was forgiveness. It was pain. It was sacrifice.

It was the Way of the Lord, the hard way. Love hurt and Magda didn't want it to.

Her ears drowned out the sound of the scoffers lining the streets. The Romans continually whipped Him as He struggled without protest beneath the weight of the wooden beam. He carried its shame. He carried its burden. The burden of splinters rested on His shoulders, a sacrifice made for love.

He loved her more than she could fathom. Magda heard His labored breathing above the roars of the multitude. His breath, God's breath, breathed out for her, for them who mocked Him along the way. Could they not see the blessing of Yahweh sending His one and only Son?

Magda scanned the crowd, ignoring the pain of her bloodied feet as she let the stones that littered the ground cut through them. In the multitude of people, she saw shadowy figures lurking. Dragons, wolves, serpents, and lizards moved in and amongst the people victoriously. Hideous creatures that she couldn't even describe circled overhead. One, a bat-like creature, set his evil gaze upon her. Magda feared them. She felt her protection ebbing away. She felt her heart's fire extinguished by the darkness that the people willingly embraced, and a cold, disheartened feeling washed over her.

When Yeshua stumbled again, the cross fell to the ground with a loud thud. Magda felt the vibration through her bloodied feet. She wanted to rush to Him, to die with Him, but the crowd kept her parted from Him. The soldiers wedged themselves between her and the One she loved.

Alongside Yeshua, another man stepped forward, offering his assistance in carrying the heavy cross. The final steps proved to be the most challenging, with each one requiring immense effort. The ascension to the place of the skull, as Golgotha was called, was steep.

Magda felt the burning of her nutrient-deprived legs. Her lungs protested, but she didn't care. The crowd may keep apart from Him her, and the Roman soldiers may hinder her from getting close to Him, but her body would not keep her from being with Him until the end.

Finally reaching the top of the hill, Magda realized that the once bustling crowd had significantly dwindled. It reminded her of the many times He preached to listening ears only to have them turn away when they felt threatened or convicted. When it became uncomfortable, unpopular to hear Him, most walked away of their own accord. Now, once the mocking was over, no one wanted to see a crucifixion.

Magda found a spot in the dirt. The ground was hard where she stood. It was nothing like the supple soil which Yeshua had led them through as He taught them about a farmer sowing seed in his field.

Magda watched Him crawl toward the cross, embracing it like a lover. She didn't understand why He wasn't fighting back. He raised others from death, why was He submitting to it?

Magda could feel anger nipping at her heart. She was determined not to let it in. *"I trust Your ways, Lord,"* she whispered in prayer. *"I am my Beloved's. My Beloved is mine."*

Magda had just calmed herself with the power of her prayer when the solace was stripped from her by a heart-wrenching cry of undergirded pain and the sound of a nail being pounded into His flesh. Magda dropped.

With her knees up to her chest, Magda rocked back and forth. Her tears flowed freely, mingling with the blood staining her injured feet. The pounding of the nails beat in perfect rhythm with her heart. She could feel the anguish in her soul, as if her heart was being pierced by a thousand sharp nails. Magda could feel the internal bleeding begin in her soul. Who would heal her now?

Magda watched as they raised the cross, His destroyed form one with the instrument of death. The shadow of the cross stretched long across the barren ground. The tip of it reached the place where Magda's feet rested. Seeing it on the ground in its shadowy form, Magda saw a sword where the cross was. The tip of the sword pointed straight at Him. According to this image, she was the one holding it by the hilt. What did it mean?

Magda raised her eyes to look at Him. He could barely breathe, struggling to raise His body up enough to take another breath. How long would His Father make Him endure this? Why did it have to be this way?

His words echoed in her heart. *"The hour of darkness comes when no one can work."*

Standing near Magda, the religious leaders wore expressions of mocking indifference. She could tell that they were uncomfortable by the way they shifted their weight back and forth. One of them spoke up, sarcasm lacing his words like the poison of his self-righteous attitude.

"He saved others, but He can't save himself. If He is the King of Israel, let Him come down from the cross now, and we will believe in Him. He trusts in God. Let God deliver Him now, if He wants Him; for He said, 'I am the Son of God.'"[215]

Magda heard the forces of evil declaring their victory through the taunts and ridicule of Israel's teachers. Even the criminals on either side of Him joined in the revelry.

Following His lead, Magda kept silent despite the fact that everything in her wanted to hurl insults, to throw the stones that they stood on, to attack them with the ferocity with which they attacked Him. Her life meant nothing to her now.

She looked into His swollen eyes. The drops of blood were tears that revealed the condition of His heart. Magda knew He wouldn't want her to defend Him like that.

"If you love those who love you, what credit is that to you? Even sinners love those who love them." He had taught them. *"But love your enemies, and do good, and lend, expecting nothing back; and your reward will be great, and you will be children of the Most High; for He is kind toward the unthankful and evil."* [216]

---

[215] Matthew 27:42-43
[216] Luke 6:32, 35

Yeshua did not respond to their taunts. Instead, He looked directly at John, who was standing by Yeshua's mother.

"Woman, behold, your son!" Yeshua, even in His disfigured state, shone love to His mother. "John, behold, your mother."[217]

John nodded, choking on his own emotions as he embraced Yeshua's mother, broken by her Son's words. The finality of them hit Magda hard, too. Resigned to his fate, he had no desire to resist the approach of death.

The mocking continued. "You who destroy the Temple and build it in three days, save Yourself! If You are the Son of God, come down from the cross!"[218]

Yeshua did not answer His accusers. Instead, He looked up to the heavens and spoke with struggled breath—breath that He fought for. "Father, forgive them, for they don't know what they are doing."[219]

Everyone was silenced. Yeshua's statement had such a profound impact that even the Romans, who were in the midst of casting lots, were silenced. Magda sensed that the whole of creation itself struggled for breath in the hours that passed. It was becoming harder for her to breathe. Yeshua was tiring.

Magda, her body heavy with exhaustion, struggled to resist the overwhelming temptation to collapse. She willed her body to remain in prayer, upright and suffering along with Him. It was so much less than she deserved. How could she ease her own pain in this hour?

The criminals continued to taunt and deride Him. "Why don't You save Yourself and us?" one of the criminals cried out.

"Hur, don't you even fear God, seeing you are under the same condemnation? And we justly, as we receive the due reward

---

[217] John 19:26-27
[218] Matthew 27:39
[219] Luke 32:34

for our deeds, but this man has done nothing wrong."[220] The other criminal spoke forcefully. Magda recognized the repentance in the man's voice. Was it too late for him?

"Ravid, you are mad! He can't save you now. Look at Him," the criminal, Hur, breathed out, expending his waning energy uselessly.

"Yeshua, remember me when You come into Your Kingdom,"[221] the criminal Ravid pleaded.

Yeshua, with great effort, turned His head to look at the man, Ravid. "Assuredly I tell you, today you will be with Me in Paradise."[222]

Overcome by a rush of emotion, Magda found herself unable to feel anything. Her throat constricted with the weight of her numbness. Even now, even in the last hour, He was still forgiving, still extending His love. Even in the last breaths of life, anyone could repent and come to Him.

"Lord, Your love is astounding. Your love is beyond compare. Your love is everything," Magda sobbed. *"This hurts, Lord. It hurts. Don't go."*

When the sixth hour came, deep darkness fell like a blanket on the land. Pain came rushing into Magda like a tidal wave of pent-up emotion. The sun was blown out like a fire doused by water. The atmosphere felt heavy, oppressive. Magda recognized the reflection of the forest of Zophos immediately. She held her breath. Was this how it was going to be? How could evil win?

She couldn't see Yeshua, but she heard His voice. "My God, my God, why have You forsaken Me?"[223]

The pain in His very human voice shattered Magda's heart into a million pieces. There was no flame of faith fired up in love anymore. She was broken. She was undone. Life didn't matter

---

[220] Luke 23:40-41
[221] Luke 23:42
[222] Luke 23:43
[223] Mark 15:34

now.

With the noose of darkness tightening around her neck, Magda stilled. The suffocating darkness lasted for three long and torturous hours. She was chilled to the bone. Without sunlight, everything went cold. Without sunlight, everything that had life was dying. Magda was ready to die, too. Better to die than be controlled by the forces of evil again.

Yeshua called out one last time. His voice was softer, more intimate. Magda heard Him through the dark. "Father, into Your hands I commit My Spirit!"[224]

Yahweh lifted the darkness from the land even as it quaked with a force so great that Magda thought it would swallow them all up alive. She wanted it to. The rocks tumbled all around her. The people who had been standing, fell to the ground. She remained anchored, unmoved by the cracked ground beneath her.

When the shaking stopped, she knew He was dead. The radiance she still saw even through His disfigured human body was gone. As the sun moved across the sky, the shadow of the cross was swallowed up toward His lifeless body like a sword that Yeshua took with Him when He went.

Centurion Longinus ordered the other soldiers to break the legs of the bodies on the crosses. They wanted to be done with this before the Sabbath. After enduring the hours of darkness, Magda could tell that the centurion was mystified. When he came to Yeshua's body, he realized that He was already dead. Just to be sure, Centurion Longinus thrust his spear into Yeshua's side. Blood and water spurted out in a steady stream upon the man's face. He fell to his knees.

"Surely, this man was the Son of God,"[225] Longinus proclaimed, placing his hands over his eyes.

John was by Magda's side in an instant. Yeshua's mother was

---

[224] Luke 23:46

[225] Luke 23:47

with him. They both looked as terrible as she felt.

"Come on," John said. "Let's make our way to Bethany."

Magda said nothing, wondering if she would ever want to talk again.

CHAPTER THIRTY-EIGHT

Strange bat-like creatures sliced through the night sky, shrieking with the victory cry of Zophos. John and Yeshua's mother jumped at the fierceness of the echo. Magda was unmoved. The blackness of the night sunk its teeth into Magda's heart, making her soul go numb. The earlier darkness of the day had been suffocating, casting a heavy blanket over everything. This darkness was utterly painful.

Magda didn't know if it was her own exhaustion or the spreading contagion of grief that sucked the life out of her, but she didn't care. She walked methodically, following John, her last connection to the One she knew as perfect love.

When the three weary travelers arrived at the familiar home in Bethany, Lazarus, Martha, and Mary were not home. Two men staying at the house greeted them. They were just making their introductions to Betzalel and Jerah when Lazarus brought his sisters into view.

Upon recognizing their guests, Mary broke from her siblings, rushing forward, falling into an embrace with Yeshua's mother.

"Tell us everything," young Mary gasped.

Curiously, Magda was unable to feel the usual happiness upon seeing her friends, Yeshua's dear ones. The usual sense of security she felt in their home was absent. When they went inside, Magda remained quiet, weary emotionally and spiritually. Martha set to finding them some nourishment for their hunger. Lazarus and Mary created a restful space at the table where they could all talk.

"They crucified my Son," Yeshua's mother said in a hollow voice.

Magda listened in silence as John relayed the story of everything that had happened over the last few hours. She didn't want to relive that day. She didn't want to see the pained expressions on their faces. She didn't want to see it again through another's eyes. The moments, though painful, were sacred to her.

Magda could feel her insides boiling as the fluctuating numbness turned to anger. Hot tears flowed down her cheeks while John spoke. John was her only link to Him. John was the one who brought her there, to the hill, to the cross. The pain she experienced directly resulted from his actions. It was his fault that she had to be scarred with images she would never get out of her mind.

No one noticed Magda as she arose from the table and went outside. She couldn't stand it anymore. She had to get out of there! How could the black hole of nothingness that clipped all human emotion from her now be brewing with anger?

The internal bleeding that began when her heart was pierced at the cross had led to this. The overwhelming grief cracked the foundation of love that had held her secure for so long. Everything she believed, she trusted in, was breaking apart inside of her.

Magda knew that blaming John wasn't the answer. She had wanted to go. She had insisted. She had taken off her shoes, walking along the road to Golgotha in such a way as to ensure she would feel the pain. Now, she couldn't feel anything at all. Or she felt everything, and it nearly consumed her to death.

Magda didn't bother to wrap her cloak around herself in order to fend off the chill in the air. The cold felt good. It made her feel pain. Was pain the only thing she could embrace now?

As Magda navigated through the deep darkness, she was amazed to discover that her eyes had adapted to the low light, allowing her to see the shapes and outlines around her. She looked into the shadows, knowing they were coming for her. There was no protection for her now. The seeping infection of grief was severing the last thread Magda had to her Lord, her Teacher.

Anger and blame consumed her as she thought of John. She felt hatred and disgust toward Judas. And what about the others? Where had they been? Why didn't they save Him? How could they just let Him die?

Magda had wandered out to the animal enclosure. The sheep there were nestled into the hay, fast asleep. Magda vividly recalled the details of her dream, every image and sensation playing in her mind. She remembered she was the one who deserved to die, not Him. Magda's anger loosened its hold. Her ears tuned in to John's voice coming through the open door. Magda listened to the disciple's words.

John was relating what Yeshua said on the cross as He hung in agony, enduring the mocking blame and ridicule from those He came to save.

"He said, 'Father, forgive them for they don't know what they are doing.'" Magda heard John sigh, a deep sigh that revealed the lesson learned. "He asked for them to be forgiven, Lazarus...the ones who put Him there."

The shackle of anger finally broke free, and Magda's dammed-up emotions came flooding back into her heart. The deluge overwhelmed her. In her exhaustion, she was too weak to take it all in. They were there, all the human emotions that her pride had stifled in an effort to survive. Magda felt the sadness, the loss, the hurt, the confusion, the heaviness, the hopelessness, and the anger fueling her grief. The grief was trying to burn up the ground that love had claimed in her heart. The grief was trying to steal her truth, kill her faith, and destroy her love.

Magda thought about her father, Amos. It had been a long time since she thought about him. At this moment, in the deep darkness, she had a glimmer of her father's pain. She understood him in ways she never had before. It was grief that claimed Amos. Grief stole the protection that a father places over his child. It was grief that stripped her father of his ability to love. Grief left him open to the infiltration of the enemy. Amos had turned grief into an idol—grief over not having a child gave birth to grief over losing a wife he loved.

Magda didn't want to end up like her father. She didn't want to permit the enemy to take any ground that Yeshua had fought for in her heart. Magda stood up. Her tears soaked the ground beneath her, leaving it damp and heavy. The anointing of her pain, of her new understanding, fell on the soil beneath her, turning the hard ground soft. Dirt oozed between her toes, reminding her of the soil she had walked through when Yeshua took them to the farm. The soil there had been freshly turned over, ready for planting.

"Father," Magda prayed toward the skies with her eyes closed so she would not see the darkness. *"I forgive him. I forgive Amos. He did not know what he was doing."*

With her eyes closed to the black night creeping in around her, Magda looked into the beauty of heaven's glory. The staircase imaged in her mind, stretching down from heaven, lifting her up above the dark clouds, revealing a higher destiny invisible from down below. Magda let the light that she couldn't see with her eyes infiltrate her body, dispelling the darkness while burning up the remnants of pride in order to spark the embers that still remained among the ashes of her heart.

"My Beloved is mine. I am my Beloved's," Magda whispered in

prayer.

She heard the loud screech of the creatures of the night, but they were only an echo, a distant sound that was fading in her memory. Magda knew she was heard. She went to join the others in the dwelling. Love would share the pain of loss. Love would not isolate. Love would endure.

Magda walked back in while they were still talking.

"What happened to His body?" Mary asked.

Magda had been so wrapped up in her own misery, that she hadn't even noticed what happened to His body. How could she have missed that? How could time have passed without her recollection? A

s a matter of fact, Magda now realized that she couldn't even remember how she had gotten to Bethany. In her befuddled mind, the last few hours had been erased from her existence.

John answered Mary. "Joseph of Arimathea and Nicodemus placed Him in a tomb, a brand new one in the garden, after anointing His body. There was so much blood upon the cross. The way it soaked into the wood made it look like..." John paused.

"Wine," young Mary said, finishing his thought.

John nodded. The room was thick with silence.

Magda wondered how they could have performed a proper burial so quickly. From what she could remember, the sun was setting when the soldier plunged the spear into His side. How could the two men have given her Lord a proper burial? The thought bothered Magda, taking root inside of her mind. He might be gone from her, but she could at least worship Him one last time in death. She could at least give Him the kind of burial a King deserved. If only she could just see Him one more time. If only she could touch Him, sing over Him, wash His feet once again, expressing her love.

"Father, help me find a way. Help me find a way to anoint Your Son one last time," Magda prayed in her heart.

At first, Magda couldn't sleep because she kept thinking about her desire to anoint Yeshua's body, wondering how she could do it. Where would she get the supplies? Who would move the stone?

Though Magda's mind didn't want to sleep, her body pulled her into it. Exhaustion won the battle, as Magda's thoughts lost all resistance to her will of staying awake. She had eaten the little food that Martha provided, drank the wine offered and settled into the sleeping mat Mary made up for her.

Immediately, Magda replayed the events of the past few weeks. The memories flitted across her night thoughts in rapid succession. She heard His voice. *"What have you learned, Mary?"* She felt His touch on her cheek, wiping away her tears. She heard the screams against the downbeat of nails being hammered into His flesh. Those screams ripped her heart, shattering her soul on the inside.

Magda's sleep became restless. She tossed and turned until her mind settled on a scene that was not a memory…

Magda saw herself, dressed in rags, barely covered. She was exposed, unclean. She walked on dirty ground, shackled and chained. She was moving toward something. All around her, there was nothing but complete darkness, making it impossible to see even an inch ahead.

She saw the cross on a hill. The One hanging on it radiated light. The sky, completely dark and foreboding, was intermittently lit up by powerful flashes of lightning behind Him. She approached, unafraid. She stood at the foot of the cross, close enough to reach toward Him. Her fingers trembled as she worked to release one arm from the cold, unforgiving chains. She extended it toward Him, reaching in praise and worship.

Her other arm hung low, reaching toward the ground, weighted down by the shackles that bound her. His blood poured out. It rained down on her, touching her fingertips, flowing down her arm of praise. Where His blood touched, her skin became pure, glowing, and stunningly beautiful. The rags turned into a wedding garment of linen, white and pure. The scene was frozen in time.

Magda stood there, at the foot of the cross, slowly being revealed for who she really was. As His blood poured out over her, half of her radiated the royalty of God's Kingdom. The other half was still in the process of breaking the chains and shedding the shackles. The work was almost complete, but it wasn't quite finished yet.

When Magda woke up, the sun reluctant to shine the morning after the death of Yahweh's Son, she felt a peace in her heart which she had not felt in the absence of His presence before. She recalled the scene that was painted on her mind in the night — the scene that taught her she was a work in progress, that she was being made new.

Magda entered into the haze of the world, but she made an effort to keep her heart within the light of heaven's hope. She joined Martha, always up early, in the cooking area. Today was the Sabbath. No work could be done. Magda would have to bury her desire to anoint His body at least for one more day. She still hoped that there was a chance to carry out this final mission which gripped her heart.

"Shalom," Magda said to Martha.

"Shalom, Magda," Martha replied. "I'm just warming bread from yesterday. Would you like some?"

"I'm not sure how hungry I am, but I suppose I should eat."

Magda and Martha sat in silence, both of them heavy with contemplative thoughts.

"There is so much that I don't understand," Martha admitted.

"Yes. It is a mystery beyond our grasp, I'm afraid," Magda agreed.

When Mary joined them, it startled both women. They had not heard her approach. Mary was an intuitive young woman. She immediately picked up on Magda's strange mood.

"Is something wrong?" she asked.

Magda sighed, wondering if she should reveal the true intentions of her heart. Looking at these women, she knew she could trust them. "I appreciate Joseph and Nicodemus for what they did but..." Magda paused.

"What is it?" Martha asked.

"It's just that they were making haste because it was close to sundown and they wanted to get the body to the tomb before the Sabbath. I'm not sure that He was anointed properly. I lay awake thinking about it."

Mary spoke up. "I have some burial spices and oils. We could go tomorrow morning to make sure that it was done properly."

Magda looked up, thrilled at the idea. "Do you think so? Do you think we could do it?"

"I don't know, but we could certainly try. Let me get the supplies we might need. I'll prepare them in my traveling satchel," Mary offered willingly.

Magda hugged her tight. She was an answer to her prayers. Yahweh had heard her. He had chosen her to anoint Yeshua's body in death. Vigorous hope coursed through Magda's veins, revitalizing her spirit. She couldn't wait for tomorrow when she could worship Him once more.

Mary had gone off to gather supplies. Martha and Magda heard the sound of approaching hooves. Abner came from Jerusalem. Martha was the first to go greet the Centurion.

When they came toward the house, Mary also joined them in the courtyard. Abner appeared extremely tired. He looked worn out to Magda. She appreciated all that the man was doing to help them. To the rest of the world, they would be enemies, Romans and Jews, but this was Yeshua's world. This was a reflection of the Kingdom where love reigned.

"I have something for you," Abner said to Mary. He handed her the cloak she had lovingly made for Yeshua.

Mary took it into her arms, cradling it. Even Magda's tears

flowed when she saw the cloak that He always wore. It brought painful memories filtered with grief at the loss of Him.

"How?" Mary could hardly get her words out.

"The soldiers had not wanted to rip it since it was such a nice garment. So, they cast lots. The man who won it was a friend of mine. He intended to wash the stains out and sell it. I was able to purchase it from him as is." Abner spoke tenderly.

"Thank you, Abner," Mary hugged him. "This means so much to me."

Magda remembered something Yeshua had said. *"Love moves. Love is not only a feeling, a taking. Love is a giving, a sacrifice."* Magda bowed her head. The examples of love still existed all around her if only she let her eyes see them. *"Help me, Father. Help me to see love."*

"What else have you heard, Abner?" Lazarus asked.

"I know that the Temple officials are trying to hunt down His followers. Pilate has posted guards at the tomb. The High Priest has convinced him that Yeshua's followers are going to attempt to steal His body and claim that He isn't dead," Abner informed them.

"That's preposterous!" John was indignant. "It would be dishonorable. Why would we do that to our Lord?"

Magda fought the lure of anger. She failed to understand the hatred of those who claimed to follow Yahweh. But she also pitied them because they didn't even know they were shackled to their hatred, chained to their sin. Questions pummeled Magda's mind. She wondered how she would be able to anoint His body if there were guards stationed there at the tomb. She wondered who would assist her in moving away the stone if she could even get close. If what Abner said was true, then it wasn't likely she would be able to carry out the plan of anointing His body. Hopelessness beckoned her. Magda fought the battle with prayer.

"Help me, Father," Magda prayed in her heart. *"I trust You will make a way."*

"Where are the others? Do you know?" Yeshua's mother spoke up timidly.

Magda was suddenly interested. She hadn't thought of where they might have gone. Were they together? Did the disciples completely abandon everything they had learned? Magda suddenly missed her brothers—the men she had spent years of her life with, learning, growing, trusting, and failing.

"They are in hiding together, I believe. I overheard a rumor in the garrison regarding the location of the followers. If the Temple authorities find out where they are, I have no doubt they will all be arrested. The soldiers don't want to be dragged into the religious dispute anymore, so they are keeping their mouths shut," Abner said to them.

"I want to be with them," Yeshua's mother pleaded with John.

Magda stepped up, wanting to be included. She wanted to be reunited with her family.

"But, it's the Sabbath. We can't travel or they will most certainly arrest us, Ima." John seemed to be wrestling with his own desire to be with his companions and the fear of being caught.

"I can get you there undercover," Abner offered. "I have my horse. I'll ride back to Jerusalem, bring some garments for you to wear to disguise yourselves, and you can travel with me once I confirm where I think your friends might be."

Before John could protest, Yeshua's mother said, "We would be obliged, Sir."

Abner nodded reverently. "Alright, I will bring three garments and…"

"Four," Mary inserted. Everyone looked at her quizzically. "I'd like to go too."

Lazarus interrupted. "No, Mary. It's too dangerous. After what happened yesterday, I don't want you out of my sight."

"Brother, I need to go. I'm helping Magda in the morning. If you don't let me go with Abner, I'll find another way. At least with him I will be safer." Mary spoke with confidence and determination that caused her brother to relent.

Magda appreciated the confident phrase, *I'll find another way.* She was determined to adopt it as her own. She would find a way to anoint Him, to worship Him once more.

Reluctantly, Lazarus agreed to his sister's insistent pleas to go and find the disciples. This gave Magda hope for her own quest, though dangerous. She hoped that Yahweh would see fit to let her accomplish it.

Hours later, when Abner showed up with Malchus, the servant of the High Priest, they all were frightened. Magda remembered seeing the man in the garden. He was the same man who had his ear sliced off by Peter's sword. Even then, Yeshua showed mercy and compassion to His enemy.

The man related the story of his time in the garden. It had changed him. Forgiveness had touched Malchus, moved him to see things differently. The High Priest's servant recognized Yeshua for who He was and not who the religious leaders said He was. After Malchus told his compelling story of transformation, their fears of his intentions were vanquished. They knew he was not there to harm them.

Abner spoke up. "Malchus's absence hasn't been noticed yet, due to all the commotion of the recent hours. He will be an asset to us as we travel back to the city. He has agreed to play the part of the dutiful servant of the High Priest if we need him to help us get past the Temple authorities. Here are the garments I have brought you to wear. They will make you look more like Roman citizens. We are going to claim that you are merchants coming to the city for business. That way, questions about breaking the Sabbath laws won't pertain to you."

With that settled, the group began changing into their disguises. Magda put on a Roman toga similar to the one she wore the day Abner had rescued her from her assailant. She had been separated from Yeshua at that time, for a while. A smile played on her face when she remembered the flood of joy upon being reunited with Him again at Passover after those days of fearing she would never see Him again.

Using an extra horse that Abner brought with him, they traveled by horseback because it was the custom for the Romans. Magda was instantly aware of the reign of evil over the land. She could feel it in her bones. She could sense it in her heart. This was the hour of darkness. Would it ever end?

Before they could enter the city, the Temple authorities halted them in their tracks. "What is your business on the Sabbath?" the man demanded.

Abner took charge. "Do you dare question Roman merchants? We are not subject to your religious laws. These people are under my guard and protection. Let us pass, now!" Abner's voice held the full force of his authority as a centurion.

The man cowered under Abner's confident tone. He stepped aside, letting them through. Abner led them as far as he could. He gave them instructions on how to find the house where he heard the disciples were staying. If a Roman soldier was found in the Lower City by himself, it would arouse suspicion. So, the group slipped out of the garments of disguise they wore over their regular tunics and parted ways with Abner.

They continued on foot with Malchus, their only protection now. Fortunately, the streets were empty and quiet because it was a Sabbath day. They arrived at the place in the lower city according to the directions Abner had given them. It was rumored to be the home of a woman named Rhoda, a young widow who had taken to following Yeshua on some of His journeys. The dwelling was small. All the windows were shut, and the door was locked. They tried to be as quiet as possible as they approached the door. Yeshua's mother was the one they decided should knock. There was no answer.

John approached the door just as a group of Temple guards

rounded the corner. There were five or six of them. The one in the front yelled out. "Halt! What is your business?"

Magda's heart raced with fear. She waited, trying to remain hidden beneath her cloak.

Malchus immediately stepped toward the man. "They are with me. The High Priest sent me on this errand to take these people to their relatives. They are travelers who could not find lodging, so they came to the Temple for help."

Malchus was knowingly jeopardizing his safety by deceiving the Temple authority, and Magda understood the gravity of his actions. If the man checked on his story, Malchus would be imprisoned.

The man hesitated, but he obviously knew who Malchus was, so he waved his men on. The look in his eyes, however, suggested that he would indeed check out Malchus's story when he returned to the Temple. Magda was worried that their presence was putting the others in danger.

At last, someone opened the door. "Yes?" an old woman inquired. She was so frail and sickly that Mary guessed it had taken her that long to come to the door.

"We are looking for Rhoda," John inquired of the woman.

"Rhoda?" It was obvious that the woman couldn't see nor hear very well.

"Yes, a young widow."

"Oh, yes. You have the wrong house. She is two streets over, third dwelling on the left, young man." With that, she shut the door, obviously annoyed at having been disturbed.

Magda was glad that they had inadvertently led the authorities to view the wrong house so that if they came back looking for Yeshua's followers, they wouldn't find them. Despite the power of evil in the world, Yahweh was still in control.

The group made haste to go where the woman directed them. After several knocks, Rhoda opened the door, recognizing Yeshua's mother and the disciple, John. They were all quickly ushered inside. All of them except Malchus, who said his goodbyes, eager to return to his duties at the Temple in order to find out more about what was happening there.

When Magda saw the disheveled group of men that followed Yeshua, her heart broke for them. Her soul hurt with her brothers. In their grief, they were united. In their lack of understanding, they were one. In their love, they would be unstoppable.

CHAPTER THIRTY-NINE

The dwelling they had found provided a sense of safety, but to Magda, it also felt eerily cave-like with its rough stone walls and dim lighting. The followers of Yeshua were knit tight in this secret space, where they attempted to go unnoticed by the forces of evil. The room was filled with a palpable sense of fear, confusion, and uncertainty. Those who had scattered to their own way when He was arrested in the garden, now sat shoulder to shoulder bearing the burden of their grief together.

Magda knew the tiredness she felt in her bones was due to the situation surrounding them, as well as to her own heightened emotions. Contemplating her conflicting emotions, she wondered if she should embrace the return of her passionate heart or long for the shield of numbness that guarded against pain.

Magda was acutely aware of the gray haze seeping in from the unseen realm, clouding the filter of faith with which Yeshua's disciples had once seen everything. The haze of confusion hung in the air, and as they took deep breaths, it affected each person in a different manner.

In her reserved manner, Magda sat quietly, lost in contemplation. Despair seemed to hang heavy on young Mary's shoulders, visible in the slump of her posture and the weariness in her eyes. James, the one who had always been the first to figure out the meaning of Yeshua's teaching, looked confused.

"I should have stopped Judas," James said into the empty air. "Or maybe if I had gone with him, this never would have happened."

"You couldn't have known, Brother," John answered him. "None of us did. The man's treachery was hidden to us."

John, the one who brought out the emotional anchor of faith when the storms of adversity plagued them along the way, sounded unsure and drained.

"Judas was always running errands. He was the treasurer. I thought he was going to get provisions like he had so many times before," Andrew added. "And we all ran. We didn't stay by His side in the garden. Only you went to the cross with Him, John. We all abandoned Him."

Andrew, the brother with a keen eye for the needs of others in the crowd, was burdened by an overwhelming sense of guilt.

"Why weren't you there?" John asked Peter in an accusatory tone that split the silence of the room like a hot dagger.

John, the one who was so confident in Yeshua's love that he followed Him to the cross, gave up the ground in his heart to blame.

"I denied Him, John. I failed Him. I can't undo what I've done. I can't tell Him I'm sorry." Peter's boisterous confidence was gone. He was a timid shell of a man, the sense of failure stealing the foundation from the one who Yeshua called His rock.

In the quiet, Magda could sense the oxygen of belief being snuffed out of the room. Yeshua's ministry had kindled a powerful flame of faith in each of them, but now it was starting to dwindle. Morning mist didn't last long when the bright sun of a fresh day fell upon it.

"Why did He not fight?" Thomas queried, turning the spotlight off Peter. "Why did He just stand there? Why didn't He perform another miracle?"

Each of his questions hit the target of every person's heart, like accurately thrown arrows. The blood of doubt infected each of them, though none dared to admit it openly. Had they been wrong about Him?

"Mary," Thomas turned toward her, "He raised your brother from death. You were there. You saw it. We all did. Why didn't He save Himself and come down from the cross?"

Thomas, the one who said he was willing to die with their Teacher, now was filled with questions no one could answer, sparking frustration in the disciple's heart.

Magda wondered herself what the plan was. She had asked those same questions when she sat at the foot of the cross. She closed her eyes, picturing the scene. The shadow of the cross had looked like a sword to her—a sword pointing toward Him from her.

"No one is to blame." Yeshua's mother spoke in a strong yet quiet voice. "This was a path He chose. This was the destiny He was sent for."

Her words, her confident understanding, dissipated the smoke from the unseen realm. A holy breath came into the room, dispelling the threat of evil, reclaiming the ground that had been lost. The light vanquished the mist of doubt instead of the other way around.

Yeshua's mother began to sing some of the mourning songs of lament. The others joined in, their voices intertwining and creating a powerful harmony that drowned out the confusion, shame, and guilt threatening to divide them. The growing melody lifted the heavy weight of emotions as their voices became one in song. Their union, their expression of love in pain, chased away the powers of darkness.

"I will bless Yahweh, who has given me counsel. Yes, my heart instructs me in the night seasons. I have set Yahweh always before me. Because He is at my right hand, I shall not be moved.

Therefore my heart is glad, and my tongue rejoices. My body shall also dwell in safety. For You will not leave my soul in Sheol, neither will You allow Your holy one to see corruption. You will show me the path of life. In Your presence is fullness of joy. In Your right hand there are pleasures forever more." [226]

The day of rest was swallowed up by night, the transition unnoticed by the group of mourners. Time was irrelevant to them now. The lyrical laments enlightened their spirits, pushing away the darkness that was trying to suffocate and divide them. As the One they had followed, the One they all loved, lie deep within the belly of the earth, those He left behind sat entombed in the mystery of the psalms they cried out.

They sang, prayed, and wept until their bodies were weary from physical exhaustion. Since the space was so small, they made no proper arrangements for sleeping. Rather, most of them fell asleep where they were.

Magda fought her own exhaustion. She nestled in the corner, using her cloak as a blanket and her arm as a pillow for her head. Sleep was the last thing on her mind. She wanted to watch the first rays of light coming up over the horizon, ushering in the dawn of a new day. She longed to carry out her mission of anointing Him in worship, being with Him in death.

Magda's eyes fluttered. She intended to just close them for a moment, to relieve the sting of tiredness which made them burn. As soon as she let them shut, her mind fell into the space of sleep, bringing her, unwillingly, to a place of rest, a place where she was open to visions of the night...

Magda saw herself walking through the forest of Zophos. She saw the dark canopy overhead, its blackness tearing at her soul. She felt the gray clouds of oppression moving in all around her, making it difficult to see where she was going. Magda fought her way through the haze. She pressed on toward the glow that was at

---

[226] Psalm 16:7-11

a distance in front of her. When she got there, she saw Him. Legions of demonic forces closed in on Yeshua from all sides, their eerie whispers and growls filling the air. They pounced on Him, tearing and ripping at His flesh, consuming Him. Magda wanted to scream out, but her voice was not there. Yeshua just stood there, letting them have their way with Him.

When it was over, when they declared their victory over His death, Magda wanted to die too. She didn't care anymore what happened to her. She didn't think there was a point in living.

"What have you learned?" Yeshua's voice, like an echo from the grave, spoke to her. Magda looked up, her tears stinging as they mingled with the smoky air, creating streams of ash falling from her eyes. Yeshua stood. All the legions of Zophos turned on Him, except this time, they were frightened.

The fires were lit. Magda could feel the heat of the blaze of evil as it neared Him, trying to consume Him. The fire created a barrier around Him, preventing Magda from getting near Yeshua. Her eyes fixated on an object that appeared beside Him. Next to Yeshua stood a cross which Magda had not seen before. He grabbed it with one hand, turning it into a sword. He pointed the sword at the flames that surrounded Him and her. The sword absorbed the fire of evil, becoming the flaming sword that Magda had seen Him use in her rescue all those years ago. Only this time, Yeshua used it against the forces of darkness.

He went toward them, demolishing them, taking back the ground they stole and freeing trapped souls. One of the freed souls Magda recognized as her father, Amos.

After the battle, Yeshua spoke, and those who had been retrieved listened attentively. Magda was unable to hear His words. Most accepted what He offered. Only a few turned back toward the pit of darkness that once teemed with the forces of evil. The rest of the freed captives were lifted up into a radiant light that pierced through the gloom of the pit. Yeshua watched them go, a triumphant smile on His face. He looked radiant and strong despite being torn up, bruised, and beaten.

Setting the sword down, He came over to Magda just as the ground beneath her feet gave way. She feared she was going to fall, but He swooped her up in His arms. Yeshua walked on the air as the ground disappeared. With His battered body, He carried her through the gray haze, through the nothingness all around them. She could sense His weariness. She knew He was getting tired. Her weight was a burden difficult to bear.

Yeshua took her to the foot of the staircase. He placed her gently on the bottom step before descending into the nothingness beneath them. Magda cried out, reaching for Him, until she heard a voice. "Mary," He said.

Magda turned to look up. Yeshua stood at the top of the stairs, glorified, whole, and majestic. His arm reached toward her, beckoning her to come. Magda glimpsed the radiant garment of light that covered her as she stood to her feet. The dream dissipated.

The light broke through the covering of her eyelids. Magda came back to the world she was a part of. One single beam of weak light was trying to force its way through the darkness of the night. Everyone was asleep still. Dawn was claiming a new day.

Magda got up as quietly as she could. The dream had been both beautiful and perplexing. Mary looked so peaceful as she slept. Magda didn't want to wake her friend. She crept over to the place where Mary had left her satchel filled with the burial spices and oils. Magda couldn't wait to go visit the tomb. She hoped Mary would forgive her for going without her.

Grabbing an oil lamp, Magda lit the flame before heading out the door, an eagerness in her heart to worship her Lord, her Savior, her King.

As Magda walked toward the tomb, thankful that she paid attention when John told Lazarus where it was, she remembered the question Yeshua had asked her in her dream. *What have you learned?*

With every quiet step in the ebbing darkness, Magda pondered the question. In the years of walking closely with Yeshua, she learned that love was patient. Even when they didn't comprehend His lessons, Yeshua never got angry at their lack of understanding. He would give them more examples until they could better grasp His meaning.

She learned the kindness of love. Even when He knew they were only there to take what He could give them through His miracles, Yeshua fed those who were hungry. He healed the sick. He cast out the demons.

Magda learned by His example that love was more interested in giving than receiving. Yeshua freely extended Himself to others, but when people wanted to make Him a king, He withdrew from them, telling Peter, *"This is not the way."*

Through His life, Magda learned that love was not prideful. Though He could have called on the forces of heaven to fight for Him in the garden that night, to spare Him from the pain He was about to endure, He never once used His authority for selfish gain or self-preservation. Yet, all of His followers had wanted Him, even urged Him to do so. Hadn't Yeshua told Peter, *"Get behind me Satan. You do not have in mind the things of God, but the things of men?"*[227]

Magda learned that love was rooted in truth. The power of love stood in stark contrast to the malevolence that relentlessly chased the followers of Yahweh's children. His sword absorbed the flames meant to consume and destroy. With it, the fires of faith could be lit instead. In this power, she could bear any challenge. In this power, she could believe, even when circumstance made little sense around her. In this power, she could endure, anchored in hope.

How many times had He told them, *"I tell you the truth?"* How many times had He saved them from disaster, rescued them

---

[227] Matthew 16:23

from harm, and promised them He would keep rescuing them?

Lost in her thoughts, Magda had covered a significant amount of ground without even realizing it. She was almost to the tomb when the sun made its first appearance over the horizon, bathing the landscape in cleansing light. Magda came around the corner. The garden burst with red and white lilies in full bloom. The light of the new day appeared like a spotlight directed specifically to this spot in creation.

Magda stood still, taking in the moment. What had she learned? Love never fails. Yeshua's sweet voice echoed in the recesses of her heart's memory. *"Behold, we are going up to Jerusalem, and the Son of Man will be delivered to the chief priests and scribes, and they will condemn Him to death, and will hand Him over to the Gentiles to mock, to scourge, and to crucify; and the third day He will be raised up."*[228]

Magda caught her breath, unable to grasp the full depth of the statement. Before she could ponder the meaning of the truth He spoke, Magda noticed something was amiss. The beam of sunlight shifted, pointing directly into the tomb. Was it open?

Going further, she saw that the stone was rolled away. There were no guards. Magda set down the satchel she had brought with her. Peering inside the tomb, she was astonished that it was empty! He was gone! The forces of evil had cruelly robbed her of the worship she held dear, leaving her heartbroken and enraged.

---

[228] Matthew 20:18-19

CHAPTER FORTY

Magda left the tomb and ran even as the sun was rising, making its power over the darkness known. By the time she reached the place where they were staying, out of breath and flooded with disappointment, the new day was upon them.

She burst into the dwelling, disturbing the sleeping apostles. Magda's gaze fell upon Peter, his eyes filled with frantic misunderstanding. She clung to John, taking a moment to catch her breath.

"They have taken away the Lord out of the tomb, and I don't know where they have laid Him!"[229]

"What?" Peter asked her, his eyes wide with disbelief, as if she had lost her mind.

Magda inhaled deeply, her lungs seeking some sort of solace in the air. The cluttered chaos of her soul wouldn't let simple breathing calm her down.

"There is no body. The tomb is empty. What could they have

---

[229] John 20:2

done with Him?"

The confusion lingered in Magda's mind as she wondered why the men stood there, unresponsive to her words. Did they not believe her? Did they not trust her? Was this what Yeshua felt when He spoke to the people who were unmoved by the urgency and truth of His message?

"Do they mean to defile Him?" Magda cried.

With that statement, Peter and John sprang into action, their movements synchronized and purposeful. They didn't wait for her. Instead, they both ran.

Magda followed behind them, too tired to run as fast as they were. Running, her mind was preoccupied once more with Yeshua's probing question. "What have you learned, Mary?"

"I have learned that evil doesn't stop," she spoke between her labored breaths. "I can't let my guard down. I need the strength to fight, Lord. How could they do this to You?" The tears burned hot in her throat, but she stifled them.

By the time Magda arrived, Peter and John were already inside the tomb. They believed her now. Peter gripped the head cloth when Magda stepped inside the cool space. Neither man said a word. They looked at the place where His body had been. As their gazes landed on her, she could see the unmistakable signs of bewilderment etched onto their faces. What did it all mean? Was there more torture for their hearts to endure?

John and Peter exited the tomb, not waiting for Magda. She remained where she was, determined to link herself to the space where He had last been. Her heart was breaking all over again. Would there be no end to the pain of this love?

As her bottled up tears poured forth from her eyes, Magda felt a bright light enter the space where she was. With a sudden surge of fear, she cautiously moved to step outside of the tomb. The light was so bright, it almost blinded her.

Through her tears, Magda thought she could make out two figures. One was at the head of the space where His body had been, the other at the foot.[230]

As they spoke, Magda could feel the words resonating within her, touching the core of her soul. Instead of hearing their voices with her ears, she felt their words echo in her heart.

"Woman, why are you weeping?"[231] they said in ethereal unity.

Magda's eyes were suddenly captivated by their breathtaking beauty. They were angels, messengers of heaven. Everything about them radiated majestic glory. As she gazed upon them, Magda felt a sense of relief wash over her, as if the sight of them erased the gruesome images of demons that had plagued her mind for so long. Their beauty stripped her of the defilement left by dark images imprinted on her mind.

Magda answered the heavenly beings in a trembling voice. "Because they have taken away my Lord, and I don't know where they have laid Him."[232]

Magda was startled by the sudden movement behind her. Her skin tingled with holiness that dripped all around her like morning dew. Magda felt a surge of energy course through her, arousing her senses to the present moment. Her soul, once drowsy and lethargic, now gradually awakened inside of her.

With a quick spin, she pivoted around and took in the scene before her. In the intensity of the radiant sunlight covering the area, she saw the silhouette of a man. He looked like a gardener.

When He spoke, Magda moved toward Him, thinking, feeling that He could help her. "Woman, why are you weeping? Who are you looking for?"[233]

Stepping toward Him, Magda replied to His question. "Sir, if you have carried Him away, tell me where you have laid Him,

---

[230] John 20:11-12
[231] John 20:13
[232] John 20:13
[233] John 20:15

and I will take Him away."[234]

The man moved His position. He no longer blocked the light from the sun. He became the light. "Mary," He said.[235]

The light flooded Magda's soul, banishing any trace of darkness and filling her with a profound sense of peace. *And on the third day rise again!* The echo sounded loud in her heart. She finally understood what He meant. She finally learned that love never died!

"Teacher,"[236] she cried, falling into His open arms.

Magda embraced Him, never wanting to let Him go. He returned the embrace, laughing with delight at her enthusiastic worship.

He held her at arm's length. "Don't hold Me, for I haven't yet ascended to my Father; but go to My brothers and tell them, 'I am ascending to my Father and your Father, to my God and your God.'"[237]

Magda obeyed Him. She loved Him through obedience. She loved Him through worship. She loved Him through a willingness to carry out His commands. Her desire to hold Him had been replaced by a desire to abide in Him.

When Magda returned to the dwelling, she told the disciples exactly what Yeshua told her to say. Her joy was impenetrable. Their doubt, disbelief, and skepticism were powerless against the impenetrable shield of newfound love that now enveloped her. It was a love that conquered death, pursuing all who belonged to the Kingdom of God, even if it meant venturing into the mysterious forest of Zophos.

Though the apostles did not believe her, the other women did. Magda took Joanna and James's mother to the tomb. When

---

[234] John 20:15
[235] John 20:16
[236] John 20:16
[237] John 20:17

they arrived in the garden, they found the stone rolled away from the tomb, just as Magda had told them. Smiling, Magda watched as the women entered in and didn't find the body.

As she looked at them, she could clearly see the confusion reflected in their expressions. It was one thing to believe what someone else said. It was quite another to experience it for yourself. While Joanna and James's mother were greatly perplexed, the two dazzling angels returned, consuming them with the goodness of their light. The women all bowed low before them.[238]

The heavenly messengers spoke with authority and love. "Why do you seek the living among the dead? He isn't here, but is risen. Remember what He told you when He was still in Galilee, saying that the Son of Man must be delivered up into the hands of sinful men and be crucified, and the third day rise again?"[239]

Filled with joy, the three women started their journey back to inform the apostles. Yeshua met them along the way. Standing before them on the narrow path leading away from the tomb, He said, "Rejoice!"[240]

Magda took the lead, falling at His feet, worshiping Him with kisses. Joanna and James's mother came as well, kneeling at His feet.[241]

Yeshua bent down, placing His hand beneath Magda's chin. He lifted her face toward His. "Don't be afraid. Go tell My brothers that they should go into Galilee, and there they will see Me."[242]

When the women returned, corroborating Magda's story, the apostles still didn't believe the women because their testimony sounded like nonsense. When young Mary appeared hours later,

---

[238] Luke 24:2-5
[239] Luke 24:5-7
[240] Matthew 28:9
[241] Matthew 28:9
[242] Matthew 28:10

sharing her own story of her encounter with Yeshua, the men were more determined than ever to disregard the women's witness.

Magda could see that the pride of their position as His chosen apostles was being threatened because Yeshua had shown Himself to women instead of to the men. Regardless, she was not afraid. She knew that Yeshua's teachings lingered in the air, guiding and equipping his disciples for the mission that awaited them.

He was alive! Death could not hold Him. The grave could not keep Him. The power of love conquered the curse of death. The dominion of darkness took a mighty blow.

When darkness engulfed the land once again, Magda knew she was no longer a part of it and never would be. She existed in a realm far above the gray shadows of Zophos, under the protection of love, Himself.

They were just sitting down to the evening meal. Thomas had gone out to get more supplies. The doors were securely locked, preventing anyone from entering. The apostles kept the windows tightly shut, their fear of the religious leaders still lingering. They were taking extra precautions, unsure of what to do. Magda was sad for her brothers. They could not enter the joy of the power of love as revealed in resurrection because of their unbelief.

"Father, help them believe. Come to them, Yeshua, so they can see and hear again," Magda prayed while she divided up the bread.

Before she even turned around, she felt the tingle of His presence. The holiness permeated the room.

Yeshua stood among them. He spoke, silencing them all. "Peace be to you."[243]

He moved among them, showing them His nail-scarred hands and His pierced side. The men who followed Him couldn't

---

[243] John 20:19

contain their joy and delight. The women's stories were not untrue. He was alive! He was with them still!

Yeshua reminded the men who they were. "Peace be to you. As the Father has sent Me, even so I send you."[244]

In the silence of their response, Yeshua baptized them with His own breath. "Receive the Holy Spirit! If you forgive anyone's sins, they have been forgiven them. If you retain anyone's sins, they have been retained."[245]

Over the next forty days, Yeshua walked among them, teaching and preparing them. He led them to the outskirts of Bethany. As they sat upon a small hill, listening to Him preach, Magda watched the gray clouds moving in.

Yeshua's voice carried against the brewing storm. "Remember what I have taught you. You are My sent ones. As you go, preach, saying, 'The Kingdom of Heaven is at hand!'"[246]

Yeshua looked up at the clouds moving in. His gaze stopped the clouds where they were. "You will be hated by all men for My Name's sake, but he who endures to the end will be saved."[247]

He came among them, touching each of those who followed Him. "But, you will receive power when the Holy Spirit has come upon you. You will be witnesses to me in Jerusalem, in all Judea and Samaria, and to the uttermost parts of the earth."[248]

As they were looking at Him, absorbing His words, embracing His commission, He was taken up. A pure white cloud received Him out of their sight. They all stood, looking into the sky as He went. Magda was the first to notice the two heavenly messengers she had seen at the tomb.

When they spoke, it startled the apostles.

---

[244] John 20:21
[245] John 20:22-23
[246] Matthew 10:7
[247] Matthew 10:22
[248] Acts 1:8

"You men of Galilee, why do you stand looking into the sky? This Yeshua, who was received up from you into the sky, will come back in the same way as you saw Him going into the sky."[249]

Magda raised her arms in praise. "Love never ends!" she declared, unafraid of the approaching darkness.

---

[249] Acts 1:9-11

MAGDALA, 34 AD

The following year, Magda was living with her Aunt Milcah, helping her with the children in the orphanage. She had just set out the morning meal for the little ones. When Milcah came in to sit with them, Magda stepped outside for some fresh air.

Spring had arrived, filling the air with the sweet scent of blooming flowers. The blossoms were forming on the almond trees, transforming the gray landscape of winter with the vibrant promise of a new season. The sun rose more powerfully each morning. As Magda looked up at the sky, she closed her eyes in remembrance of that precious morning when her world was transformed and her soul was ushered into the light by the power of a love everlasting. He was with her, even now.

She had been there that morning when the Holy Spirit descended in blue flames that became a part of each of those who believed in His Name. The warmth of His love was on the inside of her, dwelling within her, abiding in her.

"Are you alright?" Milcah asked her niece.

"Yes, Aunt Milcah. I am fine," Magda said.

"I don't believe you." Milcah put her arm around Magda's

shoulders.

"You know me too well," Magda replied. "I just feel like I am missing something. I feel like I'm supposed to be doing something else."

"Something else?" Milcah asked.

"It's not that I don't love living here with you, Aunt Milcah. And you know that I care about the children. I just don't feel like I'm fulfilling my purpose. I feel as if I am helping you with yours." Magda sighed. "Does that make any sense?"

Milcah was silent for a moment. "It does, Magda. It does. But I believe you will find your way. After your uncle died, I felt lost, too. I didn't know that this was what I was going to do. This orphanage found me. I didn't start it from my own desire to prove anything. Faith is funny that way. It has to come out, or it isn't real. But, if you do something with the intention of showing your faith, then that isn't real either. I could have started this orphanage so that people would think I was a good person, taking my faith seriously. Instead, this orphanage was started, and I responded because I love the children. Faith rooted in love blossoms."

"I only hope I am not missing anything," Magda said.

"My dear, I think the time that you have spent with me has prepared you for something. Let's just wait and see what that might be."

Just before dusk, weeks later, there was a knock at the door. One of the servants came to get Milcah. They were sitting down to the meal together.

"There is a woman at the door who thought this was a place that she could find lodging. She looks as though she is in trouble. What should I tell her?" the servant asked.

"I'll come talk to her," Magda offered, sensing the poor servant's distress in trying to handle the matter.

When Magda came to the door, she saw a young woman standing there, trembling. She only had a thin tunic on. It looked torn. Her cheek was bruised. Magda's heart was immediately touched with a desire to protect the young woman.

"Come in," Magda said, taking her arm. The woman winced.

Once inside, Magda asked the servant to bring some food and drink. She got a blanket from another room. The young woman was half-starved, hurt and afraid.

"What is your name?" Magda asked her.

She looked at Magda, obviously wondering if she could trust her. Something about the woman's look reminded Magda of herself so long ago. The woman she had been ceased to exist, only to be reborn into a new form, imbued with an immense ability to love.

"I am Jezebel," she said, looking down, ashamed of her name. "My father thought I was a curse, wicked and unclean. He had wanted a son."

Magda handed the woman some bread. She ate ferociously. "I understand, Jezebel. My father named me out of his own bitterness and grief. He named me Mary, but another woman began calling me Magda because she believed I would be a tower above the bitterness and sorrow. But what I didn't know was that the name Mary also means a wished-for child."

The young woman listened intently as Magda explained. She was eating and drinking quickly. Magda could see the energy returning to the frightened woman's eyes.

"So, even though your name is Jezebel, why don't I call you Jes which means gift?"

"Gift. I like that," Jes said, a smile attempting to form on her bruised face.

"Alright, Jes," Magda replied. "What are you looking for?"

Jes told Magda her story. Rejected by her father, Jes was married off at the young age of twelve. The man she was married to was older than her father. He died after only four years. Now, Jes had no place to turn. She had been on the streets, preyed on by men just so she could get food to eat. Someone showed her compassion and sent her to Milcah's.

Magda helped Jes get settled in for the night. The young woman was obviously glad to be off the streets and under the protection of Milcah's orphanage.

In the weeks that followed, three more young widows turned up on the doorstep. Magda didn't have the heart to turn them away. She also knew that their estate in Magdala was becoming crowded.

"Magda, my dear," Milcah said to her one morning. "I appreciate your heart for the young widows, but our dwelling isn't big enough for both the widows and the orphans. I am going to look for property…"

Magda cut her off. "No, Aunt Milcah. This was your home before it was mine. You belong here. Let me look for property. I will use my portion of the inheritance money to purchase land. I can build something that will offer these women the protection they need. It will be a place where I can share the good news, where I can bring them beneath the protection of their Father in heaven."

Even as Magda said it, she knew she had found the mission Yeshua had set before her.

Milcah looked into Magda's eyes. "I can see that arguing with you is futile. Just let me know how I can help."

"Pray for me, Aunt Milcah. Pray that the Lord will reveal where He wants me to be."

Months later, Magda finished signing the land deed to some property not too far from Magdala. She hadn't had time to see the land, so Magda trusted the outcome of her purchase to the Lord. The plans were in place. They would begin constructing the new dwelling in three days. Magda was determined to be there.

Once her tasks were complete for the morning, Magda walked toward her new property just before dawn. The journey was quiet as all of creation was only beginning to wake up to the new day. Magda made the walk in a little over an hour. She came to the small village, recognizing it immediately. How could she have forgotten? This was the place where she ended up with Jezebel, her father's servant.

Magda went over to the spot where the house of ill-repute once stood. Yeshua had brought her here years ago. He had already picked it out, even then. She remembered the space where the building stood had been covered in ash. Beautiful wildflowers had sprouted from the ashes, filling the air with their delicate fragrance. Magda walked over to the place, the land that now belonged to her. The flowers were gone. The soil had been freshly tilled. No one was there yet since it was barely light out. Magda slipped off her shoes and walked the ground in her bare feet, letting the supple soil anoint her feet with each step.

Yeshua's voice was inside of her. *The ground is ripe for harvest.*

Magda lifted her arms in praise while her feet sunk into the dirt. There was no doubt that this was the place where He would harvest freedom and plant love in the hearts of discarded women. Magda opened her eyes when she felt the warmth of the sun on her face. The dazzling beams of radiant spring sunlight fell directly on the pile of stones set aside for building the dwelling. One particular stone caught Magda's eye. It absorbed the light, becoming a part of it until it radiated from within. It reminded her of the stone that had been planted for her in the forest of Zophos—the one that she clung to in an effort to save her life, the stone that was merely an extension of the One who did save her life.

As the crew arrived, Magda went to meet with the man in charge. He told her the plan. The dwelling should be up and ready in three days. Magda agreed to the man's ideas.

"I have one request," Magda said to him.

"What is that?" the man asked.

"I want to place the cornerstone," Magda said.

"Well, it isn't customary for women…" the man began.

"I already picked it out. I am going to get it now. Just tell me where it needs to go." Magda walked over to the pile of stones, praying for the strength to lift the one she knew was the designated cornerstone.

Bending down before the large stone, Magda used every ounce of strength she had to lift it. The men were silent, in awe as they watched her carry it. Magda knew they thought that her tears were tears of pain because of the strain, but she knew they were tears of love sent forth to anoint the stone she clung to.

Magda set the cornerstone in the designated spot. It was strong, sturdy, unmovable. This place would be built on love. Through her, He would set the captives free. Through her, He would love them out of the darkness that vied for their souls.

When they finally moved into the new space, Magda had four women under her protective care. Jes had become a dedicated servant of the Lord, assisting Magda in whatever way she could.

It was late one night when another woman arrived on the doorstep of the new sanctuary for widows.

"What is your name?" Magda asked her.

"Junia," she said, crying. "I was on my way to Rome, but I'm afraid. What will my uncle say when he finds out I've been defiled? Will he throw me out? There is no such thing as love. I was wrong to hope."

Magda did her best to comfort the sobbing girl, gently patting her back and whispering soothing words. "Why don't you stay here for a few weeks? When you feel ready, you can go and see your family in Rome. If they turn you away, you can always come back and stay with us. There is love, Junia."

"What is love?" Junia looked up into Magda's eyes.

"Let me tell you about Love. His name is Yeshua," Magda began.

Even though Junia eventually went back to Rome, Magda knew the woman took her fledgling belief in Love with her.

Over the years, Magda was grateful for the Centurion Abner. He would bring her funds collected by the church in Jerusalem. His unexpected visits served as more than a means of collecting provisions. Abner was also a deterrent to the men who wanted to turn Magda's place back into a house of ill-repute.

When a young woman showed up on the threshold of Magda's refuge late one night. She looked troubled. Her eyes were black and hollow, instilling a sense of fear in Magda.

As was her custom, Magda invited her in. The young woman lowered herself onto the chair with a rigid motion, devoid of any emotion. The perspiration beading on the woman's forehead was a clear indication of her racing heart.

"What is your name?" Magda asked.

"Belial," came the raspy voice.

The attack was swift and unforeseen. Magda felt the force of the young woman's blows as if the woman had the strength of one hundred men.

"You are mine," the demon hissed, releasing the rage of defeat upon her.

"I am my Beloved's and my Beloved is mine," Magda screamed it with the forceful authority of Yeshua behind her. "Yeshua, Son of God Most High, is His Name."

With that, the demon backed off. Magda, bleeding and bruised, stood over the crumpled figure of the woman. "Be gone Satan, by the power of the Name of Yeshua. You have no authority here."

Magda slumped down to the floor. She sensed the vacancy of evil, but her injuries were severe.

The other women came rushing in.

"Miss Magda, are you alright?" They were yelling.

"Take care of her." Magda pointed them toward the new woman who needed their help.

Jes, the only one who remained with her after all the years, was by Magda's side. "Let me help you to your chambers,

Mistress," she said, tears falling down her cheeks. "I will summon a physician."

Magda had no strength to argue. She lay on her sleeping mat. Within hours, a young physician came to see her. Magda slipped in and out of consciousness.

"The injuries are serious." The physician spoke to Jes. "I did what I could to ease her pain. Only time will tell what the final effects are."

Magda recalled the night she attacked her cousin's husband. She had brutally scarred and disfigured the man, Eleazar. Yet, Yeshua had forgiven her, enabling her to forgive the young woman.

"Is she alright?" Magda asked weakly.

Jes was by her side. "Who? Is who alright?"

"The young woman who came. Is she here? Are you taking care of her?"

Jes was silent. "Mistress, she hurt you. We were all upset."

Magda sat up. The physician was by her side. "Be careful," he said, gently pushing her back down.

"I need to see her," Magda said. "The young woman." Magda tried to get up. It was so hard to breathe.

"You are in no condition to go out," the physician said. Moved by the fierce determination in Magda's eyes, he let out a resigned sigh. "Can I find her for you? What did she look like, and when did she leave?"

Jes gave the physician all the information she could remember about the woman who attacked her mistress. Before he left, Magda spoke up.

"What is your name?" she asked him.

The physician turned around. "Luke," he said. "My name is Luke."

True to his word, Luke found the young woman and brought her back to Magda. The young woman was trembling, fearfully wearing the weight of guilt around her soul as she looked at

Magda in her terrible condition.

Though her eyes were swollen, Magda could see the woman. She reached out her hand. Luke helped the woman to take it.

"What is your name?" Magda asked her. Her breath was labored, rattling.

"I am Sarah," she replied.

"Sarah, your name is lovely. It means His princess." Magda touched the woman's palm with her broken thumb. "I want you to do something for me, Sarah."

"Yes?" Sarah couldn't look Magda in the face.

"I want you to accept my forgiveness. I don't blame you for this," Magda told the woman.

Sarah's eyes filled with tears, and she couldn't hold back the sobs any longer. "I'm so sorry. I don't know why..." her sobs came fast and hard.

"Shh, I know. I know, Sarah. Don't cry." Magda paused. She could feel something filling up her lungs. Breath was hard to take in. "If I could, I would tell you about Yeshua. Do you know Him?"

Sarah shook her head. "No, I don't know Him."

"Then listen to Jes. She will tell you about Him." Magda lay back down. "One more thing, Sarah. Say this out loud so I can hear you—I am forgiven."

Sarah looked at her curiously before whispering, "I am forgiven."

Magda gave her a look so Sarah said it again, louder. By the third time, Magda believed that the young woman finally accepted it.

Magda closed her eyes, stinging with pain.

Her Aunt Milcah's voice from long ago echoed in her heart. *We will push through the pain and get home no matter what.*

Magda smiled. "I am going home," she whispered. "Out of the reach of the forest of Zophos, forever. Love wins!"

The darkness pulled her in. She did not resist. She was not

afraid. The pain dissolved. Magda was standing on the staircase, looking up into His eyes. His hand was extended toward her. "Mary," He said. "Come away with Me, beloved."

Magda ascended the staircase, entering into the eternal light, attired in wedding garments of radiant faith. She was His bride. She took Yeshua's hand as He led her into the place to which she belonged, the Kingdom of God, founded on truth, sovereign over darkness, bordered by perfect love.

OTHER BOOKS IN THE
FAITH, LOVE & HOPE SERIES:
Shimmer in Time
The Torn Veil

Being an independent author, I rely solely on my readers to get the word out about my books. If you enjoyed this novel, I would greatly appreciate your feedback in the form of a star rating on Amazon with or without a written review. Reviews can be short, only a sentence or two about what you liked. It goes a long way in helping me continue writing. Even better, recommend the book to a friend or use it for a book club and tag me to let me know. Reviews are also helpful on Goodreads and Bookbub. Thank you again for reading the book and helping me put another story in your hands.

If you are interested in sharing what God revealed to you through this book or simply would like to be on our email prayer list, contact us at: devotedsteps@gmail.com

Visit **devotedsteps.com** for daily prayer and more information.

Additional titles
by D.M. Griffin are available at
amazon.com/author/devotedstepsministry
including:

Replenish

Abiding

Ignite

Devoted Steps

Alabaster

ABOUT THE AUTHOR

D.M. Griffin is the author of several Biblical Fiction novels as well as devotionals, prayer journals, and Bible studies. Her novel, *The Crumbs off Heaven's Table*, won Literary Global's Independent Author award in the category of Religious Fiction.

She currently resides in Northern California with her husband. They met in middle school a few days after she was transplanted to the West Coast at the tender age of twelve. She has three adult children who have been an endless source of delight and inspiration. She also has a precious grandchild who brings her joy.

As a native New Hampshire girl, she fondly remembers spending her summers there as a child. Thick accents, small towns, and fascinating weather stirred the imagination of a young heart. She has always had a fondness for stories thanks to her imaginative mother, who would make up wild, adventurous tales to tell when tucking her into bed as a child.

She truly believes that a book that sits on a shelf unread is like a planted seed that never blossoms. Nothing delights her more than sharing a story.

Made in the USA
Las Vegas, NV
09 October 2024

96587715R00246